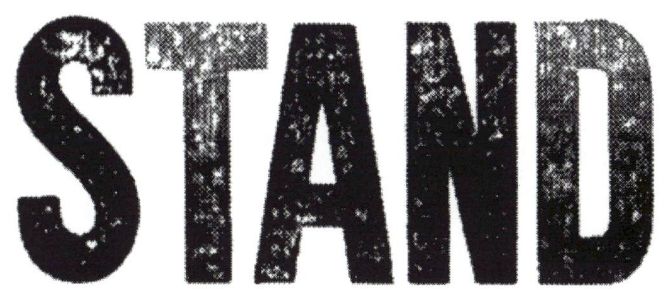

BOOK 3 – THE SEQUEL TO *STAY*

"STAND"
Written by EK Jonathan
Cover design by EK Jonathan
www.fleenovel.blogspot.com
Edition 1.0

Other books by EK Jonathan:

All Things New
The Unrighteous
Critical Times
FLEE
STAY
The Bloom of Youth

For more information on my novels, please visit my blog at:
EKJonathan.blogspot.com

I also have a podcast:
Youtube.com/c/EKJonathan

This is a work of fiction. While the events portrayed herein are based on Bible prophecy, they are not predictions. The idea that we will all be congregated in one physical location prior to Armageddon is a premise that has never appeared in our publications. In a similar vein, I am careful to avoid framing my books as spiritual food, which they are not. This is entertainment, plain and simple, and it is in no way sponsored by the Watchtower Bible and Tract Society. Any similarities between characters featured in this book and real life persons are completely unintentional.

Additionally, in harmony with the principle at Romans 15:1, readers are urged to be mindful of the consciences of those who may be uncomfortable reading this kind of fiction.

"…And I will raise up over them shepherds who will really shepherd them. They will no longer be afraid or be terrified, and none will be missing," declares Jehovah.

-Jeremiah 23:4
New World Translation of the Holy Scriptures

Previously in *STAY:*

With his coworker's doomsday bunker now to himself, CHAD HARKETT is faced with the task of survival. Thousands of miles away, THIAGO, the man Chad has hired to capture his ex-wife ANGELICA PARRY and their son EVAN, is out of reach.

As Rig 7 churns eastwards towards the Atlantic Ocean, chaos erupts. BO WHARTON, an evacuee tagalong and Bible student of PETER BURTON, falls ill and dies. TED WATKINS shows similar symptoms and is immediately sent to the rig's infirmary. Meanwhile, ANGELICA and EVAN are nowhere to be found, as is Rig 7's newest arrival, a mysterious man named JAMES.

Off the coast of Washington, JOYCE TUCKER and STACY OWEN drift haplessly in a mysterious blackness, utterly unequipped to reach their destination far to the North. After a series of blunders, their small craft is set ablaze, severely burning STACY's hands. JOYCE attempts to care for her while awaiting the inevitable, only to be discovered at sea by another vessel…

PROLOGUE

Dietrich Nash tugged at the collar of his wilted shirt as a bead of sweat swam down his spine. The perspiration on his face was beginning to smear with red dust kicked up from the wheels of the jeep. The vehicle's chassis creaked and groaned as its battered tires leapt across the grassless plains. On the sun-bleached dash, a tangle of cables, wires, and keys thrashed wildly, and Dietrich wondered with passing curiosity what might happen were their vehicle's engine to fail here, nearly forty kilometers from the nearest town, far from the reaches of cell towers and civilization.

On the wobbling GPS unit lodged between their seats, they were no more than an insignificant red triangle swimming in a sea of featureless beige. No marked roads, no railways. Not even a gas station. A solitary blue thread winded somewhere to their south to signify the existence of a river, but Dietrich knew better; it was presently nothing more than a shallow trench of rock and sand, dried out long ago by a dam a few hundred kilometers to the north. He took a swig of tepid water from a plastic canteen and thought it tasted dusty but sweet.

"We need to fill the tank," the driver roared over the engine. His name was Adani Ratief, a government worker from the Namibian capital who'd been selected to act as Dietrich's escort.

"Geen probleem," Dietrich said with an easy smile as the engine fell silent and the jeep came to rest in a cloud of dust. The driver raised an eyebrow and returned an amused look.

"It is seldom I hear a white man speak Afrikaans," Adani said as he got out of the jeep and lifted a petrol can to the side of the vehicle, the empty tank gulping the fuel down greedily. Dietrich gave a modest nod and grinned, but offered nothing more.

"Tell me more about the colony," he said, his gaze stretching back over the dunes at their back. Glassy curtains of heat swayed from the sand, creating shimmering pools.

"Bismarck, you mean? It is not so much of a colony nowadays. Once the mines dried up, the town vanished."

"No one stayed behind? No businesses? No residents? Land owners?"

"No. All gone," said the driver with a sweeping gesture. "You will understand when you see the place. There is simply nothing there. It is as dead as a bone."

"And how long has it been like that?"

"Oh, I would say four, maybe five years. That's when the last of the Chinese freighters left Elizabeth Bay."

"Chinese?"

"*Ja*, the entire mining operation was run by the Chinese, part of a huge corporation. I do not remember the name. They purchased the mines from the Germans, who took it from the Dutch. It would seem that everyone but the Africans themselves have had a turn owning this land," Adani remarked, lifting his chin into the air with a hearty laugh, though Dietrich thought he heard bitterness. "The Chinese probably did more for the land than any of the others before them, though. They laid the railways through the desert and the mountains all the way to the coast. Dug wells, built roads and dams…"

"And then left," said Dietrich with a sardonic look at the man next to him, who shrugged in response.

"No one expected them to stay. They only wanted the resources deep in the earth, and in return promised to build the infrastructure the area needed. They were good on their word," said the driver with a wag of his finger for emphasis. Dietrich nodded silently.

"So tell me, Mr. Nash, why are *you* interested in this land?"

"I just want to have a look. After I see it I'll be able to determine how interested I am."

"Yes, I suppose you will. Perhaps you will find some value from it yet. But to the eyes of a simple man like me, there is nothing here but rock and sand and death. The land has been plundered beyond healing, I'm afraid."

"It's a nasty habit of man, isn't it?"

The driver nodded, the pain in his expression clear and striking. "Nearly all of Southern Africa is the same. If you were to see it from a bird's eye, it would look as barren as the face of the moon." Dietrich nodded in acknowledgement as a doleful look seeped into Adani's expression. He dabbed a line of sweat from his forehead with the back of his sleeve and capped the gas tank.

"Rest assured, friend, I'm not here to bring any more harm to the land or to its people. Quite the opposite, in fact."

The driver strapped the emptied fuel can to the back of the jeep and glanced curiously at his passenger, who grinned calmly at the dunes, and wondered.

PART I.

CHAPTER 1

Peter stood motionless in the center of the cramped cabin, the evidence spread out before him atop the mattress. The scuffed Polaroid camera hanging from its hook above Bo Wharton's bunk now elicited a completely new set of emotions.

There was a knock on the cabin door behind him. "Come on in. But close the door behind you," Peter said. Marcus Kelly entered and shut the door as instructed. For the last few weeks, Marcus had served as one of the housing overseers. Being familiar with the conditions of the cabins and ensuring the friends' safety was his responsibility.

"I found these under his mattress," Peter said, gesturing towards the Polaroid images spread out on the bunk. Marcus said nothing as he glanced over the photographs. Most were underexposed and blurry, but the subjects were clear enough in some.

Marcus Kelly groaned uneasily. "You know any of these sisters?"

"Yeah, I recognize a few," Peter said, pointing at a few of the Polaroids.

"Where'd he take these photos?"

"It looks like a few—these three for sure—were taken in the cafeteria after hours." Peter indicated a few images on the far left edge of the bed. "These others, I'm not too sure about. Could've been taken in the corridors or stairwells. Looks like he had the camera hidden up in the rafters somehow. Maybe he had some sort of remote trigger."

"Are these all of the images?" Brother Kelly asked.

Peter nodded. "It's all I've found so far. I stripped most of the room. I doubt he could've had many more packs of Polaroid film on him."

"Any idea what he was up to?"

"Your guess is as good as mine. Maybe he was just collecting images. Could've been planning something else, of course," Peter said grimly. He felt a shiver creep up his spine.

"Well, at least they're all clothed. I guess he wasn't able to sneak into any cabins," Marcus said, shaking his head.

"No, I suppose not. And we haven't had any complaints? No sisters have come forward mentioning anything?"

"Not to my knowledge. Of course, we're constantly making announcements about safety and keeping doors locked and what not, especially after hours. Those precautions go a long way."

"I hope. Frankly, I'm still not comfortable with all these strangers aboard. Something like this was bound to happen sooner or later."

"Perhaps."

"It makes me sick to my stomach."

"Then again, there is another way of looking at things."

"Oh?" Peter asked.

"You could say that whatever threat this man posed, it's been taken care of. Mr. Wharton is no longer a reason for concern."

"Yeah. The thought crossed my mind."

"I don't want to jump to any conclusions, and I certainly wouldn't publicize the idea, but…" the overseer trailed off, scratching the back of his neck.

"You feel we're protected," Peter prodded.

"That's right. Think of the blackouts all across the country. Then the firestorms. I'm sure it's absolute anarchy back there. But here we are, all our needs taken care of. Jehovah hasn't abandoned us. We know we're right where he wants us to be. We just need to trust that whatever little hiccups there are along the way… he'll address them in due time."

Peter took a deep breath and sat on the bunk, brushing aside the pile of photos. "Thank you, Marcus," he said. "I needed that."

The older brother sat down beside him. "I know it's hard, Pete. We're all struggling with uncertainties, my wife and I included."

"How's your heart been?"

"Stable, but sometimes I can feel I'm pushing it too hard. Vivian keeps telling me to pace myself."

"You should listen to her," Peter scolded lightly.

"Probably. But it's hard with all there is to do. Even at my age I'm still working on modesty, I guess."

"We've all got something."

11

"One day at a time."

The two sat there in silence for a moment, staring out the porthole at the waves rolling by.

"What should I do with all this evidence?" Peter finally asked.

"Put it somewhere safe for now, somewhere no one else will stumble upon it. We'll have to report this to the others and see how they decide to proceed."

"Got it."

"And Peter, I'm sorry," Marcus said.

"Sorry for what?"

"Sorry about Bo. I hadn't suspected anything and had high hopes for him. You must be disappointed."

"I guess," Peter said with a distracted look. "But I'm just glad nothing happened. I'm not sure what I would've done had he actually attacked someone."

"Well, let's just be thankful it didn't come to that."

***

Rachel's anxiety had risen steadily as the evening wore on. Her search was proving futile. She'd checked the cafeteria, the rec rooms, even the common spaces where brothers and sisters frequently congregated to read and chat and catch up on news. But Angelica and Evan were nowhere to be found. It was nearing eight o'clock as Rachel made her way for the third time to Angelica's cabin. She'd skipped dinner and the hunger was starting to gnaw at her insides, but that could wait. Her instincts told her something was very wrong here.

"Angelica? Evan? Anyone in there?" Rachel said, banging a fist against the cabin door. She pressed her ear to its surface but heard nothing. She knocked again.

"Guys, I'm really starting to worry about you. I'm coming in, ok?" Rachel called out. She took a breath, braced herself, and twisted the knob. It wasn't locked.

Rachel's pulse raced as she slowly pushed in the cabin door. Light from the fluorescent corridor bulbs spilled into the otherwise dark space. An odd smell hung in the air. Rachel flipped on the lights with one hand as she swung the door wide with the other. Her heart quickened as she took in the scene before her eyes.

The room was a mess. The mattress sat unevenly on its frame, its blanket and pillows scattered haphazardly on the floor. She lifted one to find Evan's *Bible Story Book* underneath, its pages crumpled and torn. She held it close to her face—that smell again. A disinfectant, perhaps, but like none she was familiar with. It was strong, enough to make her head spin.

Rachel rose and moved to the far wall where she opened a window to let in some fresh air. She filled her lungs and slowly regained clarity. What *was* that smell? And did it have to do anything with whatever had happened here? Rachel gave the room another quick glance, noticing this time two pairs of shoes peeking out from below the bed. It didn't make sense. Why would Angelica and Evan leave so suddenly without their shoes?

No, none of this was right. Something had happened. Maybe it had to do with that mysterious man who'd shown up a few days ago? She'd overhead Peter and Ted saying something about him speaking with Angelica, something that had spooked her, but Rachel hadn't caught all the details. She would need to show this to Peter, of course, and the other elders as soon as possible. She hated to put another burden on him, but this was urgent, and if what had happened with Bo and Ted was somehow connected to Angelica, her very life might be in danger.

Rachel Burton crouched down, carefully replacing the story book exactly as she'd discovered it. She glanced at the two pairs of shoes neatly tucked under the corner of the bed, and screamed.

Just behind the pairs of shoes, two large eyes stared back at her from the shadows. Rachel felt her arms and legs scrabbling beneath her body, moving her as quickly as possible away from the bed, even as her brain was processing what she was seeing.

It was nothing to be afraid of. It was only Evan.

"Evan! Is that you?! You scared me half to death!" Rachel said, barely getting the words out between large gulps of air. But the small boy said nothing. He appeared frozen, his eyes wide and unblinking.

Rachel pushed the mattress back against the wall, temporarily unconcerned with leaving the scene as she'd found it. Evan was here. He would have the answers. Rachel felt a wave of relief, but the expression on the child's face kept the fear from dispelling entirely.

"Evan? You okay, sweetie? Why don't you come on out here? It's ok. I'm not going to hurt you." Rachel extended a hand, but Evan pulled away.

13

"Evan. It's ok. I promise."

Evan shook his head.

"Can you tell me what happened, honey?" Rachel asked. Nothing.

"I wanna talk to Teddy," Evan said, his voice barely registering.

"Teddy? You mean Ted? Ted Watkins?"

Evan nodded. Rachel frowned.

"I'm so sorry Evan, but… He can't come to see you now."

"Why not?"

"He's… He's not really feeling well. He's sick, Evan."

"What about Peter?"

"Peter? Well, I can go get him, but—"

"No. Don't leave me here. Please," Evan said, his voice on the edge of tears. Rachel's heart broke a little.

"I'll tell you what, why don't we go see him together? We'll get you out of here and get you something to eat and you can tell us everything. How does that sound?"

Rachel waited a minute before Evan nodded reluctantly. He scooted out from under the bed and into Rachel's arms. They hugged briefly, then rushed off to the cafeteria.

***

Chad Harkett stared vacantly at the assortment of beer cans and liquor bottles littered around him. He'd finished every last drop he could find in the bunker, so how was he still conscious? How was he still unable to silence the noise in his head?

Chad squeezed his eyes shut, pressing his knuckles into their sockets until there was only blackness and shooting stars. The gunshot still rang in his ears. He'd only pulled the trigger once. So why did he keep hearing that *BANG BANG BANG* in his head, like some kind of ghastly skipping record?

He felt *hot*. Chad rose from his spot on the couch and gazed around for some kind of thermostat. Why was it so *hot* all of a sudden? He lifted the back of his hand to his forehead. It was slick with perspiration, but he didn't feel feverish.

I did what I had to do, Chad thought, clearing a walking path between the bottles and cans with his bare feet. *If I hadn't shot first, I'd be the one lying out there.*

14

"And anyway, Martin wouldn't have lasted much longer," Chad announced aloud. *You can't know that for sure,* replied a voice in his head.

"I do know that for sure! I *knew* him for nearly a decade. It was *always* the same with him. He never had the guts to pull the trigger on anything." Chad snickered at his own joke as he dragged a trashcan from beneath the counter in the kitchenette. He started scooping garbage into it. *Why was it so hot?*

Your world is on fire.

"Yeah. No kidding. Maybe that's it."

Maybe that was it.

Frowning, Chad Harkett abandoned his task of cleaning up to walk back to the entrance of the bunker. He felt the heat rise as he neared the thick steel door. It was warm to the touch. Outside of the reinforced glass, he could make out undulating orange shapes swimming in the blackness. Martin's house was on fire.

"So much for salvaging supplies," Chad snorted bitterly. He backed away from the door and peeled off his sweaty shirt. He could feel the temperature decrease as he retreated to the back of the bunker, but not by much. Had Martin really failed to install some kind of cooling system? Chad went from one wall to the next, struggling to locate a control panel of some sort, something he'd missed before. There was nothing. But as he passed Martin's radio cage, he paused.

Did you imagine that?

He waited, his gaze fixed on the radio console within the Faraday cage.

You're losing it, Harkett.

"Please tell me I didn't imagine that," he muttered, slicking the sweat from his forehead and leaning into the doorway. He waited. Then he saw it again, subtle but unmistakable. The needle on the radio transceiver had spiked.

Chad Harkett stumbled through the cage's door and slumped into the chair. He donned the headphones and dialed up the volume. At first there was only the sustained hiss of static.

"*–ters –oint –evac–,*" sputtered a voice on the other end.

"Hello? Hello? Is someone there?" Chad said. A tremendous wave of relief overcame him at the sound of another voice, but it was quickly followed by the fear of never hearing it again.

"Hello? Anyone? Who's there?" Chad's eyes raced over the

transceiver and its many knobs, switches, and dials. He hadn't bothered learning how the thing worked, and now he regretted it. But he knew enough to understand that this wasn't a telephone. He had to transmit to be heard.

"*Hun–poin– evac– mili– comm. Repe–*," stuttered the voice once again. Chad's eyes squeezed shut as he struggled to make sense of the words.

***

Peter sat hunched over his meal in a dimly lit corner of the cafeteria. He'd had little to eat all day and it felt good to get something inside him, even if that something was only a cold turkey sandwich, a bag of Lay's potato chips, and a warm can of Coke. He polished off the last bite of his sandwich and tore open the bag of chips just as the cafeteria doors behind him burst open. He turned to see a frantic expression on his wife's face, and following closely behind her, Evan.

"Peter, something terrible has happened," Rachel said, her face pale and sweaty.

"What now?" Peter asked. Rachel slid into the bench across the table from her husband. Evan stuck close by her side.

"Go ahead, Evan. Go ahead and tell Peter what happened," Rachel prodded. Evan glanced warily at the other diners. It was well past serving hours and few remained in the cafeteria, giving the large space a cold, sepulchral feel. Peter caught his expression and glanced overhead.

"Why don't we get some of these lights on," Peter said, giving his wife a look. "And what about dinner, Evan? You eaten yet?"

The boy slowly shook his head. There were purple patches under his eyes and stringy, dark hair plastered to his forehead. He looked as if he'd just been woken from a nightmare. Rachel took the cue and busied herself locating the overhead light switches and preparing a small plate of leftovers from a serving table near the kitchen doors. Evan watched her carefully.

"You wanna tell me what happened this afternoon, buddy?" asked Peter once the two were alone. Evan's expression twisted, as if his face were working itself into a knot. It would clearly be difficult for him to talk about this.

"Where's Teddy?" the boy finally asked.

16

"Ted?" Peter asked. He found himself instinctively looking towards the spot on the floor where Ted had collapsed. It had all occurred only hours before. "Um. Well. Ted got sick. It was pretty sudden. He's in the infirmary now."

"Is it pretty serious?" Evan asked.

"I… I don't really know, Evan. They're keeping an eye on him. I'm sure it'll be ok," Peter said. The words left his mouth and sat on his shoulders like an uncomfortable weight.

"I really wish we could just be in paradise already," Evan said. A tear ran down his cheek; he quickly brushed it away with the cuff of his sweater.

"You and me both."

Rachel returned to their table with two paper plates of food. Peter said a prayer for them and they ate in silence.

"So, where's Angelica?" Peter finally asked. He peeled the tab back on the soda; the resulting hiss was almost deafening in the cavernous empty space. Rachel gave him a desolate look.

"Someone came for us," Evan said.

"What do you mean?" Peter asked.

"It was some guy. He was really scary. And fast. He tried to grab us. We were in the room and we thought he was just one of the cleaners or something. I got away, but my mom…" Evan's lips quivered as tears pooled in his eyes. Rachel wrapped an arm around him, pulled him close.

"Had you seen this man before?" Peter asked carefully. Evan nodded.

"Yeah. He talked with Mom and me a couple days ago. He told us to go back home."

Rachel's eyes widened. She shot a glance at her husband, who didn't seem surprised, only gravely concerned. "Look, Evan. I know all of this must be really scary, but we're going to find your mom and get her back," Peter said. Evan seemed to relax a bit with Peter's reassurance. "After all, we're on an oil rig in the middle of the ocean. They couldn't have gotten far."

Peter spent the next ten minutes questioning Evan on the man's physical appearance. Peter himself recalled the tall, dark stranger—the man who'd called himself *James*—clearly enough, but wanted confirmation on some of the details. Evan finished his meal in silence as Rachel pulled her husband aside. They kept a close eye on Evan as they talked.

"Did you know about the man who approached them earlier?" Rachel asked. Peter nodded. "And that didn't strike you as odd?" Rachel pressed.

"Sure it did, but there was plenty of other *odd* stuff happening. Still is."

"I'm just wondering why nothing more was done when you knew she was in danger?" Rachel asked. Her words were quiet and measured but the tone sharp. Peter crossed his arms and shook his head.

"Rachel. I'm doing the best I can. We all are. And for your information, it's a constant struggle, balancing practical measures with reliance on the organization. I didn't think things would be this difficult, either. I had no idea we'd be mixed in with these kinds of people here. But we have to trust that Jehovah's still in control of the situation."

"So let me get this straight: some strange man comes aboard and has a suspicious conversation with a sister and her son who are actively fleeing from an abusive, controlling ex and no one does anything? That seems like something that should've required practical measures, doesn't it?"

"We took the measures we felt were appropriate at the time. Ted agreed to tell Angelica to keep her and her son safe and never meet the man alone. The problem is that I'm not sure if he had a chance to tell her. Everything else just happened too fast. Now Ted's incapacitated, Angelica is nowhere to be found, and some madman––" Peter paused. He turned from his wife to glance at Evan at the table. The boy stared at them curiously.

"What'll happen with Evan?" Rachel asked.

"I'll have a chat with our guys. He'll probably room with us for the time being," Peter's voice trailed off as the dangers implied by this suggestion hit him. "Of course, that'll mean we could be targeted next."

Rachel bit her lip as she gave Peter a steely look. "Just tell me what I need to do."

"For now, just stay close to me."

"Yeah, that seems to be a real winning strategy," Rachel muttered. Peter pressed his eyes shut and held his tongue.

***

Thiago gazed at the frail woman crumpled on the stack of cardboard and canvas sacks in the corner of the storage room. She'd be conscious any moment now, though it would doubtless take her some time to regain her strength and her wits.

The tall man stood and stretched. The room still reeked of the sweet, pungent ethanol he'd used in his concoction. He'd been careful not to bring his hands anywhere near his face until they'd been thoroughly washed; still, his head spun from the lingering chemicals. He cracked the door open an inch, and once he'd determined the coast was clear, squeezed out into the dark, gusty night.

Black, foam-crested waves tumbled into the rig's pylons stories below. A row of floodlights perched to the lower catwalks cast ghostly, green shapes into the water. Even from way up here, Thiago could occasionally make out the dark shapes of animals in the water as they passed through the beams of light. Dolphins, perhaps, or even sharks. Anything was possible way out here, wherever here was.

Frankly, this job had been a mess, Thiago relented. He'd only managed to capture one of the two people he was sent to bring back, and the hits he'd attempted had similarly proven only half successful. His client would be furious, of course, but there was little to be done about any of that now. He could only wait and regroup and formulate a new plan.

From day one, there had simply been too many unknowns, too many variables. He'd been forced to abandon his gear and transportation, and the flimsy cover story he'd adopted aboard the supply boat had worn paper thin. If he were to stay aboard this rig, he would need a new disguise, a new name, a new identity, and all of this required time he didn't have. He could not keep the captured woman secret forever, not in a place like this. Eventually someone would come to these levels looking for her, and Thiago would reach the end of his line.

And how would he escape? He'd stood watch for hours during the previous days and nights, struggling to learn their patrols and supply drop offs, but if there was a routine in place it had remained a mystery to him. There was no way up, or down, or off this rig, and that was only half of his troubles.

The other half was the disturbing news coming from the mainland. News of massive power outages and a meltdown of infrastructure. Thiago had dismissed these initial reports as fake news, propaganda spread among the Witnesses to keep the evacuees docile and obedient. But then he'd seen the footage with his own eyes—live reports broadcast on the cafeteria monitors. Cities sitting in darkness, skies glowing red with embers and smoke. If things really were this bad back on the mainland, what would Thiago be returning to? Would he even be able to collect his payment?

Thiago turned; a noise from behind the door caught his ear. He glanced up and down the catwalk before slipping back into the room.

"You're awake," he said flatly to the woman on the floor. She struggled to sit upright, but the zip ties holding her wrists together made it difficult. A rag taped to her mouth kept her from speaking. "I'll free your wrists, but first you will promise me you won't try anything foolish," Thiago instructed, his dark eyes boring into hers. Angelica nodded slowly.

Thiago fished a pair of pliers from his pocket and snipped away the restraints. The woman brought herself upright and retreated backwards into the corner. She pulled the tape from her mouth and spit out the gag. Thiago read fear in her eyes, but not panic.

"I'm not here to harm you," he said, eyeing her carefully. She was rubbing her wrists and returning his hard stare.

"Chad sent you," she said simply.

"Eat," he ordered, throwing a bag of potato chips at Angelica's feet. His voice was icy and distant.

Angelica did as she was told, careful to avoid any sudden movements under her captor's clinical stare. She tore a corner of the bag open and began eating. It wasn't much, but it was better than nothing. She could feel her hunger stirring as her head cleared. A brief prayer for wisdom and clarity helped.

"So I take it your name isn't James," Angelica said. The man's dark eyes hadn't strayed from her for a moment.

"Water," Thiago said.

"Thank you," she said, reaching a hand out cautiously. "So, can I ask what the plan is here?" Angelica asked after she'd drank half of the bottle.

"We head back," Thiago said simply. There was no point in keeping this information from the woman. After all, he would require some measure of cooperation from her if they were ever to leave this rig.

"Back to California?"

"Eventually, yes."

"How?"

Thiago was silent. Angelica frowned. "You've seen the news, right? You know there's nothing to go back to. Chad might not even be there anymore."

"We are in contact," Thiago lied. The only item that had stayed with him since his departure from the coast in New Orleans was the satellite phone he kept at all times in a sealed bag, but since the blackouts on the mainland, there had been no signal available for calls in or out.

"Look, I know that Chad is scary. He's wealthy and connected and under normal circumstances it'd be dangerous not to listen to him. I know. I've been there. But these aren't normal circumstances. This is a fool's errand."

"Enough," Thiago said. "Show me your wrists."

Angelica stared at him for a long moment before complying. The man pulled two fresh plastic zip ties from a back pocket and cinched them together, though somewhat looser than the first time.

"I'm not going to run, you know," Angelica said.

"Why not?" Thiago asked.

"Because right now, I believe I'm in one of the safest places I could be, aboard this rig."   "Oh?"

"Tell me, what do you think of the people you've met since you've been here?"

Thiago's eyes narrowed. "In a word, *naive*."

"We seem helpless, don't we?" Angelica asked. Her bound hands were folded in her lap as she scooted back against the wall.

"I suppose so."

"And yet here we all are, safely evacuated from the mainland just in time. It's not just us here on this rig, you know. There are millions of us all around the world, fleeing on tankers and cruise ships and rigs, all being perfectly coordinated. We're not armed, we've got no police or security force, and yet we've come this far."

Thiago's gaze dropped from his captor as he pulled more zip ties from his pocket and bound her ankles.

"We're protected. And so long as you stay here with us, you will be, too."

Thiago turned to reach for the gag and a fresh strip of duct tape.

"I don't know how much Chad is paying you, but you have to

21

ask yourself if it's really worth your life."

Thiago ignored the woman's words as he replaced the cloth over her mouth and taped it tight in place. He relished the silence. Finished, Thiago stood and surveyed his handiwork. Then, without a word, he was gone.

Outside, he cleared his head and decided to try the satphone once more. Chad would want to know at least that his wife had been captured safely. Thiago reached into his pocket, but it was empty.

CHAPTER 2

Joyce Tucker opened her eyes to a soft, orange glow. Half-burned candles swung rhythmically from hanging lanterns above her head. She struggled to sit upright, but a firm hand on her shoulder pressed her back down.

"Easy," came a voice from an unseen figure.

"Who's there? Where am I?" Joyce asked. Pain shot through her temples and her vision swayed.

"You're safe. That's all that matters."

"Why is my head spinning? Do I have a concussion?" Joyce asked.

"Here, drink this." A cup was squeezed between Joyce's fingers. She felt her head lifted by a few degrees as she brought the cup to her lips. It was cold and wonderful.

"Thank you. I'm really parched."

"You're probably dehydrated. How long were you out at sea?"

"I… I'm not sure… Two days, maybe? It was dark. We lost track of time. Stacy… Wait, where's Stacy? Is she ok? What happened to her?" Joyce said, fighting the urge to sit up again.

"Your friend is stable for now. We've got her somewhere else. But her burns were severe. What happened out there?"

Joyce pressed her eyes shut and tried to remember. "There was a fire aboard the sailboat. I'm not sure how it started; it was all so sudden. It spread. It got on her jacket and hands. How did you find us?"

"A thirty foot blaze in pitch black tends to stand out pretty well. The two men who pulled you aboard said you told them you were headed to Burrard Harbor right before you fainted."

"That's right."

"May I ask why you were headed there?"

Joyce carefully weighed her possible responses. These were dark times. Over the last year, there'd been no shortage of horror stories. Witnesses being stoned while engaging in the ministry, children beaten mercilessly by classmates, bricks thrown through windows in the middle of the night, Kingdom Halls defaced with threatening messages. Identifying herself as a Witness could mean the end of this safe passage. Then again, Joyce thought, if these people had evacuated from nearby, perhaps they had valuable information and would be willing to share. After all, they'd been kind enough to rescue her and Stacy. She petitioned silently for courage and spoke up courageously.

"My friend and I are Jehovah's Witnesses. We were trying to evacuate to the camp in Burrard Harbor to be with our brothers and sisters."

The other voice, wherever it was coming from, said nothing.

"Is everything ok?" Joyce asked, her pulse beginning to quicken. The thought of being expelled from this boat, being forced back onto their vessel, was an unbearable one.

"I'm sorry. I need to speak with the captain," the voice finally responded, and before Joyce could say another word, she could hear someone retreating through an unseen door.

***

Peter stared at the circle of faces around him. Without exception, each showed the telltale signs of stress and exhaustion. It had been a difficult year for all of them, and he was sure that each elder sitting around the table had their own harrowing tales to tell. He hated to add to their burden, but there simply wasn't another way. After a prayer, the chairman gave Peter the floor.

"I'm sorry to get you all out here so late, but we have a situation that requires your immediate attention. This afternoon, we located the ten-year-old son of a sister in our congregation. He was hiding under the bunk in their cabin, crying. He says his mother was abducted."

"Abducted?" someone asked. Some of the glassy looks around him had chipped slightly. The men were leaning forward.

"Yes, that's right. We've got a description of the man who took her. I'd like to put an announcement out there out for an artist and get a sketch done. Maybe we can show it on the monitors, get people involved to track this guy down."

"Hold on a minute there, Brother Burton," one of the

overseers said, holding up a hand. He held a finger in the air while he gathered his thoughts. They seemed to come with some difficulty. "What's the name of this sister, first of all? And how was she abducted?"

"Name's Angelica Parry. Taken from her room, it seems. Her son was with her at the time. He managed to get away, but just barely."

"When's the last time someone saw her?" another elder asked.

"I saw her yesterday, but no one's seen her today, it seems," Peter explained.

"Did you check with her neighbors? Maybe they saw something, or have heard from her," someone said.

"No, haven't checked yet. I'll do that tomorrow, but I wanted to get a jump start on this now," Peter said, starting to feel a tinge of impatience.

"I can understand your concern, Brother Burton, but... Well, other than the young boy, did anyone else witness the abduction?"

"Well, no. I mean, it was just the two of them together at the time. But when my wife inspected the room, stuff was everywhere. It was clear there'd been a struggle."

The room fell silent. Peter stared at the older brothers' faces around him as they exchanged looks.

"Look, brothers, I know how crazy this sounds, that something could happen way out here like this. But I have strong reasons to believe that there is a very real threat aboard this rig, and I think our friends are in danger."

"Did something else happen?" someone asked.

"Well, sure, this afternoon we had someone collapse dead in the cafeteria. Not to mention one of our elders, Ted Watkins, falling seriously ill. He's in the infirmary now."

"Yes, we heard about your student. We're very sorry. But... isn't it true that he was a recovering addict? Is it possible that he ingested something?" someone suggested.

"And I'm not sure if I see how what happened with those two this afternoon is related to your missing sister. Is there a connection?" asked someone else, looking around.

Peter took a deep breath. He was having trouble collecting his thoughts. It was like everything in his head was jumbled and blurred. "Look, I know it seems incredible, but I do think they're connected. You see, the sister who went missing has an ex, back in California.

25

His name is Chad Harkett, he's a big shot from Silicon Valley. Very wealthy, very powerful." Peter glanced around, but the name didn't seem to register with this audience.

"Anyway, the man is dangerous. Right before we evacuated, he came to his wife's house with a gun. He meant business. We were able to keep Angelica and her son safe, but it was clear that he was determined to get her back. I'd never seen anything like it. He was like an animal."

"So, you're saying that you think he's come after her, way out here?" the chairman asked.

"Yes. Again, I know it sounds absurd, but this man has the resources to hire someone. And I think that someone was also after me and Ted—we were the two elders who disarmed him the day he tried to attack his family."

"So you're suggesting that this sister's ex-husband hired someone to board our vessel out in the Gulf of Mexico, kidnap his ex-wife, and kill you and Brother Watkins?"

Peter wanted to nod, but he had to admit that his theory sounded completely ridiculous. He lowered his head, exhausted. "Yes. That's what I think."

"Let's suppose this were possible, for a moment. How do you think someone would even get out here, Peter?" someone asked.

"James," Peter said, his head still down.

"Who?"

"He said his name was James. He boarded a few days ago during a supply transfer with one of the boats. Apparently, a rumor was going around that he was…" Peter took a deep breath. "An angel."

The words had an instant effect. The brothers sitting around the table were nodding and exchanging looks.

"James. Right. We've heard of him."

"Here's the thing. The day before Sister Parry goes missing, this James character asks to have a word with her. We supervise it closely, of course, and it turns out that he wants her to get back with her husband. She of course refuses, and suddenly he's nowhere to be found."

"I can attest to that last bit," Marcus Kelly chipped in. "His cabin's completely cleaned out."

Now the room was silent, but the overseers around the table appeared to be thinking things over.

"Well, brothers, what do you think?" asked the chairman.

"I understand Brother Burton's concern," someone spoke up. "And I agree that something ought to be done to help locate our sister. But I'm not sure I like the idea of putting up wanted posters."

"Agreed. We must maintain as peaceful an environment as possible," said another overseer. "The branch has emphasized this from day one. We're in a small, confined space out here and people are already under stress. Even the slightest panic has the potential for disaster."

"Ok brothers, I can appreciate all that, but surely we've got to take some action here," Peter pleaded. "We're talking about a missing sister and a potential criminal on the loose."

"But Brother Burton, if I'm hearing things correctly, the only eyewitness to this supposed abduction is a small boy. Ten years old, you said?"

"Yes, but he's a reliable kid. He wouldn't make up something like this."

"I'm not saying he would. But you also mentioned that he's been through some very traumatic events recently. You said he was attacked by his father."

"Yes."

"Well, don't you think it's possible that he's suffering from some of those side effects? His mother leaves his side for longer than he expects, and suddenly his mind jumps to his abusive father?"

Peter was dismayed to find a couple of heads nodding thoughtfully at this suggestion.

"Brothers, I'm sorry, but I have to disagree here. The room, as I mentioned before, was in shambles. There had clearly been a struggle. This isn't something Evan could've dreamed up. And what about this James guy telling her to get back with her husband? It only makes sense the one way! You've got to be able to—"

"Peter, please," Brother Kelly interrupted, his hands in the air. "No one is accusing you or anyone else of being untruthful. We want to get to the bottom of this as much as you do, but we've got to consider each step shrewdly. As was stated, a crisis aboard our rig would be disastrous. We're nearly a thousand miles from home and it'll be weeks before we reach our destination. The friends have to feel safe."

"But what if they're not safe?" Peter asked, his voice cracking under the emotional strain. "I promised Angelica and her boy that

27

they'd be safe if they got away from her ex. When my Bible student expressed doubts about boarding an oil rig with a hurricane just on the horizon, I promised him, too. Those people followed us all this way. We're responsible for them."

A silent pall fell over the room like a thick, black quilt. Even in the older, wizened sets of eyes across the table before him, Peter sensed fears similar to his own. It was oddly comforting.

"I know where you're coming from, Brother Burton," said the chairman. "We're all carrying our own burdens out here, and not one of us has escaped the realization of how enormous this task is. But actually, none of us is responsible for the safety of our friends. That's on Jehovah. We've been obedient down to the last detail, and that's the only reason we're here, together, having this conversation. Sure, we might've assumed that it would be smooth sailing as soon as we boarded these vessels, but *should* we have? Think of the Israelites. Just days after crossing the Red Sea, they began to doubt Jehovah's ability to provide and protect. The evidence of his power was all around them, but they became distracted by problems that, in hindsight, were very minor. You are clearly a loving shepherd worried about one of your sheep, as you should be. But don't let it distract you. Jehovah is in control."

"Perhaps there's still a way we can help without raising too much of a commotion," Brother Kelly chipped in. "Peter's idea of finding a sketch artist to put together a rendering of this mysterious man calling himself James might not be a bad one. Once it's done, we could circulate it among the overseers and the night watchmen. We don't need to provide all the details of what he's suspected of, but that way they can keep an eye out. There's only so many places to hide out here."

"Thoughts?" asked the chairman. Those around the table raised their hands in a motion to accept the proposal.

"Thank you. Thank you all. And that example of the Israelites… It's a good one. Looks like I need to do some reading," Peter said.

"It's a good reminder for all of us. We can only expect the pressures to mount as we get closer to the end," the chairman said, to which everyone heartily agreed.

***

The lanky man sat quietly in the corner of the small room. He'd introduced himself as the captain and was now wiping what looked like motor oil from the cuffs of his dark green weatherproof. Joyce Tucker had finished the plate of scrambled eggs he'd brought in with a cup of coffee. Both had been bland, but that hadn't kept her from savoring every mouthful. Anything was better than peanut butter and crackers.

"Thank you all for your generosity," Joyce said, sliding the emptied metal dish to the edge of the table. She brought the mug of coffee to her lips and took a sip. "We've been running for days. Seen lots of awful stuff out here."

The captain nodded, but it was a distracted gesture, as if heavier matters weighed on his mind. He was working on a smudge near his elbow.

"Engine trouble?" Joyce asked.

The captain glanced up at her for a moment, then down at the rag in his hands. "No. It's not oil. It's something in the air. You stay out in the fog or the rain long enough and you get covered in it."

"Odd."

"Some say it's what's keeping the light from getting through."

"Oh," Joyce said, eyebrows rising.

The captain shrugged it off. "That was a risky thing you two tried. Boarding a sailboat in pitch black without a wind at your back. What were you thinking?"

"Not much, really. We were out of options. We had to get to our destination. We'd tried the roads, but the border was closed. And of course airports were out of the question. By sea was the only way, and my friend, Stacy, happened to have a boat…"

"You could've easily died out here. Almost did."

"If there had been any other way, we would've taken it. But even the harbor was becoming too dangerous to just hang around. We were forced to leave, and so we did."

"Whole world's gone crazy," murmured the captain, then frowned. "Gina said you two were Jehovah's Witnesses."

Joyce nodded. "Yes. We were fleeing to Vancouver. A place called Burrard Harbor."

The captain was nodding patiently. "I'm familiar with the Witnesses' camp there. We passed it on our way out of Vancouver. The place was being overrun."

"Overrun?" Joyce asked.

29

"Apparently they'd shut the gates. Once the power went off, they were the only ones in the area with the lights still on. People started flooding in. It was pandemonium."

Joyce was speechless, a look of horror frozen on her face.

"So even if you'd gotten there somehow, there'd have been nothing to flee to."

"But... That can't be..." Joyce said, her voice a frail whisper. "They would've been protected."

"By what?"

"By our organization, and our... our God, Jehovah."

"Interesting. Someone who still believes in God."

"I do. I've felt his protection these last few days, despite stupid decisions."

"Like sailing off into the dark unknown?"

"Worse. I was in Burrard Harbor weeks ago. I left on an impulse. We were given explicit instructions and I disobeyed."

"Well, if we run into any inclement weather out here, I'll be sure to toss you overboard," the captain said, a mysterious smirk forming on his lips.

"Come again?" Joyce asked anxiously.

"I'm afraid whale sharks aren't native to the California coast, though."

"I'm sorry, I'm not following you," Joyce said, brow furrowed.

"You're fortunate, you know. Had any other vessel stumbled across the two of you on that burning sailboat, they would've given you a wide berth. I guess that's one of the reasons I'm buying your story so far. Chances are too great that this wasn't just a random encounter. You may have disobeyed, but it looks like Jehovah has given you both another chance."

Joyce's expression froze as the picture began coming together.

"You can call me Brother Callister. We're all friends here."

"You're Witnesses? But you said the camp was overrun..."

"It was. But by the time that happened, we were all loaded onto ships and barges on the other end of the harbor. The lights were on, but no one was home, as per directions from the branch. So far as I know, no one was harmed. I apologize for leading you on there at the beginning, but I needed to see if you really were who you said you were. Can't be too cautious these days."

Joyce's head reeled. The relief was immense, but with it came a flood of questions.

"You said no one's left in Burrard."

"That's right."

"My husband was there. Alvin Tucker. Does the name ring any bells?"

"Sorry. Last I heard, the count at Burrard was over 190,000. Not a whole lot of familiar faces. He's probably in one of the ships out here, though."

"Is there any way to contact him? A radio, perhaps?"

"We've got the equipment, but it's been useless. My guess is that whatever's blocking out the light is also scrambling radio waves," Brother Callister said, motioning to the stained rag on the bench beside him. "Navigational systems and GPS are still working, but that's about it."

"How many ships are out here with us?"

"No idea, sister. Hundreds, perhaps thousands. It's a miracle how everything was coordinated. And it's a miracle we aren't crashing into each other out here in the dark."

"My husband told me we were instructed to evacuate to Namibia. Is that where we're headed now?" Joyce asked.

Brother Callister stood, stretched, and nodded. "That's right. It's a long trip down the coast, then we cut through the Panama Canal before heading through the Gulf and then across the Atlantic. A seventy-day trip, give or take."

Joyce could feel her head spinning again. "We won't run out of fuel in that time?"

"We've brought most of what we need with us, including fuel and supplies. When we do run low, some of the supertankers out here will act as supply and refueling vessels. That's actually our job in all this—we run supply lines from the supertankers to the other vessels. Everything's been positioned strategically along the route."

"It doesn't seem possible," Joyce said, shaking her head. "All of this is so surreal."

"You'll get over it," the captain said, smiling. "There's plenty of work to be done on a supply ship. You got any skills?"

Joyce nodded. "I was a registered nurse back in Washington. But I'm happy to be of use wherever you need me. My name's Joyce Tucker, by the way," she said, her hand outstretched. Captain Callister took it and smiled.

"Sister Tucker. Good to have you. Welcome aboard *Abigail*."

***

Chad Harkett had spent the better part of the last twelve hours in the Faraday cage hunched over a pad of paper, the relentless hiss of static near full volume in his ears. The bursts of speech were few and far between, making it a struggle to decipher even a single sentence of the repeating message. And even the snippets he'd transcribed made no sense to him, the words nonsensical and seemingly random. Some kind of coded language, perhaps.

Frustrated, Chad tossed the paper to the corner of the desk and rose from his seat. He'd been so engrossed with the broadcast that he'd hardly noticed the passage of time or the pangs of hunger. He made his way to the kitchenette and warmed a can of beans over the propane stove. The temperature in the bunker had dropped somewhat as the blaze outside had consumed all available fuel, but the air inside the bunker was dry and stifling.

For all of his disdain for Martin's inability to cope with the pressures of survival, Chad was beginning to question his own tenacity. With the liquor absent from his system, a dull, formless dread was emerging in the pit of his stomach like a creature stepping from the void. Chad was arrogant but not stupid; he knew he would need to face the terrors of his solitude. The inferno outside would eventually diminish, but the blackness it would leave in its wake would create a vacuum where new horrors would emerge.

He needed out.

Chad washed away the salty taste of beans with a warm bottle of water and sat, ignoring the rising tide of garbage at his feet. He closed his eyes and tried to sleep, but in spite of his utter exhaustion his mind was a whirlpool that would not allow him even a moment's rest. He could feel Martin's eyes staring down at him from the darkness. His fingers trembled. He felt a chill creep along his spine even as a sheen of sweat stood out on his forehead.

This will be my tomb, he thought. *I've buried myself alive.*

Chad rose and wandered to the entrance of the bunker. The hazy blaze outside had lessened to a faint orange glow, but even through the thick, reinforced steel door, Chad could smell smoke. Wispy ash and flickering embers swarmed like otherworldly insects on the other side of the glass.

And then a shape emerged.

A body, walking on two legs, through the blackness,

32

silhouetted by flames.

Chad felt his heart lunge into his throat as the figure neared. Surely this was not Martin, Chad thought. Even so, a faint hope emerged, and excitement with it.

But no, this was not Martin. The head, in fact, was not the shape of a man's head, but long and bulging with large, glassy eyes. A gas mask, Chad realized. A gas mask and fatigues and a large gun. The masked face filled the frame of the small window and brought a fist to the door. The eternal silence of the bunker was shattered by a fist pounding against the outer door.

Chad stumbled backwards down the ramp, staring up at the inhuman face as if experiencing a vision. He lay motionless there for a few long moments as the pounding continued. Then, coming to his senses, he unbolted the door and swung it open.

"You Martin?" asked the man through his mask. A wave of heat flooded into the bunker with him. Chad closed the door immediately behind him, faintly aware of the danger in welcoming an armed and uninvited stranger into the bunker with him, but too eager for company to stop himself.

Slowly, Chad shook his head. "Martin was my business partner. My name is Chad Harkett."

The soldier frowned, pulled a small notepad from his pants pocket, and grunted.

"We have this address down as belonging to Martin Landretti. Is he here?"

"I'm sorry, no. There was an accident. He's dead," Chad said. The soldier studied him for a moment before nodding.

"Been trying to reach his radio. You get anything?" The man peeled the gas mask from his sweaty face and scanned the room. He looked to be in his forties or so, with a buzz cut. A feathered wing tattoo crept up the left side of his neck from beneath his fatigues.

Chad turned to gaze dimly at the radio room. "I… there was something, but… The messages weren't clear."

"Yeah, figured. Something's interfering with the signals. Not just radio waves, either. GPS is down, satellite feeds iffy. It's a real pain to get any messages in or out. Landlines are working, but that's only if both parties have power. You got any water?" The man unzipped his jacket, revealing an undershirt soaked in sweat.

Chad fetched him a bottle. "How bad are the blackouts?" he asked. The man finished the entire bottle before he responded.

"Coast to coast, it seems. We've had confirmed reports from Florida to New York."

Chad's head spun. He sat heavily.

"I'm not here to chat. You said you worked with Martin?"

"That's right. We were business partners."

"Know anything about AI?"

"Artificial Intelligence?" Chad asked, puzzled. The soldier nodded curtly. "Sure, we were working on some facial-scanning software that utilized AI. Why?"

"No time to get into the details here," the soldier said as he stood and motioned towards the bunker's entrance. "We've got an armored convoy out there waiting. I can explain everything on the way."

"On the way where?" Chad asked.

"Can't tell you that until you're in the convoy."

Chad thought it over for only a moment before he acquiesced. "Fine. Let me just grab a few things."

CHAPTER 3

Peter was transfixed as the artist's stylus glided across the screen of the tablet. He could feel the slow burn of anxiety in his chest, the embers fanned with each pencil stroke.

Of course, part of it was exhaustion. He'd been sitting in the cramped conference room now for over two hours doing his best to summon every facial detail he could from his strained memory. He'd slept little in the past few days, and the weariness was showing. He barely recognized his own face in the mirror these days. It was as if he'd aged a decade since boarding the rig, and still their destination was weeks away.

But the other part was looming uncertainty. Uncertainty about what had happened, uncertainty about what remained.

"Brother Burton?" asked the young sister. She gazed expectantly over the top of her glasses, pulling Peter from his stupor.

"Sorry, Elise. You ask me something?" Peter asked, unable to recall anything past the haze of his thoughts.

"Um, yeah. The cheekbones. You said they were a little unpronounced before. Do they look about right now?"

Peter tilted his head and squinted at the glowing screen. If he could hardly recognize his own reflection, how was he expected to remember James's?

"Umm," Peter said, trailing off. He glanced over at Evan, snoring quietly at his side. Angelica's son would have gotten the closest look of any of them at their stowaway fugitive, but after all he'd been through the last couple of days, Peter wanted him to rest. Peter let out a long breath.

"Yeah. I think so. I mean, it's pretty close. Thanks, you did a great job."

"Uh huh," Elise said. She stretched and rolled her shoulders a few times. A glance at her watch told her it was nearly ten o'clock.

Elise was a young sister from central California who'd been a freelance graphic designer and portrait artist before the outbreak of the great tribulation. She'd been eager to take a break from folding sheets and pillowcases in the laundry department to work on the drawing, even if the overseers had been careful not to reveal its purpose. Still, being recruited so suddenly and so late in the night to do a drawing invited all kinds of speculation.

"So, I don't want to be nosy or anything, but this drawing…" Elise said as the file transferred wirelessly from her tablet to Peter's phone.

"Yeah?"

"Is it like a wanted poster or something?"

Peter frowned.

"Again, maybe it's totally not my place, but if there's someone dangerous here… I guess I'm just asking, as a single sister, is there something I should be watching out for?"

Peter's frown deepened. There it was again, that pain in his gut, that reminder that not all was well, that the sheep entrusted to his care were in danger.

"I… I'm sorry. I can't really say just yet."

"Um. All right," Elise said quietly with a shrug.

"If anyone needs to be told anything, I promise you'll hear about it." Peter made an effort at a reassuring look.

"Yeah, of course," Elise replied, and left. Peter was close behind her, Evan sound asleep in his arms. He carried the boy to their apartment and set him down on a small mattress Rachel had prepared in the corner. As Peter had instructed, Rachel had kept their apartment door bolted shut all day, and several pairs of brothers had stopped by periodically to check up on her. It had been a day of fear and uncertainty, and the signs of stress were written all over her face.

"Any news?" Rachel asked as her husband locked the door.

"Not yet. We'll be circulating a drawing of the man tomorrow. Maybe someone has seen something."

"How's Evan?" Rachel asked.

"Coping, I guess. Maybe he's still in shock. I have no idea. How're you?"

Rachel pressed her eyes shut and lowered her head. "Just tired. I want this to be over. It was exciting at first, being here with the friends. But now I feel like the walls are starting to close in on me. Like I might just lose my mind if I have to stay another week. And the food…"

36

"We're on rations, Rachel. They're doing the best they can."

"I'm not complaining, Peter. I'm just... I'm just trying to express myself."

"Well, I'm listening," Peter said, slipping his coat onto a hanger and hanging it on a slim closet in the corner of the pod.

"Really, Peter?" Rachel asked, her tone of voice taking on a sharp edge. Her husband said nothing. "Because I feel like you haven't heard a word I've said in days," Rachel pressed.

"There's been a lot going on. You know that," Peter said.

"And? You don't think I've been through a lot these last few days too?"

"I didn't say that. I'm just asking you to cut me a little slack here."

"You're not the only one who lost her, you know."

"Yeah? Well, it feels like I'm the only one trying to get her back," Peter snapped, regretting the words as soon as they were spoken. He felt the air leave the room as the two of them stood in the vacuum of cold silence. "I'm sorry," Peter mumbled. "I didn't mean it."

But it was too late. Neither of them said another word before bed.

***

Chad Harkett climbed into the armored convoy to find himself surrounded on all sides by monitors and racks of weapons. Crates of supplies and ammunition were lashed to the walls with thick nylon webbing. Narrow benches on either side and two swiveling chairs near the cabin were the only places to sit. Chad took a seat near the doors and took as much in as he could while the soldiers and technicians ignored him.

Chad's escort took a seat on the bench opposite him and unstrapped his helmet. He squeezed the remains of a second bottle of water into his mouth and slid a soot-stained sleeve across his face. Chad glanced out one of the narrow vertical windows set into the back doors of the vehicle and stared numbly at a sea of flames.

"Never seen anything like this..." he mumbled.

"Makes the previous California blazes look like bonfires, don't it?" the soldier quipped.

"How far does it go?"

"As far as we've heard, up and down the West Coast. More fires are popping up all over the place, too. All the way east, we hear."

"To Nevada?"

"To Florida."

"You can't be serious."

The soldier nodded slowly, his expression hard and unflinching.

"What started it?"

"Part of it was those freak storms, I'm sure. Right after the blackouts; seemed to come outta nowhere. Weird lightning all over the place. Been another dry season here in Cali, of course. One bolt on a patch of dried lawn or a pile of leaves is all it takes and she'll burn like the Fourth of July. But there's been reports of some other... *phenomena*, too. Could be to blame for some of this."

"What kind of phenomena are we talking about?"

"Well, I haven't seen it with my own eyes, but there's been a lot of radio chatter about... What they call it, Torres?" the soldier called out to one of the technicians glued to a monitor.

"Hail fire."

"Yeah, right. Hail fire. Fire coming right outta the sky."

"Is that... like, a normal thing?" Chad asked, eyes flitting from the back of the technician's head to the cold, dark eyes of the soldier in front of him.

"What's normal anymore these days?" the soldier laughed, a little too loudly.

"So is this an attack or what? Some kind of chemical warfare?"

"That's the current theory, yes. We think whoever is behind this is connected to the chemical attacks at the airports. Probably also connected to whatever's mucking up the air and jamming radio signals, too."

"And the power outages?" Chad asked.

"Maybe that too, yeah."

"But you're talking about an extremely highly coordinated attack. There must be only a handful of countries capable of something like that, right? China? Russia? Who do you think it was?"

"Nah, neither of those. We've been told that Beijing and Moscow have reported similar attacks on their infrastructure."

"North Korea, then?"

The soldier shook his head. "Unlikely."

"Why's that?" Chad asked.

"Bring up the image," barked the solider. The technician nodded once and tapped a few keys into the computer, bringing up an aerial image of a large peninsula. "You're looking at the Korean peninsula a few days ago. The next one was a composite put together over the last twenty-four hours. Our satellite connection isn't great, but it's enough to get the picture."

The screen image flittered away, replaced by a similar one. But now, instead of a greenish landmass surrounded by blue sea, the surrounding area was black, the peninsula itself a bright orange streak of fire.

"Oh my god," Chad gasped.

"That's everywhere. Pyongyang, Seoul, Incheon. All up in smoke. Looks like they got it even worse than we did."

"So you're saying this is worldwide?" Chad asked, struggling to process what he was hearing.

"Not sure yet. We're still struggling to make contact with whoever is left. And even when Washington has news for us, our connection to them isn't always stable. But we've got enough of the picture to form some conclusions."

"And those are?"

"From the intel we've gathered, it seems like everyone got hit with the same thing: blackouts, storms, and then fires. We're talking hundreds of trillions of dollars in damage. But in each area we've heard from so far, there are these… pockets, I guess you could call them, where things were relatively unscathed. In some areas you actually had acres upon acres of completely unaffected areas. No storms, no fires. Even, in some cases, power grids still somehow functioning when everyone else was sitting in the dark. And each of those places has something in common."

"What's that?"

"They were all evacuation points for a religious sect. Jehovah's Witnesses."

Chad felt as if the air had been sucked from his lungs and replaced with gasoline. His eyes and mouth burned. He seethed quietly as he let the soldier continue.

"You still got a copy of that pamphlet?" the soldier asked. The tech pulled a folded sheet of paper from his pocket and handed it over his shoulder.

"You remember seeing these everywhere a few months back?"

Chad nodded, the sickness worsening.

"Recruitment propaganda, trying to get people to join up before they launched their attack. Looking back, the signs seemed obvious, but at the time, I guess no one thought they were dangerous."

"How were they not stamped out with the other churches and religious group a year ago?"

"Who knows? But one thing is certain: the Witnesses are far more organized and dangerous than anyone could've imagined. And they're global, too. Financially, they're probably worth tens of billions. Looks like they finally cashed it all in on some end-of-the-world nightmare scenario."

"To what end? Why would they want this?"

"Our intel tells us they're trying to set up their own country and government. Apparently some African country sold them a huge tract of land years ago. They're headed there now."

"And then what?"

"The rest of it is detailed pretty plainly in that pamphlet, actually. They believe God has chosen them to set up a world government that will destroy all other countries. They don't believe in playing nicely together, it would seem."

"No kidding," Chad said, shaking his head. "So what's our government going to do about it?"

"Not just us. I mentioned Beijing and Moscow, and there's a few others in tow as well. A coalition is being formed."

"A coalition? To do what?"

"What needs to be done, of course. We're gonna eradicate the disease of religion once and for all and take back what's ours."

Chad crossed his arms and frowned. It wasn't the proposition that surprised him, but the frankness with which it was expressed. He wondered for a moment if the soldier had revealed more than he was supposed to. "How classified is this information?" he finally asked.

"Not very," the soldier shrugged. "A formal press release is being put together about the attacks. Once people learn the truth, we expect to have the public's full backing. After all, this isn't the end of the Witnesses' plans."

"What do you mean?"

40

"You read the pamphlet. In their scenario, this ends with Armageddon."

"Which means what, exactly?"

"According to their interpretation, the Lord Jesus and the angels wiping out all who oppose them."

"And your interpretation?"

"A nuclear attack, most likely. We don't know how they'd pull it off, but given their previous coordinated attacks, it doesn't seem so farfetched. Another possibility is a biochemical attack, similar to what we saw at the airports. They could also be somehow seeding the air with something. There are still plenty of unknowns, but all of it points to the same endgame."

"And where do I come in then?" Chad asked.

"You'll be briefed when we get to base. In the meantime, I suggest you get some shut eye. We've got a haul ahead of us and a list of names."

"Names?"

"Sure. You're not the only recruit on the list."

***

Peter found his way to a stiff, plastic chair nestled between the corner of the conference room and the long rectangular table. Tired faces—some familiar, some not—occupied the chairs beside and across from him. It was eight o'clock in the morning and Peter was unsure if he'd slept any the night before. The room stank of coffee and tired bodies; one of the water distillers had gone offline earlier in the week, requiring strictly rationed usage of water, which had only added to the passengers existing stress. Tensions were high, and nowhere more so than in this stuffily cramped room where men carried the weight of thousands on their shoulders.

The chairman spoke as soon as the prayer had finished. His name was Donnie Chavez. "I apologize for not getting an agenda out to you all before calling this meeting, but given the nature of the situation with the missing sister, and the fact that we now have this sketch, I decided to call us together again. Brother Burton, can you update us?"

Peter nodded, downed the rest of his coffee to muster whatever remained of his concentration and began. "As you all know, we've still heard no news of the missing sister from our

41

congregation. Her son is safe and is staying with my wife and I for the time being. As we discussed at the last meeting, I tracked down an artist from aboard our rig and she helped me put together the profile sketch I emailed to all of you."

The heads around the table nodded respectfully, but little seemed to register behind their eyes. Was it lack of concern or mere exhaustion? Peter couldn't tell.

"Since I haven't heard back from any of you, I'm assuming no one's seen a face like this?" Peter said, struggling to control his impatience. He waited as the brothers leaned in closer to peer at the screens of phones and tablets.

"I'm sure we'll let you know if we run into anyone matching this face, but with so many unfamiliar faces aboard this rig, please understand that it's not a simple thing to track anyone down, especially someone who doesn't want to be found."

"If he's even aboard this rig in the first place," said another brother.

"Meaning?" Peter asked.

"As far as I remember, Sister Barry's child was the only one to witness the alleged kidnapping. Am I correct?"

"The name's Parry. And while Evan was the only one to see it, we had others who testified to seeing this man aboard the rig."

"Sure, I remember that, Brother Burton. But you know that these types of things can only be established with two eyewitnesses."

"I'm not trying to start a judicial hearing here, brothers. I'm simply asking for some cooperation in helping to find a missing sister," Peter said, unable any longer to control his tone. He looked down to find his fists clenched on the table.

"Look, brothers. We've all been through a lot here," said Marcus Kelly. "Each of us has more on our plate now than ever before, and the stakes feel higher than ever. And you're right, we've got nothing established here yet with only one eyewitness. However, maybe one of us has an idea of how we can help. Just imagine if it were someone in your own group, or family, that was missing."

Peter let out a breath, exhaling some of the tension along with it.

"With all due respect, Brother Burton—and I can only imagine how anxious this situation must make you feel—I'm still against the idea of putting up wanted posters all over the rig. People are already riled up. With the lack of land communication, the food rations, and now the water issues, I feel like we're sitting on a powder keg. Our friends are struggling just to keep things civil. Something like this could send everyone over the edge."

"Have there been any reports of strange sightings from the night watchmen?" asked Brother Kelly to the security overseer, Charles Garboni.

"Not that they've mentioned to me. Why do you ask?"

"I'm just trying to piece it together. If this kidnapper is still aboard—and I can't imagine how he would've escaped—he's gotta be holed up somewhere, which means he needs access to food and water. He's got to know he's a wanted man at this point, which means he probably won't be taking his chances stealing supplies during the day. Seems only logical to assume he'd try to sneak into the cafeteria at night. Is there anyone patrolling that area at that time?"

Brother Garboni shook his head. "Our night watchmen stick to the outer walkways at night. They man the floodlights and watch for pirates or anyone who might've fallen overboard."

"So the cafeteria is completely unwatched at night?" Peter asked.

"That's right. There's never been a need to."

"Perhaps we can station a couple of night patrols in the cafeteria. I understand they've got a copy of the sketch?" Brother Kelly asked.

"Hadn't gotten around to it. Brothers, what do you think?" Charles Garboni asked. The others were nodding, and for once Peter had reason for optimism.

"If possible, tell them to keep somewhat hidden. If this James character does show up, we don't want him apprehended. They'll need to follow him to wherever he's hiding so we can locate Angelica."

Brother Garboni winced. "You said a few days ago that this James character… he's dangerous, right?"

Peter surveyed the room before carefully responding. "If he's the one behind the poisoning… if that's what it was… then yes. He's dangerous."

Charles opened his mouth as if to speak, but suddenly caught himself and simply nodded. "I understand. We'll do our best."

Peter excused himself from the conference room as soon as the closing prayer was finished. His head was pounding and his

43

lungs ached for fresh air. He climbed up an outer stairwell and leaned into a catwalk railing as the waves crashed and frothed below. He closed his eyes and drew a deep breath as a frail hand settled on his shoulder. He turned to find Marcus smiling gently.

"Marcus," Peter said, struggling to match his friend's expression. Marcus nodded slowly and turned to face the sea. He closed his eyes. The two stood quietly side by side, the salt in the air sticking to their skin, making it feel coarse and weathered.

"You been feeling ok lately?" Peter asked.

"Oh, I have my ups and downs," Marcus said with a sigh.

"I hope you've been getting regular checkups at the infirmary since you've been here."

"I'd say they have their hands full at the moment, wouldn't you? You check on Ted lately?"

"Last night. Same as before. Stable but still completely out of it. They put him in a drug-induced coma until they can be sure the toxins haven't done any permanent damage."

"He'll pull through."

"Wish I had your confidence."

"You will, in time."

"Yeah? What's that mean?"

Marcus smiled at his younger friend and took another deep breath. When he spoke, his words were measured and calming. "Stand still and see the salvation of Jehovah."

Peter sighed. "Marcus... I appreciate the encouragement. And I know Jehovah's looking out for us, and that all of this will be fine in the long run, but right now..."

"Peter, right now *is* the long run. There's no time left. We've made it this far. All we have to do is *take our position.*"

"You think I'm overreacting to this Angelica thing."

"I understand it, Peter. I get that you're worried, and I get that you're frustrated that the others don't seem as worried as you."

"You're right. I don't get that at all."

"That's because you don't understand all of what they're going through. Take the chairman, Brother Chavez, as an example. Do you know his situation?" Peter shook his head.

"His two sons, Bret and Phillip, were killed on their way to New Orleans. A couple of hoodlums mugged them at a gas station. Their wives still made it safely aboard, but now they're grieving over that loss while trying to adapt to life on these rigs. Or what

44

about Charles Garboni, the brother in charge of the security department? Have you gotten to know him?"

"No," Peter said.

"Three families in his congregation—one in his own service group—have been missing since evacuation from California. Their convoy was separated when an accident diverted traffic near their hometown. He believes they may have made it safely to New Orleans and boarded another rig, but he's been unable to confirm it."

"That's awful."

"Everyone's got a story here, Peter. And listening to these stories, our congregation seems to have gotten by pretty well. We have so much to be thankful for."

"Yeah, well except for Darren and Rita."

"Yes, I think about them too. But that's not on our conscience. We did everything we could for them, especially you. Whatever happened to them, it was entirely on their own heads."

"But that's exactly why I'm so worried about Angelica. That *is* on our heads. Isn't it?"

"No one is blaming you for her disappearance, Peter. And no one is stopping you from doing what you can to track her down. The brothers are merely trying to keep an eye on the big picture and not cause needless anxiety for the friends. The perspective is simply different."

"You feel I was too harsh in there."

"Considering all that those good brothers have gone through, and all they continue to do for everyone aboard this rig, yes."

"I'm sorry, I just…"

"Listen, Peter. We're so close to the end. But before it comes, we can be sure that Satan will try to attack us with the only means he now has—each other. You can see how tensions are already getting to people. More than ever before, unity, humility, and forgiveness are going to be tested to their limits. As brothers—and especially as overseers—we have to be setting the example. We have to be peacemakers."

***

Angelica opened her eyes to the familiar four walls of the storage closet she'd been confined to for the last three days. The swaying of the sea beneath her caused the suspended halogen lights

45

to swing from the ceiling in rhythmic arcs, tugging and stretching the shadows this way and that. The furniture had been rearranged somewhat since her arrival; Thiago had moved everything but the cardboard and sacks that served as her bed to the opposite end of the room, ostensibly to prevent her from accessing anything that might aid an escape attempt. Not that she'd tried; Angelica had been content waiting for someone to stumble upon her. There were only so many places to hide on a repurposed oil rig trudging through the Atlantic, and it would only be a matter of time before she was discovered. She was most worried for Evan, as it had been made clear to her that Chad had paid for the capture and safe return of both of them. She filled the time between meals and sleep with prayer, and this kept the anxiety at bay.

"Food's been rationed. This is all you'll get for today," the tall man said as he slipped in through the entrance. He pulled the tape from Angelica's lips; she winced as flecks of dried skin peeled away.

"Thank you," Angelica said, raising her wrists above her head so that Thiago could snip away the ties. From the start she'd been careful to build the trust between them. No sudden moves. No thoughts of escape. With the ties cut, Angelica massaged her wrists as she began working on the plate of food in front of her. It wasn't much, but it didn't matter. She was voracious and there wasn't a crumb left when she was done eating.

Her captor had been nothing if not attendant to her needs, Angelica thought. It was now clear that the price on her head was predicated by her safe return to land, and so any initial fears of physical violence had vanished. James, on the other hand (or whatever his name was) seemed increasingly anxious with each encounter. Angelica had been careful not to press him needlessly for details, but it was clear to her that whatever plan he'd originally formulated had been abandoned. The farther the rig carried them out into the open seas, the more treacherous any attempt to leave would become. Time was running out for him.

"How have conditions been here on the rig since the rations went into effect?" Angelica asked, testing the waters. Thiago gave her a long look before replying.

"Little has changed."

Good news, Angelica thought. Everyone was keeping calm. It would not be easy, she knew. Even down here, in her cramped storage room closer to the waterline, she could feel the seas

46

roughening with each passing day. Thankfully, seasickness hadn't been an issue. Things could always be worse.

"Have you seen my son?" Angelica asked. Thiago's eyes narrowed as his chin lifted slightly into the air, gauging her intentions.

"No. But when I do find him, you can be sure we'll be on the next boat off of this cursed platform."

"You have a boat, then?"

"How we leave is none of your concern," Thiago hissed.

"I'm sorry. I'm not trying to cause you trouble," Angelica said, lowering her gaze. "It's just that... Well, if I'm going to be expected to leave with you, I'm afraid my legs won't be much use. I haven't walked in days, and my ankles are starting to swell."

"What are you asking?"

"Just that you cut the ankle restraints, let me stretch my legs."

Thiago considered the request for a long moment before tossing the wire cutters onto the mattress. Angelica removed the zip ties. The skin around her ankles was red and chafed and her whole body felt stiff from the lack of movement, but otherwise she didn't feel terrible. She returned the cutters and slowly began to massage the muscles in her calves, her knees, and ankles. Heat spread through her body as the circulation improved.

"This place is a death trap," Thiago growled. It was the first instance she could remember of her captor initiating a conversation and she wasn't about to pass up the opportunity.

"Oh? Why's that?"

"Thousands of brainwashed cult members adrift at sea with no means to protect themselves. Now your food is running out. Soon it'll be water, then fuel. Then you'll see these people's true colors."

Angelica smiled. "It does seem dire, but I'm not worried. We've been through worse."

"Impossible."

"During the Second World War, our brothers and sisters were attacked by Hitler. He sent them to concentration camps and death marches. He was determined to completely wipe out the Witnesses. But we took care of each other, fed each other, gave up our lives for each other. Most made it out alive. We can handle some rough seas and food rations."

"So much confidence, even as you sit here as a prisoner," Thiago said coldly.

47

"I don't know how things will turn out for me individually. I might live through this ordeal, I might not. But as a people, nothing can stop us. I have absolute faith in that."

"Faith is a dangerous thing."

"Lack of faith is even more dangerous."

"It's worked out fine for me," Thiago sneered. He fished a few zip ties from a pocket and tossed them onto the mattress. Angelica looked at them dejectedly. "Fasten those nice and tight. I have some errands to run." He stood and donned a jacket and baseball cap while Angelica complied, looping the ties around her ankles first, then her wrists. Thiago bent down to inspect her work and cinch the ties even tighter. Angelica winced as the sharp plastic bit into her raw, reddened skin.

"Where are you going?" she asked.

"Supplies," replied her captor before shutting off the light and disappearing out back into the cold outside.

CHAPTER 4

"How are you and Tina holding up?" asked the night watchman. His name was Mike Glover, though most on the crew knew him as Mikey. He broke a Snickers bar in half and handed it to his buddy, Cary.

"Little antsy, to say the least," Cary said glumly. He bit into the chocolate, savored it. "Man, I can't tell you how bad I want to get to that next supply depot."

Mikey grunted in confirmation. "Yeah, rations are taking their toll. On the plus side, I've probably dropped ten pounds in the last few weeks."

"Three more days, man. Three more days and I can forget about tuna salad and crackers."

"I wonder what our diet is going to be like when we get to Namibia," Mikey said, chewing on the last bit of his candy bar.

"Probably not Snickers bars."

"Yeah. Probably not. I'm sure we'll be taken care of, though. It's pretty crazy when you actually stop and think about everything that's happening now. It was only a year ago when the evacuation letters were read. I'll never forget that meeting. It was so unreal, getting those instructions."

"We didn't sleep at all that night. Just laid awake in bed talking about it, worrying about the house and the jobs and everything. Only a year ago. That *is* crazy."

"Feels like a lifetime ago, doesn't it?"

"Sure does. And can't say I don't miss it a little bit."

"What do you mean?" Mikey asked.

"The stability, you know? Having a job to clock in on each day, a paycheck to look forward to. Being able to drive around, go to the grocery store, come home and flip on the TV or Netflix and just veg."

"Life has become simpler. But you do have a stable job, and

49

you don't have to worry about a paycheck now. And no more rush hour traffic, right?"

"Yeah, sure, but it isn't the same. Don't get me wrong, I'm not complaining. I'm grateful… for everything."

"That's good to hear, Cary. We just had that talk about not looking at the things behind, you know? And I know life aboard this rig isn't what any of us expected. But we've got to keep fixed on what lies ahead, right?"

"Yeah, of course, I get that. Like I said, I'm not about to jump ship and try to swim home, I'm just saying. You miss those mundane things in life when everything gets flipped upside down. Don't you?"

"Once in a while, sure. But we've got so much more to look forward to. I try to focus on that."

"That's great and all, don't get me wrong, but we also have no idea how long this tribulation will last. What if it goes on for years? Have you thought about that? What if we're all crammed into some kind of refugee camp in Africa for a decade? Can you imagine that? Ten million of us or whatever. I'm just saying it could happen."

"I guess anything is possible. We don't have the details. But I'd still take that over what's happening in the rest of the world. You saw that footage from New York: no power, no sunlight, and now flash fires? It must be scary. I wouldn't want to be back there. Would you?"

"That's just the East Coast though, Mikey. There's no way of knowing how bad it actually is in California. Maybe things are just as they were when we left."

"I dunno, Cary," Mikey said uncertainly. "That seems like a dangerous train of thought."

"I'm just talking, Mikey."

"Okay."

The two watchmen fell silent as the overhead bulbs thunked off in succession until the only light was the soft glow of an electric lantern seeping from the kitchen window. The last of the kitchen crew filed out of the cafeteria. Some waved.

"So, what are your thoughts on this whole… *fugitive* thing?" Cary asked when the two were alone. He pulled his phone from a jacket pocket and swiped to the artist's sketch, combing over the details.

Mikey shrugged. "What do you mean?"

"Well, you think he's connected to those two who were poisoned?"

"I didn't hear anything about anyone being poisoned."

"What? You didn't hear about the two guys who collapsed the other day? It happened right over there," Cary said, motioning with his chin.

"No, I heard about that, but I didn't know they'd determined it was anything to do with poisoning."

"Well, it's not *official*, of course. But that seems to be the consensus. I guess they're trying to keep things under wraps, trying not to cause a stir."

"Makes sense to me."

"If you ask me, it's worse to be so secretive. Same with these wanted posters. I say stick 'em up on the walls, put them on the monitors. Get *everyone* involved. We'd nab him a lot sooner."

"I'm sure the brothers know what they're doing, Cary."

"I wish I had your confidence."

"I think the important thing is to just keep our minds on the task at hand."

"You really think the guy'd show his face in here after what happened? He's probably long gone," Cary said smugly. He took a seat on one of the cafeteria benches and threw his feet up on the seats across from him.

"Then again, maybe there's a reason the overseers assigned two of us to this place for the night shift. They explicitly mentioned keeping a low profile and staying out of sight. We should probably take a look around and figure out how to patrol the place without being too visible."

"Relax, Mikey. It's almost pitch black in here. No one's gonna show." Cary crossed his arms and tried to get comfortable on the bench while Mikey looked on in dismay. He had words for his nephew—many words—but would save them for another time. He set off by himself towards the kitchen.

***

Joyce stared motionlessly at the still body of her friend, Stacy Owen. The injured woman had been laid on one of the ship's cabin bunks and wrapped in a space blanket. The color had drained from her cheeks while a vicious fever had gripped her for nearly three days. Joyce had administered all of the antibiotics the crew of the Abigail had managed to scrounge up, and there was little left to do now but wait.

She prayed aloud for the dozenth time that day, repeating the words that had become nearly rote. Perhaps Stacy could hear them too.

"How is she?" asked the baritone voice of a man from the doorway. Joyce Tucker turned to find Captain Callister standing there, a mug of steaming black tea held in his outstretched hand. Joyce took it from him and escorted the two of them out into the corridor.

"Still fighting off some kind of infection. I've medicated her as best I can with what's available, but I'm not sure it's enough," Joyce explained softly, glancing back at her friend through the doorway. "I'm more concerned with the pain, though. She's got second and third degree burns on her hands and arms. If she wakes up, it'll be excruciating."

"She still hasn't regained consciousness then?"

"Her system is in shock. My guess is that's what's keeping her under. She may be more conscious than we know, though. It's possible that she's aware of her surroundings on some level."

"I see," grunted the captain. "Well, I may have some good news for you."

"Great. I could use a dose of that," Joyce said, feeling some of the tension release in her shoulders.

"We received a radio transmission this afternoon from another vessel."

"A transmission? I thought all the signals were being blocked somehow."

"They were. But it seems that things are improving the farther we get from the coast. We're picking up nothing from the mainland, just other ships out here with us. Skies are lightening a bit, too."

"What was the transmission for? From one of our ships?"

The captain nodded. "A supply depot. One of the massive barges that was sent out from Burrard Harbor."

"What about medical supplies?"

"Most of the supply vessels are stocked with a little bit of everything. If you can put together a list of the things you need, we can ask."

"I'll do it right away," Joyce said, already compiling a list in her head. "How far away are they from us?"

Captain Callister glanced at his watch. "At our current speed, we should reach them late tonight. If everything goes smoothly, you should have your supplies shortly thereafter."

"Thank you, Captain," Joyce said.

"Happy to help. Seeing the way you've taken care of your friend, well… It's the least we can do. You two from the same congregation?"

Joyce nodded. "Yes. Only got to know her well in the last couple of weeks though."

"Yeah, I hear a lot of people saying the same thing. Lots of friendships being forged by the fires of these trials."

"I used to think Stacy and I were such different people, back before all this started, when we were just two sisters in the same hall. It turns out we were more similar than I thought. We're all working through things, but we've all made it this far, and I guess that says some—" Joyce was interrupted by the loud clanking of footsteps coming from the end of the corridor. A tall black woman in a grey parka was rushing towards them, a fiery look in her eyes.

"Captain," said the woman. "We need you on the bridge. We've got a situation."

***

Mikey Glover stood and stretched, his mind wading through a drowsy haze. It was much easier on the normal night watch above decks, with the cold wind at his back and a regular patrol shift to keep his mind and feet busy. There, a rotating roster of brothers to chat with, an occasional hand of rummy, and plenty of opportunities for conversation kept the drowsiness at bay. Down here in the cafeteria, though, it was just him and Cary and the dark.

Mikey took a long look at his dozing nephew and could only shake his head. Not only did the younger man fail to take their assignment seriously, but some of his recent sentiments had been downright worrisome. He and his wife, Tina, were becoming growingly impatient and dissatisfied with life aboard the rigs. Mikey was grateful that the couple had made it this far, as there was little choice for them now but to stay and endure their situation. Still, he was unsure how they might react to future challenges. He was not sure they could resist the temptation to go home if such became a possibility.

Mikey stood and scanned the dark cafeteria for the dozenth time that night. No one had entered or exited since the departure of the kitchen crew. The cavernous space was utterly quiet but for the distant rumble of the rig's diesel engines and the creaks and groans of the platform itself as it waded through the waves below.

He walked to the end of the cafeteria and pushed through the swinging doors into the kitchen. All was just as it had been when he'd checked an hour prior. Mike scanned the room and stifled a yawn. He checked his watch; it was only slightly past eleven but it felt much later. Out here on the open ocean, the bodies of the crew and passengers had adapted to a new Circadian rhythm, one that utilized daylight as efficiently as possible. They rose with the sun and headed for bed shortly after dark. Despite being on the night crew for weeks, Mikey found it increasingly difficult to stay alert during the long stretches of dark and quiet.

He mentally reviewed the instructions they'd been given from their overseer, Brother Garboni, two days before. The overseer hadn't said much about the man they were to be on the watch for, but had insisted that they keep the artist's sketch to themselves. If spotted, the man was not to be apprehended or followed; they were to report the sighting immediately and await further instructions. Mikey had to admit that the direction had been odd, and it was difficult to resist drawing conclusions to link recent events aboard the rig. Maybe Cary was right about that one after all. Maybe they weren't as safe out here as they all thought.

Of course, they'd been warned of as much in recent broadcasts and reprinted study articles that were reviewed at the weekly meetings. It was unreasonable to assume that *each and every individual* would be protected through the great tribulation, only that the great crowd as a whole would pass through the other side. Infiltrators were thus a real possibility, as was injury and even death. It was a sobering thought and one that Mikey Glover preferred not to dwell on as he knelt down to perform a quick scan of the space beneath the prep tables. Nothing.

Satisfied, the watchman stood and headed back towards the dining area to rouse Cary. But then he froze. The sound of creaking hinges shattered the stark silence. Reflexively, he ducked his head so as not to be seen through the kitchen window. Then, as quietly as he could manage, he snuck to the back of the kitchen, where a rear door led into a corridor connecting the dining area. He stood up slowly, his eyes lifting to the level of the door's window, and watched.

A tall, dark figure moved silently among the tables. Thankfully, Cary was napping on the floor on the opposite side of the large room and went unnoticed. Mike clenched his teeth and winced as he pushed the door back into the dining area open, hoping it wouldn't squeak as the others had, but it remained silent. He slipped into the cafeteria and crouched behind a table stacked with serving trays.

The figure made a beeline for the kitchen, exactly where Mike had been only moments ago. Whoever he was, Mike thought, he seemed awfully familiar with the layout of the place. But was he their wanted man or merely a worker who'd returned to retrieve a forgotten item? He needed a good look at the man's face. Slowly, he rose from his hiding spot and peeked back through the kitchen window, hoping he wouldn't be spotted.

The man's back was turned towards him as he pulled a canvas sack from a shelf and began filling it with various food items from the kitchen. There were several cans, a carton of juice, and half a loaf of bread. The man seemed to deliberate over certain items. Mike watched as the man carefully replaced one of the cans, adjusting its position to match the other stacks. Suddenly, Mikey understood.

This was their man.

***

John Callister moved hastily through the cramped corridors of the supply ship, eager to reach the bridge. His first mate led the way, revealing as much as she could as they went. Her name was Monique Legrande, a French-Haitian whose family had emigrated to the States years ago. She was as seaworthy as they came, and the captain was grateful for her presence. Her competency made the urgency in her voice and the way her eyes shot nervous glances back over her shoulder especially unnerving.

"Ok Monique, lay it on me. What's happening out there?" John asked, trying to keep pace with the younger woman. At twice her weight, it was no easy task. He envied the way she slinked and weaved effortlessly through the corridors even as the vessel moved with the rhythm of the sea.

Monique threw him a grave look before replying. "Pirates."

John took a moment to process this. "Pirates? *Here?* Off the coast of California?"

"We noticed a smaller vessel trailing us at first. We ignored them at first, until we spotted a second ship ahead of us."

"What makes you so sure they're pirates?"

"They're right in our path and showing no signs of yielding. I hailed them on the radio and they asked to speak with the captain. I've got a bad feeling about it."

"Maybe they just need help."

"We're very isolated out here, Captain. If we were just a bit farther down the coast it'd be a different story, but here…"

"Have you tried radioing the others?"

"No response. I think the signals are having trouble again."

On the bridge, the captain picked up the VHF handset, careful to hide the apprehension in his voice. "This is Captain John Callister of the *Abigail.* Please state your intentions."

Monique handed the captain a pair of binoculars while they waited for a response. He was able to make out the craft clearly. It had been positioned at a ninety-degree angle to their course, exposing its starboard side. It was a luxury yacht, and with more powerful engines and a sleeker design, the captain knew immediately that there would be no way to outrun it.

He checked the forward and aft ends of the vessels and felt his heart sink. Patches of dark paint had been hastily applied to the hull. "Name's been covered up," the captain groaned uneasily.

"I noticed. Stolen?"

"Seems likely. And the one tailing us?" the captain asked, setting down the binoculars and glancing at Monique.

"Thirty to thirty-five footer. No name. That one's a fishing boat."

"Then they're both too fast for us. We'll have to talk our way through this one," John Callister said.

"Should I alert the cr—" Monique began, but a pop of static from the radio stopped her.

"Captain Callister, we read you loud and clear. You a military vessel?"

Military vessel? John mouthed to his first mate. It should've been obvious from a glance that their ship was anything but.

56

"No," the captain replied, his mind racing. "We're part of an evacuation convoy from Vancouver."

"A convoy?" asked the voice skeptically.

"Yes. We were rerouted through the bay due to poor visibility. We're going to rendezvous with the rest of our convoy soon."

"You carrying supplies?"

The captain hesitated. He had feared this question was coming.

"What kind of supplies?" he asked, buying time.

"Food, water, meds."

"Very little. We have injured aboard our vessel, which is why we need to rendezvous with the others as soon as possible."

"Yeah, well, us too. And we're running low on food."

"I'm sorry," John said firmly. "We've got nothing to share."

The following moments of silence were agonizing as John and Monique waited for a response.

"Here's the thing," the voice finally said. "We want to keep this civil, but we'll take what we need if we have to."

"Monique," the captain said, turning to his first mate and speaking in a quick but calm voice. "Rouse the crew. Tell them not to panic, but explain the situation. Have them gather any supplies we can afford to part with and leave them on the aft deck. Understand?"

Monique nodded quickly and disappeared immediately below decks.

"I copy that," responded Captain Callister into the transmitter. "We'll see what we can spare."

"Good. One of our boats will rendezvous with you shortly."

"Ok," said the captain. The branch had been explicit in their directions on how to handle these kinds of encounters. The brothers were to comply as much as possible and avoid confrontation. Lives were always to be protected over belongings. John Callister exited the pilothouse and watched as the smaller fishing boat crept alongside their starboard quarter. Two men, one with a rifle flung over his shoulder, shone flashlights along the outer hull of *Abigail*, inspecting the outer walkways and portholes.

"We are unarmed!" the captain called out to the men, who didn't bother responding. They wore dark baseball caps and jackets. John wondered if they were ex-military. He recalled the odd question they'd been asked by the captain and wondered if that's what he meant. Perhaps he'd been testing the waters, trying to figure out how protected the supply vessel and her crew were.

57

The smaller craft approached and the two men climbed aboard. The captain said a quick prayer and walked to meet them, just as several members of his crew emerged onto the weather deck with a few boxes of items.

"Set 'em down right there," barked one of the men, pointing a gloved finger at a spot on the deck. The other man stood with his legs spread apart, his rifle held at the ready. His dark eyes darted from one crew member to the next.

One by one, the brothers complied, depositing the boxes where the man had indicated. Captain Callister stood and watched, careful to keep his hands where they could be seen. He was at this moment as proud as he'd ever been of his crew. Unarmed and with only moments to prepare for this encounter, he knew they had to be scared–terrified, even—but they didn't look it.

The first man knelt on the deck and began digging through the boxes, tossing items onto the deck one by one. The first was filled with shirts and jackets and a pair of shoes. He didn't seem pleased as he began rifling through the second box. This one contained two gallon-sized cartons of drinking water, a pair of propane lanterns, and some assorted canned goods. They were precious emergency supplies from the pantry, John realized. The third box contained toiletries: a large carton of toothpaste, a family-sized pack of toothbrushes, rolls of toilet paper and paper towels, and bags of hand wipes. The captain hoped it was enough. They all did.

"Unbelievable," said the man, rising to his feet. "You all had time to run to Costco before boarding this ship or what?"

"Gentlemen, you got what you came here for. We've been more than generous with you and we don't want a fight on our hands. Now please, take your items and leave us in peace," John said, taking a cautious step forward, hands still in front of him.

"You think we're stupid or something?" asked the man with the gun.

"You all are stocked with extra clothes, paper towels, and… and *toothpaste* and you expect us to believe you've been generous?"

"I don't understand… What's the issue here?" the captain asked.

"We want your firearms and ammunition," demanded the second man.

"I'm sorry, gentlemen, but like I said, we're an unarmed vessel. I can assure you that you won't find a single gun aboard this ship."

"Well, then you won't mind us checking, will you?" the leader of the two said with a scowl. He leaned over the edge of the ship's railing and whistled down to the men in the fishing boat. Moments later, two more armed men had climbed aboard. They charged through the back doors of the supply ship. Screams erupted from the cabins and corridors within as the men began ransacking the vessel. The brothers exchanged nervous looks with the captain, but no one budged.

CHAPTER 5

Captain Callister and his crew waited patiently while the pirates combed through every nook and cranny of the *Abigail*. From the crew's quarters and the corridors came the crashing noises of overturned furniture and emptied bins and containers. The men laughed as they went, clearly enjoying the havoc.

Twenty minutes later they emerged from the rear doors of the ship back onto the aft deck, boxes of supplies piled high in their arms. There were personal items as well—watches, necklaces, and electronics—stuffed into the men's pockets and tossed carelessly into the boxes.

"Looks like y'all were holding out on us," growled one of the pirates, leaning into the captain's face and glowering.

"I told you we had no weapons aboard," Brother Callister responded.

"Maybe not, but you had plenty of other stuff. Just look!" the man teased, holding up an arm to show off an expensive stolen watch that belonged to the captain. It had been an anniversary gift from his wife shortly before her death. He bit his lip and pushed the sentiment from his mind.

"These items are of no use to you. We already gave you what we could," the captain objected, but the men ignored him and were already beginning to toss the boxes down into their boat. He wanted to step forward, to do something to stop these delinquents from taking the few personal belongings that he and crew still owned, but a gentle hand on his arm stopped him. He glanced back to find himself staring into Monique's cautioning eyes. She slowly shook her head.

"Are we done here?" the captain asked the leader of the pack. The man ignored the question as he lit a cigarette and blew the smoke into the brother's face.

"Why? You in some kind of rush?" asked the pirate.

"As a matter of fact, we have an appointment with the rest of our convoy."

"Uh huh," the man replied, glancing over the captain's shoulder. "Well then, we'll let y'all get on with it. We just need one more thing." In a flash of movement, the man dropped the smoldering cigarette to the deck and snapped his hand out to grab Monique's wrist. She struggled to resist, but even using only one arm he was much too strong for her.

"Stop it. Let me go!" Monique shouted, twisting and writhing, trying to break free. But the man said nothing as he pulled her closer to the railing of the supply boat.

John Callister had had enough. In spite of the two armed men standing at either side, he reached out and grabbed his first mate's other arm. Instantly, the brothers on deck followed his lead, grasping for the sister and halting the kidnapping. The two pirates raised their weapons.

"Back up! Right now!" they ordered.

"No," Brother Callister said firmly. "You may take our supplies and our valuables, but I will not let you take my crew."

The lead pirate whipped his head around, a menacing look in his eyes. "And how are you gonna stop me? You people are too stupid to arm yourselves, too naive to protect yourself against a handful of opportunists like ourselves. What's your plan here?"

The captain said nothing, a hard set look in his eyes, his gaze unflinching as he stared directly at the lead pirate. For a few tense moments, neither man spoke.

"Fine!" the man finally said, pushing Monique away from him. "Have it your way! Let her die with the rest of you. Mark my words–none of y'all will last long on these waters!" the man laughed as he corralled his accomplices back over the railing and into their fishing boat. The captain and crew of the Abigail could hear their raucous laughter as they disappeared over the black waves.

***

Brother Chavez welcomed the overseers one by one back into the small conference room. The scene was much as it had been days prior when they'd last met, but spirits were noticeably higher today. Even Peter Burton had managed a couple of nights' worth of sleep and was ready to be here and hear more of what had been described to him briefly on the phone as "positive developments". The brothers mingled briefly over coffee and day-old pastries prepared by the cafeteria.

"I'll get right to the point," Donnie Chavez said when everyone had filed in and the meeting had officially begun. "Early this morning I received a message from Brother Garboni," he said, gesturing towards the overseer of security. "Charles, I'll let you share the rest."

Charles Garboni nodded and rose from his seat, making his way to the far wall of the room where a printout of a 3D floor plan of the entire rig was mounted to a giant billboard. "I was contacted early this morning from one of our night watchmen. He and another brother had been assigned to the East Cafeteria on the B Deck," he explained, sticking a red pin into the diagram. "Apparently, they spotted someone sneaking into the kitchen area and stealing supplies."

"Did the brother have a copy of the artist's sketch we provided?" asked Peter.

"He did, and he checked it. It was dark, but he seems to think this could've been our man. He said he didn't stay long though; he filled a small sack with some supplies and was gone. The watchman said his behavior was peculiar; he seemed careful not to take too many supplies, perhaps to keep from arousing suspicion."

"Did the watchmen follow him?" Brother Chavez asked.

Brother Garboni shook his head. "No. They were instructed not to follow or engage in any way."

"But then how does this get us any closer to finding this stowaway and our sister?" Peter asked.

"The instructions given were for any watchmen who spotted anyone resembling the fugitive to determine which direction he was moving in and contact the nearest brother in his path. It was safer to keep an eye on him this way, rather than have someone tailing him."

"And? Did anyone else on your crew see the man?" Brother Chavez asked.

Charles Garboni pulled two more red pins from the corner of the bulletin board and continued. "Yes. We had another watchman camped out in a rec area here. There's a snack and water cabinet there and we suspected the stowaway might attempt to stock up on supplies here. That turned out not to be the case, but he did pass through the hallway just outside the rec area and was spotted through the windows." Charles stuck one of the red pins into the corresponding spot on the map. A path was now beginning to form on the diagram.

"From there our suspect kept course, taking the south exit on this level here. We know this because another watchman on the top deck spotted him from the tower crane." A final pin was jabbed into the map. "Unfortunately, the trail goes cold after that. The man kept to the shadows and wasn't seen by anyone after he passed under the walkway, here. Still, it doesn't leave too many places for him to have gone."

"So you have an idea where he might be holed up?" Donnie Chavez asked.

"I have a guess, yes," Brother Garboni said. He pulled a few green pins from the corner of the bulletin board before continuing. "On the lower decks here are a bunch of old supply lockers. They were too small to be converted into apartment pods and a little out of the way to be practical for storage, so most of the spaces have gone unused. My guess is that our stowaway somehow got into one of them—perhaps he was able to pick the lock—and that's where he is now."

"And what about the missing sister?"

"It's possible he's got her in another one of the lockers. It'd be a tight squeeze, but not impossible." Charles turned from the group of overseers and jabbed pins into the indicated spaces: tiny boxes which were barely visible from the conference table.

"This is some fantastic work, Charles," the chairman said as the other brothers nodded in unison. "The question is, what do we do now?"

"Why not just go and check all the rooms?" Peter asked, but Charles was already shaking his head.

"Not a viable solution?" Donnie asked.

"It's not what I'd recommend, no," Charles said with a grave look.

"Why?"

Charles' gaze fell to the carpeted floor as he sat heavily in a chair by the bulletin board. "To be perfectly frank with you all, I was a little skeptical of this whole stowaway story in the beginning. It just didn't seem possible. There aren't many places to hide on this rig without going noticed. The kidnapping seemed even more unlikely. But after sitting down and going over the watchmen's reports from this morning… Well, let's just say that whoever this guy is, he knows what he's doing. He's been able to slip in and out of corridors and cafeterias and supply closets without being noticed all this time. Had we lacked a very specific plan for spotting him, I doubt anyone would've noticed. Even the watchmen had a difficult time tracking his movements, and they're trained."

"So what are you saying?" the chairman asked.

"I think Brother Burton's first instinct may have been on point. We could be dealing with a trained professional, meaning he's extremely dangerous. Especially if he's got a captive. If we go straight to his hideout, we could be risking a hostage situation."

The overseers let this sink in.

"Then what options does that leave us with? We can't just ignore him."

"What if we just stake the place out, wait for him to leave again, and then go in and get Angelica?" Peter suggested.

"Also risky," said Brother Garboni. "Even if you manage to extract her safely, he'll still be on the loose. Once he finds that she's gone, he'll just find another place to hide, and I'm guessing it'll be even more difficult to track him down the second time. It would also put us all in danger. It'd just be a matter of him grabbing another passenger and you've got a hostage scenario again."

"This seems pretty hopeless, then," said the chairman with an exhausted look.

"There must be another way, something we're not thinking of," Peter said. The other men were staring at the table between them with furrowed brows.

"Maybe we can pray about it, take a little break, and reconvene after lunch, when everyone's had some time to think over the situation," suggested Marcus Kelly. Heads around the table nodded in unison and the group of overseers was dismissed with a prayer.

***

Joyce Tucker found her way to the pilothouse of the *Abigail*, where Monique sat alone in the captain's chair. A wool blanket was draped over her shoulders and she cradled a steaming mug between her hands. The consoles before her chirped and throbbed quietly.

"Mind if I join you?" Joyce asked.

Monique gestured to the open seat beside her without a word.

"What a day, huh?" Joyce said.

"What a day."

"Sometimes I wonder how long this can possibly go on for," Joyce sighed. "In the last couple of months I've fled my home, lived in a refugee camp, been interrogated by soldiers, slept in a homeless shelter, fled on a sailboat, and experienced a shipwreck. I thought I'd been through it all, and then we get hijacked by pirates. I'm almost getting used to this life."

Monique was silent.

"Mind if I ask your story?" Joyce said. Monique gave her a long look and shrugged.

"My family was from Haiti. We emigrated to the United States when I was a little girl. My mom was contacted by the Witnesses first. Dad opposed her for a few years because of some things he'd heard from relatives back in Haiti, some crazy thing about the Witnesses practicing witchcraft. He even threatened to divorce my mom, which would've probably resulted in her having to move back to Haiti, but she stood firm. Within a few years he was studying, too. Eventually we all got baptized."

"That's a wonderful story," Joyce said, smile beaming. "Where are your parents now? They on another boat here?"

Monique shook her head and stared blankly into the blackness beyond the bridge windows. "They were visiting family in Port-au-Prince when the 2010 earthquake struck. They were at a local vegetable market when it happened. We never found them."

"I'm so sorry," Joyce said.

"I was only sixteen at the time, in my second year of high school. Life in America was all I knew and I had no Witness family in Haiti to go back to. That's when the Callisters took me in."

"The Callisters? As in the captain?"

Monique nodded. "At the time it was him and his wife, Linda, and I. We were an odd-looking family for sure. Two middle-aged white people and their little black Haitian girl in probably the whitest suburb of all Seattle."

"You poor thing," Joyce said with a chuckle.

"Oh, I was used to it by that point. I'd been in public schools the whole time. I'm sure it was harder for John and Linda getting all those stares. But we made it work. John's like a father to me."

"What about Linda?"

"Diagnosed with pancreatic cancer shortly before the evacuation letters came through. She was gone within just a few months."

"Oh no."

"It was a huge blow for John. They'd been together most of their lives and expected to see the end together. But now it's just me and him."

"I see why he fought for you on that deck," Joyce said.

"Oh, he would've done the same for anyone aboard this ship. He'd give his life to save one of us if he had to."

"Sounds like a good brother."

"One of the best I've known. And what about you? You alone out here?" Monique asked. She leaned forward and gently adjusted one of the dials on the console.

"Yes and no," Joyce said. "I have a husband named Alvin. He's an overseer as well, and he's probably on one of the ships out here, but… Well, we got separated weeks ago. I haven't been able to talk with him in a long time. Actually, the last time I did… I didn't say the nicest things. I regret it every day. But I look forward to seeing him soon. I miss him something awful."

"I know how that feels," Monique sighed. The two sat in silence as the Abigail trudged on, drawing ever closer to the rest of the convoy.

***

"Turkey or tuna?" Peter asked, setting the tray of sandwiches down on the cafeteria table before taking a seat across from his wife.

"It doesn't matter," Rachel responded flatly.

"Then may I suggest the tuna extraordinaire? It's the special for the day and, if I may be so bold as to say, pairs *delightfully* with this bag of Lay's potato chips," Peter said, wriggling his fingers with a wave across the tray of packaged foods.

"Your British accent needs some work," Rachel said, grabbing the tuna sandwich and peeling open the bag of chips. She glanced up at her husband with the faintest of smirks. It wasn't much, but it was something.

"Now there's the smile I've been missing the last few days," Peter said. He raised a finger to brush a wisp of hair from Rachel's eyes but she batted it away.

66

"You haven't exactly given me a whole lot to smile about."

"Point taken," Peter said, unwrapping his turkey sandwich, his third in as many days. He shut his eyes and tried to imagine some other flavor. "You know," he said between bites, "I never understood why the Israelites complained about manna… Now I'm starting to see how it might've been a real trial."

"Don't change the subject," Rachel said with a shake of her head. Her voice had taken on a serious tone, but at least she was talking now.

"Ok. I'm sorry."

"That's a start. Sorry for what?"

Peter held his breath and resisted the urge to roll his eyes. "I've been… really *preoccupied* lately. It's just this whole Angelica thing, Rachel. I feel—"

"No, don't excuse it. Tell me why you're sorry."

"I… I've been neglecting you."

"And?"

"And… And… I'm not sure."

"Peter, let me ask you a question. Do you even know what department I'm working in?"

"Not laundry?"

Rachel shook her head and huffed. "I switched out of laundry almost two weeks ago."

"Oh. Wow. And so now you're in…"

"Housekeeping."

"Right. Ok, I think I remember hearing you say that."

"In the last week, how many actual conversations have we had?" Rachel asked.

"I… I'm not sure. I know we eat together."

"None, Peter. Not once have you asked me how I am, or even how Evan is. You volunteered for us to take him in, and while I'm happy to do it, it's been one more thing thrown onto my plate. I know you're busy, Peter, and stressed out and worried about Angelica."

"I'm sorry," Peter attempted.

"And this whole time I've still been so worried about Claire. After that one time we talked, everything was turned upside down. Suddenly we were out on the open seas and there was all the news about the blackouts. We have no idea where she is, or if she's even safe. What if something happened in Vancouver? What if Claire had

67

second thoughts and returned to her school? Literally anything could've happened in the last few weeks." "Rachel, hon, I'm sure Claire is fine. We're just out of contact for the moment."

"I know that in my head, Peter. But it doesn't stop me from worrying about her. And the Angelica situation is even worse. I'm not even allowed to talk about that with anyone. People are asking where she is and why Evan is with me all the time. Am I supposed to deflect the questions somehow? Am I supposed to lie? I know you have a lot more people counting on you, and I'm sure there's plenty that you can't tell me about. I get all that, Peter. But I need at least some of you for me. Is that too much to ask?"

Peter gazed into his wife's eyes, and for the first time in weeks could appreciate just how close she'd come to her breaking point. She looked older, suddenly, weathered and wizened.

"You're beautiful," Peter said. "You know that?"

"Oh brother. Don't try that with me," Rachel said, rolling her eyes.

"I mean it, Rachel. It's that earnest, honest quality that made me fall in love with you all those years ago. And you're right, I've been too wrapped up in my own head to really be with you. I'll do better, starting right now."

"Okay," Rachel said uncertainly.

Peter glanced at his wristwatch. "Look, I've got a meeting this afternoon, but after that, let's do a date night. We've still got that bottle of cabernet, right?"

"I thought you said we'd only open it after Armageddon," Rachel said.

"Forget it. Let's open it tonight. We'll put on some music and watch the sunset from our room. Deal?"

"That... That actually sounds kind of wonderful," Rachel said.

"I can't promise a fancy dinner, but at least we'll be together."

"That's all I'm asking for, babe."

"Then you got it," Peter said with a wink. He took Rachel's hand in his and kissed it just as a sister in blue hospital scrubs appeared next to their table.

"Brother Burton?" the young woman asked. Peter and Rachel exchanged a worried look.

"Yes, that's me," Peter replied.

"I'm glad I found you. I've been looking everywhere. It's about Ted Watkins."

Peter felt Rachel's grip tighten on his hands. Whatever the news was, they were here for each other.

"Ok," Peter said, bracing for the worst.

"The doctors would like to see you in the infirmary," she said nervously, already backing away from the table and towards the doors.

"I'm coming with you," Rachel said. The couple rose, hand in hand, and followed the nurse.

***

It was nearly three in the morning when Captain Callister spotted the pale deck lights of the distant supertanker. She sat on the sea like a giant sleeping on a bed of glass.

The surface of the water was calm and flat, and John Callister was grateful. Choppy seas made transportation between vessels difficult at best; this would be a cinch. He leaned into the console and pulled a switch, flicking on *Abigail's* cabin and hallway lights to rouse the crew. What little coffee was left in the galley was hastily brewed and distributed. There would be no breakfast served. Since their ship had been plundered just hours prior, their supplies had run dangerously low, but now it mattered not. Their rendezvous with a supply barge would mean a full restock and refuel, a task which even a groggy crew was eager to begin.

Joyce Tucker slipped into a thick fleece sweater and a pair of workman's boots. A neon green hardhat covered in strips of reflective tape completed the outfit. She navigated the corridors to the weather deck. Most of the crew had gathered in a tight line huddled over cups of coffee. They watched expectantly as the immense supertanker loomed closer.

"She's called *The Golden Age*," Monique said to Joyce.

"Clever. Not the original name, I'm assuming?"

Monique shook her head. "Most of the ships were renamed after our organization acquired them. I thought at first it was just a silly little thing, but now I see the wisdom of it."

"Oh?"

"Sure. We run across an unfamiliar ship out here and everyone's suddenly nervous. You were here for the last run-in."

Joyce nodded thoughtfully.

"But if you spot a ship with a name like *The Golden Age*,

69

Queen of Sheba, or *Millennial Dawn,* you're instantly at ease. You know it's one of ours."

"I see," Joyce said, amused.

"This tanker's fully outfitted for your friend," the captain said, appearing suddenly at Joyce's other side. "They've got a stocked medical bay and from what I hear some of the best doctors and nurses from the West Coast. I'm sure they'll be able to help her."

"Thank you, Captain."

"Once you leave this vessel, just *brother,*" John corrected.

"Right."

In another few minutes, *The Golden Age* towered high above *Abigail.* It seemed to stretch on endlessly in either direction. Tiny silhouetted figures with headlamps scampered along her upper deck. White puffs of condensation from the deck hands' mouths were ignited by the powerful deck lights.

Above them, a pneumatic telescoping boom extended slowly, a reinforced cage suspended from its tip.

"Incoming! Heads up!" Captain Callister shouted as the cage began its descent. The crew scrambled into positions, giving the cage ample room. As soon as it made contact with the deck, its door was flung open and supplies hoisted off and passed down the assembly line of crew members. Joyce fell in place among them, eager to help with the unloading of supplies. Though their time together had been brief, they already felt like family.

This loading and unloading process was repeated twice more, and within ninety minutes the *Abigail* had been completely restocked. The cage lifted once more into the air, and when it returned Joyce was surprised to see a man sitting inside.

"Who are the two transfers?" he asked once he'd shaken hands with the captain.

John Callister motioned to Joyce. "This sister here is one. The other is the injured sister. She's still below decks."

"Is she able to move?"

"Her system has been in shock since the accident. I think I'll need help getting her here. Can two people fit in the cage?" Joyce asked.

The man nodded. "I'll send you two up first. Can you take me to her?"

Joyce led the way below decks to their cabin. Stacy was just as she'd left her, just as she'd been since they'd boarded the supply ship and done their best to keep her sedated. Her fever had broken but she was pale and motionless.

"Her arms are badly burned," Joyce said. "We'll have to be extra careful when moving her."

"No other injuries? Just the arms?" asked the man. He pulled a small flashlight from his jacket pocket and gave Stacy a quick examination.

"Not that I know of. Are you a doctor?" Joyce asked. The man nodded.

"Roderick Munoz," he said, briskly shaking her hand. "We'll have to take her to the medical bay for a thorough examination, but it looks like you did a pretty good job keeping her under. The pain would be excruciating if not for that. She's fortunate to have a nurse at her side," he said, putting the flashlight away and standing. "Most of the ships out here are equipped with a small first aid kit and basic medical information and that's it."

"Have there been a lot of serious injuries since the evacuation from Burrard?" Joyce asked.

"A few. Your friend here wasn't the first to get caught in a fire. Once the blackout hit, there were all kinds of fire-related injuries. Other than that, transit between boats has proven pretty dangerous. A few broken bones, people jumping out of cages too soon and spraining an ankle, that kind of thing. Still, I'm sure it's nothing compared to what's happening back on land."

"How bad is it there?"

"Let's get your friend moved first. We can talk more on the tanker."

On the weather deck, Joyce Tucker said her farewells to the crew. She thanked Captain Callister and gave Monique a big hug. "Hang in there, sweetie," she whispered.

"I will, Joyce," the younger sister said, wiping a tear away with the back of her hand.

As the doctor, Stacy Owen, and Joyce were loaded into the cage and the groaning winches gathered the steel cable lifting them into the air, Joyce gazed down at the crew and let her mind wander. She wondered when she'd see these friends again, and whether or not they'd all make it safely to their destination.

"You said things are worse on land," she said to the doctor. "I got a little taste of it as we were fleeing a harbor in Seattle. What's it like now?"

71

"When we left, bad. Surely much worse now. We received some photos and videos earlier from the last of the evacuees. Fires and looting everywhere. I'm sure the death toll is catastrophic."

"I wonder if there'll be anyone left," Joyce said distractedly, gazing off into the murky distance.

"There must be. Otherwise who would come after us in the final attack?" said the doctor with a dour look.

"What about reports from our friends? Any fatalities?"

"Not that I've heard of," the doctor said. "But that doesn't mean it hasn't happened. We're not really in contact with the other medical bays on different tankers."

"Captain Callister mentioned you were fully staffed."

"Yes, we've got over twenty in the infirmary. About half are general practitioners and RNs, but we have a few specialists. Even a few surgeons, if the need arises."

"Let's hope it doesn't."

"You never know. We've still got a lot of sea ahead of us."

"I suppose you're right," Joyce said. The higher they climbed, the more distinct the swinging motion of the cage became. Joyce felt herself gripping the steel edge of the bench beneath her. "There's something else I want to ask," she said, controlling her impulse to gaze through the grating at her feet.

"Go ahead," said the doctor, cool as ever.

"I'm trying to find my husband. We were separated back in Vancouver and he has no idea where I am."

"Separated in the camps?"

"Well, no… It's a little more complicated than that. But I need to find him."

"There's a database of ship manifests I can access from our ship, but I can't guarantee anything. The data is still being compiled and with the spotty reception we've been experiencing out here, everything's a bit haywire."

"I understand. I realize it's like finding a needle in a haystack, but I need to try. His name is Alvin Tucker. Last I saw him, he was still in Burrard, but we talked later on the phone and he mentioned boarding a ship. I know it's not much to go on, but that's all I know."

The doctor made a mental note. "I'll search the name when we get back. But first, let's get your friend to the medical bay. If we're quick, we might even catch a bit of sleep before lunch."

"That sounds better than you realize." Joyce said. The pneumatic boom compressed, pulling the cage and its contents into a vast cargo area deep within *The Golden Age*, and Joyce Tucker exhaled a sigh of relief.

CHAPTER 6

Peter and Rachel struggled to keep pace with the young nurse as she whisked them through hallways and stairwells towards the infirmary. She seemed to have the labyrinth of passages memorized, and while Peter knew the layout of the rig well, he found himself distracted all the same. Was it good news or bad news?

At the infirmary, Peter and Rachel were greeted by a sister in a white coat. She introduced herself as Doctor Maria Bennett and invited them into a small room beside the reception lobby. It had been converted into an office of sorts, though the place was stacked with boxes of books and papers.

"Please excuse the mess," Doctor Bennett apologized. "I'm still trying to get organized here but haven't had the time with all that's going on."

Peter and his wife sat across from the doctor's desk and waited anxiously.

"I'll get right to the point. Your friend Ted is going to make it," she said matter-of-factly, moving a stack of papers to clear a space for her hands.

Peter couldn't hold back the tears. Part of it was the pent up stress and uncertainty of the last week, but most of it, he knew, was the immeasurable relief at knowing his good friend would survive. His head fell into his hands and he took a minute to regain composure.

"That's... That's a huge relief, doctor," he said.

"Before I get your hopes up too high, though, I need you to know a little about his condition," Doctor Bennett warned.

Peter and Rachel shared a look and nodded, ready.

"We performed an endoscopy shortly after Brother Watkins arrived. We were able to flush the contents from his digestive tract and analyze them. What we found was pretty conclusive. This wasn't just a case of bad food or an allergic reaction."

"He was poisoned," Peter said flatly. "Wasn't he?"

The doctor nodded, but with a cautious expression. "It would appear so. There were toxic chemicals present in his stomach that wouldn't normally be found in food."

"I knew it," Peter said, his jaw clenching.

"So he'll be ok?" Rachel asked.

"I'm going to be cautiously optimistic and say yes, but there could be side effects, some possibly long-term."

"Such as?"

"The toxins Ted ingested were corrosive. As they entered his esophagus and digestive tract, they ate away at some of the tissue lining. In essence, it burned his vocal cords. At worst, this will permanently affect how he speaks and digests food. At best, everything will heal over time and there will be no long-term side effects. We'll just have to wait and see."

"The main thing is that he's alive," Peter said gratefully.

"And that there appears to be no significant brain damage. This was a major concern of mine due to the choking. The brain can't go long without oxygen before it starts shutting down. Fortunately, he was here when it happened. But there's something else I need to inform you of."

"Oh? Is something wrong?" Peter asked.

"When we performed the endoscopy, we found something unusual in his stomach, a kind of tumor."

"That doesn't sound good,"

"We didn't think so either. We did a biopsy and it turned out to be cancerous."

"Oh no," Rachel said.

"Actually we think we caught it early enough. It was very small, about the size of a pea. We were able to remove it without doing any invasive surgery. Of course, we can only wait and see if we got it all. This could be the end of it, it could return. He'll need regular check ups in the future."

"If this system continues," Peter added.

"Of course. If this system continues," Doctor Bennett said.

"Can we see him?" Rachel asked.

Doctor Bennett nodded. "Yes, you can. But he's been under for the last few days, so his system isn't functioning completely on its own. You can talk to him, but he won't be able to respond."

"We understand. We'd still like to see him," Peter said,

75

wiping his face.   "All right, then. Follow me," the doctor said, rising from behind the stacks of papers and boxes to lead the couple out of the room.

Ted Watkins lay on a hospital bed in a small, windowless room. The space was sparsely decorated; a heavily creased Rand McNally World Map hung on one wall, the clothes Ted wore when he was admitted neatly folded beside a vase of fake flowers on a bedside table at the other. Peter wondered how many of the furnishings had been leftovers from the rig's previous owners.

The rest of the room was occupied by medical equipment. An expensive looking machine blinked and whirred quietly in one corner while various charts and diagrams were pinned to a strip of cork board above Ted's bed. Ted himself looked remarkably well, but for a messy head of hair and the evident weight loss that had resulted from being tube-fed a liquid diet over the course of several days.

Peter and Rachel pulled up chairs and sat quietly for a few moments at Ted's side. It was Rachel who finally spoke.

"We miss you, big guy," she started uncomfortably. "But we're happy to hear the good news."

"Sounds like you'll get through this just fine," Peter chipped in. "You had us real worried, though."

Ted shifted slightly in the bed and the couple froze. Slowly, the large man's eyes pried themselves open and he turned his head to look at them. His lips quivered as he struggled to say something, but Peter stopped him.

"Doc says your vocal cords are going to need some time to heal," Peter said, putting a hand on Ted's arm. Ted pulled away gently and lifted a hand slightly in the air, wiggling his thumb.

"I think he wants your phone," Rachel said. Peter pulled the device from his pocket and handed it over. Ted's movements were slow and uncoordinated and it took him a minute to type the message. He handed the phone back, and the couples' heart sank. On the screen, Ted had typed:

How is Angelica?

***

When Joyce finally awoke aboard *The Golden Age* it was nearly eleven o'clock. Warming rays of golden sunlight streamed

76

through a window beside her bed. She stretched and enjoyed her view of the sea. It felt like weeks since she'd seen daylight, and for the first time in weeks she felt rested and well. She took her time getting dressed and combing her hair before strolling to the ship's medical bay.

Doctor Munoz was the first to greet her, and seemed inhumanly energetic and sharp after having pulled an all nighter. He briefly introduced Joyce to the other medical staff before taking her to see Stacy Owen.

"How is she?" Joyce asked nervously as they walked to her friend's room and peeked through the door's window.

"Stable."

"Infections?"

"Yes, but not serious. She's on a strong dose of antibiotics. Like I said this morning, you being there was crucial. Frankly, I don't think she would've made it this far without your medical attention."

"I wish I could've done more," Joyce said.

"Given the circumstances, I think you did just fine. The staff on hand last night treated her as soon as she arrived. She's all bandaged up and heavily sedated. I think it's safe to say we're through the worst of it."

"Did she ever regain consciousness?"

Doctor Munoz shook his head. "Too soon. We confirmed that the burns on her arms and hands are second and third degree. It appears as if parts of the jacket she was wearing at the time melted into the skin."

Joyce shook her head and frowned deeply. "It all happened so fast. There was no time to react."

"There rarely is."

"So what happens next?"

"We'll keep her here as long as we need to, change the bandages every few days, make sure the infection goes away."

A weight lifted from Joyce's shoulders, one that had been there for days, perhaps weeks. In the presence of other medical professionals, she could take a backseat. Stacy's life was no longer in her hands and that was a tremendous relief.

"Any way I can be of help?" she asked.

"For now, just get some rest. You look like you could use it."

"Under normal circumstances I might be a little offended by

that statement," Joyce said, smirking.

"I'm serious. Medical personnel need their wits. You're of no use to anyone tired and stressed. The organization has been very strict with us in their directions. They don't want our doctors and nurses getting fatigued, physically or mentally. As I said earlier, anything can happen out here and we need to be ready."

"Point taken," Joyce said. "I guess a day off wouldn't hurt."

"Take two if you need it. There'll be plenty of work waiting when you feel fit."

"Thank you, brother. In the meantime, do you think you could tell me where I could get something to eat around here?"

Roderick Munoz glanced at his watch. It was nearly noon. "I can do better than that," he said, grinning for the first time Joyce had seen that morning. "I'll take you there myself."

***

"You hear the good news?" Peter asked Marcus Kelly as the two filed back in to the conference room for their afternoon meeting with the overseers. Brother Kelly shook his head.

"It's Ted. He's finally awake and through the worst of it. Can't talk yet, but we were able to communicate."

"Wonderful news," Marcus said, beaming at the younger elder. "I'll have to pay him a visit later this afternoon."

"I'm sure he'd love that. The doctors still want to keep an eye on him, but he looks pretty good, all things considered. But get this: when they examined him they found something in his stomach. A cancerous tumor. It's already been taken care of."

"Interesting," Marcus said, lost in thought for a moment. "And did they determine the cause of sickness?"

"They confirmed it was poisoning."

"You should let everyone know during the meeting," Marcus suggested.

After a brief prayer, the group of overseers heard Peter's update. The room was a sea of uneasy expressions once Peter delivered the blow. It was clear that they'd underestimated the threat, but Peter wasn't about to hold it against anyone. They'd been hit with a perfect storm of unforeseen occurrences that no one could've predicted or prepared for.

"Thank you, Brother Burton," Donnie Chavez said gravely.

He removed his glasses and pinched the bridge of his nose. They'd all aged visibly since boarding the rig, but none more so than Donnie. Peter could hardly imagine the stress he was under.

"Well, it's clear now that we need to find sister Parry and her captor as soon as possible. Any ideas?" Donnie finally asked, his red, puffy eyes roving the room. A full minute passed before any hands were raised.

"The way I see it, we haven't got a lot of options," said Brother Garboni, head of security.

"What options do we have?" someone asked.

"Either we go door to door looking for them in the area we've narrowed down, or we wait till there's another sighting of the stowaway. A third option is the one Brother Burton brought up this morning, holding a stakeout of the place, waiting for him to move, and sending in a few brothers to extract her."

"Do any of those ideas seem better than the others?" Donnie asked dubiously. Brother Garboni was already shaking his head.

"Extremely risky. The more we learn about this man we're dealing with, the more nervous I get about any kind of confrontation."

"I think confrontation is inevitable," Peter said.

"I agree," Marcus added. "Sooner or later, the time's going to come where there's a conflict between us and this man. We can't expect him to just pack his bags and leave peacefully. The key is to try to minimize the potential harm to the friends as much as possible."

More silence as the group mulled this over.

"We know that Jehovah wants us to resolve this peacefully," Marcus continued, his words slow and calm, just as Peter had always known them. "His organization did not arm us with weapons to defend ourselves out here. There must be another way."

"What if we could sedate him somehow?" Peter said quietly. The others turned curiously to look his way.

"Sedate him?"

Peter nodded slowly, the pieces still coming together in his head. "The doctor who treated Ted Watkins also ran a chemical analysis on the residue we found in Sister Parry's cabin."

"Residue?" someone asked.

"Yeah. When my wife discovered Angelica's son hiding under their bed, she also reported smelling something strange. When I

79

checked it out, I found there was some discoloration on one of the pillowcases. The doctor has a chemical lab set up in the infirmary and was able to run some tests. She believes it was chloroform."

"Chloroform? As in the stuff they use in movies to knock people unconscious?"

Peter nodded. "I asked the doctor how anyone could've snuck something like that aboard, but she explained to me that it's easy to make, so long as you've got access to common cleaning supplies and know the right procedures."

"So you're saying this man not only snuck aboard, avoided detection, and kidnapped one of our sisters, but he also managed to set up a little lab someplace and make a batch of chloroform?" Donnie Chavez asked, visibly disturbed.

"I mean, if this guy is a hired professional, it'd fit the profile," Brother Garboni said, raising his eyebrows. But then his expression shifted. "Does our doctor know exactly how to make it?" he asked.

Peter shrugged. "Possibly. She seemed to know a lot about the process, but most of it was over my head."

"What are you thinking?" asked the chairman.

"Well... I think I may have an idea. But I don't know if you're all going to like it."

"Try us," the chairman said.

***

Joyce Tucker was awestruck by the sheer size of the sprawling cafeteria. It stretched on so far into the distance that she couldn't see the back wall. Beyond the endless rows of dining tables stood towering steel shelves stacked with crates, chairs, plastic containers, and dozens of other items Joyce could scarcely name, let alone recognize. Further beyond that, she spotted what she guessed were vehicles and machinery covered by thick tarps. Hundreds of Witnesses filled the dining area, many standing in snaking lines waiting their turn, trays in hand.

"Everything all right?" Doctor Munoz asked, handing Joyce a cafeteria tray. She took a minute to reply.

"I'd forgotten how much I missed this—being with the friends. Feeling safe."

"You mentioned getting separated from your husband. How'd that happen?"

"I made a stupid decision," Joyce said.

"Oh?"

"I left the camp."

Roderick nodded thoughtfully. "Why would you do that?"

"We had a sick girl with us. She'd shown up at the hospital I worked at just before the evacuation and turned out to be a Witness. Couldn't remember a thing, not even her own name. She got caught up in that explosion at the Seattle airport. It was awful. The poor thing was so scared, so alone, family probably worried sick."

"So you took her in."

"Of course. Then we evacuated, drove up to Vancouver. Thing is, she wasn't getting better. If anything, her symptoms seemed to just keep worsening. I was in contact with a doctor at my hospital back in Seattle; he was interested in the girl's case but needed a blood sample to run his tests. Alvin—my husband—was very against the idea."

"But you went anyway."

"Like I said, it was a stupid thing to do."

"Very stupid."

"When I tried to get back across the border, it was already closed. It's a miracle I'm here, Doctor."

"So, why'd you do it? Why did you leave?"

Joyce found the way Roderick spoke both jarring and galvanizing, like waking up in a cold shower. She could almost feel his clinical mind prying at her own, probing the symptoms one by one until he'd delivered a diagnosis.

"I guess… I mean, I *thought*… I thought I had to save her. It didn't feel like I had a choice."

The doctor stopped moving with the line to turn and peer into Joyce's eyes. "Oh, there's *always* a choice."

"What I *mean* is I felt like she was my responsibility. I couldn't just let her… *die*."

Roderick turned back towards the queue and proceeded a few steps. "Tell me, Sister Tucker, what got you into nursing in the first place?"

"Just that, I suppose—a desire to help people. To try and save some lives."

"Jehovah saves lives. We just prolong the inevitable."

"That's a rather macabre way of looking at it," Joyce said with a grimace.

"It's the truth though, isn't it?"

"I mean, from a certain point of view, I suppose so. But it's a very bleak way of looking at things. Why did you become a doctor if you didn't think you could help people?"

"It wasn't my choice, actually. I was in Bethel at the time and there was a need for doctors. I was chosen. They sent me to a local medical school to get licensed."

"Was this in the United States?"

"South America."

"It doesn't sound like you much enjoyed it."

"To the contrary. I've learned to enjoy all of my assignments in full time service. It's simply that being a doctor wasn't my choice, nor was it something I'd ever considered."

"Well, that might explain why the two of us have different outlooks on helping patients."

"Sister Tucker, don't get me wrong: I enjoy taking care of patients and I take my responsibilities very seriously. The difference is that I don't believe their lives are in my hands."

"You don't?"

Roderick shook his head. "I was fortunate enough to meet a brother who'd served for years as a GP at headquarters. We met shortly after I'd graduated and he quickly overturned much of what had been drilled into my head at medical school."

"Like?"

"So much of it was a worldly way of thinking: the idea that advances in medicine could save the world, an inflated view of one's self, that doctors and nurses were somehow heroes above the rest of society, the saviors of mankind. It doesn't take long for that warped thinking to make inroads."

"You're saying doctors and nurses are trained to be arrogant?"

"To some extent, yes. I think it's a tendency that's built into the culture of medical care. It can be a pitfall, and you have to fight against the idea that we have been charged with saving lives. That's not our job."

"Then what is our job?"

"Helping the body to heal itself and providing quality care."

"I don't see the difference," Joyce said skeptically.

"Medicine is powerless without the body Jehovah created. We are merely helping bodies to do what God intended them to do perfectly from the beginning. But when an imperfect body has had enough, there is nothing more that we can do. We are not miracle workers."

"Okay."

"Once we start focusing on trying to 'save lives' or start feeling like we are responsible for everyone around us, we begin to lose perspective. We are no longer modest. No matter how spectacular a doctor's abilities are, her patients will still die eventually. Keeping this in mind helps us provide quality health care while maintaining a spiritual outlook. Additionally, it keeps us from feeling like failures when a patient's body fails to heal, or we lose them entirely."

"Easier said than done. Have you ever lost a patient?"

"More than I can count. Before evacuating to Burrard Harbor I served for years in a Bethel where the majority of our patients were elderly. It was never easy, seeing those dear brothers and sisters eventually succumb to sickness and death."

"How did you cope?"

"It was difficult at first to not feel like a failure when a patient died, to not second guess decisions that were made and determine what could've been done better. But that kind of thinking will sap your spirit in no time. The branch was there for us, always giving the needed emotional support and shepherding. I had brothers sit down and tell me the same things I'm telling you."

"Too bad I never got that Bethel training."

"Well, we condensed a lot of the training we received in headquarters and put it into the medical training videos."

"Videos? Were those available online?"

Doctor Munoz gave Joyce a puzzled look. "Oh, no. They were designed for training doctors and nurses in the evacuation camps. Weren't you with the medical unit in Burrard?"

Joyce shook her head slowly, a sad realization dawning on her. "I never checked in. I was too busy caring for Claire."

"Ah, I see," said the doctor, frowning.

"And Alvin kept trying to get me to go… If only I'd listened."

"Not to worry," Roderick said, smiling. "I've still got the videos on my laptop. You're welcome to have a look. Perhaps it'd be a good little project for your days off."

"Yeah, ok," Joyce said.

***

Rachel dragged herself up the winding staircases to her and Peter's apartment pod. It had been another exhausting day of scrubbing hallways and bathrooms and shower stalls. The salty sea air clung to every surface, leaving behind a gritty residue that presented a constant battle. After only a week on the custodial crew, Rachel's lower back ached. She sat on the edge of the bed, massaging her lower back as she tried to relax.

The thunderstorm playlist helped some. It played from a portable speaker connected by Bluetooth to her phone and filled the small apartment with the otherworldly sounds of raindrops slapping on a canopy of leaves and slipping down ancient boughs into streams and rivers and eventually finding the great ocean atop which Rachel now sat.

She turned from the sink and fished a couple of plastic wine glasses from a narrow cabinet space beside their closet. Glass was a material seldom seen aboard the rigs; it was considered too delicate and risky for life aboard the unsteady vessels, and its safe disposal in the case of breakage was nearly impossible. One of the few exceptions was wine bottles, although they were increasingly becoming a scarcity as well.

Rachel sighed wistfully as she pulled the Cabernet from a rolled up towel in their closet drawer. The idea had been to save it for the Big Day—or perhaps just after—when the old system was finally behind them, but she hadn't been particularly put off by Peter's suggestion to break their pact and enjoy it earlier. Who knew, really, what would even be left of their belongings when that time finally came?

She set the two glasses down beside the bottle and pulled one of the chairs to the center of the room, facing the picture window overlooking the setting Atlantic sun. And waited.

By the time Peter finally arrived, Rachel had been dozing for nearly an hour. There was a kink in her neck where her head had rested at a funny angle, but at least some of the back pain had abated. Peter slipped out of his coat and kissed his wife on the forehead before washing his hands in the sink and joining her at the window.

"I come bearing gifts," he said, reaching into his pockets.

Rachel covered a yawn and turned with a curious look. She could hardly believe her eyes: in his hands Peter held a half stick of salami, a small block of extra sharp cheddar, and a sleeve of saltines.

"Where? How?" Rachel gasped, her mouth already watering.

"A gift from the chairman. I mentioned after our meeting this afternoon that I had a date night with you. I think it pricked some consciences."

Rachel snickered. "I'm sure there are a lot of wives feeling a little neglected these days."

Peter nodded, carefully tearing into the pack of crackers and setting them neatly on an overturned cardboard box between them. "Some of these brothers are in four to five meetings per day. That's on top of the supervision they have to carry out, and the inspections of the different departments. There's just so much going on."

"Who knew it'd be such a big task caring for a couple thousand people aboard a floating city?" Rachel said dryly.

"Yeah, no kidding."

"Any updates on the Angelica situation?" Rachel watched as Peter worked a cork free from the wine bottle. It wasn't easy with a pocketknife corkscrew; Peter's hands trembled as he struggled to pull it free without tearing the cork in half. It wasn't looking good.

"As a matter of fact, we came up with a plan," Peter said, casting his wife a quick look. The cork came free cleanly and he smiled triumphantly.

"Oh? That's good news."

"We'll see. To be honest, it's a little crazy, but we decided it's the only viable option. But you know what, I'd really rather not get into it now."

"Oh. Okay," Rachel said, frowning. She held out her glass and Peter filled it.

"I just want to put all that stuff aside for tonight and enjoy the moment."

Peter filled his own glass and gazed out of their picture window at the vast sea before them. A ruby sun was dipping into the farthest waters on the horizon, dyeing the clouds red and violet. A handful of other rigs' silhouettes could be seen in the distance, their long shadows extending across the trembling waves.

Rain sounds washed down around them. Peter could almost feel the drops tickling his spine. "I'm proud of you," he said quietly.

"Oh? What for?" Rachel asked.

"I know how tough it was for you to step aboard that ferry back in New Orleans. We haven't been on solid ground since, but I don't think I've heard you complain even once."

"What choice did I have?"

"There's always a choice. Could've headed back home."

"If it's a choice between obedience and disobedience... It's not really a choice."

"Like I said, I'm proud of you," Peter said, leaning over to place a kiss on his wife's forehead.

"And I'll admit, this view is something else," Rachel said, ignoring Peter's advances. He was still gazing in her direction.

"Yep, quite a view indeed."

CHAPTER 7

Their plans had been nothing short of meticulous. Under Brother Chavez's oversight, Peter Burton and Charles Garboni had worked carefully to ensure that the plan was as failsafe as possible. No detail had been overlooked. The entire night crew was brought in for a lengthy debriefing that afternoon, each phase of the plan carefully delineated so that all were on the same page. There could be no mistakes.

Peter and Charles took their positions at the crow's nest—a small, glass box perched beside the rig's tower crane. They had ascended the ladder just after dinner so as not to stand out to suspecting eyes. They'd brought with them everything they'd need to get through the night: water, snacks, sandwiches—even a bedpan. There could be no descending for a bathroom break during such a crucial night watch. Together, they kept their eyes glued to their binoculars, watching the walkway on the perimeter wall where the lockers were.

"What if he doesn't show?" Peter asked.

"Then we'll be back tomorrow night. He has to surface for supplies sometime."

"Should've gotten more details from the brothers who spotted him the first time in the cafeteria. If we knew how much food he took, we might be able to better approximate how long it'd take him to run out and have to make another run."

"Yeah, I thought of that too, but it doesn't really matter. We'd be out here tonight just the same."

Peter knew he was right, and was thankful for it. Having the backing of the overseers had lifted a tremendous weight from his shoulders.

"Hey, Charles?"

"Yeah?"

"I just wanted to say thank you."

"Okay. For what?"

"For being out here with me tonight, for doing all this. For coming up with this plan and all."

"Our sister is in danger. I'm just doing what needs to be done."

"No, I realize that. I just really appreciate how serious you're taking this. I know you've got a lot on your plate."

Charles Garboni said nothing, and Peter was about to drop the conversation when the man let out a long sigh.

"I probably owe you an apology."

"What for?"

"For not taking this threat more seriously from the beginning. Maybe we could've got her back sooner if it hadn't been for me stonewalling you."

"I didn't take it that way."

"I just couldn't accept it, you know? I'd been over all the security procedures a million times. I mean for crying out loud, the branch had training seminars and everything, and I was one of the instructors!"

"No one's blaming you, Charles."

"I'm blaming me. I was so caught up in other things around the time that imposter boarded that I didn't pay it much attention. We should've asked for credentials—a congregation number, a full name, contacts that could verify him—*anything*. But no, we just let him right onto our rig and didn't give it a second thought."

"There's no way we could've known who he really was. It caught all of us off guard."

"Pete. It's my job to *always* be on guard. And then, a few days ago, when you started talking about kidnappings… Man, that really scared me. At first I thought there was no way, thought we were way too airtight for something like that to happen. Pride before a crash, I guess."

"Well, that's all behind us now. I'm just glad we're here, and we've got a plan."

"Even if it's a crazy one," Brother Garboni chuckled.

"It is pretty wild. To be honest, I'm surprised the overseers okay'ed it."

"It's the lack of options, that's all. You know, when the tribulation first started, we once had an armed man enter our Kingdom Hall."

"No kidding?"

"He had a nasty-looking kitchen knife under his coat. Came in right before the meeting started so the doors weren't locked yet. I happened to be an attendant that night. There was something fishy about him, even before we saw the weapon. We knew something wasn't right. I rounded up a couple of other brothers—big guys, all of them—and we approached the man. Tried to keep it real friendly, asked if he'd like to sit with us, that we'd find him a chair, all that stuff, just the way the branch trained us."

"What'd he say?"

"Not much. It was clear he was up to no good, kept trying to squeeze past us into the main hall. We asked him to leave, and he refused, started getting real hostile. At this point the opening song was playing but people kept looking back at us through the doors. It was all very tense. I don't think I've ever been so scared in my life. It was then that I had someone call the cops, though we didn't really expect anyone to show up. We grabbed a few more brothers and formed a tight line between the man and the auditorium doors, and that's when he pulled the blade."

"Did anyone get hurt?"

"Nah. Directions from our organization are pretty clear. As soon as someone gets violent or shows an intention of violence, we use whatever force necessary to keep the friends safe."

"Which meant what?"

"Well, we kept trying to reason with him, but when it was clear that wasn't going anywhere, we jumped him."

"Amazing no one was hurt."

"It was quick and painless. One of the brothers used his suit jacket to cover the man's face as the others went for the knife hand. It was over in an instant. The police never did show up, so we let the man go."

"That's it? You just let him go?"

"Sure. We kept the knife, of course, along with the footage from the cameras. Told him to never show his face again in our Kingdom Hall, of course. So far as I know, he listened."

"That's quite an experience."

"And it's not so different from what's happening here. We're taking a little more initiative, sure, but the principles are the same. We know this man is a threat, we know he has ill intentions. It's up to us to remove the threat with whatever means necessary."

"But what happens after? Suppose we catch him? Then what?"

"We let him go, I suppose."

"But where?"

Behind his binoculars, Charles shrugged and chuckled. "We'll see when we get there."

***

Chad Harkett had been on the road for days. What would've been an hour long drive under normal, pre-apocalyptic conditions had turned into a grueling sojourn over dangerous highways, across treacherous bridges, and around countless blazing infernos. As the fire chewed through the landscape, it sent choking plumes of contaminated smoke and swirling embers into the air hungry for fresh tinder.

Chad knew he'd only made it this far thanks to the armored military convoy and trained soldier escorts. Had he been alone venturing these roads, his life would've been taken within miles of Martin's bunker. Had the fires not consumed him, the gangs surely would've. They moved in droves, leaping from the shadows at passing cars and hurling bricks and whatever else they could find to startle drivers and commandeer their rides and supplies. Even with the military escorts they'd been ambushed twice, both attempts abruptly interrupted when the soldiers had brandished weapons. There'd been screams and the heavy thud of projectiles being thrown at the car, and then silence after the fusillade of automatic artillery. Whoever these people thought they were, they were no match for professional military troops.

Still, they were forced to make frequent stops. In one instance, they'd spent hours removing a fallen oak tree from the middle of the road. In another, they'd spent the night in a small clearing beside a highway when their vehicle had run out of fuel and a small team of soldiers was dispatched to look for more.

The civilians—Chad and a few others who'd been picked up from their homes along the way—were ordered to bed down for the night in the back of the supply truck while the remaining soldiers took turns keeping watch outside. Chad gorged himself on a standard issue MRE, complete with a pouch of piping hot black tea, but even a full stomach wasn't enough to ease his nerves. Judging from the furtive glances he caught from the others, he knew he wasn't alone.

"So how'd you get reeled into all this?" a man asked him. He was heavyset with a graying beard and a braided ponytail.

Chad shrugged. "They came knocking. I answered."

"I guess it's better than being burned alive in your own house," said a woman. Mascara smudges left two dark runways on her face. Her face was puffy and red but she seemed to be all out of tears. She seemed to be a shell of some other person who once existed inside.

"Worst fires I ever saw in Cali, that's for sure," said the man. He scraped the last of the beef stew from his MRE pouch. Some of it drizzled on his beard.

"How do you two play into all this?" Chad asked.

"Something to do with my work in AI, but that's all they've told me. Jay's the name," he gave Chad a long hard stare but didn't offer his hand.

"And you?" Chad asked the woman. A sound from outside the truck had caught her attention. She stared tensely at the back doors. Chad finished off his tea as he waited for her reply.

"Her name's Sadie. She's a digital security whiz. Big cryptology buff. Used to win Sudoku competitions, that kind of thing," Jay said, rolling his eyes. Sadie didn't comment.

"You two know each other?" Chad asked.

"Yeah, we started at Google the same year. You?"

"App developer. Mostly encrypted communication stuff. We were working with AI, too. Did the army tell you who they think is behind this all?"

Jay nodded, his expression shifting as if a shadow had fallen across it. "The Witnesses. Doesn't surprise me in the least."

Sadie shifted, her gaze fixing on a spot between her feet. Chad thought she looked uncomfortable.

"You see that video that was going around few months ago, back before all of this started up? Fire and brimstone, and all those world leaders getting incinerated? I said it right then and there— these people are terrorists! And then what do they do? Up and leave, abandon everything to go live who knows where! We're talking here about a *massive, global* organization with *millions* of followers. You know their video had over two billion views when YouTube finally decided to take it down?" Jay was shaking his head in disgust.

"I didn't," Chad said.

"Well, it's about time the government takes action. It was a mistake to not label them a terrorist organization before, because that's exactly what they are."

"Should've gotten out," mumbled a frail voice. Chad and Jay turned to find Sadie, her eyes shut, tear streaks glistening in the dimly lit space.

"What?" Jay asked, annoyed.

"I got one of those invitations. I should've just packed up and left."

"You kidding me, Sadie? Have you heard anything I just said?" Jay demanded.

"It doesn't matter. Doesn't matter what you think, what the government thinks. Doesn't even matter if they are terrorists. They were right."

"They were *right*? She's lost it," Jay scoffed with a look at Chad. "Two kinds of people in this world. Survivors and followers. I've always believed that."

"You saw the videos," Sadie said. "They predicted this. All of it."

"They predicted it because they made it happen!" Jay shouted.

"Hey! Quiet down in there!" came the voice from one of the soldiers outside. Chad wondered what difference it made.

"Maybe, but it still makes their side the safest," Sadie continued, unfazed.

"Watch it, Sadie. What you're saying is beginning to sound like treason."

"I don't care," Sadie said weakly. Her expression was distorted, somehow off kilter.

At that moment, the back doors of the truck flew open, revealing the snarling face of one of the soldiers. "Y'all forget your orders?" the man snapped. Fresh stitches ran like a railroad down one side of the man's face. They tugged at the flesh as he opened his mouth to talk. "We're all out here risking our necks to keep y'all protected, and y'all were told to keep quiet. This ain't no Menlo Park no more. Do I make myself clear?"

"Actually, sir, I've decided to leave," Sadie said. Everyone fell silent.

***

It was just past three in the morning when Peter Burton spotted movement on one of the lower catwalks of the rig. A dark, lanky figure had emerged from the shadows and was making his way up a switchback of stairwells.

"That's him," said Peter.

Charles Garboni flipped on his walkie talkie and pressed the transmitter. "We've got movement on the walkway. Team B, prepare to move in."

"Copy that, Team A," came the succinct response from the brothers below. Peter watched as they emerged from a doorway one level up and quickly descended the stairwells to the locker level.

"Uh, Team A, you see which door it was?" came the request as soon as the men had assembled on the lowest walkway.

"Sorry, no. He came out of nowhere. You'll have to try them all. Start with the south door."

"Copy," the voice said, the tension palpable. Small flashlights were illuminated, the yellow rods of light slicing through the blackness of a starless night as the clocked ticked down. The afternoon before, a brother had done a trial run on the opposite side of the rig to see how long a brisk walk to and from the cafeteria would take. He'd completed it in six minutes and they'd cautiously added another three for the time it took to pilfer the kitchen.

"How're we doing on time?" Charles asked. Peter glanced at his stopwatch. "Ninety seconds down. Seven and a half minutes left."

Charles let out a thin breath. "Team Charlie, what's your status? Do you have eyes on the suspect?"

"Team Charlie here. Yeah, suspect moved through the northern corridor about twenty seconds ago," whispered the brother on the other end. Charles closed his eyes and retraced the route in his head, then he frowned.

"No good. He's moving faster than we anticipated," he muttered. Then, into the walkie talkie: "Listen up: Team Bravo, you might have less time than we expected. How are those doors coming?"

The response took a moment. When it came, the brother was out of breath. "The first one was barricaded. Got it open finally with a crowbar, but nothing's inside. We've got seven... no, eight more to go."

Charles and Peter exchanged an uneasy look.

"Team Delta here, just saw him pass our location," came another quiet voice on the radio.

"Time, Peter," Charles mumbled.

"Six minutes forty left."

"Second door open, nothing here," reported Team Bravo. Charles pulled the binoculars from his face to wipe the sweat from his brow. Peter was feeling it too; suddenly it was as if someone had turned the heat on in the crow's nest.

"They'll never get all the doors at this rate," Charles said anxiously. It was a seemingly impossible situation, and Peter well understood the complications. The doors had to be checked, one by one, but it was important to damage them as little as possible so as to avoid detection when the suspect returned. To this end, only one crowbar was assigned to the team. They were to avoid using force if at all necessary. But with nine doors and as many minutes, things were moving too slow.

"Third door open!" came the exuberant voice from Team Bravo.

"What'd you find?"

"Uh… We've got some shelves in here, bunch of items stocked up. Empty packaging, bottles. Broken light bulbs. Looks like someone was here recently."

"That's probably the locker he was hiding in," Peter commented.

"No one else there?" Charles asked.

"Negative. It's empty."

"Then keep moving! You've got only five minutes left!" Charles said. Then: "Team Echo, report in. You have eyes on him?"

Team Echo had been assigned to the cafeteria. It was the same pair of brothers who'd originally spotted the stowaway a few nights prior, Mikey Glover and Cary Doyle. They along with the other brothers on the ground wore earpieces connected to the walkie talkies to make as little noise as possible. They'd been strategically positioned away from the intruder's expected course, but even the slightest sound had the potential to carry far in the cramped metal chambers that were the innards of Rig 7.

Two bursts of static piped through the airwaves and through Charles's radio. This was a mute code; it meant Delta had made visual contact but were too close to the subject to communicate verbally. Charles was glad they'd gone through the rigors of

94

accounting for a variety of scenarios and training the teams accordingly, prouder still that the brothers remembered everything.

Charles gave Peter a look. "Just under four minutes," Peter said, taking the cue.

"Bravo here, doors three and four open, no one's inside," crackled a voice from the radio.

"Team Echo reporting in, suspect has just left the cafeteria. Repeat, subject is heading your way!"

Peter felt his heart jump into his throat as commotion erupted from Team Bravo's end of the line. "We've got five doors left down here, there's no way we'll get them all in time!"

Charles shot Peter a glance. "Do we call them off?" Peter asked.

"If we don't and he returns, things could get ugly. Those men are defenseless and he probably knows it," Charles said grimly. Peter nodded, the stark realization washing over him. To be this close and come away empty-handed was a painful defeat.

"Finish the door you're working on now, then get out of there," Charles ordered.

"So close," Peter said regretfully.

"We can try again tomorrow night. If he goes again for supplies, we'll find her. We've eliminated—" but the overseer's voice was cut off by a loud voice on the walkie talkie.

"Brother Garboni, we got the door open. You won't believe it—we found her!" exclaimed the excited voice from the Bravo Team. Charles allowed himself the briefest moment of relief but no more. This was, after all, only the first phase in a complex plan; things could still go terribly wrong.

***

"You wanna run that by me again?" the soldier growled at Sadie. A second soldier had appeared at his side. He spit something from the side of his mouth, eyes flicking from face to face.

"A misunderstanding, gentlemen," Jay said. He cleared his throat and gave Sadie a hard look.

"No. I've made up my mind," Sadie insisted. "This isn't where I want to be. I don't know what you're all up to, but I don't want any part of this."

"Shut *up*, Sadie," Jay hissed. He grabbed at her but she shook him off and stood. She scooped up her luggage in her scrawny arms.

"I've been quiet long enough. I know what I'm doing. Now let me out," she said.

"Can't let you do that, ma'am," one of the soldiers said icily.

"What do you mean? I was told this was a volunteer situation."

"Don't care what you were told. Our orders are to keep you here."

"So what, are you saying we're prisoners or something?"

"Call it whatever you like," the soldier said, shrugging.

"Just sit down, would you?" Jay said, his tone more imploring this time. Sadie glanced around at the faces staring her down and shook her head stubbornly.

"Tell me, then. What happens when we get to whatever base you're talking to? What do you want with us? How do we fit into your plans?" Sadie asked.

"I'm not privy to that info, ma'am. I'm just an escort."

"Well, it sounds like you're planning an attack against the Witnesses."

The soldiers looked at one another and shrugged. "That's above my pay grade."

"My family are Witnesses," Sadie said finally, her voice starting to shake. Sitting next to him, Chad saw Jay slowly lowering his face into his hands. "I was raised a Witness, in fact. I didn't stick with it, but I remember enough. I know what's coming. I know you're planning something big. But it won't succeed. God isn't on your side."

"Well, you're right about that, ma'am," said the soldier, his forefinger tapping the safety on his rifle. "God isn't on our side, and he isn't on theirs either. That's 'cause there is no God."

"Yeah, that's what everyone's saying these days," Sadie said. "Tell me, what's the punishment like if one of you turns out to be religious?"

"Ma'am, I'm going to ask you just once to sit down and keep your mouth shut."

"Are you fined? Does your pay get docked?"

"I won't ask you again," the soldier warned, eyes narrowing.

"Or is it worse? Do you get thrown in prison? Executed?"

"Enough!" Jay shouted, desperate eyes darting between his colleague and the soldiers. But to Chad it was clear that no one was backing down. This wasn't going to end well.

"I don't want to be here," Sadie said one last time. Bags in hand, she took another step to the back doors. And to her surprise, the soldiers made no move to stop her. Instead they backed away, allowing space for her to squeeze between them.

"Thank you," she said quietly, smiling nervously at each of them. She struggled with her luggage, moving into the darkness of the night. The soldiers allowed her several paces before quietly shutting the rear doors of the vehicle, and taking aim.

There was a single pop, and Jay covered his face and wept.

***

"Great news, Team Bravo," Charles Garboni said, relieved. "Get the girl out of there immediately."

Peter Burton watched as the team of brothers below them scrambled down the catwalk and out of sight. He supposed Angelica was sandwiched somewhere in between them, but he could see nothing. He heard Charles draw a deep breath beside him.

"Here comes the tricky part," he said, pulling the walkie talkie to his mouth. "Team Foxtrot, are you in position?"

"All ready to go, Brother," came the voice on the other end.

"Good. Stay put until you hear my order. We've got eyes on the catwalk," Charles said. "How's the clock looking?" he asked Peter.

"A minute thirty to go."

"Foxtrot, we're cutting it close. He'll be there any second now."

"Copy that, Team Alpha. We're ready to go."

"Team Charlie, have you made visual contact yet?" Charles asked after another fifteen seconds had ticked by.

"Negative. All's quiet here," came the voice, barely a whisper.

"Odd," commented Peter with a glance at his watch. The time was nearly up, but still their suspect had not made it to the final checkpoint. "Maybe he took a detour," Peter suggested uncomfortably.

"Let's hope not," Charles said. The heat was rising again. Another minute ticked by and still there was nothing.

"I don't like this one bit," Charles finally said.

"You think he caught on to us?"

97

Charles nodded slowly. "It's possible he spotted one of the surveillance teams."

"Well, at least we got our sister back," Peter said hopefully, but the mood was tainted. Until the intruder was caught, no one would be truly safe.

"Team Charlie, update us," Charles said. The suspect was now a full two minutes behind schedule. They'd officially lost him.

"Sorry, still nothing," came the response. "Should we go looking for him?"

"No, stay right where you are."

No sooner had Charles spoken these words when the shadowy figure reemerged. "Alpha Team here: we've spotted him," Charles said immediately into the walkie talkie.

The figure walked briskly, clearly familiar with the route. A canvas sack was slung over his shoulder. As he walked, he tossed a food wrapper over the railing. It fluttered along with the sea wind and disappeared into the night.

The man slowed. Something had caught his attention. He paused at one of the locker doors, crouching to inspect the locking mechanism. Peter and Charles held their breaths. It was not the room that had held Angelica Parry, but it was one that the brothers had entered only moments before. Clearly, not all had been left the way they'd found it.

Peter's heart was a jackhammer in his chest. Everything hung on the following moments. The man backed out of the room, then began to jog down the walkway. Clearly he knew something was up. Plans would need to change.

"Team Foxtrot, be advised, our suspect appears to be on the alert. He's checking rooms."

"What do we do?" asked the panicky voice.

"Hold your position," Charles ordered. "Team Bravo, is our sister safe?" he asked.

"Team Bravo here, we're with her in one of the generator sheds. She's shaken up but conscious."

"Did your team leave the decoy?" Charles asked. The decoy was a long pillowcase filled with life vests. It wasn't convincing by any stretch of the imagination, but it was enough to pass for a body in an unlit room full of shadows; that's all they needed.

"Affirmative, decoy is in place and covered with a bed sheet."

On the catwalk, the figure checked a second door, and then a third. Neither Peter nor Charles knew where the intruder had gotten his keys from. Then again, if he'd managed to make it this far, being able to fashion his own lock picks from supplies lying about the rig didn't exceed the realm of possibility.

After three doors, the man made a beeline to the room where Angelica had been kept.

"Get ready. He's headed for the bait," Charles said.

The man glanced several times over his shoulder, then pulled the key from his pocket and entered, slipping in and closing the door immediately behind him.

"Move!" Charles commanded into the radio. On the catwalk below erupted a flurry of activity. From the southernmost room, three brothers raced towards the room where Angelica had just been extracted minutes before. Their boots clanked loudly on the metal grating, but it didn't matter. Stealth was no longer the game here; speed was. A metal rod carried by one of the running brothers was threaded through the handle of the door and jammed against the doorframe on either end, effectively pinning the inward-opening door. Armed with a power drill and steel screws, a second brother affixed a row of clamps around the bar and into the metal doorframe. There was now no way in or out.

This first task completed, the brothers took a step back to make way for the third brother. He wore a large plastic canister on his back. From the top of the canister led a thin rubber hose. He pulled the pack from his shoulder and set it down, donning an air filtration mask before working a hand operated pump at the top of the canister. As he readied the canister, the two others stuffed a knot of rags under the door jamb, leaving only a small hole for the rubber tube.

The tube was inserted, and once the brothers had retreated to a safe distance, the canister's release valve was pulled. Within two minutes, the suspect's room had filled with chloroform.

CHAPTER 8

Settled on a sprawling six hundred acres of flat waterfront southeast of San Francisco sat the Hunters Point Naval Shipyard. The property had through the years transferred hands multiple times, from private shipbuilders to government entities to condominium developers. Shortly before the outbreak of the great tribulation, the environmental protection agency deemed the land hazardous after discovering that despite years of concentrated rehabilitation, soil and water samples revealed high counts of radiation. But now, with most major US cities brought to their knees, and with the greater national infrastructure reduced to shambles, environmental protection was at the top of no one's list of concerns.

Within two days of the initial blackouts in California, a joint force of US Army and Navy troops had burst onto the waterfront, secured the perimeter with a chain link fence and sentry towers, and set up camp. Previously abandoned structures were quickly boarded up or covered in canvas sheets and turned into makeshift command centers, armories, mess halls, and barracks.

Within one month, Hunters Point became the United States' most important military base on the West Coast, and what troops were left from California to Arkansas were instructed to rendezvous here, regardless of which military or paramilitary division they belonged to. The armed forces, it was assumed, would be better off defending a central location until the fires died down and whatever was left of society could slowly begin to stabilize.

The inevitable result was a frenetic, overcrowded hive buzzing with helicopters and police motorcycles ferrying in personnel and supplies. Tents—both military and civilian—had sprung up in every available space to house the troops and their families. But space had been at a premium, with many non-immediate family members being refused entry at the gates. Violent fights ensued over this and other policies, resulting in the erection of a large roadside sign that explained in no uncertain terms that any attempt at forcible entry would result in a swift, lethal response.

To further protect the base and its occupants, multiple layers of fences and palisades had been erected, along with a half-mile walled-in alley of gates and checkpoints stretching from the entrance to Hunters Point all the way to the exit ramp from Highway 101. Any vehicle attempting entry could only do so here, navigating the checkpoints one at a time before finally being granted entry to the base. Armed soldiers perched atop towers laced in razor wire pinned down the vehicles in their floodlights, the blue beams bathing the cars in an ethereal glow as they underwent meticulous inspection. Slowly they crawled through the security gauntlet. Above them, helicopter rotors hacked at the air, slicing into the black night with their own searchlights. Swirling plumes of dust and smoke moved through the base.

Chad Harkett finally emerged from the armored truck to find himself surrounded by tanks, Humvees, supply trucks, and an assortment of police and SWAT cars. Many bore the unmistakable scars of violence: charred siding, shorn sections of metal and tarpaulin, bullet holes. Fire trucks with long, winding hoses roved constantly around the premises, misting the air with water.

A woman in army fatigues shoved an oiled poncho into Chad's arms. "Put it on," she barked. "You'll be soaked to the bone in no time."

"What's with all the water hoses?" Chad asked, slipping into the poncho and slinging his bag over a shoulder. His face was already wet with salty, stale water.

"Helps keep dust and ash out of the air. Also keeps the gasoline situation at bay."

"Gasoline situation?"

"Lotta these vehicles are leaking oil and gas. One of those drifting embers from the fires hits a puddle and it's over. Gotta keep it all diluted and running off into the bay."

"Wonderful. All this gets dumped right into the ocean," Jay said bitterly from over Chad's shoulder. No one responded.

"Your barracks are over there, to the south of the camp. You'll be boarding with other civilians, but you're expected to live just like the rest of us. Don't expect any special treatment. Now hit the showers, get some shut eye, and we'll reconvene here at oh-six-hundred tomorrow morning. Understood?"

The two civilians nodded uneasily and wandered to their tent. There were others inside waiting—some reading books, others chatting or napping. A man wearing a pair of headphones warmed food over an electric stove in the corner. A few glanced up at the newcomers, but no one welcomed them. The expressions on the faces here were all the same: sallow, dark, and hopeless.

The end was near, that much was clear.

***

In spite of yet another sleepless night, Peter didn't feel tired, nor did he much feel like sleeping. A tremendous weight had been lifted from his shoulders with Angelica's safe extraction. He could hardly believe, in fact, just how smoothly things had gone. Not only was she safe and sound and reunited with her son, Evan, but she appeared to be doing remarkably well, both physically and emotionally.

After the extraction the night before, Team Bravo had whisked the sister straight to the infirmary, where a small unit of doctors and nurses had been on standby. They had been told to expect a semi-conscious woman with a strong possibility of physical abuse, and so the thin, chatty sister who arrived at their doors walking on her own two feet was something of a surprise. She was neither injured nor visibly traumatized, and while she asked for something to eat and drink, she didn't show signs of malnourishment. Clearly, she'd been well taken care of.

Satisfied that she was in no pressing danger, the doctors left for the night, though Angelica agreed to stay in the infirmary for a couple of nights to be monitored. A second bed was wheeled into her room at her request, so that she and Evan could spend the night together. It was a teary reunion, and Peter left them alone. It was nearly eight o'clock in the morning when Peter Burton finally slipped back into his apartment and collapsed onto his bed.

He was woken late that afternoon by a knock on his door. It was Charles Garboni. He held a turkey sandwich wrapped in cellophane in one hand and a bottle of water in the other. Peter ate as the two walked to the conference room. Peter was still waking up as he took the first bite of his sandwich.

"So tell me, Charles, was everything from last night real or did I just dream it up?" Peter said, only half joking.

"Not a dream, Pete. We got both of them. Unharmed, too," Brother Garboni said, grinning widely.

"I can't believe the chloroform worked. Frankly, it seemed like a long shot. How is he, by the way?"   "Conscious and quiet from what I've heard. The brothers delivered a meal this afternoon; he's not eating."

"I hope they know to be careful."

"Absolutely. We won't make the same mistake twice," Charles said with a stony look.

The two bothers descended the levels of Rig 7 one by one, eventually coming to the outer catwalk which led to the locker rooms where the infiltrator had been hiding. The doors had by now been unlocked and opened, although the brothers were careful not to disturb the contents of the rooms. There would be no official investigation made now that Angelica was safe and her captor locked away, but the overseers were still curious about how this stranger had remained hidden for so long. Whatever details could be gleaned from this event would be carefully documented, compiled, and shared with the branch.

Peter knelt in the room where Angelica had been kept. Apart from a stack of cardboard on the floor, a few dusty sacks, and a storage shelf littered with cans and food wrappers from the cafeteria, the room was bare. The second room offered a little more. Against one wall, a tiered shelf beside a narrow workbench and stool held an assortment of strange items: disassembled light bulbs, small sections of rigid rubber hosing, a handful of lighters, and several bottles of cleaning chemicals.

"We think he pilfered most of this stuff from the kitchen," Charles said, leaning against the doorframe as Peter pored carefully over the items.

"I'm surprised no one reported any of this missing. There's a lot here."

"I doubt anyone would've noticed if he was taking things at different times and from different areas. The cleaning supplies could've come from anywhere."

"Looks like he set up his own little chemistry lab," Peter observed.

"I'm thinking that's exactly what he did. Clever, using the light bulbs as beakers. I certainly wouldn't have thought of that. Pretty crazy, this all being under our noses the whole time."

"Scary to think what he was capable of," Peter agreed. He felt a chill run up his spine and had to remind himself that it was all over. Or was it? With the man now in captivity, what would happen next?

"Well, I think we've learned about all we can from here," Charles finally said, rubbing his eyes. He'd been on his feet for at least as many hours as Peter had been.

"Now what?" Peter asked, pulling his gaze away from the contents of the shelf long enough to see the exhaustion in the older man's eyes.

Charles Garboni smiled wanly. "Now we go talk to him."

***

Joyce Tucker had spent the better part of the last two days in her cabin sprawled out on her bunk, sipping Earl Grey from a thermos and watching medical training videos on her iPad. She'd taken extensive notes. In many ways, she couldn't help but feel like she was back in medical school, sitting through her professors' lectures and cramming in late night study sessions to pass her exams. It was odd, to be so far away from that old life while evoking its memories and emotions so vividly. But perhaps even more poignant to her now were the echoes in her head, the words that kept rattling around from the conversation she'd had with Roderick Munoz. Though she'd held her tongue at the time, she couldn't help feeling slighted at the way he'd described the medical community she'd been a part of for so long.

Now though, having watched so many of the videos from the branch, with their carefully delineated instructions and cautions on medical procedures and health care, she had to admit that this was something entirely different from what she'd studied in school. This was superior. The fact was, as difficult as Roderick's words had been to stomach back in the cafeteria, even then Joyce had detected kernels of truth.

For one, Roderick's portrayal of the medical community was accurate: headstrong, arrogant doctors and surgeons had been the norm at West Hill. Even those whose bedside manner exhibited calm, caring demeanors frequently clashed with colleagues behind closed doors. Diagnoses and procedures were topics of hot debate, and it was common for doctors to go for months without talking to each other after some tantrum had been thrown. So much was predicated by the doctors' reputations that mistakes were rarely owned up to. Errors were instead swept under the rug, their aftermath dumped into the arms of whatever overworked nurse or scrub tech happened to be standing by at the time. Some of those mistakes hurt patients.

And medical school hadn't been much better. In her four years at the University of Washington, Joyce's professors had displayed traits similar to the doctors she would later work beside. She recalled only now, though somewhat distantly, how grating their condescending, conceited attitudes had felt at first, but how she'd eventually grown accustomed to it, and even in some subtle ways grown to admire it. After all, they were simply determined to put the lives of patients' first, weren't they? Why should they worry about a little thing like stepping on others' feelings to provide the best possible medical care?

Such behavior had seemed excusable at the time, but Joyce could see now how poisonous that atmosphere had been, and how it had affected her thinking as the years trickled by. The fact was, the longer she worked at West Hill, the more strained her relationship with Alvin and certain others in the congregation had become. At times, she even suspected that Alvin suffered from depression due to their marital stress, but they'd never discussed it. She wondered now how much of that pressure she'd brought home with her after long, grueling shifts at West Hill.

It was only now, viewing the medical training videos on her iPad that she appreciated the contrast between the health care offered in Jehovah's organization and that of the world. The humility and genuineness conveyed by each of the speakers and doctors was unmistakable. Roderick was right.

Joyce Tucker wondered how many other doctors, physicians, surgeons, and nurses had reached this same revelation; how many of her brothers and sisters had breathed a sigh of relief realizing that now they could attend to their patients without the fear of being belittled by some colleague, or the fear of a scalpel thrown their way by an angry surgeon in an operating room. Joyce guessed it wasn't a small number.

She took a deep breath, drawing her attention from the gradually lightening morning sky outside her cabin back to the tablet before her and pressed play again.

***

Peter climbed down the grated metal stairways, winding his way down to the bowels of the rig where the diesel generators groaned and hissed—large, grumbling machines that faithfully kept their platform powered on its slow course through the Atlantic. Several steps ahead of him, Charles Garboni led the way. Bands of yellow light raced over the back of his head and shoulders as he passed beneath a trellis of pipes and conduits. The men said nothing; Peter's mind was still formulating the questions he'd want to ask as soon as they reached their destination, and he figured Charles was doing the same.

The cage had been assembled in a cramped but well-ventilated room adjacent to the generators. A steel door offered some barrier to the incessant mechanical din from the engine room. Their captured intruder sat on the floor of the cage, legs outstretched, ankles crossed. If he was fearful or apprehensive, he certainly didn't show it. His gaze was black and empty. Looking into his eyes, Peter felt as if he were leaning precariously over a cliff to peer down an endless hole. Next to him on the floor sat a paper plate with a sandwich and a bag of chips. Neither had been touched.

"Not hungry?" Peter said with a glance at the food. The pitch of his voice was higher than he would've liked.   The man shrugged.

"It's not poisoned, if that's what you're thinking. We have no desire to harm you," Peter added, trying to be reassuring but feeling little in the way of compassion. The man glanced down at the sandwich, shrugged again, and finally relented, opening it slowly and taking a bite. He chewed thoughtfully as his eyes examined the faces of each man in the room. Rotating pairs of watchmen had been assigned to keep guard. The two now on duty stood at the far wall silently, wary expressions on their faces.

"So, I'll take it that James isn't your real name," Peter said. He pulled up a chair and sat a few feet from the cage. The man said nothing. He finished the sandwich slowly. Peter wondered what it felt like to be a trained professional and be bested by a small team of inexperienced, unarmed men.

"What were you planning on doing with Angelica Parry?" Peter attempted. This seemed to catch the man's attention. He paused, narrowing his eyes as he peered at his captor.

"If I tell you everything, what happens to me?"

"Same thing that happens if you keep silent. You stay in this box until we figure out what to do with you."

"Not much incentive to talk, then."

"It's your choice."

"I'd like a phone call."

"Wouldn't do you any good. Last we heard, phone lines are down all across the US. No way to get calls in or out of the mainland."

"Do you know that for yourself, or are you simply relying on the what others have told you?"

"I saw enough when I was on land to know where things were headed. And I've seen recent images as well. There's no reason for me to doubt the reports."

"You people sure are trusting of your superiors," the man said with a faint smirk.

"That's a funny thing for you to say," Peter shot back. "Wasn't it exactly that—trust in your employer—which led you on this crazy mission in the first place?"

The man smiled now. "Go on."

"I may not have all the facts, but I have a theory: you were sent here by Angelica's ex—Chad Harkett, if I recall the name correctly. You were sent to bring the two of them back to him, but things went wrong."

"If you know so much, why ask me what I was planning on doing with the woman?"

Peter shrugged. "I wanted to give you a chance to clear the air. And I'm curious: exactly how did you expect to escape from this rig with two captives in tow?"

"It was a work in progress."

"Well, not anymore. The road ends here."

"Let me ask you something, then," the man asked. Peter frowned and nodded.

"Is it really true that none of your men are armed?"

Peter mulled over the question before replying. "Why do you ask?"

"Curious is all. It just seems unbelievable, that you'd risk so much on these waters and then neglect to arm your guards."

"What about you? Were you armed?"

"When I boarded your ferry back in New Orleans, yes. But I had to get rid of most of my equipment when I boarded the supply boat."

"So neither of us is armed, then."

"I can make do without weapons," the man said, his expression darkening.

"As can we."

The man paused, his gaze penetrating. "Do you really believe it? That your God is protecting you somehow?"

Peter nodded without hesitation. "Do you think I'd board a fleet of rigs in the middle of the ocean and head to a strange continent if I didn't have that kind of faith?"

"I've seen seemingly normal people do strange things, sane people do crazy things. Faith and stupidity are sometimes two sides of the same coin."

"Blind faith, maybe. But my faith—*our* faith—is different. We are acting based on facts and years of observation. The world is in its final stages, I'm afraid. And we fully expect to outlive it. We're not rolling dice."

"Time will tell."

Peter nodded. There was no point in arguing. He doubted now that much more could be gained from a conversation with this criminal.

"How much longer will you keep me here?" the man asked as Peter stood and put away the chair.

"I don't have an answer for you," Peter said. "You've got us in a predicament. We aren't about to let you go, but we don't really want you here, either. Unfortunately, there's no place for you now. We will treat you as civilly as possible, but we're not stupid. We won't be taking any chances. For now, this is your home."

The man smiled. "Fine. I can respect that."

Peter tried to ignore the uneasy feeling coursing through his veins. He nodded with a grunt and turned towards the door.

"By the way, Peter, my name is Santiago Pérez," the man called after him. Peter paused, the hair rising on the back of his neck. The fact that this man knew his name solidified his malaise. He turned.

"But you can call me Thiago."

***

"What a night, huh?" Mikey Glover said, plopping down onto

the sofa beside his nephew, Cary. Comprising Team Foxtrot, the two had been instrumental in the discovery and capture of the rig's intruder the night before. Though the operation had kept both men up for most of the night, Mikey didn't feel tired. If anything, he'd found the experience exhilarating. He offered the younger man a small packet of peanuts but was waved away.

"Tina?" Mike asked. Cary nodded slowly, his expression stoic.

"Got into another fight. Soon as I walked in the door. It was like she was waiting for me," Cary said sourly.

"What's her deal?" Mikey asked. The couple had been married only two years, but the problems had been many. They'd wed too young, Mikey thought; neither was very experienced or mature. He worried about them often and frequently acted as a confidant.

"Same old stuff. She's just not adjusting to life here. Sick of the food, sick of the people. Sick of me."

"The people? Why's that?" Mikey asked.

"Some issue between her and a couple of other sisters on her work crew. Tina said they've been spreading rumors, they say Tina's lazy and entitled."

Mikey bit his lip. He was sure Cary had accused his wife of the same thing at least a dozen time in their two years together, and not always behind her back.

"Did she try sorting it out with them, maybe sit down for some coffee and hash it all out?" Mikey suggested.

"Yeah, right. This is *Tina* we're talking about," Cary said, rolling his eyes. "And anyway, that's just part of the problem. This whole place is getting to her, man. It's driving her crazy, and I'm the one that has to deal with the aftermath. And it's not like I can blame her, either. I mean, it's not like any of us knew we were gonna be stuck out here at sea for months, let alone moving to some continent halfway across the globe. And then we start rationing the food, and now the water!"

Mikey tried to ease the tension with a chuckle but Cary didn't notice. "Well, it could be a whole lot worse," Mikey said.

"I don't see how," Cary scoffed.

"We could still be back in LA. Fires, blackouts, the sky going dark. Can you imagine the riots, the looting, the crime? We've got none of that to worry about here."

"Yeah, except for the kidnapper we just helped catch."

"That was an exception, Cary. Overall, don't you feel pretty safe?"

"Sure, until the overseers come to us about the next criminal hiding out somewhere on this rig. And who knows what else they aren't telling us? And how can we really trust those reports from the mainland? Things may not be half as bad as we're led to believe. America's experienced plenty of disasters—wildfires, terrorist attacks, hurricanes—at worst it's a few billion in damages, a few months of cleanup, and then things get right back to normal. We've been there before."

Mikey took a deep breath. He knew Cary had been upset for some time now. The seed of discontent had been sown months earlier when preparations for their evacuation had begun, and over time that seed had germinated and sprouted. The discord between he and Tina had only expounded his negativity, and in the wake of his discontent, the rig, the overseers, and the organization had become an easy target for his attacks.

"Well, look at it this way," Mikey attempted, "we won't be out here forever."

"Nope. We get to look forward to living in Africa," Cary said sarcastically. "Won't that be just great? Going from the most affluent, advanced country in the world to the poorest, most backwards."

Mikey forced a laugh, but he knew Cary wasn't joking.

CHAPTER 9

"Well, by now you've probably all heard the news," Donnie Chavez began, taking stock of the room around him. "Our security brothers did a fine job last night. Not only was the culprit apprehended, but more importantly, Sister Parry was rescued and no one was hurt. I understand you were able to pay her a visit, Brother Burton?"

Peter nodded. "Aside from some chafing on her wrists and ankles where she'd been tied, the doctors haven't found any injuries."

"What's her mental state?" one of the other overseers asked.

"It might be a little early to say, but her spirits seem high. Frankly, I'm surprised at just how well she's doing. It seems the kidnapper—Thiago is his name—handled her with kid gloves."

Eyebrows raised around the room. "Thiago? How'd you find out his name?" Marcus Kelly asked.

"He told us. Charles and I paid him a visit this afternoon. We wanted to inspect the holding cell and make sure it was secure. Got a chance to talk to the guy," Peter explained.

"I'm surprised he was willing to talk," Donnie said.

"He wasn't, at least not at first. But Pete made it clear there'd be no interrogations, no torture, nothing like that. We promised that he'd be treated humanely, fed regularly," Charles explained.

"He did want to know what our plans for him were, though. In the long term, I mean," Peter said.

Donnie Chavez nodded and gazed around the room. There were no suggestions. He finally asked for Brother Kelly's input. The elder was the oldest in the room and ostensibly the most experienced, but even he had never imagined being faced with such a scenario.

"This is a perplexing situation," Marcus said after some thought. "Releasing him and letting him roam freely is out of the question. I suppose we could move him to a more standard cabin on the housing floors, but that would be a risk as well. Keeping him separate is wise."

Charles Garboni was nodding in agreement. "We haven't gotten the full story on this man's business here, but he just about admitted to Peter and I that he was hired by someone, meaning he's a professional. And if he was able to set up a functional chemistry lab with odds and ends lying around the rig, there's really no telling what he could manage in a cabin. It would be a difficult space to secure, not to mention that it'd put him in close proximity with the friends."

"And the space he's in now?" Donnie Chavez asked.

"Same space we prepared before the stakeout. The brothers welded a couple of the transport crane cages together and fitted the door with a padlock. The room it's being held in is monitored constantly by a couple of brothers on constant watch. The cage has a sleeping bag and a pillow and we've offered to provide him with literature to read. He gets three meals a day."

"Anything else the man revealed worth mentioning? What's his overall demeanor like?" the chairman asked.

"He was tight-lipped, but he doesn't seem particularly angry or hostile. Just very cold and calculating. Personally, I think the sooner we can get him off this rig, the better," said Charles.

"What if he asks to stay?" Peter asked, his eyes rising suddenly, as if the question had surprised even himself. "I'm not saying it's likely, but it is a possibility. When we talked this afternoon, there was something in his eyes—maybe a realization—that this world was in its final stages. He knows why we're out here, he's seen how things have unfolded. What if he asks for a spot among us? How do we respond?"

"I think he forfeited his spot here when he kidnapped one of our sisters and attempted to poison two of our brothers," Charles said. The others agreed.

"Then what do we do with him? Do we keep him locked up until we reach the coast of Africa, then send him off into the wilderness to fend for himself?"

The room fell silent. There were no answers.

***

Joyce Tucker emerged from her cabin after three days of

intense study. She took a leisurely stroll down the deck of the supertanker. It stretched on for what felt like miles—so far that the other end appeared somewhat hazy, shifting through a fog that rolled in as the frigid Alaskan waters mixed with the more temperate seawater off the South California coast.

The sky had lightened by degrees with each passing day; the farther the convoy travelled from land, the brighter the skies overhead became. The sun was still not visible—not even as a fuzzy pale shape far overhead—and yet the illumination seemed to surround them, as it might on a gloomy, overcast day. Yet today, no clouds were visible.

It took her nearly twenty minutes to traverse the length of the ship. At the bow she leaned into the wind and felt the salty morning air caress her. It was early still and most of the crew and passengers slept soundly in their cabins below deck. It felt as if she had the entire ship to herself.

Joyce thought back to what she'd heard of the supertanker's history when she first boarded. For decades it had served as a faithful crude oil transporter for a major oil company. During the recession of 2008, the ship had been sold off when its parent company, embroiled in a series of ecological scandals, liquidated a large portion of its assets. The company that had purchased it had fallen on similar hard times nearly a decade later, and the tanker was sold again, this time at a fraction of its original price. The new owner, a subsidiary of a small Hong Kong-based shipping company, then donated the vessel to the organization. After a thorough cleaning and some renovations, including a vastly expanded area for crew living quarters, galley, rec center, meeting hall, and medical ward, the tanker made its way to Vancouver, where it would take on a new role—that of a resupply vessel, refueler, and floating medical facility. There were only two like it among the entire Witness fleet, and the only of its kind on Pacific waters by the time Joyce Tucker climbed aboard.

The guttural bellow of *The Golden Age*'s fog horn erupted from somewhere behind her and Joyce jumped; she could feel its vibrations through the soles of her feet. As if in response, distant belches of varying timbres and textures echoed back to her over the waters.

It was incredible, really. Had anyone told her, even two years prior, that this is where she'd be at this moment, she would have laughed. The migration of over ten million Witnesses from around the world to a single location over the course of a few months seemed impossible. And *Africa*, no less! Even now, with her feet firmly planted on the two-inch steel plating of the enormous supertanker, Joyce could hardly believe how things had unfolded. Then again, wasn't that always how it had been, even in Bible times? Could Noah have ever guessed that he would be commissioned to build a huge box, fill it with food and animals, and ride out a year long global flood? Could Moses have ever predicted that he would lead three million Hebrews across a miraculously dried seabed, only to be followed by an army of horses and chariots who would, moments later, drown in that same sea? Could anyone imagine, just months later, that food would rain from heaven, or that water would flow from rock? Precedent had shown time and again that all things truly are possible with Jehovah.

In just a few short months, everything had changed in Joyce's life—her surroundings, her job, so much of what had seemed so immutable, so constant, so important. It was true, what they said: in times of crisis, that which really mattered became clear. Material things meant nothing; all that mattered was her relationship with Jehovah, her hope, her brothers and sisters, and Alvin.

Alvin. How she missed him!

***

Through his binoculars Peter could make out the US Coast Guard's insignia on the tail of the orange helicopter. He estimated it to be about a mile from them and clearly circling towards the rig's position. As it neared, a man in an olive jumpsuit and helmet hung from the helicopter's cabin cargo door, an arm pointing down, motioning directly towards the rig. A radio transmission followed shortly after. They were requesting permission to land.

On this point, directions from the branch had been clear: the brothers were to follow the orders of any governmental agencies, so long as those orders were relayed within the territories under their jurisdiction, and so long as they did not interfere with the evacuation process. In the case of conflicting orders, the brothers were to state their legal right to a peaceful evacuation and stand their ground. In many countries, officials around the world had tried every possible tactic to dissuade, intimidate, threaten, and coerce the Witnesses to abandon their travel plans, but so long as they remained determined to leave, they'd been blessed with a way out.

"Aren't these considered international waters?" Peter asked the men beside him. Their rig was roughly two hundred miles east of the Florida coast.

"Technically, anything beyond twelve nautical miles from shore lies outside the US's maritime jurisdiction, but they routinely go beyond that. *Way* beyond," a brother said drolly beside him. An experienced seafarer and ex-Naval officer, Archie Morgan had been training Peter Burton on the ins and outs of a CRO, or Control Room Operator. "The only other country out here is The Bahamas, and they rarely bat an eye when US ships wander into their waters. Other than them, there's no one out here, which makes the US the de facto authority."

"So do we let them land or not?" Peter asked.

"We're technically within our rights to refuse, but I'll need to confer with the Overseers' Committee and the platform operator." Archie reached for a blue phone from the console and made a couple of calls. Moments later, the Coast Guard helicopter began its descent.

"Should we be worried?" Peter asked, eyes locked on the orange shape as it approached.

"We'll see. There will only be four or five guards aboard that chopper. It's not like they can force us to turn around. But I am curious as to why they're so far out at sea. They're too far out from land, which means they've probably flown in from another vessel. And there aren't many Coast Guard ships with helipads."

Peter followed Archie from the communications room to the platform's elevated helipad, a 600 square foot octagon that reached over the western wing of the rig like a waiter's platter. The steel platform was painted dark green with a bright yellow circle at its center. The Coast Guard chopper landed deftly right on target. The screaming engines were shut off and the rotors gradually wound themselves down as a small contingent of men and women piled from the cabin doors. Archie and Peter met them at the edge of the helipad, where a stairwell led up from the upper decks of the oil rig.

"Chief Petty Officer Miranda Sachs," said the woman leading the pack. Peter only now noticed the dark blue uniform peeking out from inside her jumpsuit. He and Archie nodded respectfully but no handshakes were exchanged.

"Officer Sachs, welcome aboard. I'm Archie Morgan, chief

barge engineer. How can we be of assistance?"

Officer Sachs frowned. "I'd like to speak with your superiors."

Archie and Peter exchanged a glance. "We can arrange that. Please, follow me." Archie led the group of guards down the stairwell and into the rig. On their faces, Peter read expressions of uneasy contempt. He felt his pace quicken.

"How many civilians are aboard this platform?" Miranda asked, her voice like the crack of a whip.

"A little over two thousand, ma'am," Archie said. Peter heard one of the men gasp.

"That's an awful lot for a rig. You realize that violates maritime regulations for a platform this size?"

"We're not a functional oil platform, ma'am. We're not drilling and we're carrying no crude oil. The rig has been completely renovated and everyone is housed comfortably. If you'd like a tour––"

"I'm not here to tour your rig," Officer Sachs said impatiently. "Just take me to whoever's in charge."

"Very well," Archie said with an easy smile as he led the group through the double doors and into the corridors of the upper deck.

***

The overseers of Rig 7 had assembled shortly after the news of the helicopter's landing had broke on their radio airwaves. They'd chosen a slightly larger venue than their usual cramped conference room—a rec room in the common area on the north end of the rig. They'd folded up the ping pong tables and pushed the pool table to one of the far walls. The place still didn't much look like somewhere suited for a meeting with government officials, but it would have to do.

Someone put on a pot of coffee and a tray of mugs was rushed in from the cafeteria along with a meager platter of snacks and sandwiches. It was all the kitchen crew could offer on such short notice, especially with the food rations which were growing stricter by the day.

Chief Petty Officer Miranda Sachs entered with an air of authority. Nose held high in the air, she glanced around the room

116

with unconcealed disdain. The attitude of the rest of her team, though, was different. Although they kept silent, their eyes scanned the room in what Peter estimated was a kind of startled awe. He wondered.

"Coffee, anyone?" Peter asked. Everyone's hands but Miranda's rose quickly into the air. He filled cups and handed each of the men a sandwich. They ate hungrily.

Miranda quickly reintroduced herself to the overseers, adding the point that she'd been with the US Coast Guard for over a decade and hailed from a Floridian port. The overseers nodded amicably. She then introduced the others on her team, men outranked by herself and clearly much younger. Peter could see the intimidation in their eyes.

"I'll cut right to the chase," Miranda said once she'd finished with the introductions. "There's been a lot of talk of you people and these rigs, and not all of it is good." Her eyes roved around the room, gauging reactions.

"I'm sorry, ma'am, but we're fairly isolated out here. Typically the only talk we hear is among ourselves, and occasional messages from other rigs," the chairman responded.

"Where's your base?" Miranda asked, leaning back in her chair and crossing her arms.

"Up until recently, our headquarters were in upstate New York. But that facility was closed recently."

"You're not in communication with your superiors now?" pressed the woman.

"We get updates from representatives from time to time, occasional bits of news, warnings and instructions, but it's been difficult, especially as we get farther out to sea. And with the blackouts…"

Miranda's underlings shifted uneasily, casting surreptitious glances at one another, though the woman seemed unfazed.

"Exactly what have you heard about our rigs that brings you aboard?" one of the overseers asked. Miranda gave him a cold, long look before responding.

"Human trafficking. Involuntary servitude. People held here against their will. I myself have a hard time believing that so many thousands of you would board these rigs and sail across the ocean. It's a death wish."

"Well, we'll be the first to tell you that this is a pretty

unconventional way to travel. But I can assure you that we've done everything possible to keep the housing and working environments safe, and no one was forced to evacuate with us."

"Evacuate?" one of the male Coast Guards blurted out. Officer Sachs shot him a look.

"Sure. We were part of a mass evacuation. Most of us are from the West Coast, but I imagine that now we've got people from all over the South, too. Why? Did you hear something else?"

The man shot an imploring look at Miranda but she was stoic. "Why you left is beside the point. I want to know about those aboard this vessel. How could you convince so many to come here? What did you tell them to get them to follow you?"

"Ma'am, we didn't twist any arms. We are acting out of faith. We believe that mankind is experiencing an unprecedented era of tribulation foretold in the Bible, and we believe that our organization is being guided to safety for our survival."

"Don't preach at me!" Miranda screamed suddenly, her face turning bright red as pulsating veins erupted on her forehead and neck. She smeared a loose strand of hair from her eyes and lowered her head for a moment to gain composure. The room had fallen deathly silent, the overseers leaning backwards, as if bracing for another verbal assault. Oddly, though, the men on the other side of the table wore dull, numb expressions. Perhaps this was normal.

"I think," said the woman finally in a low voice, "that it would be best if my guards and I had a look around for ourselves. This meeting is going nowhere."

The overseers exchanged glances and nodded. What could they do but comply?

***

The crowd of diners turned and stared at the peculiar group that filed through the cafeteria doors.

"It's the first time we've had military personnel board our rig," Donnie Chavez explained. Chief Petty Officer Miranda Sachs didn't seem to be listening.

"Where does all the food come from?" one of the male officers asked, ignoring the diners to stare at the trays of wrapped sandwiches.

"Much of it was prepared in advance and stored in dry

pantries and freezers below deck. When that runs low, supply ships will help restock us. There's been some foul weather in the gulf, though. They're a little behind schedule."

"What about you all? How are you getting supplies with all the stuff happening on the mainland?" Peter asked. An odd, nervous expression appeared on the man's face. He glanced at his superior and then looked away without answering.

"We need to talk to some of these people," Miranda announced suddenly to her officers, sticking her chin out with an imperious look. "We'll set up in the corner over there." She pointed. "Smith, I want you to round up a few of the passengers. Get their names, ages, whatever else you can think of. And Kowolski, you'll stick with me. We'll get to the bottom of this."

"Ma'am, with all due respect, is this absolutely necessary?" asked Brother Chavez quietly. "Our brothers and sisters have assignments to attend to once they finish lunch. Others have the day off. Is there another way we can—"

"Sir, don't interfere. This is now a US Coast Guard investigation. Do I make myself clear?" Miranda said in a voice that turned heads.

Seeing as the rigs were already far out into the Atlantic Ocean, Peter wondered to himself why they couldn't object to this intrusion. Perhaps the overseers were simply trying to keep peace. He knew, as they all did, that all of this would eventually culminate in the foretold coalition of world powers bringing about the attack of Gog of Magog. That conflict would be inevitable, but the events preceding it were still mostly unknown. Presently, it was the brothers' job to protect the friends by all means, and apparently that meant complying with unreasonable demands in order to facilitate a peaceful arrival at their destination.

"Understood," Donnie was saying diplomatically. "We'll set you up with a pot of coffee and give you the time you need."

Miranda nodded, clearly pleased with her victory. But there was something else in her expression that Peter sensed, something uneasy and unsure. As the officers shuffled towards their spot in the corner, one of the men broke away from the pack.

"You got a bathroom nearby?" he asked. Peter nodded. The man glanced over his shoulder and his superior officer nodded at him. Peter led the way as the man followed him out of the cafeteria doors. But as soon as they were alone, the man's demeanor changed.

Fear was written in his eyes and he spoke in a low voice that only the two of them could hear.

"We need your help."

CHAPTER 10

"My help? How?" Peter asked, pausing to look at the guard with a puzzled expression.

"Don't stop. We'll walk and talk. My CPO will notice if I'm gone too long."

"Ok," Peter said, confused and worried. He led the officer in the direction of the hallway leading to the lavatories. "So, what's going on here?"

"Chief's lost it."

"You mean Officer Sachs?"

The man nodded. "This is crazy, us being here. She should know that."

"We're out of your jurisdiction," Peter said.

"That's not even the half of it. Given everything that's happening out here, this should be nowhere on our list of priorities."

"What do you mean, 'everything happening out here'?" Peter asked. The man said nothing for a moment as he stared wide-eyed into Peter's face.

"You really don't know?" he asked. Peter shrugged.

The man shook his head. "We were dispatched from the Coast Guard Station in Fort Lauderdale when everything hit the fan. Power went out, then the cell towers. Looting started up almost instantly. It was like a powder keg, man. One little spark and the whole thing went up in flames.

"The National Guard and local PD were called in to defend the military bases. We didn't think we'd get much action—we're the Coast Guard, for god's sake. But no, people showed up all the same. *In droves*. They parked on the lots, started scaling fences, demanding to get in. I guess they figured that with the fires and all, heading out to sea was the safest bet. A lot of them were armed. It was complete mayhem. People were shooting and screaming and fighting and getting trampled.

"We couldn't hold our position. There were simply too many people. We were ordered to retreat to the cutter. But even that didn't stop them. People were trying to scale the ropes, trying to jump from the dock to the prow as we pulled out. That's when she gave the orders…"

"The orders?"

"Sachs told us to open fire on the dock. There were just way too many people… We couldn't have taken them all aboard."

"You were told to shoot civilians?" Peter asked. He saw that the man's hands were shaking.

"I was so scared, man. I didn't know what I was doing. I still can't believe it. It happened so fast."

"But why are you here, then? How are we in any way involved?"

"You aren't. But there's rumors going around about you people. A lot of talk. People think you must've known something, that that's the only way you could've evacuated before everything went down."

"But human trafficking? How does that make any sense?" Peter asked, feeling an odd mix of sympathy and anger.

"That's just Chief Sachs talking. Like I said, she's not right. Hasn't been since we left Lauderdale. Maybe she just needs a new purpose out here, a reason to keep wearing that uniform."

The two men paused before the bathroom doors. The officer entered as Peter waited outside, feeling the weight of this newfound knowledge sinking in his chest like lead.

"So what happens when your chief realizes that she's wrong, that everyone here volunteered to be?" Peter asked once the officer had returned and the two began the trek back to the cafeteria.

"Anyone's guess. Maybe she'll just leave it alone and find herself another mission. But there's another problem."

Peter took a deep breath. "What's that?"

"We're going to run out of supplies."

Peter nodded slowly "When?"

"I don't know exactly. It's a thin crew—half a dozen officers left on a stolen patrol boat the night after we left port, and a few others are… No longer with us. I don't know the exact situation with the supplies, but we were never meant to survive for weeks at sea. If the food doesn't run out, it'll be the fuel, or ammo."

"Well, we've got no ammo on board here. We're unarmed,"

Peter explained.

"You're joking," the man said with a disbelieving look. Peter shook his head.

"Then how've you fought off the pirates and looters?"

"Pirates and looters?"

"Sea's crawling with them. Anyone who's got a boat out on these waters has practically been forced into piracy. There's no other way to get supplies. And it's not like anyone's gonna risk making landfall."

"Well, we've had no run-ins. Not so far, anyhow."

"You will. There's no way to avoid them. Maybe they've just been intimidated by the challenge of boarding an offshore platform. Not exactly as simple as throwing a rope ladder aboard a boat passing in the night."

"Maybe."

"What about food and water then, or fuel? You must have something to spare. I see how you're eating here."

"That's not really my decision to make," Peter said. "I'd have to discuss it with the other overseers. But frankly, we're not in a position to be giving out food supplies. Our brothers and sisters come first."

"What about a trade?"

"A trade for what?"

"We could offer protection. Our cutter is not far from here. She's armed with machine gunners bow and aft. We could keep you safe."

"Thanks for the offer, but we're already safe. Like I said, I'll mention it to the others and we'll discuss it."

The two men paused in the hallway as they came to the doors leading to the cafeteria. The officer cast a fretful look at Peter and said, "We never talked, you got it? If you and the others decide you're able to help us, go through me directly. There's no telling how my CPO would react if she found out I'd asked for help."

"Understood," Peter said, and the two returned side by side into the cafeteria.

***

"So tell me, how exactly was it that you found out about this 'evacuation'?" Chief Petty Officer Sachs asked the couple. They'd been chosen at random by one of Miranda's officers for an interview and appeared uncomfortable sitting across the cafeteria table from her. Other diners had moved tables to keep their distance.

"A letter was read at one of our congregation meetings. It explained the situation and gave us directions on how to prepare."

"So your church initiated a mandatory evacuation?"

"It wasn't mandatory, really. We weren't forced to do anything. They merely told us that things were about to become more difficult around the world, and that a place had been set up for us to flee to."

"Who is 'they'?" Miranda asked, making a note in a small book taken from her jacket pocket.

"Our brothers. The organization."

"Do you know these men personally?"

The couple shook their heads.

"Then why should you listen to them?"

"We knew this was going to happen, even before the letter came through. It's foretold in the Bible that there would be a great tribulation, and the start of that would be a global attack on false religion. We all saw how that unfolded, so we knew that more directions would follow. This was something we were waiting for."

Miranda bristled at the mention of the Bible. How had these people managed to evade the government forces that had efficiently swept through the nation, closing churches and mosques and confiscating church properties? How were they still around, and still so well organized? She fumed silently, biting her tongue.

"So, how is all this funded?" the CPO asked.

"Donations," the couple said after a glance at one another.

"Explain."

"Months before the evacuation, we were instructed to sell as much of our non-essentials as possible and donate that money to our brothers. They were in charge of purchasing, refurbishing, and restoring the rigs, the ships, everything. That also paid for the fuel, the food, and all the supplies."

"I have a hard time believing that anyone in their right mind would give up everything to live on some platform crawling through the Atlantic," Miranda said with clear disdain.

"It hasn't been the easiest life, but we're alive. And for now, that's enough," the husband said, taking his wife's hands in his.

Miranda Sachs had heard enough. She rolled her eyes and

waved the couple away to move onto the next interviewee, a young woman with a small child in her arms. But before the woman could sit down, a man slipped into the bench in front of her.

"Name's Cary Doyle," the man said, offering his hand. Miranda took it reluctantly. "It's good to finally meet someone from land. We need to talk."

"All right, Mr. Doyle, what do you want to talk about?" Miranda said hopefully. The discontent in the man's eyes was a contrast with the placid, rueful expressions around her. Maybe with this man, finally, she'd get the answers she was looking for.

"I want to know the truth. What's happening back in America?" the man asked with a glance over his shoulder.

"What are you referring to, exactly?" the CPO asked.

"The looting, the fires, the chaos," Cary pressed. "It's all anyone's talking about. No one's questioning it, but I want to know the truth."

Miranda raised her eyebrows and said nothing, as if this was the first she was hearing of this news. "Well, I hate to break it to you, but things aren't half as bad as you're being told."

"You're kidding."

Miranda shook her head sadly. "There was a blackout, yes, but it didn't last long. And as far as the rest of it, I can assure you that our country is quite capable of handling itself in times of crisis. Can you say the same about your people?"

"I knew it," Cary said, simmering quietly. "I knew it had to be exaggerated."

"How long have you been aboard this rig?" Miranda asked, sensing her moment had come.

"Too long," Cary said, burying his face in his hands.

"Weeks? Months?" Miranda pried gently.

"Over a month. It's been… A nightmare. Food's being rationed, and now the water, too. Can't even take a hot shower every night. And that's not to mention feeling totally stir crazy. I need to get off this rig and back to solid ground."

"Sounds like a rough time," Miranda said with feigned empathy.

"I'll bet you all have it much better," Cary said, shaking his head.

"The United States government takes care of its own."

"I miss home so much. Should've never gotten on those

ferries. Should've never gone along with… all this," Cary said, motioning to the room around him. "You have any idea what we left behind?"

"Tell me," Miranda said, soaking it in.

"We had a house right on the coast, prime real estate. Gave that up, along with two cars. One of which is parked in New Orleans. Who knows what happened to it after we boarded the rigs. Probably stolen by now. And for what? To board this floating pile of junk and work some crummy graveyard shift?"

"You're working here?" Miranda asked.

"Of course. Everyone's got a job assignment. What, you think this is some kind of Atlantic cruise?"

"What kind of job?"

"Night watchman."

"Night watchman? Here on the rig?"

"Yeah. Usually on the top deck manning the lights and the tower. But lately we had to pull a bunch of all-nighters. Trying to catch some infiltrator, they said. Who knows now, though? Maybe that was all a ploy, too."

"An infiltrator? Did they catch him?"

"So they say. He's being held somewhere on the lower decks. Apparently, they've got him locked up."

"How very interesting," Miranda said.

"Wait, that's gonna stay between you and me, right?" Cary said suddenly, looking up into the chief petty officer's eyes like a child who'd just been caught stealing.

"Well, actually, as a sworn officer, I'm bound by my duty first. As it happens, this isn't the first I've heard about people being kept prisoner in your convoy. I have reason to believe that there are plenty of others. And that's a problem. Are you familiar with human trafficking laws?"

"Hold on a second, I didn't say anything about human trafficking. This guy was up to no good. He's probably a criminal."

"So you're harboring criminals?"

"No, that's not what I meant either. You're twisting things!" Cary said, flustered and at a loss for words. He turned to glance at the doors behind him, and Miranda feared that he'd bolt at any moment. She needed to keep him put.

"Look, Cary. Calm down. You're not in any trouble. In fact, you're in a great position."

"I am?"

"You are. You're in a position to make a deal. Care to hear the terms?"

"Um. Ok."

"Tell me everything you know about the prisoner here, and anything else I want to know. And in exchange, I'll grant you a ticket off this rig and back to land. What do you say?"

The man thought it over before speaking. "Make it two tickets and you have a deal."

***

"It's come to my attention," Chief Petty Officer Miranda Sachs announced triumphantly to the men seated at the table across from her, "that some important details were left out of your version of accounts."

"What are you referring to?" asked Donnie Chavez.

"Well, for starters, you told me that everyone is here voluntarily. But that isn't the case, is it? Is it not true that you've got someone held captive below decks? Someone you failed to mention?"

The men exchanged glances, their gaze finally settling on Charles Garboni. "That's true. His name is Santiago Pérez. He's a criminal, hired by someone to harm our passengers. We had no choice but to contain him."

"Don't military ships have a brig of some sort to contain unruly crew members?" Archie Morgan added. Though not an overseer, his presence in the meeting had been requested due to his naval experience, a fact that the other men were now grateful for.

Miranda didn't respond to the question. Instead, she asked: "How long do you plan on keeping this man?"

"That's a good question. Perhaps you have a suggestion. Frankly, we'd like to be rid of him as soon as possible. Keeping our friends safe is a top priority, and him being here is a threat to that," Donnie said.

"We're just like you, ma'am. We take seriously our responsibility to care for those in our protection," Archie said respectfully.

"What evidence do you have against him?" Miranda asked after some thought.

"Well, we have his kidnapping victim. She was recovered from the room he'd been holding her captive in. You're welcome to interview her."

"Where is she now?"

"In our infirmary being looked after by our doctors."

"Infirmary?" Miranda repeated, her expression shifting. Seated behind her, her officers exchanged startled glances. It was like looking at an expanding ripple in a glassy pool of water.

"Yes. Yes, I'd like to speak with her," Miranda said distractedly.

Fifteen minutes later, the team of Coast Guard officers walked through the doors of Rig 7's infirmary. It was a modest establishment, with a small waiting room lined in folding chairs leading to a hallway of closed doors. The brothers had called ahead, and two nurses were on hand to welcome them as they entered.

"How many doctors do you have here?" Miranda asked as she walked through the doors. Her demeanor had changed.

"Seven medical volunteers. Three are general practitioners, and we've also got a surgeon. The rest are registered nurses," explained Marcus Kelly. As the housing and personnel overseer, he knew these details by heart.

"I'd like to talk with the woman that you found," Miranda said after some thought.

"Is she ok to talk?" Peter asked one of the nurses. She nodded and led him and the officer down the corridor.

"I've never known offshore platforms to have such big infirmaries," Miranda said under her breath as they walked.

"They don't. This entire floor was expanded to add more rooms. With so many passengers, we couldn't take chances on running out of space in case of an emergency."

"Are all your rigs like this?"

"I've only been on this rig since we left land, but I believe this is a standard design. Safety regulations were rigorous. Our tankers are even more impressive. They have full medical wards. I'm told they're like small but fully functional hospitals."

The interview with Angelica did not take long. Peter had seen her only the day before, and she had looked well then. Now she appeared almost fully recovered, but for the bruising on her wrists and ankles. She showed them to the CPO along with a detailed retelling of her capture and rescue. Miranda listened to the entire

128

account, interrupting only occasionally to ask questions.

Peter said a silent prayer of thanks. While it was unclear how this unexpected run in with military forces would turn out, Peter suspected that Jehovah had his hand in matters.

***

Chief Petty Officer Miranda Sachs and her Coast Guard officers spent the night aboard Rig 7, housed comfortably in a row of empty cabins. The next morning they enjoyed a breakfast of oatmeal and dehydrated eggs. They mingled with the crew and passengers and met for a final meeting with the overseers before their departure.

A unanimous decision was reached. The USCG cutter would dispatch a patrol boat to retrieve Santiago Peréz the next day. He would be placed in their brig until he could be delivered to the authorities for a proper tribunal. Chief Petty Officer Miranda Sachs would be in charge of presenting the evidence she'd gathered from Angelica Parry, including video testimony. In turn, the doctors of Rig 7 would donate a small bundle of medical supplies to the Coast Guard. Shortly after their visit to the infirmary, it was revealed that one of their officers had been injured in an accident on deck days prior and that supplies were needed to treat him. Peter suspected there was more to the story, but had discreetly chosen to keep this opinion to himself. He would meet later with the other overseers to explain the story he'd heard from the officer and try to arrange a small gift of extra food supplies to be delivered via the patrol boat the next morning. Although stores were running low aboard their rig, the resupplying depot was only days away, and Peter did not expect much resistance to his idea.

"There is something else that I need to discuss with you," Miranda said once the details of Thiago's transfer had been nailed down.

"Please," Donnie Chavez said. The atmosphere in the room had improved significantly from their first meeting, and tensions had eased considerably.

"I need to ask what your policy is for passengers requesting to leave. Is there a formal process, or are they free to depart whenever they choose?"

The overseers were puzzled. Brother Kelly was the one to respond: "As you know, no one is forced to be here. If they choose

129

to leave, that's their decision. Finding the means to leave, however, is another story."

"What if we were the means?" Miranda asked.

"Are we speaking hypothetically here, or…?" Donnie asked. Miranda shook her head.

"I've agreed to provide passage to land for two of your passengers," she said, gauging the expressions of the men before her. They were clearly upset, but none seemed angry. Behind her, Peter noted, her men shifted uneasily. Clearly they hadn't been privy to this information.

"May I ask who?" Marcus asked. Miranda pulled a notepad from her pocket and flipped through the pages.

"Cary and Tina Doyle." Charles Garboni lowered his head. He'd seen this coming.

"Did they specifically ask to leave?" Peter asked. Miranda nodded.

"He said he's unhappy with the way things are run here. He wants his old life back."

"His old life? Doesn't he realize that—" Peter was cut off by a hand placed on his arm. It was Marcus Kelly.

"It's their choice. If they want to leave, we can't stop them," said the older brother.

"The patrol boat will pick them up tomorrow morning along with the prisoner. Oh-nine-hundred. Can they be ready by then?"

"We'll inform them," Marcus said. And with that, their meeting was dismissed.

CHAPTER 11

An eerie red mist seeped past the windows of the civilians' barracks at Hunters Point on the south side of San Francisco Bay. The red light had gradually replaced the total darkness that engulfed the camp and most of the continent around it. To most, this was an improvement over the featureless, pitch black that had surrounded them for weeks, but not by much.

The civilians had busied themselves while they waited for explanations as to why they'd been summoned here. They passed the hours struggling to make contact with friends and family, but good news was rare. Voice messages were left; calls were scarcely returned. What little news trickled over the airwaves only served to intensify their anxiety. The East and West Coast were engulfed in flames. There was little left to protect and no means to do so; fire departments and the military had pooled what resources they had left to evacuate survivors and flee to safer areas. Entire cities and counties were abandoned. Millions more would be burned to death as the encircling fires inched ever closer.

In the Midwest, freak tornadoes cut unapologetic paths through areas where such storms had previously been unheard of. Experts would speculate that they were the result of powerful heat waves from the fires mixing with cold arctic weather patterns. Still, no one could explain the persistent electrical storms, the blood red skies, and the fire storms. These were calamities of Biblical proportions, and while a nagging suspicion of supernatural forces was unavoidable, it was scarcely mentioned.

Instead, people began to point fingers. In their agony, what they craved most was a scapegoat: someone to blame for the countless extinguished lives and ruined wealth. And who better than the Witnesses? They were, after all, nowhere to be seen, having conveniently fled just prior to the first wave of disasters. And hadn't they been proclaiming the very doom that now engulfed all of humanity? How could they have known, if not for somehow playing a part?

Suspicion quickly escalated into accusations. Ecoterrorists. Anarchists. War criminals. False prophets, bent on exterminating the human race. A seething, fearful populace poured fuel to the fire. A brief witch hunt ensued. In America, those known to have had ties with the Witnesses in the past were brought before militant tribunals and interrogated. Only by swearing allegiance to their government and promising to take arms against the Witnesses were such ones spared their lives.

"Should've taken them out when we had the chance," Jay grumbled. He'd been sitting in the corner sharpening the blade of a hunting knife on a block of carbide. News from a tribunal across the bay had just come through. A family had been found guilty of sedition for attending a Witness meeting years prior. The death sentence was stayed only after they swore to uphold the sovereignty of the state. "Not like I didn't have an opportunity. Must've showed up at my door at least twice a year, back in the day," he said.

"Maybe you'll get that chance again," Chad said. He was leaning against a doorframe beside the radio, staring blankly at the red sky.

"Yeah?" Jay asked.

"Sure. That's why we're here, isn't it? Government wants our help dealing with the situation, right?"

"That's more than I heard," said another voice. A young woman was sitting cross-legged on the floor, a game of solitaire spread out before her. Chad's eyes hurt looking at the cards; the suits all looked the same color in the red light. "What do you know?" She asked.

"Not much, just what the colonel told me in the truck on the way over. They want our expertise in dealing with them."

"What, like an attack?" Jay asked. Chad shrugged.

"I doubt a physical one, unless you all were in the weapons industry." Chad took a look around. Heads shook.

"AI," said the girl on the floor.

"Yeah, I was in artificial intelligence too. Machine learning, specifically," someone else said.

"Google's DeepMind developer here. Also AI," said another.

"Ok, so that's probably why we're all here. We've got expertise in machine learning."

"Some kind of cyberattack?" Jay asked.

"That's what I'm thinking."

"If fighting is sure to result in victory, then you must fight," said a new voice. A man wearing a suit emerged from a back door. He held a briefcase in one hand and a stack of papers in another. He cleared space on one of the tables and set his items down as the others watched curiously. "Surely with all the brainpower in this room, someone can identify that quote." The man donned a pair of glasses and surveyed the faces.

It was Chad Harkett who spoke up. "Sun Tzu, The Art of War. Who are you?"

The man smiled, impressed. "Name's Driscoll. Formerly with the USCC, the United States Cyber Command. Not sure what my new title is yet, but here I am."

"So we are here for a cyber attack," Chad said. Driscoll waved him away.

"We'll leave the attacking to the soldiers and generals. Our task is more preliminary, more subtle." He pulled a laptop from his briefcase and plugged it into the wall. The debriefing began.

***

The crowd of passengers and overseers carefully descended the winding staircase beneath Rig 7. It led to a long, metal walkway suspended between the pylons and the spider deck. White caps agitated noisily a dozen feet below them. Diesel engines powering the machinery groaned steadily somewhere overhead.

"I don't see anyone out here!" Cary grumbled, struggling with a pair of suitcases. His wife followed close behind.

"We're ten minutes early. They'll be here soon," Peter responded from the rear. He and Charles Garboni flanked Thiago on either side. The tall man was bound by a pair of handcuffs, an item loaned to them by the Coast Guard.

"Please, Cary. Don't do this. Don't leave this place," pleaded a third voice. It was Mikey Glover, Cary's uncle. He'd been up most of the night trying to reason with Cary and Tina as the two packed their bags, but their minds were made up. Mikey reached out to grasp at the younger man's jacket. "Just think about what you're doing, Cary!" HIs voice was hoarse.

"I *have* thought about it! This is *my* life, *my* decision, Mike! I won't let you run our lives anymore!" Cary snapped. His wife gazed at the two men unaffectedly, as if oddly detached from her surroundings. Peter could only wonder what was going on in her head. He hated to see anyone leave, but it was their choice. No one had been forced on to the ferries back in New Orleans and no one would be forced to remain on the rig.

Minutes passed. A boat appeared on the horizon, and as it neared it became clear from its white and orange insignias that it belonged to the Coast Guard. Three men in brightly colored life vests and baseball caps brought the patrol boat to a stop and tied off to one of the pylons.

Using a battery-operated winch, Peter lowered the tip of the walkway, a small set of steps unfolding from beneath it.

"One at a time," Peter cautioned. "You don't want to take a dip in these waters."

Peter tightened his grip on the cold metal handrail as the sea surged below his feet. A jagged wave rose suddenly, closing the gap between the walkway and the waterline and soaking everyone's shoes in seawater.

"Keep an eye on your feet," Peter cautioned as Cary and Tina neared the stepladder. The trek was made all the more difficult by the bulky backpack slung across Cary's shoulders and the rolling suitcase he dragged behind him, its wheels rendered useless on the metal grating. Tina eyed the water warily and gave her husband a wide eyed look. Peter could sense that she wanted to say something, but her lips remained pursed tightly together. But then she screamed.

"What was that!" Tina yelled, her bag slipping from her shoulder. Items clattered on the walkway.

"What was *what*?" Cary snapped, glaring at his wife over his shoulder.

"Something moved below us. Something in the water!" Tina pointed, glancing at the men behind her for some sort of confirmation. Peter and Charles exchanged a glance.

"Sharks," Peter said matter-of-factly.

"Sharks? There are *sharks* out here?" Tina said, aghast. Peter nodded.

"Sure. They've come and gone as long as we've been out here. The kitchen crew disposes of food waste from this same walkway. It attracts scavengers."

"And you didn't think that was something worth mentioning?" Tina said, her face flushed with outrage.

"You were told explicitly that attempting to board a smaller ship in these waters would be dangerous," Brother Garboni said from the back of the group.

"Yeah, well, no one mentioned *sharks*," Tina muttered, her eyes now glued to the water beneath them, though she saw nothing but the churning black waves.

"You fall in this water and I can guarantee you the sharks will be the least of your worries. You see the way the waves are bouncing around like that? You get caught in this water and you'll be sucked right under. That happens and you get knocked around, maybe smashed into one of the pylons, and you're out cold. There's no pulling you back out."

The couple said nothing as they watched the powerful waves bash and topple below them. Sea spray coughed up at them.

"What's the hold up?" Yelled one of the coast guard officers from the patrol boat. Two men on the opposite end of the boat held long gaffing poles out at the submerged structure of the platform to keep the hull of their boat from crashing into the pylons. They wore nervous, impatient expressions.

"Are you sure about this?" Peter heard Tina ask. Her husband's resolve seemed to waver, but only for a moment. He raised his chin into the air and nodded.

"This is the only way," he insisted.

"Listen to her," Mikey pleaded one last time. But Cary didn't respond. Instead, he lowered their bags one by one down to the officers. Then, timing his movements to match a rising swell, he dropped down the few feet from the stepladder down to the deck of the patrol boat. The officer grabbed Cary's arms and steadied him. It seemed to take him a moment to get his bearings. He'd been aboard the rig so long that he'd grown accustomed to the gentle sway of the floor; he hardly felt its movement anymore. But now, aboard this much smaller vessel, he could feel every dip, every degree of list. He slipped quickly into a life vest and made his way unsteadily to the rear of the boat.

Tina was next. It was clear from a glance that she lacked the coordination of her husband. She couldn't anticipate the movement of the water, and in the end had to be told when to jump. Two officers caught her as she fell to the deck and nearly toppled into the

135

seas. She sat heavily on the stern of the small boat, gulping for air and nursing a twisted ankle with tears in her eyes.

"You're up next," Peter said, meeting Thiago's stony gaze.

Thiago lifted his wrists and wiggled the chain between the handcuffs. Had it been up to Peter, he would've been fine leaving the handcuffs for the officers below to deal with; surely a criminal skilled enough to transfer from one ship to another in the pitch black of a stormy night could handle a simple acrobatic maneuver with a mere chain between his hands. But the CPO's directions for Thiago's extraction had been clear: all restraints were to be removed prior to transit.

Peter pulled the key from his jacket pocket and gave Thiago a hard look.

"I'm going to remove the cuffs, and you're going to turn around and board that patrol boat. Then you're going to leave this place and never come back. Do I make myself clear?"

Thiago nodded once. Peter and Charles exchanged a glance and Peter inserted the key. The handcuffs fell away, and the men took a step back. Thiago rubbed the skin of his wrists between his fingers before turning to face the steps down to the patrol boat. But then he turned to face Peter.

"It made no sense for you to spare my life," Thiago said, his expression blank. "Why did you?"

"We're not executioners. We leave that up to the God we serve," Peter said simply. Thiago looked up at the sky, as if expecting to see this God in the flesh. He shrugged, glanced back down at the waves, and descended the ladder.

The commotion that unfolded in the following seconds happened so quickly, so suddenly, that Peter would often think back to them, wondering exactly what had gone wrong. Had Thiago simply lost his footing when he stepped onto the patrol boat? Had a sudden gust of wind tipped him off balance? Or had there been something else at play? Thiago was agile, light-footed, and athletic. For him, the transfer to the smaller boat should've been a cinch.

And yet he'd stumbled. His feet had come out from under him, his limbs scrabbling for purchase, fingers clawing at the deck, at the lines, at the handrails, at something—at anything—to save himself. But all that had failed, and he'd toppled straight into the water, his body arcing backwards over the safety rail and he tumbled headfirst into the black waters.

More commotion followed. He went under fast, just as Charles had warned. The waves, thrashing unpredictably as they bounced off of the pylons, sucked the tall man in his heavy coat straight underwater. The coast guard officers shouted orders at one another. A life preserver was tossed into the sea, but when Thiago resurfaced he was far from it. The line was pulled in and it was tossed again, but by now he'd been sucked under again. People were yelling. Tina was sobbing in Cary's arms as he gazed on in silent shock.

But the worst was still to come.

If there was anything merciful about Thiago's last moments, it was that he did not spot the sharks moving in his direction. There was thus no way to dread his impending fate. Attracted by his erratic thrashing and the sense of his panic, the creatures circled once before attacking. The attack happened so quickly that Thiago's brain could hardly process the sensation of pain. Instead, he experienced only an enormous, crushing pressure as three sets of serrated teeth clamped onto his limbs and pulled him under. His eyes caught the stare of their black, unblinking eyes and realized at once that the predator had become the prey.

And then he was no more.

***

Stacy Owen had been in and out of consciousness the last few days. The sedatives and painkillers had kept her mostly under, and keeping her bandages changed and her bed clean had kept Joyce busy. Thankfully, with few other patients requiring attention— mostly friends who'd wandered in asking for more Dramamine patches or requested OTC's for headaches and minor colds—Joyce had spent most of her time on the clock at her friend's side. She read aloud old *Watchtower* articles from her phone and played original songs to keep her spirits high.

It had done the trick, but Joyce was getting restless. She walked the perimeter of the tanker each morning at sunrise and toured the cavernous storage compartments below decks after hours, where forklifts and palette movers whizzed around like insects, systematically moving crates of supplies to open areas on the floor marked out in brightly colored tape. Occasionally, a supply transfer would offer a much-needed break in the monotony. The doors of the supertanker would slowly roll away to reveal a gaping rectangular hole in the hull, where small but strong cranes on rails would pluck the crates from the floor and lower them to the waiting ships below. It was a mesmerizing process to watch, and Joyce soon found herself splitting shifts between the medical ward and volunteering on the supply floor.

The convoy trudged southward, just twenty miles off the Southern California coast. With radio signals between ships still unreliable, the communications room of *The Golden Age* had been unable to determine the whereabouts of Alvin Tucker, Joyce's husband. And so, with the arrival of each group of passengers, transfers, and workers, Joyce would make the rounds, asking if anyone had news of Alvin, of where he might be. It was unpleasant to imagine spending the entirety of her transit to Africa without her husband, but if worse came to worst she would accept it; she was just glad to be alive and reunited with her brothers.

It was to be a busy day in the loading dock of *The Golden Age*, and all available hands were requested to assist. Volunteers from the various departments arrived obediently, donned Hi-Vis vests, and were dispatched to the various stations to prepare for a rendezvous with another vessel.

"She's carrying over a thousand passengers," explained a brother that morning as everyone finished their breakfast trays. The man stood beside a giant projector screen, where a picture of a vessel similar to their own was displayed.

"This supply run will work a little differently than the others, though," the brother added, clicking through to the next screen. In this picture, a broad metal walkway suspended by cables jutted from the side of the ship. "The ship's equipped with a retractable gangplank, which means we won't be using our rail crane. She'll simply pull up next to us, extend the plank like a bridge, and we'll exchange supplies." The brother pushed the button, revealing two columns of items.

"We'll be sending over the items on the left. The crates and containers will be color-coded to help you keep it all straight. The right column is the items we'll be receiving. Some frozen goods, clothing and footwear, and of course, medical supplies." The speaker cast a glance in Joyce's direction, where she sat at a cafeteria table with a handful of other medical staff.

"There's going to be a lot of back-and-forth as we transport the items, so it's crucial that everyone follows the instructions of the overseers. Also, be aware of the marked footpaths and stay in your lanes. We don't want anyone getting run over by a forklift."

The speaker paused as an uneasy chuckle rippled over the audience.

"Due to the volume of supplies we'll be moving, we estimate that this will be an all-day task. There will be plenty of people coming and going, including brothers and sisters from the other vessel. We know you'll all want to sit and chat and you're welcome to associate during the lunch break, but please keep in mind that our work takes precedence. Once our rendezvous with this vessel is complete, we'll be making a bee line for the waters of Mexico, where we're expected for a supply drop-off in just two days." The brother paused as the audience nodded in understanding.

With the debriefing finished, the crew went to work immediately. The air was filled with sounds of beeping forklifts, squealing dolly wheels, the groan of wooden crates sliding across the reinforced steel floors. Nearly twenty tons of supplies were transported between the two vessels that morning, carried by dozens of volunteers ferrying materials back and forth.

The gangplank itself was hardly two meters wide, often with space for only a single worker moving supplies at a time. Joyce took a deep breath and stepped on, nerves buzzing as she felt the walkway sway below the soles of her shoes. The platform rose and fell like a bridge in high winds. It yawed left and right with the shifting positions of the ships. Steel suspension cables pinged and twanged with tension as a tempestuous sea heaved several stories below. Joyce double-checked the safety line clipped to her waist and crossed cautiously, eyes fixed on the other end of the suspended walkway.

Two burly brothers were waiting for her. They grasped Joyce's arms in their hands as she stepped off of the swaying walkway and onto the wonderfully firm deck on the other side. She removed the clip from her belt and handed it to a sister headed in the opposite direction.

And then Joyce Tucker froze. She could hardly believe the sight before her eyes. Not ten feet in front of her stood her husband, Alvin.

"Joyce?" Alvin asked, his voice nearly lost among the cacophony of sounds on deck.

But Joyce could not respond. Her knees felt suddenly heavy, like two lead weights pulling her down. She mouthed Alvin's name and collapsed, but he was there to catch her before she hit the deck. He pulled her close to him, wrapping her in his powerful arms. The two stared into each others' faces for a long moment without speaking. It was simply too much for either to take; hot tears streamed down their cheeks and they embraced.

"I can't believe it's really you," Alvin said over and over, pulling away momentarily to gaze back into his wife's eyes. "But how? How did you get here?"

Unable to speak and overcome with emotion, Joyce could only shake her head and smile, eyes puffy and wet. "I'd love to catch up," Joyce finally managed, struggling through a sob. "But I'm still on the clock."

Alvin pulled his wife in close for another hug as the two laughed and cried happy, warm tears.

PART II.

CHAPTER 12

Dietrich Nash gazed down at the sprawling settlement nestled in the valley. In spite of his close connection to every detail of the project over the previous six years, he still had difficulty believing that it was all real. Seeing Jehovah's hand constantly maneuver matters and watching the pieces fall into place had been nothing short of miraculous.

He thought back to those initial talks, when Namibian officials had been stupefied by the brothers' proposal to purchase the first four hundred thousand-acre swath of land. Half of it was scorched desert, they said, impossible to aerate and impractical to build on, while the other half was covered in a gravelly sand where only the hardiest of African plants could hope to survive. Even African farmers avoided this land; foreigners would hardly survive a season. Crazier still were the details of the brothers' plan: to build a multi-national, multi-lingual community to house and train worshippers from around the globe.

Behind closed doors their plans were mocked and ridiculed. Surely the foolhardy enterprise could only end in a costly, embarrassing failure. Still, the promise of quick money in exchange for worthless land proved irresistible, and a deal was quickly settled upon. If nothing else, the Namibian officials reasoned, perhaps such a strange building project would boost their tourism industry and lead to further foreign investment, a desirable source of income that any African nation hoped to secure.

When the brothers arrived just months after the deal was signed and the payment delivered, their first task was to build a reliable system of transportation between their budding settlement and the Namibian coast, a nearly two hundred kilometer trek to the East. In many cases, this was simply a matter of repairing a winding network of railways laid by the land's previous tenants, a Chinese mining operation. In others, it meant building entirely new swaths of track. Within a year, a working hybrid train was running trips to and from Elizabeth Bay and the Witnesses' colony of Bismarck.

More volunteers followed. Brothers and sisters from African countries arrived by the tens of thousands, working side by side to quickly erect spacious mud-brick structures to serve as dormitories, classrooms, and meeting halls. Those without skills were trained in weekly classes, covering everything from bricklaying to plumbing, electrical wiring to HVAC and roofing.

The settlement grew. Within just three years, it was clear that the Witnesses were here to stay. Visiting government officials gawked at the growth. Their small nation, previously the second least-populated in the world, had grown considerably with the expansion of the Witnesses' compound, and there was no end in sight. The small community of Bismarck had swelled to nearly fifty-thousand permanent residents and temporary volunteers. A second railway was built, providing transportation to newer settlements to the south.

Then the earth movers arrived—the bulldozers, excavators, graders, and haul trucks. More land was cleared as foundations for future buildings were installed. Soil from distant lands was spread in huge, acres-wide tracts and carefully tended. Trees were planted along brick walkways that weaved their way through the growing communities.

But as amazing as these industrial developments were, Dietrich Nash had always felt that the most significant sign had been the change in weather. Their first two summers in Namibia were the coolest in recorded history; more importantly, they'd brought record levels of rainfall. The barren stream bed threading its way through the colony swelled to a river so powerful that part of it was diverted, dammed, and harnessed for energy. The fertile artery of land surrounding the river began to expand outward. Trees and shrubs never before seen in this part of the Namib grew and thrived. Before their very eyes, the ecosystem was shifting.

It was around this time that the colony's true purpose was revealed to the overseers there. It had been a trial period used to determine whether Jehovah's blessing was on their plans, and the results were clear. This land would serve as home not to tens or even hundreds of thousands, but to millions. Shortly thereafter, the attack on false religion would signal the outbreak of the great tribulation, and plans for the Namibian colonies were expedited.

As Witnesses the world over began simplifying their lives and donating what they could directly to the organization, the funds began pouring in. Additional land was purchased, though unsurprisingly at a much steeper price than before. Legal arrangements were made with the Namibian government, too, ensuring that passport holders of any country would be allowed entry, so long as they remained on the Witnesses' land. It was an unprecedented development that Dietrich could have never foreseen, but if there had been one thing he had learned about the celestial chariot, it was to never question the direction and always expect the unexpected.

Which is why Dietrich was not entirely surprised that a representative from the government's tax bureau had asked for a meeting. He had, in fact, suspected such a meeting to happen sooner or later, but he had not expected to recognize the man that entered his office. It was Adani Ratief, the same government worker who'd first showed him the land years before. He wore a shorter haircut, now, and was dressed in a dark blue suit with thick grey pinstripes. He removed his white straw hat and shook hands with the brother, who greeted him with the traditional *'Goeie more'* and poured his guest a cup of South African rooibos.

"Congratulations on your promotion," Dietrich offered.

"Ah, it is nothing," Adani said, waving the compliment away. The guest took a sip of the red tea and smiled. "Only in your commune does one find a white man serving a black man to be a common thing," Mr. Ratief said with a demure shake of his head.

"We are all brothers and sisters here, Adani. Skin color has no bearing on things. You know that."

"And am I your brother, too?" Adani asked.

"You are a friend and my guest. You receive the same treatment as my brothers, and you are always welcome here. Chocolate?" Dietrich asked amicably. It was a game he was accustomed to playing with the local officials. Their playful banter, he suspected, masked a desire to uncover what the Witnesses were really doing on their land. In spite of the years spent working to build a respectful relationship, Dietrich sensed a growing mistrust between them, thanks in part to the events since the outbreak of the tribulation.

Adani helped himself to a chocolate candy from a tin and popped it into his mouth. He held it between his gums and his cheek as he spoke.

"I like you, Dietrich. And I like your people, too. They are good, clean, honest."

Dietrich nodded and braced himself. "But..." he prompted.

"Yes, well. You know why I am here."

"To collect taxes, I presume."

"Precisely."

"I believe we've discussed this in detail with the bureau on previous occasions. The agreement we signed on was clear. We are a non-profit organization. We make no money here."

"On paper, no, of course not. But it does not look good, all of these people coming, and buildings rising up from the ground. And the machines,"

"I understand, but this doesn't change the fact that we are not running a business here."

"Yes, yes, you and I know this. But the bureau... they see it differently."

"Mr. Ratief, I'm sure you've been over the paperwork. Everything here was either donated or purchased and that no one is making a salary here. Myself included. There is no legal basis for taxing us."

"But when will it end, Dietrich? I was at the harbor at Elizabeth Bay last week. I counted over thirty ships! People were leaving the boats and boarding the trains and coming straight here! Surely you cannot expect our government to turn a blind eye to endless expansion."

"But we are self sufficient. We produce our own energy, filter our own water, grow most of our own food. What we do not produce we purchase directly from your communities. We have asked for no preferential treatment or discounts. If anything, we have already contributed greatly to the local economy. I've seen the public works in Windhoek with my own eyes. I can only assume that was possible in part to the funds we've spent in the capital."

"Your economic support is appreciated. We are a grateful nation. You have brought wealth and beauty to the land."

"Then what's the problem?" asked Dietrich, still smiling.

"The problem is that your community—a city now, by all standards—is half of our entire nation's population, and not one of you is being taxed. It does not look good, Mr. Nash."

"How can we be taxed when we are not making any money?"

"The Namibian Tax Bureau has discussed the situation and come to a consensus," Adani Ratief said, pausing to pull a folder from his briefcase. "I think you will find it fair."

"With all due respect, Mr. Ratief, you and I both know this is illegal."

Adani shrugged, his smile beginning to falter. "And we also know that these are extraordinary times. There are no more churches in all of Namibia, no Christians apart from your people. Beyond our borders, we hear of economies collapsing, societies toppling. During desperate times, laws change, Dietrich. Please try to understand."

"So this is a religious tax?"

"Please, look at the document for yourself. We will be in touch," Adani said. He rose and offered his hand with a smile. Dietrich shook it and watched his guest disappear.

***

The fleet from Burrard Harbor had been on the open seas for nearly four months now. Their toilsome journey had taken them down the western coast of the United States and Mexico, through the Panama canal, and into the vast Atlantic Ocean. From there they sailed eastwards straight for Namibia. But conditions on these waters would be much different than they had been for Peter, Rachel, and the rest of Rig 7's crew and passengers.

When the earlier convoy had moved through these waters months ago, they'd encountered few other ships. Most vessels simply had no means or motive to venture so far out into open waters. As the blackouts struck, few were equipped with the supplies to survive or the expertise to set course for some overseas destination. These Witnesses' journey had thus been, for the most part, quiet and uninterrupted. But for those traveling from Vancouver and farther north, a very different experience awaited.

Comprised mostly of former fishermen and their families and neighbors, smugglers from Venezuela had been active since the mid 2010's, when a faltering Venezuelan economy and collapsing government drove many to desperate, unthinkable measures. Smuggling everything from guns to diapers, these former fishermen abandoned their nets for the promise of greater profits. But as the situation in their country and neighboring territories continued to disintegrate, new sources of income were needed. Thus began a

146

ruthless cycle of piracy, hijackings, and murder.

By the time the Witnesses fleeing from Burrard spilled from the Panama canal into the Caribbean, pirates from across South America were waiting. Reports of the fleet of unarmed, well-stocked vessels had spread quickly. Originally superstitious about targeting vessels belonging to an organization believed to be in some way connected to supernatural celestial events, the first waves of ships had gone untouched. But those ships had sailed months ago at a time when the pirates were focusing their attacks on easier prey, small vessels like luxury yachts piloted by rich American businessmen fleeing the fires and riots. But as time went on, such targets dwindled. The pirates became desperate. Returning to land was no longer an option, and many had taken to the seas with their families aboard. Just approaching land was perilous, where their decks would surely be overrun by their former Venezuelan countrymen waiting in rafts—old planks and flotsam lashed together with wire and rope.

Joyce Tucker sat on a bench on the upper deck of *The Chariot* deep in thought. She'd boarded Alvin's barge shortly after the two were reunited, and Stacy Owen had been moved along with her. It was a warm Sunday morning, the air heavy with Spring. The open seas were a welcome change after the rigors of Mexico and Panama, where angry citizens had cursed and jeered from shore as the convoys passed. Announcements were made for all passengers and crew to stay below decks until the boats pulled away from land; some on shore had reportedly shot firearms at the passing vessels, though no one had been injured.

That morning's meeting had been timely: the discourse, prepared by a helper to the Governing Body, emphasized the importance of caution, good judgment, and obedience. Now was not the time for rash, emotional decisions. As pressures mounted from the gathering forces that would culminate in the Gog of Magog, keeping a cool head was paramount. There was no place for anger and retaliation among God's people—vengeance belonged to Jehovah. Never before had Jesus' words to 'turn the other cheek' been more appropriate, and never before more challenging.

The prerecorded talk was followed by an older *Watchtower* article about cultivating peace within the congregation. Supplementary information provided by the branch made application to the evacuating convoys, where brothers and sisters, often in tight confines and high-stress situations, would need to display Christian qualities as never before.

It had been just the spiritual food that was needed. Joyce thought back to her time with Stacy, when the two were trapped in Seattle, how tense things had been. And then again, on the deck of the *Abigail*, when Monique had nearly been kidnapped. And yet again, on *The Golden Age*, when Dr. Munoz's terse words had rubbed her the wrong way. If she'd experienced all this over the course of a few short months, surely millions of other Witnesses had faced similar trials. Years ago, when Joyce contemplated the great tribulation, she'd never anticipated such things to be a challenge, but of course it made sense now. They were, after all, still imperfect, and the immense stress of these last moments of Satan's system would only aggravate whatever discord existed between them.

"Mind if I join you?" asked a soft voice from over Joyce's shoulder. She turned to see Claire Aberdeen standing behind her, two cups of steaming coffee in her hands. She held one out to Joyce with a shy smile. They'd been together now for weeks, but Joyce still had trouble believing just how much the young sister had come along since she'd first found her, badly injured and amnesic at West Hill Medical. It wasn't just the physical progress that Joyce found impressive. The fact that the girl was on her own two feet and walking without a limp was miraculous enough, but it was her spiritual growth that truly struck her former nurse. She was only sad that she had not been a part of it.

"Of course, darling," Joyce said, making room on the bench. Claire stepped over and sat. She closed her eyes and filled her lungs with the warm breeze of the sea. From the corner of her eye she caught the older sister staring at her.

"What is it?" she asked.

Joyce sighed. "Just can't stop thinking about the first time we met. Do you remember?"

Claire made a face. "It's a little fuzzy to be honest. I don't think I was myself."

"That's one way of putting it. You couldn't even remember your own name."

Claire chuckled. "Glad it's behind me."

"I'm glad it's behind both of us."

"What do you mean?"

"Everything. That old life. That old me. It sounds crazy to say it, but this is exactly what I needed."

148

"The great tribulation?"

Joyce nodded solemnly. "It's exposed all my weaknesses, all my flaws. I have so much to work on."

"Well, from where I'm standing, you seem to have it together. I don't know what I would've done without you."

Joyce shook her head. "Jehovah would've found another way. You had made the decision to come back and were taking action. He would've blessed that."

"Yeah, maybe so."

"No, not maybe. He would've," Joyce said. "I never should've left the camp."

Wrinkles appeared in Claire's expression and she nodded slowly.

"I learned my lesson the hard way," Joyce sighed, her gaze returning to the ocean.

"You know, Brother Tucker never told me the whole story about why you left. I mean, I figured it had something to do with that blood sample you took from me, but he never went into the details. I could tell he was hurting the whole time, but he never said why. Just said that you were away, that something had come up suddenly. I guess he didn't want me feeling like I was somehow responsible."

Joyce bit her lip as she felt the tears pushing up behind her eyelids. For all his faults, Alvin was a man she loved completely. She knew how difficult Claire's presence had been on Alvin, how much extra stress it had put on his shoulders. And yet, in the end, despite her own absence, Alvin had taken the young girl under his wing and cared for her like the daughter they'd lost. Joyce would never forget it.

She smiled at Claire and wrapped an arm around the young sister's shoulders and together they watched the waves dip and crest over an endless horizon.

***

The broad stretch of gravel plains and sand dunes known as the Namib Desert stretches for the entirety of the West Namibian coastline. Its name, taken from the Khoekhoegowab word for "vast place" is fitting; at its widest point, this arid swath of land spans hundreds of kilometers before climbing to the country's highest

149

elevation atop the Central Plateau. Beyond the Plateau, the land diversifies into many-fingered canyons, grasslands, rivers, and a sub-tropical woodland known as the Bushveld, where white rhinos, giraffes, wildebeests, and kudu freely roam.

To access the fertile areas from by sea, however, one must first make landfall on the Skeleton Coast. Here, strong winds formed by cold Atlantic currents push the sifting desert sands high into the air, creating the tallest dunes found anywhere on planet Earth. With these coastal winds come heavy surf—towering waves strong enough to swallow small ships whole or else dash them against rocky outcroppings camouflaged among the white sands.

A walk down this sun-blistered desert coastline reveals hundreds of rusty shipwrecks in varying stages of decay, 'skeletons' which serve as an unmistakable warning to captains and crew with intentions to come ashore. Like much of sub-Saharan Africa, Namibia is a land of countless natural perils.

Fortunately for the brothers and sisters, the Skeleton Coast was not to be conquered by boat. Far out at sea, long before the waves realized their full potential, the repurposed offshore platforms powered down their turbines and nudged close to one another. Thus positioned, prefabricated collapsible bridges were used to link the platforms, so that once assembled the rigs jutted from the sea like a network of floating towers.   The brothers thus made their way from the platforms down onto dry land, where electric trams sporting oversized dune tires carried passengers, luggage, and supplies up and over the dune cliffs and onto the waiting train carriages.

The trains themselves, like so many of the structures here, were not built for luxury or comfort, but for practicality and cost-efficiency. Open air passenger compartments with slanted aluminum overhangs provided vital shelter from the sun, while the speed of the train itself created a warm—though not unpleasant—breeze to keep its passengers cool.

The steel railway, built on solid bedrock, weaved through the towering dunes, some as high as thirty-story buildings. They cast long, cool shadows along the track, a brief respite from the unrelenting African sun.

"It feels like a dream, doesn't it?" Peter said, wrapping his arm tightly around Rachel's shoulders as their train carriage passed into the dune's shadows. He found it surprising how quickly the temperature plummeted in the shade. A young African brother carrying a sack of bottled water paused briefly at their side to hand them two bottles.

"Dankie," Peter said. The young brother nodded meekly and continued on his way. While English was to be the official language of the colony, the organization had encouraged new arrivals to learn a few simple Afrikaans phrases, and a series of short videos shown on the rigs shortly before their arrival had taught them the basics. It was the language of many of the local brothers and sisters, and they'd sacrificed much to prepare for the constantly growing population.

"If you had told me two years ago that I was going to be sitting on a train in some African desert, I would've thought you were crazy," Rachel said, snapping the top off the bottle and taking a sip. "Who could've imagined?"

Peter chuckled. He heard the sound of boyish footsteps racing up the carriage behind him and turned to see Evan Parry's beaming smile. The boy held a curved white shard in his hand.

"Brother Burton! Guess what this is?" he asked, eyes gleaming. Peter took the fragment in his hands and turned it over, inspecting it carefully.

"Looks like a bone of some sort. Am I right?" Peter asked.

"Yeah! It's part of a zebra jaw! One of the guides gave it to me. Isn't it cool?"

"Very cool," Peter said. He had an urge to reach out and tussle the boy's hair, but he stopped himself. Evan didn't seem like a child anymore. After months spent at sea and everything he'd been through, it was like looking at a young man now.

"I told him that maybe when we get settled in, we can drill a tiny hole in it and turn it into a necklace," Ted Watkins said, walking up the aisle behind Evan. Peter took a moment to look over his friend and smile. Though he'd lost some of his weight and vigor in the weeks during his hospitalization, he'd recovered quickly, and there'd been no permanent damage to his vocal cords as the doctors had worried. "What do you think, Pete? That'd be pretty neat, huh?"

"Very neat," Peter said.

"Yeah!" Evan said, eyes even wider now. He disappeared excitedly from where he'd come.

"To be young and carefree again," Ted said, throwing a thumb over his shoulder in Evan's direction.

"Wish I had his energy," Rachel said.

151

"You will. Not long now at all," Peter said. Ted walked off to find Angelica as Peter took his wife's hands in his own and gave them a squeeze. "You've made it this far," Peter said. "Just think, we're that much closer to the end."

"One day at a time," Rachel said.

"One day at a time."

And with that, their train left the shade of the dunes and began the second phase of its journey: a winding trek through the canyons. Behind them, the sun was beginning to dip below the dunes and into the horizon and the temperature dropped. A pair of African sisters moved quietly through the carriages, encouraging passengers to bundle up; any who needed extra layers were given wool blankets.

Peter and Rachel extracted a pair of coats from their luggage and slipped into them.

"Didn't think the desert could get so cold, eh?" asked a brother sitting on the bench across from them. They nodded sheepishly. "Might dip all the way down to ten degrees tonight! That's the Namib for ya."

"Ten degrees?" Peter repeated.

"Yes. Celsius, that is. Not sure what that is in Fahrenheit."

"Oh," Peter said, unsure himself of the conversion. It would be yet another thing to learn about their new home. "So, you from around here?"

"Pretoria, South Africa, originally. Relocated with my wife to Bismarck when the branch asked for volunteers, been here ever since. Name's Winifred Osborne."

Peter introduced himself and his wife and the three shook hands.

"So, what can you tell us about the colony?"

"Which one?" Winifred asked with a crooked smile. The couple exchanged a glance.

"How many are there?"

"Well, there's the largest colony, Bismarck, where I'm from. North of that is Meringhousen, where much of our food is grown. To the south are the colonies of Kosi and Sheim, and below that is Grunau. I'm sure you'll remember all those names," Winifred smiled.

"Yeah, right," Peter said, shaking his head.

"There will be maps when we get to our stop. Usually the brothers distribute them on the trains, but I'm afraid you're the last group of the day; the pamphlets have run out."

"I don't know if a map would help me much at this point, to be honest," Peter said. "We're still having difficulty wrapping our heads around just being here at all."

Winifred made an empathetic face, but the expression was somehow distant. "You'll adjust. Frankly, there's so much to do that there isn't much time to think things over. Everyone has a job."

"What's yours?" Rachel asked.

"Train mechanic," Winifred said, kicking the heel of his boot against a metal toolbox beneath his bench. "I'm on the trains each and every day, back and forth from the bay to the colonies. If something goes wrong, it's my job to get it fixed as soon as possible."

"Sounds important."

Winifred gave a curt nod. "Trains weren't meant to run constantly in these conditions. On the one end, salty sea winds are constantly trying to corrode everything, and on the other, the desert heat does a number on the batteries. That's why the trains are hybrid—can't rely solely on electrical in this climate."

"What's the worst you've seen out here?" Rachel asked. The mechanic squinted up at the ceiling and scratched his chin.

"A year or so ago, when some of the first volunteers arrived, we got battered by some heavy winds. The winds are especially problematic out here for us, because given enough time, they can actually move sand dunes. So these strong winds were kicking up all this sand, and we didn't realize it, but the track up ahead was covered in sand. That's a big problem. Either of you know how train wheels work?"

Peter and Rachel shook their heads.

"It's a very simple design: two wheels attached to an axle, with the top of the wheels angled slightly inward to keep the carriage centered on the rails. They're not like roller coaster wheels, with an up-stop assembly to keep the carriage from flying off the track. Basically, it's the sheer weight of the train that keeps it in place. So if there's something on the track and the train approaches with enough speed, you're in danger of derailing."

"Is that what happened? From just some sand?"

Winifred wagged his finger. "Lesson number one of living in the desert: never underestimate the sand. It can shift under your feet, it can move as if it had a mind of its own, and it can certainly derail a train. Fortunately we weren't moving very fast when it happened, but it was still frightening. The carriages were carried right over the hump of sand, as if we were moving up a ramp, and then we slid off the tracks. We coasted for another kilometer or so. Fortunately no one was injured, but everyone was shaken up and it took weeks to repair the damage."

"What's to prevent something like that from happening again?" Rachel asked uneasily, suddenly wishing the driver would slow down. As it was, they were barely moving sixty kilometers per hour.

"A good question. First, sand spotters are required for operating the engines. They keep an eye on the track ahead and make sure there are no impediments. Second, the front of the engines are fitted with special rail guards design to sweep away any debris on the tracks. Since the trains run regularly, they keep the tracks clear for one another."

"Well, I'm glad to hear it," Peter said. But no sooner had he spoken those words of relief than a sudden gust of wind whipped through the train carriage, draping the compartment in a sheet of dust and sand. The passengers shielded their eyes and faces as the sand stung any exposed skin. The wind passed, but the momentary relief was interrupted by another, more powerful gale.

Winifred rifled through the contents of his toolbox, producing a pair of hand cranks. He stood and handed one of them to Peter.

"We'd better lower the awnings," he explained, pointing to a socket embedded on the wall at the far end of the carriage. Peter obeyed, though not completely understanding. He inserted the crank into the socket and rotated. Gears and levers groaned to life within the wall of the train, bringing the slanted overhangs downwards until they covered the window openings. With a two-inch gap remaining between the cover and the opening, wind and sand were still leaking into the compartment, but the amount of each had lessened considerably.

Winifred Osborne walked over to inspect Peter's handiwork. "Should there be a gap like that?" he asked.

"Oh yes. We don't want the friends to suffocate in here."

"But the sand…" Peter objected.

Winifred gave him a look. "My brother," he said with an impish grin as he set his hand on Peter's shoulder, "you'd better get used to the sand. There's plenty of it where we're headed."

154

CHAPTER 13

"Let me take a wild guess," Brother Lucas said as he entered Dietrich's fourth-floor office and sat on a small couch beside a bookshelf. The old friends shook hands and Dietrich poured the man a cup of red tea. "They're trying to tax us again, aren't they?"

Dietrich nodded tiredly. The recent visit from Mr. Ratief had not been the first attempt made by the Tax Bureau, but it had felt different from previous ones. Van Lucas took a deep breath. Originally an on-call attorney for the South African branch, Brother Lucas had eventually found himself relocated to the growing complexes in Namibia. They'd run into few legal roadblocks during the initial purchase of land, and things in the years following had been remarkably smooth. But that was then, before the outbreak of the tribulation. It was no surprise that now, finally, in the last moments of Satan's system, tensions between the brothers and the government of Namibia were beginning to worsen.

"I'm sure you walked him through our status as a non-profit," Van said.

"Yes, of course."

"And their rebuttal?" Van asked. Dietrich had to think for a moment.

"I suppose they didn't really have one. Just kept saying that it was time, that we'd been here for so long and the colonies keep growing. I tried reasoning—told him that our simply being here, supplying business to the locals, is a huge boon to the economy, but…" Dietrich threw his hands in the air with a sigh.

"But they want more."

Dietrich nodded grimly.

"You contacted the branch reps?"

"They told me to call you, see if we have any sort of legal recourse." Dietrich Nash set the tax papers on the table between them.

156

Van Lucas shuffled through the documents for a few minutes before leaning back and staring up at the ceiling.

"Is this anything like what the French government tried against the Witnesses a few years back?" Dietrich finally asked.

"Yes and no. They were trying to demand back taxes amounting to tens of millions of Euros. The Namibian Tax Bureau isn't quite so bold. This tax wouldn't be retroactive."

"But it's still illegal."

"According to this, not technically. The document they have here indicates that they are attempting to redefine the law. My guess is that from here on out, only smaller non-profit organizations would be exempt from taxes, which would exclude us."

"What about appealing to the supreme court?"

"We could try that, but we could only take it as far as the Supreme Court of Namibia. That's another difference between us and France. In France, the brothers eventually appealed to the European Court of Human Rights, where they were handed a victory. But nothing like that court exists here in Africa."

"But it's still worth a shot."

"Of course, but before we go the legal route, let me confer with the branch. They may suggest us first sitting down with the Tax Bureau behind closed doors to see if some other arrangement can be made. Legal action is usually the last resort."

"Okay," Dietrich said, feeling a tinge of relief. He took a sip of his tea and gazed out his window down into the valley. "I just can't believe they're pulling this now, when we're so close to the end. What do they expect to achieve?"

"From a worldly standpoint, it makes sense, really," Van countered. "To be honest we've enjoyed a fairly conflict-free relationship with them for years. It doesn't surprise me in the least that a government would try to squeeze us for extra cash, especially when they see how we've thrived."

"Not monetarily."

"Sure, but they don't know that. They only see buildings and railways popping up everywhere and hundreds of thousands of people crossing their borders. They must be scratching their heads."

"I suppose," Dietrich said through a sigh. Van Lucas glanced at his watch and raised his eyebrows.

"Almost two o'clock. I've got an appointment in just a few minutes downstairs. Mind if I keep these?" he asked, raising the tax documents in his hand. Dietrich nodded. Van stood and Dietrich showed him to the door.

The two men shook hands again before Van said, "Cheer up, old friend. Even if they manage to tax us for every cent we're worth, it's all temporary. They'll be tossing it right back into the streets in no time."

"Of course," Dietrich Nash said with a smile.

"And remember, if all else fails, there's always the back up plan," Van said, pausing at the door. Dietrich frowned for a moment before catching his friend's meaning.

"Of course. The mines."

"If nothing else, that'll settle this."

"You think so?"

Van Lucas nodded, waved goodbye, and exited Dietrich's office.

***

Luis Escobar had once been a fisherman. The decades spent out at sea hauling in catches of tuna had left his skin dark and leathery. Deep wrinkles in his face and neck made him appear much older than his fifty-three years. The sea was his mistress, Luis liked to joke, back when jokes were still exchanged among the fishermen on the piers of Caracas, back when there was still some semblance of camaraderie between them. Back before the pirates.

Luis hadn't believed the stories at first. Surely the tales of fishermen murdered while gathering their nets were just that—tall tales born of bored minds and active imaginations. But as the weeks and months passed, the deteriorating conditions on land spilled over the coast and into the seas, and it soon became clear that this profession was no longer safe. He walked into a pawn shop near his neighborhood and—despite a recent ban against private gun ownership—was able to discreetly purchase a small pistol and a box of ammunition. He shoved the items deep into his pockets and left. His hands wouldn't stop shaking.

He felt safer with the gun, but not much. He kept the pistol locked away in a small metal tin at his side on the boat, and simply glancing down at it filled him with a rush of confidence, but it was temporary. Months passed and Luis was never attacked, but the same could not be said for the other fishermen. Many would quit the seas altogether after their horrendous run-ins with pirates. These were the fortunate ones. Many simply disappeared out at sea, their abandoned boats sometimes discovered adrift at sea, their fates unknown.

Things worsened. As the fishing industry fell apart, those once in its employ were forced to make a decision. Would they return to a crime-ridden land and struggle to pave a new way for themselves, or would they turn to more lucrative opportunities at sea, however illegal? For many the choice was an easy one, and one by one, Luis found his old friends aligning themselves with various smuggling gangs and syndicates.

But smuggling came with its own risks. Pirates still roamed these waters, and boats loaded with contraband slipping through South American territories were irresistible targets. From an illegal arms dealer at sea Luis purchased a second firearm, a far deadlier automatic weapon that could be mounted on the prow of his rickety fishing boat to fend off would-be attackers. He hoped he would never have to use it. Luis was not a killer, nor did he consider himself a criminal. He was simply a man trying to make a living. Which is why, when the Sosa brothers appeared one day off the prow of his meager fishing ship with a proposal, he was willing to listen.

Of course, Luis was familiar with Rafael and Stefan Sosa. Everyone in all of Caracas knew of them. Their father, a cunning businessman with government connections, had for decades run a profitable cannery before his death in the late nineties. Uninterested in continuing the Sosa legacy, Rafael and Stefan sold the company, squandered much of their inheritance, and purchased a small fleet of luxury sailboats, hoping to stake a claim in Venezuela's tourism sector.

Their success was short lived. As the country's government destabilized, they sold off all but the largest of their ships, a dual-jet-powered speed craft that could cover the distance between Venezuela and Trinidad in record time. They were two of Caracas' first to turn to the smuggling trade and by many estimates, some of the most successful at it.

"Oye! Amigo!" one of the younger men called out, his arms waving in the air as he stood on the prow of the sleek, black and silver vessel. Luis wondered how many of his lifetimes it would take to purchase such an extravagant boat. In spite of the man's smile,

Luis leaned forward to grip the automatic rifle mounted to his boat.

"Qué deseas?" Luis yelled. *What do you want?*

"We mean you no harm!" came the response in Spanish. Luis could see now that it was Rafael, the older of the two boys. A pair of aviators rested on the brim of his Yankees baseball cap. A halved triangle of a handkerchief hung below his chin. He'd grown a beard, too, though it had grown in unevenly.

"How do I know you aren't here to rob me?" Luis asked, the stock of the gun still pressed tight against his chest.

"Really, friend? You know how expensive this speedboat is? You really think we are patrolling these seas going after the little guys?"

"I've heard of worse things."

"Not us. I swear it on my father's grave," the man replied, crossing his heart with a bandaged finger. The boats drifted closer. Luis couldn't spot anyone else through the boat's tinted windows and the top deck appeared empty. He didn't trust the Sosas one bit, but he was curious. If they wanted to make a deal, it would be difficult to refuse. Luis knew that his days of running smuggling errands on his own were limited.

"What do you want, then?" he asked.

"We have a proposal for you. Come aboard and we'll talk."

Luis thought it over for a moment. It smelled like a trap, yet he couldn't conceive of a reason for it. It made no sense; he had practically nothing but a tiny stash of cash and food hidden under one of the benches.

"If I come aboard, I'm bringing my gun," Luis said, trying to sound brave.

"Suit yourself," Rafael said without missing a beat. He cracked a crooked smile and disappeared into the cockpit.

***

Fifty kilometers from their destination of Grunau, the newest and southernmost colony, Peter and Rachel Burton's train slowed to a stop. The winds had picked up, tossing heaps of dust and sand onto the tracks, and it was deemed unsafe to continue. Local volunteers passed through the carriages and explained the situation. Many were not happy with the news. For months they'd toiled tirelessly toward their destination and they were anxious to arrive and begin their new lives.

Peter tried to remain positive, but even he was exhausted. He'd spent the previous night with much of the crew preparing the rig's collapsible bridges, and the next morning they'd gathered their belongings and come ashore. It had taken another half day to board and pack the train. There was desert grit in his ears and his hair and he wanted nothing more than a warm shower and a long night of sleep in a clean bed.

"Any idea how long the winds will last?" he asked Winifred, who'd just returned from another carriage. He was wetting a handkerchief with a bottle of water to wipe his face. He made a face and shrugged.

"No telling with an *oosweer*."

"Sorry?" Peter asked.

"Oosweer. It's Afrikaans for 'east weather'. It's what happens when a hot, dry wind blows from the Namib to the coast. Causes sandstorms, very common this season."

"And we don't know when it'll let up?"

Winifred shook his head. "Anyone's guess, brother." And with that the brother bent down to gather his toolbox in his arms and disappeared with a wave into another carriage. Peter watched him go, feeling lost and dumbfounded in this strange country.

Marcus Kelly appeared a few minutes later, taking Winifred's spot on the bench. He wore a dark green parka, a wide-brimmed hat, and a big, boyish smile.

"I forgot how much I missed it," Marcus said, grinning from ear to ear as he shook a fine layer of sand from the folds of his parka. It took a moment for Peter to recall that Marcus and Vivian had spent many years serving in Africa before finally returning to the States.

"You two were in Namibia?" Peter asked.

"Botswana. It's a bit more temperate of a climate than here, but much is the same. Same wildlife, same indigenous tribes, same way of thinking."

"And what way of thinking is that?"

Marcus Kelly was lost in thought for a moment as he chose his words. "When Viv and I moved to Botswana, one of our first challenges was adjusting to the way the local brothers viewed time. They knew sunup and sundown, they knew when meals were eaten, but they had little concept of specific times. Many brothers did not even own a clock or a watch. So for meetings, Vivian and I would often be the only ones in attendance at the correct time. Even brothers who had parts that night would frequently arrive late, or just in time, and many times the meetings started only once they were all there! There was a clock in the shed we used as a Kingdom Hall, but the batteries had died, probably long before we arrived."

Peter shook his head in disbelief.

"It took us a while, but eventually we learned that in Africa, people are accustomed to a much slower pace of life. They do not try to force their environment to conform to their will; instead, they try to adapt to the environment. When it is too hot to work outside, you go home and sleep. When the rainy season comes and the streets flood, you walk to the Kingdom Hall barefoot."

Peter took a deep breath and managed a smile. "And you like this way of life, huh?"

Marcus nodded. "It reminds me of how small and insignificant we all are. In our old home, we were used to being in control. But here, we are at the mercy of the elements."

A strong wind rushed past. The carriages grumbled in protest and were jostled from side to side. The metal siding shuddered as if clinging to the walls of the train with all its might. Peter winced as more sand found its way into the carriage and was whisked along the floor on a current of air.

"Once you let go of the control and do things as the Africans do, it all becomes much easier," Marcus said with a smile.

"I'll work on it," Peter said. "But I'm not making any promises."

Marcus only smiled. "I'm proud of you, Peter. I know this feels overwhelming, but you'll do just fine."

"We've all been through a lot."

"But you've come out stronger. And I have no doubt you'll continue on your path." Marcus smiled again, and Peter was surprised to see the corners of the older brother's eyes glimmering with water. They sat in silence as the carriage shifted in the wind.

***

It had taken months of nonstop work at Hunters Point to complete the project, and the results had not come without costs. Fights broke out nearly daily over some glitch in the replay or some audio problem. Fingers were pointed and blame thrown around the room. No one was completely satisfied with the final project—least of all Chad—but they'd all been staring at their screens for too long; any objectivity had been lost long ago. To the uninitiated viewer, it looked and sounded like the real thing, and that's all that mattered. For the time being, their job here was done.

Of course, Chad Harkett wasn't sure exactly where that left him; he'd earned his keep by working days and nights side by side with a ragtag team of coders and USCC hotshots, but no one knew exactly what happened when their project was pushed out the door. He certainly couldn't head home. Judging from the scattered reports trickling out of the Valley, it was more or less a guarantee that his mansion had been reduced to rubble and ash. After pouring millions into the property and renovations, it made him furious to think that there'd be nothing left but a black smudge on the ground.

Then again, this was probably the safest place he could be, and at least he now had some connections. The military would know what to do, how to rebuild, and perhaps on the other side of all this there would be business opportunities. If he played his cards right, Chad thought, he was in a prime position to come out, once again, on top. He just had to be patient and cunning.

"Here's your share, Harkett," said a gravelly voice. It belonged to Driscoll, who'd served as the commanding officer on the project. He tossed a padded mailer onto the table beside where Chad was packing his things. Chad peeled the flap open and thumbed through the bonds.

"Will this be worth anything once this is all over?" Chad asked dismally. Driscoll grunted.

"Government isn't going anywhere, Harkett. Be glad it isn't cash. My bet is that we'll have to mint an entirely new currency. That's a ways down the road, of course."

"Where are you headed now that this is over?" Chad asked the older man. He turned to glare out at the red sky and shrugged.

"I've got new orders, I'll be shipping out soon. No real reason to stick around here anyway. Nothing to go back to. My ex divorced me years ago, took almost everything. I'll bet she's regretting that now, if she's even alive," Driscoll chuckled crudely. "You?"

"Same here. It's just me. I don't trust anything outside the walls of this complex. If there's a position for me, I'm interested."

Driscoll gave a slow nod, still staring at the blood red clouds outside the window. "I'll ask around." Driscoll finally broke his gaze from the outside world, eyes drilling into the younger, haggard-looking man before him. "How far you willing to go with this?" Driscoll asked carefully.

"You mean going after this religion?"

Driscoll gave a slow nod.

Chad drew a long breath through his teeth. "I didn't mention this before, but we've got history."

"Oh?"

"Yeah. Those people took my wife and kid."

Driscoll's eyes widened. He crossed his arms and leaned against the wall. "Surprised you didn't mention that before."

"Didn't want anyone to think it'd affect my dedication to the project."

"Well, no one's questioning that now."

"You do realize, of course, that a single video, however convincing, won't win your war."

"Of course not," Driscoll said, his expression hard. "This is just the first strike. We expect confusion, anger, feelings of betrayal. Ranks will split, divisions will form. It makes the next phase a little easier."

"Mind games," Chad said with a grin.

"Ideological warfare," Driscoll said, shrugging.

"I'm with you," Chad said simply. "Whatever it takes."

"You don't mind getting your hands dirty?"

Chad shook his head with a cold stare. "They were never that clean to begin with."

CHAPTER 14

Luis Escobar could hardly believe his eyes. From the ceiling and walls surrounding him hung a menagerie of animal trophies: stuffed marlin, gaping shark jawbones, even an alligator skin rug, complete with black marble eyes and a full set of teeth. Luis stepped around it cautiously as if it might still possess the ability to strike. Rafael caught him staring.

"She's from the Louisiana bayou. Almost four hundred kilos. Stefan was the one who shot her," Rafael bragged, pointing a finger at his brother, who was standing behind a wet bar fixing himself a drink. Stefan didn't bother looking up.

"You were in America?" Luis asked, immediately feeling stupid. For a humble fisherman like himself, traveling to America was out of the question. For these two *fresas*, getting a passport and a visa and booking a flight there would have been a simple thing.

"Had an uncle there. He'd take us hunting. That's where we shot the beast. He's dead now, of course," Rafael said emotionlessly.

"Oh. I see," Luis said, wondering if that was the appropriate response.

"Most of the people in that area are probably dead, come to think of it," Stefan said casually.

"Oh?" Luis asked.

"That hurricane from a few months ago. Completely wiped out Louisiana. Again."

"Your uncle died in the hurricane?"

Rafael shrugged. "We don't know. A relative fleeing from America told us. No one knows exactly what's happening there. The Americans are in a panic."

"It can't be worse than here, can it?"

"Fires, hurricanes, mobs, gangs. It's all the same," Stefan said, laughing bitterly. He finished the rest of his drink and sat. Rafael walked over to the bar and removed a cold beer.

"You?" he asked Luis, offering a glass. Luis shook his head. Up till now he'd been holding his rifle at the ready. Now the two younger men were staring at him. They wore nonchalant, unconcerned looks, and Luis guessed that they were a little drunk. Still, he felt silly holding the firearm, and so he swung it back over his shoulder and tried to relax. He declined the drink and asked instead for a Coca-Cola. It was wonderful. Luis hadn't tasted anything like it in months, just as he hadn't sat in such a comfortable chair or felt the cool, dry breath of air conditioning on his skin.

For nearly three years he'd been living mostly in his boat, anchored a few miles from the coast of Caracas. Occasionally he'd sneak back to the shore during the night, where he'd trade for supplies before slipping back to sea. On those midnight runs there was never time for sitting, and certainly no time for Coca-Cola.

"Is it just you two aboard this ship?" Luis asked.

Rafael nodded. "Can't trust anyone else these days."

"I know the feeling. I wasn't sure what to think when I saw your ship pulling up. I thought you might be trying to rob me."

The brothers shared a look before bursting into laughter. It was a ridiculous assumption, of course, that these two would target such a meager fishing vessel. Soon Luis was laughing along with them.

"I do not know what you've heard about us, Luis, but we do not steal from our countrymen."

"Ok," Luis said.

"Now, Trinidadians, perhaps. That is another story," Rafael said. The brothers shared a chuckle.

"What about you, Luis?" Stefan asked. "Have you turned to the life of a pirate?"

Luis shook his head. "Too dangerous. And I am only watching out for myself these days. I don't need much. Trips back and forth across the channel are enough for me."

"What do you run?"

"Diapers and gasoline, mostly," Luis said, immediately feeling ashamed.

"It's as honest a living as one can expect to make out here," Rafael said with a respectful nod. Luis appreciated the gesture.

"Yes, but how long will it last?" Stefan asked, his eyes suddenly sharp, as if the alcohol had evaporated instantly from his blood.

"I… I don't know," Luis said.

"You should think about it. You are just scraping by out here, picking up little scraps like a mouse skittering this way and that. You snatch up your little piece of cheese and run away to wherever your mouse hole is. But mark my words, Luis, it is always the cat that wins in the end."

Luis nodded thoughtfully. "Your brother said that you two had a proposal for me."

"Yes."

"Are you sure you want to work with a little mouse?" Luis asked sheepishly.

Stefan grinned. "The thing about mice," Stefan said, draining the last ounce of golden liquid from his glass, "is that they can get into tiny holes, and the fat cats cannot."

"I'm listening," Luis said.

"Good. We have plenty to talk about."

***

Regardless of which stage of evacuation each of the groups of Witnesses found themselves in on the evening of Nisan 14th, they were prepared. For many, this memorial would be held aboard supertankers, barges, and other vessels crawling across earth's vast waters. For a few of the smaller scattered groups, such as those crossing Asia by private bus and van, this special event would be held on the road. And for the thousands already gathered within the five colonies making up the Witnesses' sprawling Namibian complex, the memorial would be held much as it had in times past— in large meeting halls.

These meeting halls, of course, had been designed with large crowds in mind. Sliding wall panels linked separate rooms into giant spaces where thousands could gather simultaneously. Overhead screens gave each attendee a clear view of the speaker, and the audience was held in rapt attention; being this deep into the tribulation, many guessed that this would be their last time passing the emblems. The mood was somber.

Of course, even with the enormous gathering space provided by the halls, not all could be accommodated at a single sitting. Thus, as one group filed out one set of exits, the next group entered from the opposite side, quickly taking their seats as the speaker and stage crew rotated out to make room for a new team of brothers. The last groups finished just before midnight.

Meanwhile, in the canyons of the Namib, Peter and Rachel's train was still immobilized. Until a crew could be dispatched the next morning to clear and inspect the rails, they would have to stay put. Of course, having travelled into the desert this close to the memorial, this possibility had been anticipated and prepared for. The train crew produced a crate of wine and packaged unleavened bread. A discourse was given over the PA system, followed by a procession of brothers to distribute the emblems.

Peter could not help but watch as his close friend, Marcus Kelly, partook of the bread and wine. There was an inexplicable, overwhelming sense that told him it would be the last time this millennia-old tradition would be observed, and he was honored to have been a part of it, particularly in such a special setting for this last time.

At Marcus' side, Vivian gazed at him serenely. Whatever emotional struggles she'd faced in the past, she had come to terms with reality and accepted it. Knowing that her marriage had no chance of lasting on into paradise and thus into eternity as it would for so many other couples, had been a hard pill to swallow, but she trusted in Jehovah. Whatever happened, she knew she would live a happy and satisfying life.

Hours later and six thousand miles to the east, Joyce and Alvin Tucker—along with Claire Aberdeen and the hundreds of other souls aboard the barge—gathered on the upper deck of the ship as it passed under a full moon and a sky full of stars. As the speaker described the incomparable love Jehovah had shown by sacrificing his only begotten son, Joyce couldn't help but gaze up at the Milky Way. It seemed only fitting that on such an important night, in such an unparalleled time in history, that they should feel so close to their Creator. Out here there was nothing but the endless expanse above and the endless waves beneath.

But just over the horizon, danger loomed.

***

"I don't like it," Luis said finally, pushing the maps and sea charts away from him. Rafael had traced the planned route of the fleet of ships in a red pen.

168

"You don't like the idea of recovering more supplies than anyone could hope to smuggle in a year on these waters?" Stefan said, baffled.

"I don't like taking it from *them* is what I'm saying."

"What's the problem?" Rafael asked, throwing his hands into the air. "These people are worth more than they know what to do with! Cruise liners, supertankers, oil rigs all moving through the ocean. They must be worth billions!"

"Maybe so, but—"

"You've heard the reports, Luis."

"What reports?"

"The reports about these people. People are coming forward. They are telling the truth about them. They were tied up in all of this somehow. They are the ones to blame."

"What, for hurricanes and fires? Are they gods?" Luis asked, scoffing.

"They are *connected* is what I'm saying. The crimes that we used to hear of—random muggings, shoplifting, even murder. That all pales compared to what is happening here."

"If they are so dangerous, what makes you think that the three of us would be able to take anything from them?" Luis asked.

"We have information on them. A couple of their smaller ships have been hit, and so far there have been no signs of resistance. Easy pickings, my friend." Stefan grinned, clearly expecting Luis to mirror the expression. Instead the older man frowned and shook his head.

"I'm sorry, it doesn't make sense. First you say these people are dangerous and so we have a right to take from them, but then you tell me that they are unarmed. So which is it?"

Rafael threw his hands up in the air. "What difference does it make! The important thing is that they are loaded with supplies, and things out here are bound to dry up sooner or later. We are not in a position to pass this up. We act now or we lose an easy opportunity forever."

Luis stared down at the map in front of him before returning his attention to the men before him. He regretted coming aboard this ship and hearing their proposal, but he wasn't sure if he ever really had a choice. Their ship was much faster, their weapons far deadlier. His fate had been sealed the instant they had spotted him.

"Explain to me again why you need me and my little fishing

169

boat," Luis Escobar said, staring at the two younger men before glancing again at the charts. "Why not just do it yourselves?"

"We believe it would be too suspicious. If they see you first, drifting in a small fishing boat, you're more likely to be picked up. We don't think they'd stop for a big yacht like this."

"And once I'm aboard? Then what?"

Stefan opened a bulkhead and removed a set of small two-way radios. He handed one to Luis. "You will be our eyes on the inside. You tell us which areas of the tanker are guarded and which are not."

"We don't believe they have many guards on these ships. Just from watching them come and go in the night, they seem pretty defenseless," Rafael added, drawing a look from his brother.

"Then what?" asked Luis.

"That's it. You just provide us the information we need. Then we sneak on board, take what we need, and leave. It's all very simple. No one gets hurt," Stefan said, grinning easily, as if planning a fishing trip with friends.

"You can guarantee that?"

"Well, no, of course not. Things can always go wrong. But we are running out of options here. Smuggling won't be viable for much longer—you know that as well as anyone. We have to turn to other measures to survive, and this fleet is a golden opportunity. Frankly it'd be irresponsible to sit on our hands here, especially given the nature of the targets."

"And if it's so easy, why aren't more people doing this?" Luis asked, still skeptical.

"Superstition is a powerful thing," Stefan answered. "Some say these people are... *Protected*. That it's *bad luck* to go after them."

"Is it?"

The brothers shared a look before dismissing the question with a laugh. "Of course not. Every man is in charge of his own luck. The ones who are successful in this world are the ones who know what they want and will stop at nothing to get it," Stefan said. He pointed to the trophies hanging on the wall. "A predator does not stop to think about whether a weak animal deserves to be eaten or not. He takes it or else he starves!" He leaned forward and peered closely at Luis. "So the question is, Mr. Escobar: Do you want to survive or not?"

170

Peter's eyes opened slowly to the sight of Marcus Kelly sitting on a bench in the train compartment. The older brother had his reading glasses on and was hunched over a stack of papers in his lap. As Peter sat upright, a flash of hot pain streaked down his neck and back. His sleeping position the night before hadn't been ideal and now he was paying for it.

"What're you working on?" Peter asked Marcus through a grimace. His friend looked up over the rim of his glasses and smiled with typical coyness.

"Just a little something," he said with a shrug.

Suddenly, there was a strange noise coming from outside of the train, as if someone was banging on the walls and roof with sticks and rocks. Alarmed, Peter threw his sleeping bag off of himself and stood, listening. Most of the others in his carriages were still asleep, spread out on mats and sleeping bags or laid out on benches and the floor.

The sounds continued. They sounded like footsteps on the ceiling above him, but they were too light and quick to belong to people. Surely there weren't children running on top of the train?

"Rachel, hon, get up," Peter said softly, stirring his wife to life. Her eyes opened and she frowned as she, too, heard the sounds. Gradually, others in the carriage awoke to the noises, sitting up and mumbling amongst themselves worriedly.

"Baboons," came a gruff voice from beneath a sleeping bag. It was Winifred Osbourne. He pulled the wide-brimmed hat from atop his face, sat up, and stretched.

"Are they dangerous?" Rachel asked.

"They can be. A full grown baboon can possess the strength of several men, and they're clever animals. I wouldn't worry about these baboons though."

"Why not?" asked someone else.

"They're only curious. They watch the trains come and go from the shade of the canyons every day and are probably thrilled to finally get the chance to explore it." Winifred stood and rolled up his sleeping bag. The footfalls were now just above them. Peter couldn't be sure, but it sounded like dozens of little scampering feet were up there.

171

"Oh!" someone cried out suddenly. Heads in the carriage turned to see an older sister sitting against one of the walls, where an opening between the adjustable awning and the side of the train produced a tiny, hairy appendage. The sister blushed at the sudden attention and scooted away from the opening. The fingers were wiggling and grasping, like a child reaching for candy.

"Baboons are one of the most common native animals of Namibia," Winifred explained. "You will see them daily. They manage to survive just fine in the wild, but they are drawn to the colonies. Once we arrive you will learn more about them and about the other animals, like the cheetahs."

"Cheetahs?" someone asked uneasily. Winifred nodded enthusiastically.

"Oh yes, baboons, cheetahs, oryxes, wildebeests, jackals, meerkats. The colonies draw quite the variety of wildlife."

"I wouldn't have thought that," Peter said, massaging the back of his neck. "I would've guessed that the animals would be wary of strange humans settling on their land."

"Years ago they were. When I first arrived, only the baboons were around—they were the boldest of the bunch. Still are," Winifred said with a glance up at the ceiling. Judging from the sound, a group of small baboons outside were jumping and hooting at one another. "As time passed though, more and more animals began showing up."

"Was someone feeding them?" Rachel asked.

"Not at first. The brothers had strict rules about that, in fact. They obviously didn't want wild animals wandering through the colony, especially at night. But they showed up all the same, usually keeping to the fringes of the property, just sitting and watching the brothers and sisters come and go, as if they were curious about all that was happening on their land. Months went by like this, and their numbers climbed. In one area the brothers built a wire fence around the perimeter as a precaution once some lions were sighted, but to this day there have been no reports of attacks. We've since given up on trying to wall them out.

"Eventually, the brothers did set up a program for feeding and caring for them. Since we were producing food garbage, not all of which could be used for fertilizers, they decided to leave some in certain locations, sort of like feeding grounds. As you might imagine, they are quite popular, and the animal population continues to grow."

"Will I get to play with monkeys?" Evan asked with wide, expectant eyes.

"Oh, you'll be able to do more than that—you can sleep with monkeys if your mom and dad say it's ok!" Winifred said jauntily.

"Oh, we're not..." Angelica began, glancing awkwardly between Winifred and Ted, but Winifred's head had already turned away as something towards the front of the train caught his attention.

"What is it?" Ted asked. Winifred moved his head to get a view through the opening above the awning.

"Ah! Yes, I believe we're moving again!" he exclaimed triumphantly.

And with that the train lurched forward and resumed its sojourn through the Namib canyons.

CHAPTER 15

For years the town of Grunau had struggled for its survival. Fewer than five hundred people had lived in the minuscule settlement, connected to the rest of Namibia via a lonely thread of railway. On their way to some other destination, wealthy travelers would occasionally stay at one of the town's few lodges and chalets, but these were bleak and joyless places. The land was flat and featureless and covered in yellow, arid sand. Trees and shrubs offered scarce shade from the unabating African sun. There was little to see or do in the town, and guests would rarely stay for more than a day or two.

By the time Peter and Rachel's train finally pulled into the town, however, the land had been transformed. Orchards in the northern colonies had grown trees of various species and relocated them here, so that the main roads were lined with unique African greenery. Red brick walkways wound through the town, lined with occasional benches and solar lampposts. The land was still dry and desert like, but there was something uniquely inviting about it.

As the train carriages pulled up one at a time to the platform, local brothers and sisters waited with wheelbarrows, handcarts, and dollies to help unload luggage. African sisters in colorful patterned *dashiki* balanced enormous wicker baskets on their heads filled with bottles of water, fresh fruit, and toiletry bags. They handed the items out with wide smiles as the friends exited the train. The passengers were exhausted, but things were made instantly better by the sight of the welcoming locals. Many embraced warmly, collapsing in their new friends' arms with tears of joy and exhaustion.

After months of traversing seas and deserts, they had finally made it.

Soon the exhaustion was forgotten. Hundreds of Witnesses gathered around the train platform, merrily snapping selfies and taking videos with their new friends. Some began singing, and when the African brothers joined in, the tears flowed even harder. For many, it was the loudest, most beautiful singing they had ever heard in their lives.

"Ok, ok! We need to get you to the dormitories!" an African brother was shouting above the crowd. He'd found a stack of crates at a corner of the platform and was waving his arms to get everyone's attention. It was no easy task. "The next train will be arriving soon so all of you need to clear the platform!" It took another fifteen minutes, but finally the luggage was heaped onto the dollies and trucks, the groups reformed, and the trek to the housing area began.

It was eight o'clock in the morning by the time Peter and Rachel stepped off the train platform and onto Grunau's sandy gravel road, suitcases in tow. A guide led them through a grove of fruit trees and down a winding brick path. Rachel was surprised by how much cooler the town felt than anywhere else they so far had traveled in the country.

"The morning air is very moist, full of dew," their guide explained. "The dew sticks to the leaves of shrubs and trees. This is how they survive. But it also keeps the air cool and pleasant. It is one of the reasons the brothers wanted to plant so many trees in the colonies. Much prettier, too." She turned and smiled.

"Where does the drinking water come from?" Peter asked.

"Oh, there are many water tanks in Grunau. A water train comes by every week or so to refill them. Sometimes it rains here, too. This used to be very rare, but in the last couple of years we have been seeing record rainfall. The brothers are nearly complete with the construction of a basin to collect this water for filtration. If the rains keep up, perhaps we will not need the water train much longer."

"Yeah, someone mentioned earlier on the train that the weather has changed a lot since the brothers purchased the land here," Peter said.

"Oh yes. Big changes. Primarily the rain. Usually the Namib sees less than a centimeter of rain per year. Sometimes it doesn't rain at all. But since the brothers arrived, it has rained more than ever before. Bismarck, the capital, hardly looks like it belongs in this part of Africa anymore. There is actually green grass there, and farms! It is beautiful. And of course this has had a big impact on the indigenous tribes."

"Why is that?"

"Much of their culture and belief system is based around the scarcity of water. The Bushmen, for example, prize ostrich eggs, since they can be used as water containers. To receive an ostrich egg as a gift in Bushmen culture is considered a great honor. So you can imagine their reaction to all the rain! They immediately took it as a good omen, and believed their fortune had greatly improved with the arrival of our brothers. Many of the tribes began studying the Bible with us, and a great number of these indigenous people are now with us in the colonies, although they often prefer living in their traditional grass cottages and surviving off of the land. It is difficult for them to adjust to a more modern way of life."

"What about clothing?" Rachel asked.

"That has been a difficult adjustment as well, since many of the tribesmen and tribeswomen customarily wear no more than a loincloth. But they have made a great effort to change. It still isn't unusual to see the children running naked, but often this is further out in the bush, nearby their homes."

"So much to get used to," Rachel said, experiencing a mix of excitement and uncertainty.

"Ah! Here we are!" exclaimed the guide as the brick walkway spilled out into a wide, grassy plain. Tall trees cast dappled shadows onto their trunks, which were encircled by stones and flowering cacti and polished wooden benches. It was, like the rest of Grunau, somehow both strange and inviting.

The homes themselves were a familiar sight—they displayed the same angular shapes that had been seen in the shipping containers aboard the rigs, yet these appeared to be built from a natural material. Peter asked about it as they climbed a steel stairwell to the third floor.

"Oh, these are also shipping containers," the sister explained. "But structures out of metal would become too hot after hours sitting in the sun, so the apartments here have all been coated in *slyk*. It is a kind of mud paste made from dirt and water. It becomes nearly as hard as rock when dried, but more importantly, it keeps the rooms cool."

The group divided by couples and families and settled into their new homes. It wasn't long before the children from the train were racing through the grounds, exploring the trees and rocks. After months of being cooped up on the rig, this was exactly what they

176

needed.

Running circles around the camp was the farthest thing from Peter's and Rachel's mind, however. Their backs and necks still ached from sleeping aboard the train the night before and they were beginning to stink. More than anything, they wanted a hot shower, a square meal, and a comfortable bed. Their guide explained how to get all three.

"Although we have access to water here, it is still in limited supply. Each shower will only last for five minutes. After that, the water shuts off."

"What about hot water?" Rachel asked. She winced, bracing for an answer she wasn't hoping for.

"The pipes carrying the water from the tower run through shallow desert sand and gravel, so they are heated naturally by the sun. To my knowledge, no one has ever complained about the temperature," answered the guide. Rachel's relief was an audible sigh.

"Just like the rigs, breakfast and lunch will be served twice a day in cafeterias. For dinner, you are welcome to leftovers from the previous two meals, or you can prepare your own meals in your room. There is an electric hot plate beneath the sink. And usually the cafeteria is stocked with fruit, vegetables, yogurt, and muesli. We just ask that you only take what you need. We try to produce as little waste here as possible."

Peter and Rachel entered their apartment. The design was modest and comfortable, if a little small. The guide removed her shoes and demonstrated how the couch could be pulled out into a bed. Then, removing a small pamphlet from a nook in the wall, she said:

"Most of what you need to know about the apartment and the area surrounding it can be found in here. I'm sure you're both exhausted, but try to have a look through it as soon as you can so that you'll be familiar with how things work. If you need anything or have any questions, feel free to ask one of the local guides." The sister tapped a plastic badge attached to a yellow lanyard around her neck, bid the couple farewell, and was gone.

Peter and Rachel stood side by side in their new apartment, gazing out the picture window in front of them and soaking in the vista. The children had made friends with some of the local kids, who'd brought along a soccer ball and a handmade kite. Their energy seemed endless.

"Still doesn't feel real, does it?" Peter asked softly.

"Nope," Rachel said, laying a tired head on her husband's shoulder. "But I'm ok with that."

***

The broadcast from the branch was a surprise. There had been no previous announcement of it; no alert had appeared on the brothers' messaging app. It had merely appeared one morning on the closed circuit stream with a notification to play it at the following morning's pre-breakfast program. The fact that it was filmed from what appeared to be the usual TV studio was stranger still; the last anyone had heard, Warwick had been evacuated shortly before the fires had overtaken the state of New York months ago.

A familiar face appeared on screen, a soft-spoken brother who'd hosted many previous monthly broadcasts and morning worship programs. When he spoke, the cafeteria was deathly silent.

"Brothers and sisters, we bring you this special broadcast from our headquarters here in New York. We know it has been a difficult, exhausting journey for you. Many of you sold everything you had to be here. The Lord appreciates the generosity you showed, you can be sure of it.

"However, we are all imperfect, and none of us are impervious to sin. Thus, it is with heavy hearts that we must inform you of some changes to our initial plans. As you know, we originally intended for you all to be housed in Namibia, a desert country in Southern Africa. However, we now regret to announce that this plan is an impossible one to fulfill.

"Much of the land there is simply uninhabitable, and it is full of dangers. Droughts constantly plague the country, making access to water very difficult. There are wild animals which attack in the night." On screen, the video cut to a slow pan of a pack of fierce-looking hyenas squaring off with an unarmed family.

"But wild animals are only one of many threats. Most dangerous are the *people*. Due to the instability of nearby governments, militia fighters frequently wander through our camps. Many of our brethren have been attacked, some even kidnapped." On screen, the video cut to a photo of a man being brutally beaten by a group of militia fighters.

178

"Clearly, this is a dangerous land not meant for us. Thus, it is with heavy hearts that we urge those of you who have not yet arrived at your destination to turn back immediately and begin the journey home. We know many of you have heard reports of violence and crime, but these reports have been exaggerated. Rest assured, your government is doing everything in its power to restore peace and order. Your country has experienced hard times in the past, and this period is no different. It will rise from the ashes.

"So please, as your leaders, we urge all of you to abandon your evacuation and return. The sooner you turn back, the sooner you will be home. Thank you, and may God bless each and every one of you."

The screen before them faded to black and the familiar logo and end credits appeared. The room remained silent for another few seconds before bursting into conversation. At Alvin's side, Joyce turned to her husband and shook her head with a puzzled look. "Well, that was the strangest broadcast I've ever seen."

Alvin said nothing. He was too lost in his own thoughts to respond. Across the table, Claire turned to look at the couple.

"You're not telling me that now we're heading back…" she said.

"Alvin?" Joyce asked. "What do you make of it?"

But still Alvin had no words. He stood and put away his tray, unable to finish the rest of his meal. Joyce was right on his heels. "Honey? What are we going to do?"

"I… I don't know… I need a moment." And with that, Joyce's husband disappeared into the crowd.

***

Rachel poured herself a cup of tea and sat in one of the apartment's padded folding chairs. Outside, a crisp red sun was peaking over the horizon, draping sheets of crimson over the desert complex. She finished her Bible reading for the day and looked for something else to read. She'd finished all the paperbacks on her Kindle, including two African travelogues she'd received from friends aboard the rig. She thought it might prove helpful in preparing for life here, though she was finding things far more pleasant than she'd expected. Their home was tiny but adequate; the complex itself was populated without feeling cramped. Life was

179

simple but not unbearably so. Then again, Rachel thought, perhaps the previous year of adjustments and the months at sea had helped prepare them for this. Anything was better than spending weeks on end in a floating box with hundreds of other people.

Rachel rose and stretched. A thermostat on the wall told her the outdoor temperature was 11.6°C/53°F, surprisingly cold for this part of the world, she thought. She'd wait till the morning sun warmed the place up before taking a walk, an idea that had appealed to her as soon as she'd arrived. There was so much to explore here, so many new faces to meet. Then she remembered the pamphlet on the wall. She returned to her seat and began reading.

She hadn't expected the reading to be so absorbing. The pamphlet began with a brief history of the small town of Grunau, ending with its purchase by a subsidiary of the organization in 2016. The next section featured an overview of the plant and animal life, complete with bits of artwork for each species. Next came the dining schedule, regulations for cooking and water usage, and rules for trash disposal.

"Morning," Peter said as he walked behind his wife and planted a kiss on her forehead. He helped himself to a cup of tea and a bar of granola from a basket on the counter.

"So, I figured out why we have five different trash cans," Rachel said.

"Oh?"

"Recycling is pretty strict here."

"Even more so than California?"

"Oh, yes," Rachel said. She lifted the pamphlet from her lap and showed her husband the recycling diagram. "Two kinds of plastic, then paper, aluminum, then food waste. And apparently from there the trash is sorted through and divided up even further at a recycling center. And we're supposed to wash everything."

Peter raised his eyebrows and nodded thoughtfully. "Makes sense. I guess we're taking our first steps into paradise."

"What do you mean?" Rachel asked.

"It's something Marcus and I were talking about on the train. This whole idea of us all being together in one place and building these huge colonies didn't make a whole lot of sense to me before, but now I see the benefit. It's not just about us being together for Armageddon. It also makes things that much simpler for when we begin our life in the new world. We're all together, so that keeps us united and well-organized. But it also means that we need our own infrastructure. We need to figure out all these things that we've never really had to handle before, because the governments of the countries we lived in took care of them. Things like transportation, food production, and waste disposal. We have to learn all this stuff now."

"I guess so. Oh, and get this," Rachel said, flipping quickly through the pages. "Some animals roam freely in and around the colony of Grunau. They appear tame, and to date there have been no reports of aggression. However, we still consider them to be wild animals, so caution is advised. We do not encourage anyone to initiate contact with such wild animals unless specifically directed otherwise."

"Sounds like what Brother Osbourne was mentioning on the train."

"I've spotted some monkeys since we arrived, but haven't seen any other animals. Have you?" Rachel asked. Peter shook his head.

"Haven't really been paying attention. I was a little out of it yesterday."

"How do you feel after a good night's sleep?"

"Wonderful. You?"

"Yeah, really good. You want to go for a walk after breakfast?" Rachel asked.

"Sounds wonderful," Peter said, already beginning to get dressed.

***

Less than twenty minutes after the airing of the strange broadcast, the overseers of *The Chariot* called an emergency meeting. Tensions were higher than ever as the hundreds of passengers and crew aboard their vessel vented frustrations and struggled to understand the new directions. Failure to act immediately would lead to permanent consequences, and the brothers needed to decide on the next course of action.

A fervent prayer began the meeting. The brother begged Jehovah for wisdom and clarity, and for those aboard their ship and the many others still at sea to stay calm and obedient. The discussion followed immediately, and the group had much to say.

"Can we contact any branch reps for confirmation on the message?" someone asked.

"The first thing I did was to try to raise them on the radio. I couldn't get through. I'll try again soon," reported the communications overseer.

"How could this be? How could they have gotten this wrong?" someone began, his voice trembling. "Our friends sold everything— cars, houses, businesses. There's nothing to go back to!"

"What about the friends already in Namibia? What happens to them? Are they just supposed to find a way home?"

"Brothers, please," the chairman spoke up. His name was Paul O'Donnell. He'd previously served as the overseer for Alvin's circuit and the two had become close friends. Their travels aboard *The Chariot* had only solidified that bond. "There are many things we don't know yet. Let's stick to what we do know, and proceed from there."

"Did anyone receive an alert on the messaging app prior to downloading the stream?" Alvin asked. He watched as the others pulled phones from their pockets and checked. Moments later they were all shaking their heads.

"I was wondering about that too. And something about the broadcast just felt very... *off*... somehow," said another brother.

"What do you mean?" Paul asked him.

"Just the terminology used. I've never heard anyone say 'brethren' in a broadcast before. And the way the government was described, as if it would fix everything."

"I thought that was strange too," Alvin admitted.

"Perhaps we'd benefit from a second viewing," Paul suggested. The room nodded, and so a TV in the corner was turned on and the broadcast shown again. Dozens of pairs of eyes scrutinized every frame. More details quickly came to light.

"You're right. It's presented as if the government has a handle on everything. I don't think I've ever heard that sentiment in a broadcast before."

"Not to mention the way he signs off, with that 'God bless you'. Very strange."

"I think it's odd that he never once opened the Bible," Paul said. The others mulled over the evidence they'd uncovered. No one knew how to proceed.

"I think we have to consider the possibility that... *somehow...*

what we're seeing on this screen isn't a message from our organization."

"You think he was forced to say those things to us? Perhaps under duress?" someone asked.

"No. Never. The brothers would give their lives before sending out false information. I think this is much more sinister. I think we might be looking at a fake."

"A fake?" someone said, their tone almost derisive. "How can you call that a fake? It's his face, his voice, isn't it?"

"Possibly not," said another one of the overseers. He was leaning on a wall in the corner of the room, eyes studying the paused image on the large screen. "Anyone familiar with deepfakes? They were becoming a real problem shortly before the great tribulation broke out. Scared a lot of people, especially governments."

"Deepfakes?" someone asked. The brother nodded.

"Basically the way it worked was, you could make a video of anyone saying anything you wanted. You just needed enough footage of the subject, and an impersonator who could mimic the subject's voice. Then, using some kind of AI software, the computer could map the altered face onto the body of the original subject. I remember seeing footage of some examples on YouTube. People were switching out faces of actors or changing their genders. Some were very convincing."

"I don't know, that sounds pretty farfetched," someone objected.

"Not more farfetched than a member of the GB telling us that world governments are going to fix our problems. Not this close to the end, when we know we're on the brink of Armageddon," Alvin said.

"A fake broadcast... Ok," Paul O'Donnell said, frowning deeply as he massaged his temples. "What would something like that take to accomplish?"

"A lot of time and effort, probably a very skilled team of programmers to get it to look just right. And a voice actor, of course. You'd also need a lot of reference video, and the lighting would have to be pretty even in the source footage."

"Well that last one wouldn't be a problem, especially given all the talks the brother has done. They could've just used that footage," said Alvin.

"I'd imagine so. I'm no expert, though. I just know what I've read online."

"We really need confirmation from the branch as soon as possible," Paul said finally to the communications overseer. "In the meantime, if our consensus is that this is a hoax, are we all in agreement to maintain course?" Paul waited as hands raised around the large circle of men.

"Ok, then. That settles it. We keep course. I'll confer with the rest of the convoy and let them know what we've discussed."

"What about the crew and passengers? People are real anxious out there," Alvin asked.

"Tell them the truth. That we're maintaining course until we have more information from the branch. It won't be easy, but do your best to keep everyone calm."

CHAPTER 16

Luis Escobar was ready. He'd stashed the guns in a locked compartment beneath the benches of his boat and had wrapped old bandages in place over his head and ankle. The plan was that the ships would stop for the old, injured fisherman mixed in among the other evacuees and he would be helped aboard. The idea of taking advantage of the kindness of strangers still did not sit well with Luis, but perhaps Rafael and Stefan were right; perhaps this changed world required a man to do whatever necessary to survive. He shook away his lingering misgivings and steered his small fishing boat towards the path of the incoming vessels.

It was a dark, moonless night, the water calm and glassy beneath a blank sky. Luis much preferred this to the strange, blood-colored skies of daytime. The common belief was that it was the result of the fires in North America filling the air with ash and red embers, but that explanation didn't quite make sense to him. These were not normal times and he sensed it all around him.

Pulling a pair of binoculars to his face, Luis struggled to see through the darkness any signs of movement on the horizon. He sat and watched and waited. And as his boat drifted, so did his thoughts. He thought about the Witnesses. He was, in fact, no stranger to them.

The last time they'd come knocking at his door he was still living in his small apartment with Camilla. They did not have much, but the roof over their heads kept them dry and warm and they had each other, and for Luis that was enough. He was happier than he had been in a long time, though he'd been too proud to admit it. Like so many of the fishermen in his village, he'd turned to drink to fill in the hours and days spent between shifts at sea.

In the beginning he would occasionally return home to find religious literature tucked away here and there, but he thought nothing of it at the time. Whatever Camilla's religious beliefs were, they were her business, and he had no intention of interfering. She was raised Catholic, and as a young girl she frequently attended mass with her family, and so Luis found it somewhat odd when her heirloom crosses and *Santa María* candles began disappearing around the house. Odder still was that Camilla became suddenly interested in the Bible, speaking endlessly on the topic whenever the two were together.

Luis brushed her religious talk away. He had never been a religious man and he certainly had no use for Jesus now. In this world, one's wits alone were responsible for one's fate, and the idea of an all-powerful Supreme Being was wholly unnecessary.

The rift between them grew. Religion, while important to Camilla from a young age, had never played more than a superficial role in her life, and Luis could not understand why that would suddenly change now. Eventually she moved out.

A lesser man may have blamed the Witnesses for this, but Luis recognized his part in the breakup. His lack of interest in the things important to her coupled with the drinking had ultimately driven them apart. Camilla had been different from the other girls he had dated, and he thought of her often even after all of these years. Now a sober, wizened man, Luis wondered how things might've turned out had his attitude then been different.

In the distance, ships began emerging on the horizon. They came in every variety of shape and size, from large sailboats to old fishing trawlers and supertankers. They moved in a tight, quiet pack through the water, and in their path lay a surprise: another smaller convoy of boats.

Aboard these vessels, snippets of the passengers' Spanish conversations carried over the water to his ears. These were Venezuelan boats, Luis realized. Still several kilometers apart, the knot of local boats released a flare into the air. It burned bright green in the dark night. The effect was instant. The large incoming vessels turned on powerful deck lights, shining it in the direction of the flare.

Clearly, all of this had been carefully orchestrated, and it was a golden opportunity he would not miss. With a frantic yank on its cord, Luis brought the outboard motor to life. It coughed up foamy sea water and the smell of gasoline, and shoved Luis on his way. He slipped in among the undulating web of local ships and waited as the convoy approached.

Oddly, there were few lights aboard the boats; only a handful of flashlight beams penetrated the black of night, carried by men

186

carefully stepping and climbing their way from one vessel to the next. As he edged closer, bits of hushed conversation caught his ears. The men were helpers of some sort, perhaps guards. They were reminding each of the hundreds of passengers to put on their life jackets and prepare to board the incoming ships.

And there weren't just men out here, Luis realized in amazement. He could make out the hushed voices of women and children, even babies. Luis shook his head at their foolishness. These seas were no place for families; they were the haunt of pirates and traffickers.

Lost in his thoughts, Luis failed to notice the young man emerging from the sailboat beside him. He nearly toppled into the water from the side of his boat in shock when a life vest was thrown at his feet.

"Put in on. Tankers will be here in no time," the man said, pointing at the approaching lights. "You must have a jacket before you can board."

Luis nodded thankfully and slipped into the rigid vest.

It was another twenty minutes until the large ships finally came to a stop. Luis knew that stopping such large vessels was no easy task; the massive propellers moving the ships forward would have to be switched to reverse to counteract their momentum. In the shipping liner world, this was a costly maneuver as it expended inordinate amounts of fuel, and was only used out of necessity. That such massive ships would come to a dead stop in dangerous waters just to pick up stranded seafarers was a difficult thing for Luis Escobar to comprehend.

"*Are you in position?*" crackled a tinny voice from his pocket. He fumbled beneath the vest to turn down the volume dial on his walkie talkie.

"What was that?" asked the young man beside him. Luis turned and smiled.

"Nothing. Just thinking how peaceful this night is," he lied. He turned from the man and quietly whispered into the radio: "Yes. But keep quiet. I am boarding soon. I will contact you later." And with that he switched the radio off and buried the thing deep in a zippered pouch lashed across his shoulders.

In spite of the darkness all around them and the fact that their numbers went far beyond anything Luis Escobar first estimated, the boarding process was smooth and well organized. What Luis had expected to witness—a panicked, chaotic scramble from the sailboats and rafts onto the larger, safer ships—hadn't happened at all. The passengers crept slowly up the dozens of steel ladders leaning over the edges of the ships' bulwarks. Others, such as the elderly and mothers with small children, were helped into cages lowered onto their boats from giant telescoping cranes atop the ships. And as the passengers emptied the boats below, young men wearing vests and headlamps scampered from boat to boat, piling what appeared to be boxes and luggage into the lowered cages to be hauled up into the ships.

Luis could hardly believe his eyes. Never in his life had he seen anything like this. The years of desperation in his home country of Venezuela had taught him that nothing was more dangerous than crowds of despairing people with nothing to lose, and that in the end, governments and organizations could not be counted on to save anyone but themselves. Why were these people so different?

"It's your turn, brother," the young man said, still standing not three meters to Luis' side. Luis stood, his bandaged legs coming into view of the young man.

"Oh!" exclaimed the younger man. "I did not realize you were injured! I will call for one of the cages to pick you up," he said, beginning to make some sort of signal with his hands across the beam of the flashlight.

"No, no, *hijo*," Luis insisted, waving the man away. "I am fine. It is nothing serious. I will climb the ladders like everyone else. Save the cages for the women and babies."

The young man nodded somewhat reluctantly before leading Luis to the boat nearest the steel ladders. A thin cable was lowered, which the man threaded through a pair of carabineers attached to Luis' vest. "Hang on tight to the ladder as you climb and take your time. The brothers aboard the tanker will pull the wire in as you go, so if you lose your grip you won't fall far."

"They thought of everything," Luis said, meaning it. And then he began his climb. At the top, two muscular men pulled him over the bulwark. It felt good to be on board such a large, sturdy ship. It felt like land.

***

After two nights of restful sleep and a full day exploring their new environment, Peter and Rachel Burton were eager to get to work. They were joined by Ted Watkins, Angelica Parry, and Evan in the courtyard between the dormitories. A bulletin board here listed current departments in need of volunteers, and the assignments to choose were long and surprisingly varied, ranging from everything from plumbing and construction to animal care.

"Animal care!" Angelica exclaimed. "What do you think that's all about?"

"That brother on the train did mention baboons and other wild animals. Maybe something to do with that?" Ted suggested.

"You think it's like feeding them and training them? Wouldn't that be something!" Rachel said.

"Could be. But there could also be work horses here. Might just be cleaning out stalls and shoveling manure," Peter said with a grin, eliciting a laugh from Evan.

"Well, I for one am willing to take the chance. I'd love to work with animals," Angelica said, tugging on Ted's sleeve.

"Looks like there's also a big need with the construction crews. That'd be up my alley," Ted said, ignoring Angelica's hint. Before long the group had come to a decision: Peter and Ted would sign up with the construction crews while the girls would track down the animal people. For Evan, however, who was not sixteen years old, the day would be spent with the youth classes. Designed to orient the young ones to their new surroundings, these classes were organized and taught by experienced local brothers and sisters. The curriculum included learning to build shelter in the bush, identifying edible plants and sources of water, navigating and tracking, and interacting with local wildlife. Though at first hesitant to be away from his mother, Evan would quickly adapt and thrive.

After a brief orientation meeting, Peter and Ted were taken to the site of a brand new housing complex. The overseer explained that another five thousand Witnesses were expected to arrive over the next week, and the dorms needed to be ready by then. Boom cranes and forklifts would do most of the heavy lifting, plucking pre-fabbed shipping containers from cargo trains and setting them into the building footprints. But for the dozens of brothers on site there was still plenty to do, like connecting electrical and telephone wiring, assembling water and drainage pipes, and then coating each of the finished blocks in a thick lather of *slyk* for insulation.

The blocks were completed rapidly, and as the construction

teams moved to the next lot, a team of landscapers would file in on their heels, planting shrubs and small trees and rock gardens. At the same time, finishing crews and decorators would move rapidly through the buildings, checking outlets and sealants, placing furniture, and stocking cabinets with utensils and dishware and other essentials. The crews worked with an efficient precision that reminded Peter of the old days, when a quickbuild Kingdom Hall could be completed in a weekend. Of course, the scale of this was unimaginably larger. With Jehovah's blessing, nothing was impossible.

Two dozen kilometers to the south, at the very edge of the Grunau colony, Rachel and Angelica found themselves in similar awe of what they were experiencing. Peter had been wrong. There were no horses or stables or piles of manure to shovel.

Instead, the two women found themselves cuddling a pair of cheetah cubs in their laps. Their names were Chai and Java, and they were barely two months old but already as heavy as full-grown beagles, with shiny black eyes and white, puffy manes running from the top of their head down their backs.

One of the caretakers, whose name was Karen, plopped down beside the two and handed each a plastic jug topped with a thick rubber nipple. It wasn't long before the cubs were hungrily slurping and batting at the bottles, droplets of milk leaking from their black mouths.

"I just can't believe this," Angelica said, feeling beside herself. "They're so tame, just like big house cats."

"Yes, cheetahs are the tamest of the African cat," Karen said, gazing into the cubs eyes with a warm look. "Some even raise them as pets, though it's not so easy. The cats need to roam, and they've got an inborn hunter instinct."

"Where's the mother?" Rachel asked. The caretaker shook her head and frowned.

"No one knows. The cubs were found by a railway maintenance crew when they were just babies and brought here. It's likely the mother was killed by hunters for her fur."

"Are these the only two?"

"No, unfortunately. It's common for orphaned animals to be brought here, and it was one of the reasons this department was started in the first place. Animals just kept showing up. Some, like the baboons, were just curious about all this development in their backyard. Others clearly needed our help. The brothers went back and forth quite a bit trying to determine what to do, but eventually it was decided that since these animals were here first, we ought to do what we can to take care of them."

"Training for the future, too," Angelica said, scratching Chai beneath his chin. He'd contentedly closed his eyes and his spotted belly was beginning to bulge with milk. Her lap vibrated with the cub's loud purring.

"Yes, many have said that," said Karen.

"I'm surprised you're still in need of volunteers. I would think that everyone would be jumping at the opportunity to work with the animals."

Karen smiled knowingly and shook her head. "It's a lovely assignment, but it does come with its challenges. I wouldn't say it's for everyone. Care to see what I mean?"

Rachel and Angelica exchanged a look, not wanting to trade the adorable animals in their laps for whatever unpleasant task awaited them. Still, they shrugged. "Sure."

***

"American?" Luis Escobar asked one of the men standing at the bulwark. A powerful flashlight in his hand was roving over the surface of the boats, presumably to be sure no one had been left behind. A dozen more men further down the line were doing the same. Luis spoke poor English, but the man seemed to understand.

"We're from the State of Washington," he replied in impeccable Spanish. A woman walked past, offered Luis a blanket, and walked on. All around him, people were gathering their luggage and doing head counts. Satisfied that all had come aboard, a signal was given to a man standing high atop the supertanker's bridge wing. He disappeared a moment later into the pilot house and below their feet they could feel the powerful grumble of diesel engines firing back to life.

"Your Spanish is good. Your parents from Mexico?" Luis asked the man, curious about this whole affair.

He shook his head. "Did some need greating in Bolivia. Spent nearly a decade there. A wonderful experience."

Luis smiled dumbly, unable to understand. The man before him glanced at the screen of the radio in his hand.

191

"Sorry to run, but we've got to prepare for the next pickup," he said.

"More passengers?"

"Of course. Every thirty miles, just as planned. Nice meeting you!" and with that the man was gone.

Luis wrapped the blanket around his shoulders and sat, struggling to make sense of these strange people. How did they have so much when so many others had so little? How was any of this possible? Was the altruism real or merely some kind of front? His head spun. Nothing made sense and he was hungry.

"ID badge, please," asked a woman. Luis glanced up to see a dark-skinned woman with flowing, curly hair. He had no idea what she was referring to, but made a great pretense of searching through his pockets.

"I'm so sorry," he said sheepishly. "I must've dropped it in the water."

"I see," the woman said, flipping through papers pinned to a clipboard. "You from Venezuela or Trinidad?"

"Venezuela," Luis said, frowning.

"Can you give me your city and congregation number?"

Luis gazed blankly at the woman. Then he slowly shook his head. "I... I... I'm sorry... I can't remember."

The woman cocked her head and made a face.

"I've been at sea a long time, you see. Just me and my boat. The sun, it beats down on my head... And I forget things."

Bending down, the woman pulled a small light from her pocket and shined the beam directly into Luis' eyes. He winced with the sharp pain.

"Hold still," the woman instructed. "I'm checking your pupils."

Luis waited patiently as the woman performed the brief examination. She flicked off the light and turned to a young man standing behind her.

"Raul, take him to the infirmary for a check up. He's complaining of memory loss. And let them know he's got no ID."

The young man's eyes darted nervously at Luis before he nodded quickly and led the way down a stairwell and into the lower decks of *The Chariot*.

***

Rachel, Angelica, and Karen got off the dune buggy and approached the site slowly. The carcass before them had been an oryx, a large antelope species native to the Namib. Now, though, it was nothing more than a heap of bleeding flesh swarming with flies. The head had been cut clean off, clear proof that it had fallen victim to hunters. With its striking black and white facial markings and narrow, straight horns, head mounts were popular trophies.

Karen shook her head with the click of her tongue. "Terrible. Just pointless," she said.

"They don't even take the meat?" Rachel asked, a hand pressed over her face to keep the flies away. It didn't smell as bad as she'd imagine something like this might, but she supposed that meant this was a fresh kill, and the idea of armed hunters roaming the nearby area was not a pleasant one.

"No, they don't care at all about the meat. They're not hunting to eat. They just want a mount."

"Hunting like this is allowed?" Angelica said.

"No, of course not. But hunters in Africa are notorious for skirting the rules. They roam more or less wherever they want, shooting whatever pleases them. Even threatened and endangered species aren't safe. They have no respect for life."

"But don't the brothers own this land?"

"It doesn't matter who owns it. It's not like owning a property where you're from, where you can put up a fence and keep unwanted people out. The land is simply too vast here. Anyone can come and go. There's simply no way to monitor this kind of thing."

The three women fell silent as they took in the pitiful headless creature before them.

"So, we're here to bury it?" Rachel asked uneasily. Karen gave her a grim look.

"No, I'm afraid not." Rachel and Angelica glanced at one another as Karen returned to the buggy. She removed a toolbox from the trunk and a roll of thick plastic. Opening the toolbox, she produced a pair of hacksaws and facial masks and handed them to the wide-eyed women.

"Oh no. No no no," Angelica said, shaking her head with a step in the opposite direction.

"I know it isn't pleasant, but it must be done."

"Why? Won't other wild animals come along and take care of

it?"

"Yes, of course. But we need the meat for the conservatory. We've got hungry cheetahs, caracals, and a hyena to think about."

"Wait. I thought those animals eat our leftovers. That's what we were told, anyway. Isn't that right, Angelica?" Rachel asked. Angelica nodded eagerly.

"Yes, of course. But this is their natural diet. It's better to feed them this when we can. And immediately attending to these carcasses helps to keep disease down in the camp. I'm sorry, but this is part of the job. Don't think of it as an animal. It's just food that needs processing at this point. Ever buy a steak or hamburger meat at the grocery store? Well, this is what it looked like before it was placed on the shelf."

She was right, of course, but it didn't make the task any easier. Karen gave the two new recruits pairs of rubber gloves and scrunchies and instructed them to tie back their hair.

And then the three got to work.

When it was done, they loaded the pieces onto the plastic sheets and tied everything to the back of the buggy. It was a grisly, messy sight, and not one that any of them would soon forget. Rachel and Angelica wore stony expressions all the way back to the base.

"You'll get over it," Karen yelled over the whine of the buggy's engine. "First time's the hardest. But when you see the feeding process, well... I think that'll help."

***

Of course, they'd kept him waiting. Dietrich had been punctual, as always, sweating through his cotton suit in the hot upstairs lobby of the Windhoek Tax Bureau Building. When asked, the receptionist insisted that the officials were busy in a meeting, and it would be just another minute. Dietrich had been waiting nearly three hours.

He would've preferred the company of another brother for this meeting with the tax officials, but he understood the reasons for him being sent on his own. Ever since the beginning of his assignment here in Namibia, Dietrich had worked closely with the various departments of the Namibian government. He understood the culture of Southern Africa and knew how to work within the system. A level of respect had thus grown between the Witnesses and the government.

Over the years, Dietrich had even attempted to witness to the various officials he'd dealt with, but while many respected him, the misconception that the Witnesses were an American organization with no connection to the heritage of Africa had prevailed. There was little reason to stick to this belief after the colonies had swelled in population to include peoples from around the globe (including many Africans), but the officials stuck to their prejudice. The only thing they really cared about, Dietrich knew, was money.

Unlike most other Southern African countries, Namibia had enjoyed a consistent level of prosperity over the years. Originally a German colony, the capital city of Windhoek was a symbol of this prosperity, known for its clean, well-kept streets, modern infrastructure, and thriving local enterprises. Bolstered by ore and diamond mining and a growing tourism sector, this was a city Namibians were proud of.

"They are ready for you now," said the receptionist, smiling as if Dietrich had only just arrived. He nodded, followed her into a conference room full of men, and sat at a long, rectangular table. He recognized most of the faces on the other side of the table, including Joshua Angula and Ezekiel Qonja, representatives from Namibia's tax and commerce bureaus, and his old acquaintance Adani Ratief, the tax official who'd summoned him here in the first place. Dietrich did not, however, recognize the only person in the room not smiling, a heavyset man in a dark green military uniform. The man watched Dietrich with a steely, uncompromising stare as he sat and poured himself a glass of water.

"Thank you for coming, Mr. Nash," Adani said warmly, reaching across the table to shake hands.

"Of course. Thank you for having me," Dietrich replied.

"You took one of your trains?" Adani asked. Dietrich raised an eyebrow. None of the colony's rails even came close to Windhoek, a fact these men were surely aware of.

"Oh no, Mr. Ratief. Our railways keep strictly within the confines of our property," Dietrich said, still smiling.

"Ah yes, of course. To be perfectly honest, I cannot keep track of your building projects. Everything is always expanding down there. Zoom! Zoom! Zoom!" Adani said cheerily, gesturing broadly with splayed fingers. The men chuckled at the joke and Dietrich allowed himself to join in.

"Yes, well, as you know there is much to do. Satisfying the needs of millions of people is no easy task."

Heads tilted back and eyebrows were raised on the other side of the table, as if this was the first time any of them had heard this figure.

"Millions!" Joshua Angula said, leaning forward against the table, eyes wide with shock. "Just think! Millions living in our desert!" He looked around at the men beside him.

"It is no desert," Adani said to the other officials. "The land has been transformed. Some even say it is a *miracle*. The river has grown. Last I heard, you were even farming some of that land."

Dietrich nodded. "We can't sustain everyone on the food purchased from the capital and what is shipped in from other cities. We need to plan for our future."

"And what future, exactly, is that?" asked Ezekiel Qonja. He was the oldest of the four men, with a head of wiry, greased-back hair.

"I believe we've been over this, gentlemen," Dietrich said, sensing a trap, especially with the military official present.

"Please. Humor us," Adani said. Dietrich nodded, drew a breath, and explained as succinctly as possible. The Witnesses believed that the end was near, that they were living deep in a period called the great tribulation, and that soon they would be attacked by a coalition of world governments.

"When I was a small boy, I went to church often with my mother. I do not remember ever hearing such a thing from the pulpit," Mr. Angula objected. "Why?"

"Well, did your church ever mention that world governments would suddenly turn on the churches, the mosques, and all major religions?"

"No," Joshua replied.

"Well, we did. It's been talked about in our publications for years. We knew false religion would fall in a sudden attack. Few believed us, but look how things turned out."

"So you are prophets? Like Moses?" Ezekiel asked.

"No. We are merely Bible students. The chain of events that we are seeing today was recorded millennia ago. We are merely delivering that message to others."

"It is true, things have happened suddenly. Difficult to

196

believe," Joshua said with a solemn shake of his head.

"Regardless, we didn't bring you here to talk about religion," Adani said. "I trust you have had time to look over the tax papers."

"I did," Dietrich said simply.

"We do not plan to tax everything. We are reasonable people, Mr. Nash."

Dietrich bit his tongue. He was still smiling, but now it was an act of will.

"But the property, Dietrich... It is not what it once was. It was worth little when we sold it to you, and you bought it at bottom dollar. But now, that land is unrecognizable. It is arable, fertile for agriculture. Do you know how many farmers and ranchers we have coming in here asking why foreigners are living on this land? Some have even asked to buy parts of it."

Dietrich shook his head. Of course, such a transaction would be an illegal one. Still, he didn't doubt they'd at least considered it.

"Many, Mr. Nash. Many. We cannot simply let you go on, with such massive populations, without any kind of taxation. It would be foolish of us, and negligent to the rest of Namibia's people," Adani said earnestly.

"It is a mark on the pride of Namibia," Ezekiel said, a serious look engraved on his face.

Dietrich Nash took a deep breath and considered his choices. He could simply refuse and walk out, but he'd been authorized to make another offer, if worse came to worst. He sensed it would placate the bureau, though he doubted it would last forever.

"I cannot authorize payment of this tax," Dietrich said, choosing his words carefully. Across from him, expressions turned to disappointment and impatience. "We simply do not have the monetary means to pay. We are not a cash-based society. Everything is based on the exchange of goods and services."

"Mr. Nash, you and I both know that cannot be true," Adani said, always the negotiator. "You yourself mentioned how much money your people have spent in the capital."

"Yes, but we spend as we receive it. When new colonists arrive from oversees, whatever cash they're carrying is taken to your banks, converted to the local currency, and spent carefully on whatever supplies are needed. But in most cases, we receive what we need through trading with your farms and businesses. As I've mentioned before, no one is making an income in any of our

197

colonies."

The officials sat back, the wind stolen from their sails.

"However," Dietrich paused, watching as the men leaned forward expectantly. The word hung in the air until he was sure he had their attention. "There is something I *can* offer you. And in fact, it is worth more than the price of your proposed property tax."

Dietrich watched as the expressions of the men shifted. They glanced curiously at one another before Adani finally leaned forward. "Well? What is it?"

CHAPTER 17

Since joining her husband aboard *The Chariot*, Joyce had been busy. The convoy stopped often on its way through the Caribbean seas, zigzagging this way and that to pick up brothers and sisters at pre-scheduled points and times. While many of the Witnesses in South America, Haiti, and the Dominican Republic had left months prior with the first wave of evacuees, civil unrest had made fleeing unsafe for others. They were instead divided up into small groups and cared for by local elders until passing convoys from other areas could offer safe passage. These brothers were the last of the last, and their condition was pitiable.

Some had suffered physical violence at the hands of mobs and opposers while others had contracted illnesses, an outcome made all the more likely by lack of nutrition and, in some cases, even sunlight. Every man, woman, and child now boarding would need a thorough checkup and a nutritious diet, and precedence was given to children and the elderly.

Joyce sipped strong coffee from a thermos as she braced herself for yet another influx of patients. At least she had help. She gazed at the small team of doctors and nurses around her, many of them new arrivals since their passage through Panama. Spanish was quickly becoming the primary language of their department, and Joyce wished hers was a little better.

"Feeling ok?" Joyce asked the sister sitting across from her. Though not a formally educated nurse, she'd worked for a time in a South American branch caring for elderly and infirm patients, a practical form of experience. The woman looked up at Joyce from behind her dark curly hair and smiled.

"I'm fine," she said in accented English.

"It's going to be a long night," Joyce said.

The sister nodded. "Yes. I don't mind it. Actually, I'm looking forward to seeing them."

"Oh? That's good."

"I'm from Venezuela, you know."

"I didn't."

"It's been many years. I left shortly after I was baptized. I always thought I'd get a chance to see it again, but…"

"I'm sure you'll be back someday. Someday in the new world."

The woman smiled. "Seeing my brothers and sisters is enough, for now."

Just then a brother appeared in the doorway. He spoke rapidly in Spanish and then disappeared. Joyce looked at the faces around her for an explanation.

"He said the brothers are starting to come aboard now, and we should be ready."

The room was a flurry of activity. Cots were unfolded and lined against the walls as bottles of pills and vitamins were prepared on countertops.

Within another five minutes their first patient had arrived. He was led by a young, timid looking brother who explained the situation briefly. "He says he was injured at sea. No memories. Oh, and no ID card," the brother stammered before making way for the elderly brother behind him to pass.

Joyce felt her heart seize in her chest. Another patient with trauma-induced amnesia was not what she'd been expecting. A flood of emotion and memory came over her as her thoughts went immediately to the day Claire had been admitted to West Hill Medical. She brushed away the distraction and nodded.

"Please, brother, have a seat," Joyce said in Spanish. The man glanced at her with sharp, green eyes before taking in the rest of the room slowly. A bandage was wrapped around his head and leg, but there didn't seem to be any swelling or bleeding. Slowly, Joyce helped him onto one of the cots. He sat heavily with a sigh.

Behind her, Joyce heard the clack of a plastic bottle crashing onto the floor. Dozens of pills scattered in every direction. She turned to find the nurses' assistant frozen, her hand still poised in the air where it had been holding the bottle. The woman's lips quivered, a deep crease forming in her forehead.

"Luis?" she whispered.

The old man looked up. "Camilla!"

***

"Diamonds?" Adani asked, leaning forward so far into the table that it slid into his gut.

"Impossible," Joshua Angula said, waving the notion away with the flick of his wrist. "The Chinese would've found it. They scoured the entire area."

"How did you find them?" Ezekiel asked, ignoring the other two officials.

"We discovered them when we were blasting part of the canyon out to build a recent section of railway. It was an accident."

"Have you had them appraised? Do you have samples on you?" Joshua asked hungrily.

"I will leave that up to you. I am sure you know men in the business."

"And what is your proposal, Mr. Nash?" Adani asked.

"Simple. We will hand over control of the mines. Not just this mine, but any others we might stumble upon in the future."

Dietrich waited as the men sitting across from him exchanged glances and laughed nervously. To their ears, he knew, this was a fool's offer. No sane landholder in all of the African continent would knowingly turn over land ownership when diamonds were involved, let alone reveal that the precious stones had ever been found. In the past, families who'd discovered such things on their land would go to great lengths to keep it a secret, often spending small fortunes flying in oversees prospectors on private planes in the middle of the night to value the stones and leave before dawn so as not to arouse the suspicion of neighbors. Precious stones were a risky business, and everyone knew it.

"How can we trust any of this?" Ezekiel asked, his fingers tugging at the grey whiskers on his chin.

"You don't have to," Dietrich said simply. "I invite you to come see for yourselves. Bring your diamond expert, have him appraise what we've found. I don't think you'll be disappointed."

"And that's it?" Mr. Angula asked. "You just hand over the diamonds, no questions asked?"

"That's it. Our only request is that you drop the property tax."

Dietrich paused as the men shared another long look. They still seemed skeptical.

"Look, gentlemen: we are simple people. We have no need for

201

diamonds in our colonies. We care only for practical goods. If it doesn't help us build our residences or prepare for a sustainable future, we're simply not interested."

"You are a gambling man!" Adani said, his expression once again exuberant and joyful as he slapped the table with his palms. "You came here all this way to tell us this, and what a risk you have taken! What would stop us from simply entering your land by force and taking the diamonds ourselves?"

"Namibians are a pragmatic people," Dietrich said, summoning his most respectful tone. "You wouldn't risk confrontation like that. You know how numerous our colonists are, and you know we will protect the lives of our people. Besides, you have no idea where to dig. All you know is that the diamonds are somewhere near a railway. With over five thousand kilometers of track, you'd never find it."

Adani's smile dimmed by a few degrees, but Dietrich knew he'd won the man's respect once again.

"I like this man!" he announced in his loud, booming voice. He stood, signaling that the meeting had come to a close. Dietrich Nash rose to meet him and the two shook hands heartily.

"We will waive the tax! It is no more!" Adani said, as if accomplishing some great benevolent deed. Dietrich thanked him. And then, reaching in the breast pocket of his suit, he produced a small pouch sewn from purple velvet. He loosened the drawstrings and handed the pouch across the table.

Carefully, Adani reached in and extracted the diamond. It was rough and uncut and hardly looked like anything now, but the men still gasped at the size of it—it was as big as a man's thumb!

***

Rachel lay sprawled across the mattress of their small apartment pod. The sliding glass window was opened as far as it could possibly go, letting in a cool, dry evening breeze that felt good, but it wasn't enough. The Namibian sun had baked her exposed shoulders, arms, and neck to a tender red. A local Namibian sister had lent her a bottle of aloe to cool the burns, but only after chiding her for not covering herself better. Rachel attempted to explain that women in California rarely wore long-sleeved shirts and so she'd been unprepared on arrival, but it didn't stop the sister from shaking her head and laughing.

"Brought you a little something," Peter said as he slipped through the front door. He set down a small, boxed meal of leftovers from the cafeteria. Rachel responded with a low groan. "That bad, huh?" Peter asked, sitting on the corner of the bed beside his wife's legs.

"My body feels like a radiator," Rachel said.

"Were you out in the sun the whole day?"

"Practically. We had to take a drive out to the desert in a buggy. Didn't have much of a roof over it. Then we worked in direct sunlight for a few hours. Ugh. I feel sick."

"Try eating something. You'll feel better," Peter offered gently.

Wincing, he watched as his wife slowly rose from the bed and joined him on the corner. He fetched her a cool glass of water as she ate.

"You wouldn't believe the speed and scale of the building projects here," Peter said as he added a few ice cubes to the glass from a small refrigerator unit. "In just Grunau alone, they're adding accommodations for two thousand people per day! I finally understand why all the pod apartments were based around these shipping containers: the same containers we were using on the ships and rigs are being lifted off of them and transported here by train. It's an enormous operation, but incredibly efficient and very cost effective. I would've never thought of this solution."

"Uh huh," Rachel said as her husband returned with the glass.

"And the way the construction teams are organized is simply incredible. You've got brothers from all over Europe—Germany, Austria, Finland, the Netherlands, England—working right beside African brothers, Indian brothers, and the few of us from North and South America who've already arrived. During the lunch break they told us the most unbelievable stories, how the congregations protected the friends and managed to evacuate everyone in time. It makes our journey *pale* in comparison. Oh, and even though English is the universal language here, you're constantly hearing chatter in every possible tongue. I even learned a few phrases in Afrikaans!"

"That's great, Pete," Rachel said.

"It's tiring work, of course, especially running up and down those stairs with the finishing crew, making sure the wiring and plumbing is working correctly in each of the units. Would you believe there will be brothers and sisters moving into the units we built today by the end of the week?"

"Wow," Rachel said sluggishly.

"It's just... Just amazing, babe. I don't know how to describe this feeling. It's almost like... I don't know. Like paradise has already begun, in a way."

"That's nice. I'm happy for you, hon," Rachel said.

"What about you? A whole day working with animals, huh? Speaking of paradise."

"Yeah, I guess."

"Not exactly what you were expecting?" Peter asked.

Rachel shook her head. "I had carcass duty."

"Uh... Ok. Is that what is sounds like?"

"You bet. We got to saw up a dead animal in the blazing desert heat."

"Whoa," Peter said softly. "Why?"

Rachel repeated the explanation Karen had given her.

"Well, I guess that does make sense," Peter said.

"That doesn't make it easy."

"I suppose someone has to do it."

"Sure, but I'm not sure if that someone is gonna be me."

"How did Angelica fare?" Peter asked.

"Surprisingly, a lot better than me. I always thought I was the tougher of the two of us, but she got in there and got it done. Even had a smile on her face."

"Angelica's been through a lot. She's tougher than a lot of people give her credit for."

"Certainly tougher than me. I'm thinking of trying a different department next time. After my burns heal, of course. I need a couple days in the shade." Slowly, Rachel laid back on the bed.

"It certainly is kind for them to let us choose which assignments we take. I wonder if that'll change in the future," Peter said absently, scooping up the emptied food carton and rinsing it out in the sink before sorting it in the designated bin.

"Why would it change?"

Peter shrugged. "I kind of assumed we'd all be given a job, similar to the way Bethelites are. If everyone could choose their assignment, it seems things could get a little lopsided."

Rachel sighed.

"You wanna hear my suggestion?" Peter said, returning to the corner of the bed. He squeezed a dab of lotion on his hands from a bedside table and began gently massaging his wife's feet.

"If I say no, will the massage end?"

"Of course," Peter teased.

"In that case, I'd love to hear your suggestion, Brother Burton."

"Stick it out a few more days. Get more of a feel for the assignment, talk to some of the ones who've been doing it for a while and see how they've coped. There might be a lesson in there somewhere."

***

A wave of relief washed over Dietrich Nash as he stowed the papers in his briefcase and prepared to leave the conference room. He had wanted to leave this way, with the Namibian officials gawking over the enormous diamond and hungry for more. They would undoubtedly come clamoring for the tour he'd promised, and everything he'd offered would be fulfilled. Whether the men would report their findings to their superiors or embezzle the stones to line their own coffers, Dietrich could only guess. Regardless, he suspected the existence of such a prized commodity under their noses would keep them allies. At least, for a time. And for now, time was all they needed.

Dietrich had nearly made it to the doors when he felt a powerful hand gripping his arm. He turned to find himself staring up into the eyes of the military official. He'd spoken not a single word during their entire meeting, but now Dietrich knew he'd been waiting for exactly this moment. He glanced authoritatively over his shoulder, and behind him the other officials scattered like cockroaches from a kitchen light.

Now it was just the two of them alone in the room. The official gestured for Dietrich to sit, then returned slowly to the other side of the table. He straightened his uniform before taking a seat. He spoke in a low, monotone growl that reminded Dietrich of a lion prowling the grassless Namibian dunes.

"You will find, Mr. Nash, that I am no simple tax collector."

"Okay," Dietrich replied. "What can I help you with?"

"I am troubled by the reports being spread about your people. Especially those from the Americans."

"What are they claiming, exactly?"

"That your people are terrorists involved in a conspiracy to overthrow the government." The officer paused to gauge Dietrich's reaction. "You don't seem surprised."

"We've been called worse. Do they have proof?"

"Yes, they claim so. I want to know how many in your camps are from America."

"That would be a difficult number to procure. Our population is changing daily, as you know. Barges and tankers are arriving by the dozens each week in Elizabeth Bay. No one knows the exact numbers, I'm afraid."

"Yes. Another worrying detail."

"Your concern is understandable," Dietrich said with a touch of sympathy. "I'd be worried too if I were in your shoes. Which is why our doors are always open to you. Ride the trains, take a tour of our premises, see how we do things. I think it will provide more answers than I could sitting at this table."

The official pursed his lips tightly together as he studied carefully the man before him. "Even the pouncing leopard has a beautiful coat."

Dietrich chuckled. "Well, if that wouldn't convince you, I'm not sure what else there is to say. We're not dangerous, and we're not armed. No one is plotting or conspiring in our colonies. Frankly, even if we were bent on some kind of militaristic action, we wouldn't have the resources."

"And yet the Americans are scared."

"Fear is a powerful tool. You get people afraid and you can make them do things they would otherwise never consider."

"Still…" the man said, letting the word dangle in the air like a poised dagger, "our government wishes not to take chances."
Dietrich said nothing, but he was starting to feel anxious. Across the table from him, the official tapped an embroidered badge sewn into his lapel. Dietrich did not recognize the insignia.

"I am Commander Daniel Ngoma and I represent the NSADF. We are a joint defense unit of Namibian and South African armies. We have been keeping a close eye on your colonies, and we feel the time has come to step in."

"May I ask what that entails?"

The official reached behind him and unraveled a map of the Namib. Each of the Witnesses' colonies were clearly marked, and

206

the buildings were unnervingly up to date. Two of the structures pictures had been completely only days before.

"It is your capital, yes?" asked the official, pointing with his pen to the area marked Bismarck. Dietrich nodded slowly.

"We will begin our building project here, on top of the canyons," Ngoma said, dragging his pen to a nearby red dot.

"I'm sorry, what building project are we talking about?"

"The NSADF will be building a military base here for surveillance and state security."

"I'm afraid that's not possible," Dietrich said quickly. "This land belongs to us. It was not a lease from our government, but an outright purchase. The Namibian tax bureau went far beyond its legal rights to try and levy that property tax. The diamonds were a gift, an act of goodwill to keep the peace. But a military base on our land is simply out of the question."

"I'm afraid the decision has been made."

Dietrich's head spun. He felt like he'd been broadsided by a truck. Commander Ngoma glanced at his watch and nodded.

"In fact, the military convoy should be arriving soon."

"I can't believe this," Dietrich said softly.

"Not to worry, Mr. Nash. If all is as you say, you have nothing to fear."

CHAPTER 18

"You two know each other?" Joyce asked, glancing at Camilla, who nodded.

"It's been almost thirty years," she said, instinctively responding in Spanish. Through the grey and wrinkles, she could still see the young man before her.

"You've aged well, Camilla. Just as beautiful as you were in your twenties," Luis said, his eyes beginning to water.

"I had no idea that you became a brother. How did you find the truth? When did it happen?"

Luis shook his head, his face blank. Joyce stepped between them and put a hand gently on the woman's shoulder.

"I hate to butt in, but you'll have lots of time for catching up later. For now, we need to perform a physical. There'll be a line forming out that door in no time."

"Of course," Camilla said, coming to her senses.

"You speak English now?" Luis asked, impressed. Camilla smiled.

"We'll talk about all that soon, Luis. For now we need to examine you." She took a step back as Joyce gingerly unwrapped the bandages, but Luis pulled away.

Joyce gave Camilla a look. "Explain to him that we need to get these bandages off to see the extent of the injuries. There's no need to be afraid." Camilla translated the message into Spanish. Luis shook his head.

"The injuries are not serious," he objected. "I can take care of it myself."

"Yes, Luis, but the nurse needs to check for any signs of infection. If so, you may need antibiotics."

"No infection, it's not that serious. I will be fine."

Camilla turned to Joyce and explained. Joyce frowned. "What about the memory loss? Can you ask him what kind of head trauma he experienced?"

Camilla nodded. "Did you hit your head? We heard there are some things you can't remember," she asked Luis.

"Yes. It is a jumble. I don't remember... Exactly what happened on the boat. How I hit my head... I woke up... and I had forgotten."

"And you can't remember what congregation you're from? What about any of the brothers with you?"

Luis shook his head, his eyes darting from one nurse to the other. "I was alone. I remember nothing about my church congregation."

Camilla turned to address Joyce, but as she did the nurse's radio went off. Through it, a voice was squawking about medical attention needed on the deck. Someone had injured their leg climbing aboard and couldn't be moved to the infirmary. Around her, the other nurses were already busy with their own patients.

"I'm going to run up and have a look," Joyce told Camilla. "He doesn't look too serious. I'm leaving the rest of the examination to you. Be sure to check his pupils for signs of a concussion, and let me know if he experiences any nausea, all right?"

Camilla struggled to understand all the words but nodded anyway.

"I'll be back as soon as I can," Joyce said as she grabbed her coat and disappeared from the infirmary. Luis and Camilla watched her go before Camilla pulled a light from her pocket and checked Luis's pupils. He put a wrinkled hand on hers and gently pushed the light away.

"Camilla. I am fine," he whispered.

"What do you mean?" Camilla asked with growing suspicion.

"I never hit my head."

"And the memory loss?"

Luis shook his head.

"Why are you doing this? You know how many others need help—why would you waste the nurses' time?"

"I'm sorry. It is a long story. But we need to talk. I don't want to disturb your work; I can wait for you. Where is a good place?"

Camilla's frown deepened. "There's a small cafeteria down the hall and to your right. You can wait for me there. But don't expect it to be anytime soon. We have many patients to care for."

"I'm in no rush," Luis said. He hopped from the bed and

walked out of the door without, Camilla realized, any noticeable limp.

***

Against her own inclination, Rachel Burton took her husband's advice; she would give her assignment with the animal care department another shot. She applied a generous coat of aloe to her sunburn and slipped carefully into one of Peter's long sleeve shirts, tying the shirttails into a knot and rolling up the sleeves just enough to expose her hands and wrists. She lathered every bit of exposed skin in sunscreen and set off. It was seven-thirty in the morning and already warm outside. Karen was waiting for her beside the gas-powered buggy with a present.

"The final piece of the outfit, huh?" Rachel said as she took the floppy, wide-brimmed hat and tried it on.

"You definitely look the part now," Karen said, grinning. Angelica appeared a moment later. She'd dressed a lot more sensibly than Rachel had the day before, donning a long sleeved athletic outfit and a baseball cap. Rachel had teased her for looking like she was joining a bowling league, but she wasn't laughing today. Only the back of Angelica's neck and ears had burnt, and she was practically as chipper as she had been the day before.

"So, what's on the agenda for today?" Angelica asked as she hopped into the backseat of the small vehicle.

"Breakfast!" Karen announced as she started the engine and drove off.

The cafeteria they dined at that morning was a simple construction. The only visible walls were the ones surrounding the food prep area; the actual dining space was an open-air concrete platform with timber pillars supporting a thatched roof. A hand-carved sign at the entrance lovingly designated the area 'The Watering Hole'.

"Do each of the departments have their own dining area?" Rachel asked as they entered the pavilion and took their seats among a few dozen others.

"Not typically," Karen replied. "But our department is a little unique, seeing as our work brings us into such close contact with wild animals. This cafeteria is actually located within the conservatory's space, so we sometimes are visited by... curious creatures. It's something that can take a little getting used to, and so we eat separately. Well, us and the waste disposal department."

"Waste disposal?" Angelica asked.

"Yeah... It's a hygiene thing. We're kind of all in the same boat," Karen said with a hearty laugh. "Not so easy to keep clean at the end of the day when you're working with animals in the hot sun."

"Especially dead ones," Rachel quipped. Karen smiled as she looked carefully at the two recruits.

"You both did pretty well yesterday. Many bail after their first turn of carcass duty."

"Really?" Angelica asked. Karen was nodding vigorously.

"I've seen it all. Some make excuses—fur allergies, fear of disease, fear of getting attacked by vultures and hyenas. Others simply won't get out of the car. And a few have fainted."

The three women shared a laugh.

"Would you think any less of me if I admitted that a few of those options went through my head yesterday?" Rachel asked.

"Of course not. It's not an easy assignment. A lot of people jump right in when they hear we work with animals; they imagine we're rolling around in the grass with lion cubs and riding elephants all day. And while occasionally we do have those kinds of opportunities, a lot of it is simply hard physical labor. And some of it is gross: shoveling manure for fertilizer processing, getting drooled on by the giraffes, and, of course, cutting up carcasses for food."

Breakfast was simple but filling: oatmeal fortified with berries and nuts and sweetened with wild honey. The girls didn't recognize all of the flavors but enjoyed them all the same. They topped up their water bottles from a tall tank at the far wall and headed out into the bush.

"So, was yesterday a test?" Angelica asked from the backseat.

Karen laughed. "In a way, I guess so, but not an intentional one. It just happened that we were the closest and we had to take care of it before the heat and the vultures got to it. Meat doesn't last long in the Namib. Either I was going to have to drop you two off first and do the job myself or take you along with me. I figured it would be best to just throw you in the deep end and see how you fared."

"What happened to the meat after we cut it up?" Rachel asked. From the corner of her eye, she caught Karen grinning.

"The brothers stowed it in an underground pit to keep it cool, then loaded it back up early this morning."

"Loaded it back up? Where?"

"It's with us, actually. And it's our first task of the day."

"Ooh!" Angelica squealed from the backseat. "Who are we feeding?"

"The caracals," Karen said, glancing at the women. Judging from their blank stares, neither had ever heard of the animal before.

Standing a couple of heads taller than the average house cat and possessing many of the same facial features, caracals are characterized by their stocky bodies, black tufted ears, and their incredible jumping skills. Able to leap over twelve feet into the air, caracals routinely prey on low-flying birds, snatching them unsuspectingly in midair.

Angelica's mouth fell open when Karen described their jumping feats. "That's higher than the roof of a house," she gasped.

"Yep. They can hop right into trees if need be. Very agile. Especially Rory. He's easily our most athletic," Karen explained proudly.

"Were these orphans as well?" Rachel asked, remembering what Karen had mentioned the day before about the cheetahs.

"Some, but not all. Many have just wandered in out of sheer curiosity, it seems. It's peculiar, though—caracals are typically very shy. They're one of the lesser seen wild animals of Namibia, and they usually live by themselves or in pairs, never in packs. They're also usually very territorial, and can be dangerous to approach in the wild. But our caracals are nothing like that. They're incredibly tame and docile, almost as if they were raised around humans. Still, I'd recommend caution—they can get a little nippy when they smell food."

They drove for another ten minutes before Karen shut off the engine and parked the buggy in a patch of dried grass. A ladder led up to a raised wooden platform about two stories tall. Karen instructed the two women to slip on their gloves, and the three made their way carefully up the ladder, hauling several large hunks of meat with them as they went. A cleaver hanging from a hook on a table at the top of the tower was used to hack the meat into smaller pieces. Rachel peeked over the edge of the tower as they divided the meat and was surprised at what she saw: a small group of black-eared cats had gathered at the base of the structure and were clearly eager for handouts.

"Go ahead," Karen told her. "Drop one of the pieces for them."

Rachel grabbed a piece of meat about the size of her fist and dropped it over the edge. Her breath caught in her throat as two long-fanged heads raced up from the ground to meet her, two sets of wide, green eyes locked on the falling food. One had timed his leap slightly better; his claw stretched up just a few feet from the platform they stood on, snatching the meat from the air and bringing it down into his mouth.

"Amazing!" Angelica said breathlessly, eager to have a try. She dropped two pieces of meat this time, and three new furry heads leapt from the ground to intercept it.

"Try throwing it like a frisbee," Karen suggested. As soon as Rachel brought her arm back to prepare the toss, the cats poised themselves to sprint. As the meat was flung high into the air, they raced to intercept it, leaping into the air like dogs playing fetch.

"You sure they're not dangerous?" Rachel asked warily, trying not to imagine what it would be like to be chased by one of the creatures.

"Oh yes. They're only hungry. Care to have a closer look?" Karen asked. She led them back down the ladder. They sat in the grass with their legs crossed and waited as the cats encircled them curiously, sniffing at their heads and arms.

"Elsa is by far the friendliest," Karen said as one of the female caracals brushed the top of its head along Angelica's shoulder. The woman was surprised at the cat's strength. She turned to gently scratch the rust colored cat beneath her chin. Lifting her head, Elsa closed her eyes contentedly and began to purr. It was a powerful, continuous thrum and Angelica couldn't help but smile contentedly.

"Looks like you're part of the pride, now," Karen said.

"It's incredible," Angelica said. She found, for some strange reason, that tears were welling in her eyes. She laughed with embarrassment and wiped her face with her sleeve.

"It's ok," Karen said softly. "It's emotional for a lot of people. Being this close to these majestic animals triggers something in us, something that's been dormant for many, many years. Jehovah created us to take care of them."

Rachel felt it too, a powerful pressure in her chest that made her yearn all the more for the future. As the cats sprawled out one by one for a mid-morning nap, the women stroked their coarse red coats and listened to the Namibian breeze rustle through the grass.

***

It had been a day of backbreaking work. Sweating under his cotton shirt and jeans, Peter felt like a wet noodle. The entire day had been spent with the container placement crews, a task which involved transporting dozens of newly arrived shipping containers from the railways onto the loading platforms, and from there, via forklifts and flatbed trucks, to the housing lots.

These shipping containers had previously been used for storage rather than housing, meaning that each needed to be cleaned thoroughly and then outfitted with doors, windows, and all other necessary commodities. The teams had been rotated regularly to avoid exhaustion and heatstroke, but Peter still felt like collapsing.

He sat heavily on a shady bench beside a brick walkway, both of which had been installed only that morning. He pulled a bottle of water from a wooden crate beside him. Taped to the crate was a handwritten sign: *Keep hydrated!* He opened the bottle and finished the entire thing before leaning his head back and resting his eyes. He hoped Rachel would return the favor of massaging his feet that night, but he wasn't getting his hopes up. He was surprised his wife had dived back into her assignment after such a difficult first day, but he was expecting her to be just as tired as he was.

At least tomorrow is Sunday, Peter thought. It was the one day that all the work crews rested. Friends could get together for relaxation and association, and of course they would have their meeting in the morning, as had been their habit all throughout this ordeal. Peter wondered what the program would involve. On the rigs, various overseers had rotated giving discourses each week, often focusing on the need for unity, for forgiveness, and for humility, qualities especially important given the friends' close proximity and high levels of stress. With their arrival in Africa, they now had a lot more space to roam around in, but the challenges were no less prominent. Getting used to the environment was one thing—few had any experience living in a desert like climate—but the physical demands of life here were another entirely. And along with those changes came needed adjustments in diet, recycling, and even water and electricity usage. No one here could afford to be wasteful; in even the smallest of behaviors, the livelihood of the entire community had to be considered.

"Looks like you could use one of these," said someone in a deep voice. Peter lifted his head to see his old friend, Marcus Kelly. In an outstretched hand he held a beer bottle dripping with condensation.

"I must have heatstroke, because I think I'm hallucinating," Peter said. Marcus laughed heartily. He handed the beer over and sat.

"Really? We're allowed to drink on building projects?" Peter asked incredulously.

"Don't look at me," Marcus said, shrugging. "I don't make the rules. A whole truckload of the stuff was there at the platform, and one of the overseers from Bismarck was handing them out. We got to chat a little, seems like he's been here since the beginning."

"Oh?" Peter said. He pried open the top and took a swig. It was heaven.

"Name was Brother Nash. I recognized him from that broadcast we had months ago about Namibia."

"Right," Peter said. "Still feels a little weird, drinking on the job."

Marcus nodded. "Lots has changed. I guess that's to be expected, seeing how close we are. This is a real taste of the future, huh?"

Peter nodded. "I can't get over it. I just keep wondering how it's all possible, transporting millions of people across the world, building cities here in the desert. Feeding everyone, housing everyone. The whole thing. It's the last thing I would've expected."

"It's an incredible amount of work. But it sure is satisfying, isn't it? Knowing that each storage container you place, every pipe you lay, every little piece of it, is going directly to help your brothers and sisters."

Peter thought for a moment. "You're right. I keep thinking about how life here is like all the special forms of service from the past—Disaster Relief, LDC work, Bethel—all rolled into one. I guess that was training for this."

"And this must be training for what comes next," Marcus said. The two stared off into the distance, where most of the workers had sprawled out in the shade for naps and quiet conversation. A small group of especially energetic younger ones had organized an impromptu soccer match with local workers. From the looks of it,

215

the barefoot locals were winning.

"Join me on a walk?" Marcus asked.

"Of course," Peter said. The two slipped their hats back over their heads and set off down the brick path together. They paused to admire the large block of container apartments they'd just finished before moving on. Marcus led the two of them up the path, where it climbed to a hilly grove of trees and then a rocky outcropping. From here they gazed down at the southern side of Grunau, a landscape laced in red walkways and dotted with structures. Their own apartments were among them. Peter had to admit that it was an attractive place to live, even if the desert would never be his first choice.

"Incredible, isn't it?"

"Rachel and I tell ourselves the same thing each morning when we wake up. Sometimes we pinch ourselves to make sure it isn't a dream."

Marcus chuckled with a knowing nod. "You're not alone there, Peter."

They gazed down into the valley for a few moments of contemplative silence. In the shade of a quiver tree, they found a bench and sat.

"Can I ask you a personal question, Marcus?" Peter said. Marcus turned with a smile and nodded.

"Of course, Peter."

"Do you feel ready?" Peter asked. Slowly, Marcus tilted his head up towards the sky and closed his eyes. Dappled afternoon sunlight danced on his face.

"That's a difficult question to answer," he said finally with a deep sigh. "On the one hand, I'm eager to see what comes next. Being able to participate in those final moments at Armageddon… It's an indescribable privilege. Still, I've enjoyed my time here. It's all I've known, and I must keep my integrity to the end. And of course I do sometimes worry about Vivian."

The two fell silent. Peter was surprised by his friend's candid answer. His honesty drew Peter even closer to him.

"The thing is, when I look around here at all that is happening, it's like Jehovah is personally reminding me not to worry. Everything is under control. Just think: he cared for nearly a third of our current population over three thousand years ago under similar conditions—wandering in an arid, waterless wilderness for decades.

216

But so long as they kept their integrity to him, they were provided for, protected, and blessed.

"And don't we see the same thing now? Look at the ones who listened and followed directions, despite how difficult and unrealistic the sacrifices may have seemed at first. But now they are here, their lives still intact, living happily among their brothers and sisters. Can the same be said for those who did not obey?

"So that's what I'm focusing on now—my own integrity. I want to see the end of this system, Peter. I want Jehovah's name to be vindicated more than ever before. I want to see these colonies grow and thrive and spread over the globe for the glory of our Creator. Nothing else matters. And when I start worrying about things—about how people will fare without me, about how Vivian will manage—something always reminds me that it's not my job to take care of those things once I'm gone."

"It's our job," Peter said.

Marcus smiled and shook his head. "It's Jehovah's job, actually. It's his guarantee that if we put the kingdom first, he cares for everything else. Likely, he will use you and the other overseers and Vivian's close friends, but ultimately, it's up to him."

Peter said nothing more. The two watched as the sun slowly dipped behind the pink dunes.

***

Since the completion of the mission, Chad Harkett had spent his days carefully considering his next move. Whether their tactics worked or not, Chad knew that he was living in a transformed world. The old ways would not work in whatever new society emerged from the ashes. The technical knowledge of the old world, with its computers and machines and microchips, would be of little use going forward. The IoT—or Internet of Things—that inevitable harbinger of the next technological wave that Chad and his company had worked for years to bring to fruition, was now a forgotten memory. This new society would be a physical one, Chad could see. A man's own strength, wits, and instinct for survival would mean everything. Ones and zeros had been relegated to just that—inert bits trapped in digital prisons. Chad would not become trapped with them.

It wasn't long before Driscoll tracked him down and explained, sadly, that their ruse had failed. In spite of the weeks spent rebuilding the complex facial-recognition software that had been used to produce the fake broadcast, and in spite of its realism—convincing enough to have been signed off on by every necessary government badge—they'd failed. Perhaps there'd been an oversight—a wrinkle in the script or some telling visual detail—but the reason mattered not. They'd played their hand and the Witnesses had called their bluff.

Satellite drone footage revealed signs that the message had been received and broadcasted as instructed on each of the vessels; there had been a clear two-hour interval where several ships had slowed or even completely stopped. Likely, this had been a time of consultation between the vessels when the next steps would be decided on. Whatever the case, the consensus was clearly to ignore the message and hold course.

"So, where does that leave us, then?" Chad asked.

"Washington is shutting us down," said Driscoll, staring blankly at the wall at the back of the room where a frozen satellite image was still being projected.

"Shutting down the deepfake project?"

"Shutting down USCC completely. There's no more use for Cyber Command, they say. And time's running out."

"How's that?" Chad asked. Driscoll swiped through to the next set of images on his iPad.

"Here's the latest aerial images from Namibia. See for yourself."

Chad could hardly believe his eyes. The entire area was covered in winding train tracks and walkways, blocks of apartment housing, and vast groves of trees and plants.

"This is the compound you were talking about?" he asked coldly. Driscoll nodded.

"Growing every day. We had a UAV circling on a twenty-four hour watch and it counted seven trains coming and going, each with over fifty passenger cars. The rate of population growth is mind-boggling."

"It must be a madhouse," Chad said, appearing concerned.

Driscoll nodded grimly. "From what we've observed, arrivals are sent immediately to the dormitories, and from there they're sent out to build apartment blocks, till fields, lay railway, that kind of thing."

"Labor camps."

"That's the idea, I'm sure. They brainwash their followers into leaving everything behind, then they use them for free labor once they arrive. Classic cult behavior. Only this is on an entirely new scale. It's like a mega cult."

"And no one's had second thoughts? After the broadcasts we put together and all the thousands of people that must've heard them, no one decided to turn around?"

"We're keeping an eye on it. Some appeared to stop and even make detours, but in the end they were just picking up more followers from various areas. But no, so far not one ship has reversed course."

"Then what happens next? Surely our government isn't going to just sit on its hands. These people are terrorists, and I'm sure whatever they're planning next will be worse than anything we've seen yet." Chad grimaced. Of course, the truth was that he cared little for the well being of anyone but himself. Still, his future prospects relied on his being closely affiliated with these armed soldiers, and he would do whatever it took to remain with them.

"The deepfake project was never meant to end this, only buy us time," Driscoll finally said, removing his hat and brushing back his thinning hair.

"Time for what?"

Driscoll gave Chad a long, hard look before smiling, turning on his heel, and walking away. "Stick around and you'll find out," he said over his shoulder.

CHAPTER 19

Luis waited for hours, long into the night, fighting the urge to doze off right there in the cafeteria where crowds of diners were coming and going. Finally, he spotted a familiar face.

"Ah! You made it safely," said the young man Luis had first met while still on his boat. A backpack was slung over his shoulder. A blue Yankees cap was snugged over his head; tufts of curly black hair poking out from the sides.

"Yes, *hijo*. Thank you for your help," Luis said.

"Did you get your injuries looked at?" the man asked.

"The nurse gave me a brief examination and decided it wasn't serious. She told me to wait here."

"Ah. I see. Where's your luggage?"

Luis shrugged sheepishly. "I have none. It's just me."

"Oh no," the young man said, looking worried.

"It is fine. I don't need much."

The young man looked at him for a moment before removing the backpack from his shoulders and rifling through its items. He pulled a long, shiny garment from within and handed it over.

"What's this?" Luis asked.

"A poncho. I think it'll fit you. And it's waterproof," the man said cheerily.

"I can't take this," Luis said. He attempted to hand it back but the man brushed him away.

"Sure you can. It's a spare—I've got another in my pack. It's not much but it'll keep you warm and dry if we run into any wet weather."

"I see. Well, thanks," Luis said, nodding gratefully.

"Well, I'll be seeing you around, I'm sure," said the young man.

"Yes, I suppose so," Luis said, and with a wave the man was gone. Luis watched him leave, feelings of guilt again pricking his conscience. He did not like being a part of this scheme.

"Luis?" asked a woman's voice from somewhere behind him. He turned to see Camilla staring down at him, a deep furrow in her brow. She seemed tired and angry, and yet she was still as radiant as he'd remembered her in her youth.

"Camilla. Please, sit," he said. She joined him across the table. She wore no wedding band, Luis noticed with a glance at her hands. "You look exhausted," he said.

"It's been a long day."

"Yes, caring for so many patients... I had no idea you had become a nurse. That's quite an accomplishment!"

"Not a registered nurse. I'm only a helper. I can't administer medicine or certain treatments. Mostly I perform routine check ups."

"Like you performed on me," Luis said, smiling.

"Yes, like I performed on you... Actually, I want to ask you about that. Why did you have those bandages if you weren't injured?"

"It's... It's a long story, Camilla," Luis said evasively.

"Well, if you're not willing to tell me, I've got another question I'd like answered."

"Go ahead."

"Are you really a Witness?"

Luis' blank stare was response enough. Camilla's frown deepened and she shook her head. "I can't believe this," she said softly.

"I'm sorry. I didn't mean to lie to anyone. I just got swept up in things."

"What does that even mean?" Camilla asked. "Why are you here? Was this just so you could talk to me?"

"Of course not, Camilla," Luis said adamantly. "I had no idea you would be on this ship! How could I even know that? Maybe it's fate, you know?"

"There's no such thing," Camilla scoffed.

"And yet here we are, two old partners separated for decades, suddenly finding ourselves on opposite sides of the same table."

"Opposite sides indeed. Do you have any idea what we are doing here? Where we are headed?"

Luis nodded. "I've heard the stories. Everyone is talking about it. Some are afraid of you people. Some think it sounds crazy."

"It's not crazy," Camilla said, shaking her head with a grave expression. "This is the end, Luis. Do you know what things are like in America? The entire country is on fire. Anarchy is everywhere. Millions are dying. If that's how things are in the richest country in the world, how do you think everywhere else is? How was it when you left Venezuela? What about Trinidad? Colombia? Brazil?"

Luis said nothing. He carefully studied Camilla's expression. Her earnestness reminded him of just how things had been that last day when she'd left him.

"Some say that your people had a hand in it," Luis said, a halfhearted attempt to play devil's advocate. In fact, the accusations he'd heard about the Witnesses seemed like a lot of hot air.

"And do you really believe that talk? Do you really think any human organization could be responsible for making the sun disappear from the sky and blocking radio signals? Does that make sense to you?"

Chastened, Luis shrugged.

"As long as I've known you, you've always been a smart man," Camilla said, her tone softening. "Look around you and tell me if you think any of this seems normal."

"If I was so smart, how come you walked out?" Luis said, lifting an eyebrow playfully. Camilla did not reciprocate.

"You know exactly why I left, Luis."

"I quit smoking ten years ago, you know."

"It wasn't just the cigarettes. You weren't interested in studying the Bible with the Witnesses."

"I'm interested now."

Camilla took a deep breath and sighed. When she looked back up, Luis was grinning hopefully.

***

True to their word, the Namibian-South African Defense Force had wasted no time setting up camp. Within three days of Commander Ngoma's conversation with Dietrich Nash, a fleet of desert-camouflaged trucks had arrived with radars strapped to their roofs. Tents were erected to house the troops and technicians, and the entire base was lined in a chain link fence topped with loops of barbed wire.

Dietrich, of course, had immediately informed the other overseers in Bismarck, and an emergency meeting was held as soon as he returned from Windhoek that night. It was determined that little could be done. The government of Namibia, while long acting as a kind of ally, was nevertheless part of Satan's system, and it had been expected that at some point their relationship would sour. Clearly, that point had come.

Stepping from his jeep, Dietrich strolled up the dusty road leading to the NSADF base. He'd been summoned by Commander Ngoma, though the reason given had been vague. Two armed guards in red berets and military fatigues aimed automatic rifles at him as he approached. The soldiers barked at him to stop in his tracks and state his intentions.

"I am merely responding to a call I received from your superior, Commander Ngoma," Dietrich said loudly, his arms held high in the air.

"What's your business here?" one of the soldiers demanded. Dietrich found that shrugging was a difficult gesture to make while his hands were in the air.

"Wish I knew myself. His message was vague. Any way you can contact him and verify?"

The soldiers exchanged a glance and one shouldered his weapon as he jogged over to a black metal crate. He opened it and removed a phone. A few minutes passed and a large man approached from the other side of the security fence. It was the commander.

"Our first guest!" he roared jovially. Dietrich attempted a smile. The soldiers opened the gate and Dietrich was whisked inside. "Not bad for less than four days of building, no? I'll bet even *your* people couldn't accomplish that," Ngoma joked. Dietrich gazed uncomfortably at a rack of rifles that was waiting to be loaded into a brand new wooden shed.

"Of course, this is only the beginning. Soon, the bushmen will clear that land over there," Ngoma pointed, "and we will construct a proper helipad. No more taking jeeps and transport vehicles. Flying to and from the capital will save time."

"I'm sure it will," Dietrich responded, envisioning the constant overhead drone of military helicopters, day and night, as the brothers and sisters labored tirelessly to beautify the land. He wanted to shake his head.

"And this over here—do you know what this is?" the commander asked proudly, pointing to a long, black truck.

"No idea," Dietrich said.

"This is a surveillance vehicle. Cutting edge. British-made. Very expensive," Ngoma said, shaking a finger in Dietrich's face.

"Very impressive," Dietrich said graciously.

"Of course," Ngoma continued, "you are not on a public telephone grid out here. You have your own telephone lines, yes?"

"Built with our own resources by our own volunteers, yes."

"And it connects to your other cities?"

Dietrich did not like where the line of questioning was going but found himself nodding.

"Very fine. Then we will simply plug in."

"Excuse me?" Dietrich said.

"In order to conduct our surveillance, Mr. Nash, we will need access to your phone lines."

"You're asking for permission to tap our phones?"

The smile vanished from Ngoma's face as he stepped forward, towering several inches above the brother. "The NSADF does not 'ask permission.' We *do* what needs to be *done*. The telecom trucks will arrive within the next few days to connect our systems. I trust you will not get in their way."

***

It had been nearly two days since Rafael and Stefan Sosa had heard any news from Luis Escobar. The last they'd talked, the old fisherman had been preparing to climb aboard a Witness barge. The boats left behind by the evacuees had been completely stripped, a detail Rafael had discovered the next morning as they'd passed through the waters where the large ships had been the night before. Hundreds of smaller crafts—from wooden dinghies to fiberglass schooners and everything in between—had been lashed together with ropes and then abruptly abandoned.

As planned, the Sosas followed several miles behind the convoy as it inched through the Caribbean Sea. But without definite news from their spy aboard the barge, they were sailing blind.

"Perhaps he was discovered," Rafael suggested, his feet propped up on the yacht's console as he sharpened a hunting knife.

"Unlikely," Stefan said. "He had nothing on him that would incriminate him. No weapons, no written instructions."

"He had the radio," Rafael interjected.

"Any fisherman worth his salt on these seas carries a radio."

"That was *our* radio Luis was carrying. You know he wouldn't be able to afford such an expensive device. It could've given him away."

"A stretch. You see how many new passengers these ships are bringing aboard each day? I'm sure there are plenty of passengers with suspicious items. More than likely he is fine. We just need to be patient and keep our ear to the radio."

"And what if he never turns that radio on? What if he just decides to leave us high and dry?"

Stefan did not answer. From his captain's chair he leaned into the throttle and felt the tip of their craft lift into the air as they gained speed.

Suddenly, their VHF erupted in a burst of static. "Anyone there?" said the voice on the other end.

Stefan snatched the transmitter up in one hand as the other manned the wheel. "We've been waiting," he growled. "What's your status?"

"I'm on board. Everything is fine here."

"What took you so long?"

There was a pause. "I ran into an old friend."

The Sosa brothers glanced uneasily at one another.

"Have you had a chance to stake out the place? Do you know where the supplies are kept? How many guards?"

Another long pause. "I'm sorry. I... I can't tell you that."

"You can't? Or you won't?" Rafael demanded, leaning over his brother's shoulder to yell into the radio.

"You don't understand. These are good people. I won't betray them like this," Luis said, his voice gaining confidence.

"But you'll betray *us*?" Stefan hissed.

"Rafael. Stefan. I'm sorry. I used to think the whole world was full of people that thought and acted only for themselves. But now I can see there's some hope left, and I'm not about to throw that away. I may have done a lot of things in my life that I'm not proud of, but I'm an old man now and I've got no interest in making more mistakes. I've made my decision."

"We had a deal, old man!" Rafael shouted, his rage reaching a boiling point.

"The deal's off. I stashed my guns in a compartment underneath one of the benches aboard my boat. It's yours if you want it. I'm sure it'll cover the cost of this radio. But we're done, do you understand? I'm washing my hands of this entire scheme."

"Don't think it'll be so easy, Luis," Stefan said menacingly. "We know exactly where you are. Don't think we won't come pay you a visit and take what we were promised."

But there was no response. Luis' radio had been shut off.

***

After two weeks with the animal care department, Rachel was finding her groove. While there'd been more calls for carcass duty, these instances hadn't been nearly as emotionally taxing as the first. Rachel had found herself strangely disconnected from the bodies in front of her, letting the fluids drain and detaching the limbs in a purposeful, almost mechanical fashion.

Strangely, personal study had helped.

It had all started with Karen's suggestion that she read up on the duties of Levitical priests. After all, there were many similarities between the work she was doing now and that of the Levites. Theirs was not an easy task, perhaps made all the harder by the physical act of slaughtering the animals to be sacrificed, something Rachel Burton was thankfully not required to do.

How had they managed? Rachel found herself wondering as she dug through the topic of 'Sacrifice' in the *Insight* book. After all, Jehovah had originally created man to act as caretaker and protector of the animals. Killing them was far from his intent. The key, of course, was the value of the job those priests performed. They were not killing for the thrill of it, nor were they ruthless sportsmen out for trophies. Their job held deep significance, a reminder of their need for an eternal savior. It was part of sacred service.

Rachel began to understand. Just as those Levitical priests were working to fulfill Jehovah's will, so were they now, albeit thousands of years later and under much different circumstances. Carcass disposal, however unpleasant, kept the land free of disease, making it safer for millions, and it provided some amount of sustenance for the animal population growing at the colony's fringes.

It had helped. Better still was the deep, satisfied purrs of the adult cheetahs fed that evening. Like the fluffy cubs from the first day on the job, these mature felines acted like overgrown house cats, brushing their whiskered cheeks and ears against the sisters' backs in unmistakable appreciation. At the slightest bit of attention, they rolled happily in the grass, bellies exposed.

Rachel was glad she'd stuck it out.

As was Peter. The construction work was physically demanding in a way he'd never experienced before, but after the initial week of muscle pains he found himself craving it more and more. Losing weight and building muscle helped, a physical improvement that did not go unnoticed by his wife.

Moreover, in an effort to save electricity, many in the colonies found themselves gradually adjusting their routines to fit the sun's natural rise and set. They rose as early as four-thirty to start their day, a routine that often began with quiet walks around the compounds and up into the winding hills and canyons. Many others read or pondered quietly in their apartment pods, sliding open their windows to let in the cool morning air and warming shafts of sunlight.

On their third Sunday in Grunau, their rest day, a giant picnic was organized among the newly arrived brothers and sisters in Peter and Rachel's apartment block. They shared experiences and grilled skewers over a bonfire. After an early dinner, music was played for the gathering, with many joining in singing and dancing. Mixed in among the crowd were Ted and Angelica. Both looked happier than Peter and Rachel had seen them in a long, long time.

The band finished their set and the crowd offered a round of applause. Ted found an empty chair beside Peter and sat. He was breathing hard.

"Whew! Never knew line dancing could work up such a sweat," Ted said, taking a swig from a bottle of water in his hand.

"And I never knew you were one to dance," Peter said, shaking his head.

"What?" Ted asked.

"Oh nothing. Just marveling at the crazy things a man will do when a woman is involved."

"She's amazing, isn't she?" Ted beamed.

"She's a fine sister. You seem to fit well together."

"Yeah, it's been smooth sailing so far. Not that it's been that long, of course, but you know… I just have a good feeling about it."

"Take your time. There's no need to rush," Peter gently counseled.

"I still can't believe she said yes to dating me. I think that was the most nervous I'd ever been in my life."

"More nervous than when you were staring down the gun of

227

her drunken, murderous ex-husband?" Peter joked.

Ted gave this a moment of consideration. "Yes."

The two shared a laugh.

"To think the guy actually hired a hit man to knock the two of us off," Ted said.

"Saying it out loud makes it sound so ludicrous."

"You ever wonder what happened to him? Chad, I mean." Ted asked.

"I wonder about a lot of people. Was thinking of Darren and Rita just the other day. I keep hoping one day they'll step off one of the train platforms."

"I hear it got ugly pretty fast once the lights went out," Ted said, lowering his gaze. "Someone on my work crew heard that between the crime, the accidents, and the fires, an estimated ten million died in the first month."

Peter shook his head. He was at a loss for words.

"Hey, by the way, you heard about what's happening up in Bismarck?" Ted asked.

"You'll have to be more specific," Peter said. There was no shortage of news from each of the cities as they quickly expanded and transformed.

"The Namibians are building a military base right on-site."

"Oh?"

"They say it's for surveillance. Apparently the population growth is making them uneasy."

"They're probably buying into the lies circulating about us."

Ted shook his head with a wince. "How anyone could believe that nonsense is beyond me. Calling us a terrorist organization? Blaming us for the blackouts and the rioting?"

"Don't forget, we control the weather, too," Peter added.

"Peter?" came a soft voice from behind them. They turned to see Vivian Kelly standing there, a shawl wrapped around her shoulders.

"Hey Vivian," Peter said, standing. "Care to join us?"

"Another time. I need you to come with me," said the older sister, her expression blank. Peter nodded and followed her back down the pathway and to their apartment block. They walked in silence as a feeling of dread began to set in.

Vivian opened the door to their apartment pod and motioned for Peter to enter.

Marcus lay peacefully on the bed, his hands neatly folded against his chest. There were no signs of pain or struggle on his face. Without saying a word, Peter crouched at the side of his friend's bed and wept.

CHAPTER 20

Chad Harkett could feel his blood boiling. It coursed through his veins hot and sticky and felt like it might just erupt from his skin at any moment from the pent up anger. San Francisco was in ruins. Silicon Valley was a smoldering ember pot. Everything he had worked for and built and sweated over now lay in piles of soot and ash. It was gone. All of it.

He grit his teeth and winced as a putrid, acidic wind blew across the base and into their camp. It was a poisonous miasma of melted plastics, evaporated chemicals, and industrial waste, and it smelled like death.

"You about ready?" Driscoll asked from behind him. The chiseled old man had switched from his usual suit and tie to military fatigues and a bulky backpack that seemed to pin him down underneath its weight.

"Can't get out of here soon enough," Chad said with a scowl. He wheezed into his sleeve as a particularly acrid scent filled his lungs.

"Just as well. Not much left of this place," Driscoll said bitterly.

Chad shouldered his bags and stepped onto the gangplank. Before him towered the Nimitz-class supercarrier USS *Ronald Reagan*. If there was a silver lining to this hellish nightmare, this was it. At well over a thousand feet long and weighing an impressive one hundred thousand tons, Chad knew he'd be safe within her walls.

As he climbed the gangplank, below him on the docks one vehicle after another entered the side of the massive vessel, where a powerful aircraft elevator would store the military vehicles in below-deck compartments or on the upper deck. On the top deck of the *Ronald Reagan*, Chad stared in awe at the flanks of neatly poised jet fighters and helicopters. He'd never been especially patriotic, but the sight of such undeniable military power stirred something deep within him. In that moment, he knew that in spite of its current turmoil, his country would surely emerge from the ashes, and he would emerge with it.

"First time aboard a carrier?" Driscoll asked without turning back to look at him.

"Yes, sir," Chad said.

"Impressive, ain't it?"

"Never saw anything like it before."

"She's got enough firepower to fight off an army. No one messes with a Nimitz-class. These ships are legendary. Just one of these things stationed in Yokosuka, Japan peeved the Chinese so much that they commissioned the construction of their own aircraft carriers to defend against it. I'd still put my money on US-made, of course," Driscoll said with a wink. "And speaking of the Chinese…"

Above them, a pair of gunmetal helicopters cut through the smoke-filled skies and descended deftly onto a helipad. Emblazoned on their fuselages were red flags dotted in yellow stars, clearly denoting their Chinese origin.

"Should we be worried?" Chad asked, his pace slowing as they neared the deck. The surface of the water was now a good fifty feet below them. But Driscoll was shaking his head.

"Nah. We're on good terms. It's that coalition, you remember? China's part of it, even Russia, Iran. A truce has been called so we can deal with this threat."

Chad watched as a coterie of men in dark blue uniforms unloaded from the helicopters. They were greeted immediately by a team of US naval officers and quickly whisked away into the control tower.

"Well there's something you don't see every day," Driscoll joked. Chad ignored him.

It took another three days for the USS *Ronald Reagan* to take on its full manifest of personnel, vehicles, and weaponry. As they departed from Hunters Point and cut through the smoke and fog sitting on San Francisco Bay, Chad finally understood the full extent of the damage done here.

San Francisco was in ruins. The familiar skyline had been blackened by the raging fires, and some structures had disappeared completely. Where skyscrapers once stood, tall charcoal plumes rose like oil leaking upwards into the sky. On the shores, survivors gathered under tarps and tents, waving cardboard signs in the air and begging for help from the only ones left to offer it—the armed forces. In other areas, mounds of clothing had been piled high on the banks of the Bay and were being systematically burned. It was only upon gazing through a pair of borrowed binoculars that Chad realized these were not bundles of clothes at all, but rather the bodies of the dead.

The supercarrier churned on through the bay. It hugged the northern shore of Hunters Point, far from the crazed, panicked citizens on the far end of the Bay. But even at this distance, their cries could occasionally be heard from the bulwarks of the ship. At her edge, military personnel and technicians watched with tears in their eyes. Everyone was hurting, their only consolation the fact that they would soon have their revenge.

"What happened to it?" Chad asked in astonishment, only now realizing that the iconic Golden Gate Bridge had been severed at its far end. Thick red cables dangled in the water, chunks of steel and crumbled concrete suspended in midair.

"The base was getting overrun by idiots trying to cross the bridge. We had a sign out there saying to keep out, that no one would be admitted without special permissions, but that didn't stop people. So the Air Force had to be called in. A few sidewinders did the job."

At the edge of the mangled bridge, Chad could see rotting wreaths of flowers, stuffed animals, and deflated balloons.

"Don't pay any attention to that stuff," Driscoll chastised. "We gave 'em plenty of warning. They knew what they were risking being on that bridge. Guess they thought we were bluffing. Their mistake."

Chad shrugged. "War is war. That's what people don't get. Times change and you need to adjust. The fittest survive. The weak and the stupid will die off one way or another."

"Well said," Driscoll grunted, sizing the man up. The two stood silently side by side as the supercarrier slipped past the Golden Gate and into open waters, where a thick fog waited.

***

"I'm sorry, I'm not following completely," Alvin said, shaking his head. The words were falling much too quickly from the sister's mouth and it was difficult to piece everything together.

232

"He is saying the men will attack us," the woman said, a frantic look fixed in her eyes.

"And what men are these?" Alvin asked. Camilla translated the question to the wiry, deeply tanned man beside her. He spoke with animated gestures that belied his apparent age.

"He says they were men he was working with, before he boarded our ship."

"So they are coworkers? And they want to attack us?" Alvin asked.

"No no no," Camilla said, waving her hands in the air. "Not like coworkers. It is not this kind of situation in Venezuela now. Many of the fishermen have become pirates. They are dangerous!" she insisted.

"And your friend here, was he also a pirate?"

Camilla appeared to have not thought to ask this question. Her expression shifted as she turned to the fisherman beside her and began grilling him in Spanish.

"Luis said he never attacked people before. He was a… Ay, I don't know the English word—a *contrabandista*?" Camilla said, running frustrated fingernails through her curly hair.

"Smuggler," Joyce said, showing Alvin the screen of her phone where a translation app was running.

"Ok, so let me get this straight," Alvin paused, collecting his thoughts. "Your friend here came aboard our vessel to see if there would be anything worth stealing. And then he planned to let the pirates know. But now he's telling us this because he is having second thoughts about working with pirates. Is that about right?"

"Yes, that is it," Camilla said.

Alvin and Joyce exchanged an uneasy look.

"Camilla, I need to ask… Do you believe him?" Alvin asked.

Camilla thought for a moment, glanced at Luis, and nodded. "I do."

"How long have you known each other?" Joyce asked.

"Many years. But we haven't seen each other in a long time. I don't believe he is crazy. If he says there is a threat, I think so."

"Here's what we'll do," Alvin said finally. "I'll inform the overseers and the captain. I'll make sure the night watchmen keep an eye out. As you know, they've got lights on deck at all hours of the night. If anyone even attempts to get close and board, I assure you they'll know about it," Alvin reassured.

"Luis says the men are armed. And he thinks they may be working with other pirates in the area," Camilla countered.

"I understand, Camilla," Alvin said calmly. "There are thousands of pirate vessels in these waters. I'm sure many have attempted to attack our ships, but so far there have been no reports of injuries. If they ever do make it aboard, we'll meet their demands as best we can and keep on our way. At this point I'm sure they're only after food and water. We can help with that."

Camilla nodded appreciatively, then added: "Luis also believes they may want revenge."

"Revenge?"

"They said they would come and get him."

Alvin let out a sigh. This is where things could get dicey.

"Camilla. As you know, these vessels are for the protection of our brothers and sisters, and those who have heeded the call to flee with us. We do not provide protection for just anyone. Whatever dispute your friend has with those men, we will not get involved."

Luis spoke up suddenly, as if he somehow sensed where the conversation was headed.

"What did he say?" Alvin asked.

"He says he wants to come with us."

"And is that because it's safe here? And there's plenty of food and water?" Alvin asked. Joyce shot him a look.

"No," Camilla stated. "He says he believes that God is with us. He says he believes we are good people and he wants to go with us."

Ten minutes later, Alvin and Joyce parted ways with Luis. His general situation was explained to the housing overseer, and he was given a small cabin and a change of clothes. A Spanish speaking brother would be paired with him to oversee his studies and orient him with life aboard the ship.

"What do you think about him?" Joyce asked her husband as the two slipped into their cabin. It had been a hectic evening and they hadn't even had time for dinner. Joyce produced a small paper bag of fruit wedges and ham and cheese sandwiches and the couple plopped onto their bunks to eat.

Alvin mulled over the question as he chewed the first half of his sandwich. It was nearly midnight.

"Not the first we've seen of his type," he said finally.

"No?"

"There are all kinds of stories coming in from the other ships about people joining the evacuations. Even stories of stowaways, folks found curled up in crawlspaces and storage closets."

"No kidding."

Alvin shook his head.

"But a pirate? Surely that's a first," Joyce said.

"Hard to say, but it wouldn't surprise me if there were others. I keep thinking of the Egyptians when the Hebrews left Egypt. Exodus says that many tagged along with them. They could see that the true God was with Moses and his people, and that their gods had been powerless to protect them. It only makes sense that people would come to the same conclusion now, regardless of their background."

"I wonder if we'll have enough space when we arrive, then," Joyce said, frowning.

"I'm sure it'll be fine. Everything will be taken care of."

Joyce pondered her future quietly for a few moments before finishing her meager meal.

"Something I wanted to ask you," Alvin said suddenly.

"Sure," replied Joyce.

"How well do you know Camilla?"

Joyce blinked a few times, a blank look on her face. "We've been working together for a week or so... She's a diligent worker, seems like a solid sister. Why?"

"Just got a weird feeling tonight with the two of them. She married?"

Joyce shook her head. "No, single."

"Huh. She say what her relationship with Luis was, previously?"

"Not specifically. Just that they were friends years ago."

"Right. Think you could ask her about that tomorrow?"

"I can try. Why?"

"It'd just be nice to have the full picture. As you know, we're happy to have newcomers, but we need to be cautious. Our dedicated brothers and sisters come first."

"You think he could have ulterior motives."

"I want to rule the option out if possible, yes."

"I'll ask. Also, what about those other pirates Luis was talking about? Is there a plan in place for something like that happening?"

"I'll let the brothers in the security department know about it, but they're already keeping a sharp eye out. They patrol the decks twenty-four hours, rain or shine. And those bright deck lights scare away most would-be pirates. I'm not too worried."

"Well, then I'm not either," Joyce said, managing a confident smile in spite of her exhaustion. She could feel her eyelids growing heavier by the minute. She changed into her sleeping clothes and walked over to a basin to brush her teeth and prepare for bed.

"If it makes you feel any safer, it seems we also have a protector out here on these waters," Alvin said. Joyce turned to raise her eyebrows at him.

She spat the toothpaste into the basin. "A protector?"

Alvin nodded. "I don't know the full story, but apparently one of our ships offered aid to a Coast Guard vessel months ago. Ever since then the vessel has been patrolling these waters keeping our brothers safe."

"A Coast Guard ship? How strange," Joyce said, slipping into her bed. She thought she heard Alvin say something in response, but she was already drifting off to sleep.

***

Chief Petty Officer Miranda Sachs sat on the bow of the Coast Guard cutter, a wool blanket wrapped tight over her shoulders. She closed her eyes and felt the spray of the sea mist her face. And she tried to forget. Their months at sea had been painful and tragic. It had begun with the massacre at the harbor and had only continued to spiral out of her control as the weeks and months passed.

Most of the crew had abandoned their post by now, and Miranda didn't blame them. She knew they thought she'd lost her mind; she knew what they said behind closed doors. Perhaps they were right; perhaps she'd lost her way and carried with her only the memory of what she was fighting for.

When the crew finally cornered her and demanded that she turn the vessel around and return to Fort Lauderdale, she refused. She barely escaped with her life in the scuffle that ensued, something that could not be said for two of the women who attacked her. In the end, she maintained control of the ship and forced the mutinous crew off of her ship when the next shore was spotted, an island not far from Costa Rica.

Now it was just Miranda and Damon Valdez, her first mate, as if designations and rank meant anything anymore. Miranda sipped instant coffee from the thermos between her knees and watched as the sun climbed over the horizon. At least there was still a mission. At least there was still a reason to be out here.

"How far behind them are we?" Miranda asked. The footsteps approaching from behind her could only belong to Damon.

"About twelve nautical miles," he replied.

"Anything suspicious on the radar or radio?"

"Not that I picked up. But, you know, it's hard to monitor everything and steer the ship. A cutter wasn't designed to be driven by a single person."

Miranda said nothing as she finished her morning cup of coffee and stood. The blanket fell to her feet and was nearly carried by a breeze off the side of the ship before Damon stopped it with his boot. He bundled it up in his arms and cast a displeased look at the woman for her carelessness, but she missed it.

Miranda brushed past the younger man as she climbed the stairway to the pilothouse. She pulled herself into the captain's chair and started scanning VHF frequencies while Damon fetched breakfast from the galley. If there was a silver lining to the disappearance of the rest of the crew, it was that their rations had stretched a little farther. Damon returned ten minutes later with a defrosted bagel and more coffee. He set them on the console beside Miranda and sat.

"Permission to speak freely, Captain?" he asked. Miranda cast him a sidelong glance and snickered.

"It's only the two of us, Damon. You're free to say whatever's on your mind."

"Okay then," Damon said, taking a deep breath to steel himself. Miranda swiveled to face him. "What's our plan out here?"

"My plan?"

"I mean, how long are you planning to keep this up? Sailing around aimlessly, looking for pirates and trying to stop them... We can't do this forever."

Miranda gave the younger man a long, hard stare before answering. "You joined the Coast Guard pretty young, right?" she asked.

"Twenty one, straight outta college."

"And why did you think this was your calling?"

"Same as anyone. Serve and protect."

Miranda shrugged, as if he'd answered his own question.

"Ok. I understand that, but we can't survive out here forever like this. We've been lucky the last few times—the pirates we caught just happened to be transporting fuel, but that's not gonna happen again. We're already taking our chances out here."

"You're saying you want to head back to Lauderdale?"

"I'm saying I don't want to die a vigilante."

"There are worse deaths. One of them is probably waiting for us back in Florida."

"How can you be so sure?"

"No detectable radio signals from our old base, for one. Nor any commercial signals, for that matter. In all the months we've been at sea, the only broadcasts we've received from back home were automated emergency signals. That's evidence enough that all is not well."

"We have received other broadcasts, though."

"I'm not counting those," Miranda said stubbornly.

"And why's that?"

"Because they're lying to us, Damon. The Witnesses had nothing to do with the terrorist attacks and you know it. The things the government is claiming about them... Those are the kinds of things that lead to genocide, and I've had enough killing to last a lifetime. I won't fire on civilians again."

"That didn't stop you from following orders the last time. You lied to the people on that rig," Damon said quietly.

"A decision that I regret. I won't interfere with these people again. I saw more humanity and kindness on that rig than I thought possible in these times. I ever tell you about my time stationed in Texas?"

Damon shook his head.

"Corpus Christi. Coast Guard Sector-slash-Air Station. Lot of our work was patrolling the gulf looking for people trying to illegally cross from Mexico. You wouldn't believe the stuff I saw. Little kids—not even old enough to be in kindergarten—burnt to a crisp in their mothers' arms from the midday sun. Old people dying of heatstroke.

"A lot of those rafts would be sent out, the runners knowing full well that the conditions weren't suited for the weak and the sick. But that didn't stop them from selling those tickets. Some of those people paid just a few hundred for a seat on those rafts. Three hundred bucks. That's how much a life was worth to those men.

238

"But that wasn't even the worst of it. The worst was the ones we caught trafficking girls. Girls young enough to still be in elementary school, sometimes. Who knows where they came from, or if they ever got back. I liked to hope that their families weren't the ones who sold them off to the traffickers, because if so, we weren't doing them any favors by sending them home. Those faces, Damon… Those eyes… They'll forever be seared into my brain.

"Human trafficking thugs, violent drug runners, monsters who'd kill anyone who tried to get in their way without batting an eye… I've seen it all out here. After a while, you start to suspect there's no more good in the world, that we're all truly screwed. You wonder if any of it is worth fighting for."

"Is it?" Damon asked.

"Those people make me think it is. Maybe in a different life I would've been one of them. I don't know. Whatever the case, they showed me we still have a purpose out here. You wanted that uniform, Damon. You wanted to serve and protect. Well, this is your opportunity. You'd better take advantage of it before the world burns."

Damon had no response. Miranda had a point. Had it not been for the Witnesses' kindness, the infection in his leg would've only gotten worse. In all likelihood, he'd now be an amputee. That at least counted for something.

A sound from the console grabbed their attention. The VHF was picking up a signal. Miranda leaned forward and cranked up the volume.

"¿Están ahí?" asked a man's voice. Miranda glanced at Damon for a translation.

"He's asking if someone is there," Damon said. A second voice responded. The message had been received. The first man rattled something off quickly in Spanish. Damon frowned and looked slowly over at Miranda.

"What is it?"

"He said something about their plan backfiring. Their infiltrator betrayed them and now they're moving on to plan B. It sounds like they are preparing an attack."

***

It had been a difficult week for Peter Burton. Marcus' death,

239

while not unexpected, was nevertheless sudden and devastating. His absence left an indescribable hole in Peter's life. Who would he turn to for advice and support now that his close friend and mentor was gone? More excruciating still had been Marcus' funeral talk, a favor that Vivian had asked of Peter.

The service was held in one of the smaller open air halls not far from their housing unit. A cool evening breeze swept over the Namib as the sun set behind a crimson sky. There was so much beauty here, both in nature and in the hundreds of faces in the audience before him.

And yet Peter struggled through the discourse as he never had before, choking up frequently as powerful emotions and memories welled up from within. He could not stop thinking about the countless times his old friend had been there to support and encourage him, of all the lessons he'd learned through the years, of all the mistakes he would've doubtless made without Marcus' guidance.

Several times Peter found himself unable to continue, gripping the edges of the podium as he bit his lips to keep them from quivering uncontrollably. He knew there was joy to be found in this occasion, that Marcus' passing meant his successful endurance till death. He'd attained a nearly unfathomable reward, and perhaps he was even present there in spirit, watching with typical Marcus' amusement at the scene unfolding down on Earth. But even this did not bring him comfort. Peter finished the talk, returned to his seat beside Rachel, buried his face in his hands, and wept.

"Thank you, Peter," Vivian said once the service had finished. She sat beside the younger elder and placed a delicate, wrinkled hand on his shoulder.

"It was a disaster. You should've asked someone else," Peter said, shaking his head. The skin beneath his eyes was puffy and swollen and he wanted nothing more than to return to the quiet solitude of his apartment pod. Beside him, Vivian pulled a handkerchief from her purse and dabbed the wetness on his cheeks. He glanced up at the older woman and was surprised to see a smirk on her face.

"What?" Peter asked.

"Just thinking about something Marcus said shortly before he died," Vivian said, gazing down at the handkerchief. It had belonged to her husband.

"What did he say?"

"He said that your greatest strength was your love for others. 'Everyone has their shining qualities,' he said. 'Peter's is his love. He loves the friends with his whole heart.'" Vivian beamed at the younger man and placed a comforting arm around his shoulders.

"I don't know if it's enough," Peter said, shaking his head slowly. "Marcus had so much more to teach me. I wish I'd listened harder. I wish I'd asked more questions."

"We're all learning, Peter. Even after arriving here in Grunau I saw him growing. And I can only imagine now what he's learning…" Vivian trailed off, her gaze drifting out at the velvety sky.

"I wish I could be as strong as you," Peter said with a heavy sigh. "You were his wife and here I'm the one blubbering like a baby."

"I've had years to come to terms with things. It wasn't easy for me in the beginning either. I had to learn to cherish every moment we had together and be happy for the fact that an exciting new assignment was waiting for him, and that Jehovah would take care of me always. And now that he's gone, I feel that care and protection. Part of it was seeing you on stage tonight delivering that talk. I could see how difficult it was for you. But seeing how much you loved my husband was so comforting. I feel so safe here. So protected. Jehovah has answered my prayers."

"I'll have to try harder."

"You're doing plenty as it is, dear," Vivian reassured, but Peter was shaking his head.

"By the way," Vivian continued, pulling a small envelope from her purse and placing it in Peter's hands. "This is for you. It's from Marcus."

As the crowd dispersed after the service, Peter found himself wandering up into the hilly grove of trees where he and Marcus had last conversed. With no one to see him here, he didn't bother holding back the tears anymore. Instead they flowed freely down his cheeks and neck and below the loosened collar of his shirt. He didn't mind. It felt good, in a way.

At the top of the rocky outcropping, Peter sat in the exact spot he had before, gazing over at the empty space beside him, remembering clearly their last moments together. He pulled the envelope from his pocked and opened it.

Dearest Peter,

So this is finally it! As you read this, I'll be well into the next phase of my service to Jehovah. That old body with its creaks and groans and wrinkles will be no more—no more back pains, no more aching joints, and certainly no more heart problems! That which was corruptible will put on incorruptibility, as Paul would say. (Looking forward to meeting him, by the way! So many things to ask!)

I hope you're doing well. I know it'll take a little getting used to my not being there, but I'm confident that you'll manage. Never forget what a terrific wife in Rachel you have, and that you're surrounded by brothers and sisters who want you to succeed. You will be OK!

I've known you for years, Peter, and in that time I've seen a young man mature into a fine Christian shepherd. You may be young, but never let that deter you. You successfully helped so many in our congregation over the years!

When Eleanor Blum's husband passed away, you were the first one there to console her. When Angelica was going through the divorce, it was always you and Rachel first in line to take her meals and offer comfort and support. Evan looks up to you like the father he never had. And when Ted was first appointed as a ministerial servant and then as an elder, you were the one to take him under your wing and train him, despite being only a few years older than him.

But I'm especially thankful that you've always been there for Vivian and I. After the heart attack it was you and Vivian whom I saw first when I opened my eyes. You do so much for so many, Peter, and I know you will continue to serve selflessly down to the end.

I'm on the train to Grunau as I write this. It's early in the morning, and we've stopped on the tracks. I'm sure you'll recall this morning. You're curled up on the floor next to the others, your arms outstretched as if even in sleep, you'll be ready at a moment's notice to come to their aid—just the Peter I know and love!

It has been an honor to serve with you. I will never forget our many days spent in service, our dinners together, and our beers sipped out on your back porch while we chatted late into the evening. Nothing can take those cherished memories from me!

Do not be sad, Peter. I've conquered the world, and victory for you is right around the corner. Stay awake, stand firm, grow mighty! (1 Cor 16:13, 14, 1 John 5:4)

-With the warmest affection,
Your brother, Marcus K.

Peter carefully folded the letter, placed it back in its envelope, and gazed down at the sea of glowing lights in the valley. He gazed up at the stars in wonder—the vast Milky Way winking down at him—and prayed.

As always, Jehovah had given him just what he needed.

CHAPTER 21

It had been a long time since Claire Aberdeen had felt this happy. The labor was tiring but rewarding, nothing like the hours spent in lecture halls listening to teachers drone on about the Renaissance and wondering how any of it would impact her own life. She'd been taught to question everything; as a result, nothing made sense. She thought she'd find freedom by following Alexis, but had only ended up in a new kind of prison. Who could've known what the following weeks and months would bring? It was incredible how one thing had led to another. Jehovah had been watching out for her after all, and now here she was, wiping the deck and railings of *The Chariot* clean as they sailed for Africa.

Africa! Of all the places in the world! It was a difficult idea to wrap her mind around, but in the end it didn't really matter. The fact was that she'd soon be reunited with her sister Rachel and brother-in-law, Peter. She had so much to apologize for. What she'd put them through over the last couple of years...

"How're you holding up?" asked a familiar voice from over her shoulder. Claire turned to see Alvin standing over her, a cool bottle of water in his outstretched hand. She took the water and thanked him.

"Doing fine. I was just thinking how this beats my old life."

Alvin crouched beside the young sister and took the rag from her hands. He dipped it into the cleaning solution and wrung it out. "How are you feeling about things?" he asked as he began wiping the salt encrusted railing, giving her a break.

"It gets a little easier each day," Claire said quietly, looking out over the water. "I still feel bad about what I did... I don't know if I'll ever completely forgive myself."

"Guilt can be a powerful motivator for keeping on the strait and narrow," Alvin said without looking up. "Just don't let it get out of hand. Remember that what counts is the future, not the past."

"Thanks, I'll try to remember that," Claire said. Alvin grunted in acknowledgement, a sound that made Claire smile. It'd taken time, but the two had grown on each other. In some ways, he even reminded her of Brother Kelly from her old congregation back in California, though Alvin was perhaps a little rougher around the edges.

"You know, you really oughta be wearing gloves," Claire chided gently. Alvin looked up and frowned.

"I'll be. Nearly fifty-seven years old and women are still telling me how to clean."

Claire laughed, and Alvin joined her. He settled his gaze on the young sister before her and gave his head a slight shake.

"What is it?" Claire asked.

"Oh, nothing. Just that look you just had in your eye. Brought back old memories."

"What memories?"

Alvin paused, gazed out at sea, and took a deep breath. "Years ago, Joyce and I were parents. Our daughter's name was Jasmin. She would've been about your age, come to think of it."

"What happened?" Claire asked carefully.

"Cancer," Alvin said flatly. "It ate up her tiny little body without any kind of mercy. She was gone in less than a year."

Claire reached out a hand to touch Alvin's arm. "I'm so sorry."

"You know, for years I couldn't even say her name. Couldn't look at the pictures of her around the house that Joyce just refused to take down. It was too much for me. Too painful. It's been almost twenty years since we lost her, but not a day goes by that I don't think of the time we had together, her little voice, or that look she'd get in her eye when she was up to something." Alvin glanced into Claire's eyes and pointed a finger at her. "That same look you've got."

"I can't wait to meet her," Claire said softly.

"I'm sure you two will have plenty to talk about," he chuckled.

Claire stood at the railing and stretched her back and arms, staring out at the vast sea, when something in the distance caught her eye. Several miles out, two white streaks stood out on the water. They were the foamy tails of speedboats racing towards them.

"Our brothers?" Claire asked, looking to Alvin for

confirmation. He turned to look and shook his head slowly, protectively stepping forward between the girl and the bulwark.

"Claire, I need you to go below decks right away. Tell the brothers we've got company, and they're coming in fast."

Claire was on her feet before Alvin had finished speaking. She skipped down the steps of the stairwell three at a time, nearly losing her balance and tumbling down the rest of the way before catching a handrail and steadying herself.

"Easy! Easy!" warned a stern voice at the landing below her. The brother's hands were held up and he wore the green vest of a safety overseer.

"We've got speedboats approaching outside and they don't look like ours!"

"Speedboats?"

"Brother Tucker told me to alert the overseers as quickly as possible. He said to be ready!"

The brother's expression changed at the mention of Alvin Tucker's name. He snatched the walkie talkie from his vest and immediately gave orders to the rest of the crew. In under a minute, brothers had emerged from the depths of the boat, leaping up the stairwells and ready to protect the passengers and crew of *The Chariot* at all costs.

Aboard the Coast Guard Cutter, Miranda was giving it all she could. Freed of its crew, its patrol boats, ammunition, and most of its supplies, her ship was achieving nearly forty-five knots—more than the chief petty officer had ever seen before. She slid open the windows of the pilothouse and let the fresh sea breeze clear out the stuffy cabin air.

"Feels good, doesn't it?" Miranda asked with a nod to Damon Valdez. He could only grimace in return. "Stop worrying. We'll be fine. Keep your eyes on the radar and keep us on their tails, would you?"

"Yes, sir," Damon said. He studied the digital screen before him and frowned. "We're looking at two vessels. They're moving fast."

"Good," Miranda said. "Keep me updated. My question is if they're armed or not."

"When have pirates ever not been armed?" Damon challenged.

"It happens. Some pirates carry toy guns painted to look like the real thing. Most crews who are attacked won't take their chances and rarely call the pirates' bluff."

"Somehow I suspect that if these guys can afford speedboats, they can afford firearms."

"They might be out of ammo. Could be they've been out here for a long time... like us," Miranda said, with what Damon thought looked like a crazed grin.

"With all due respect, that's a whole lot of optimism, sir," Damon said with a nearly imperceptible shake of his head. Though he trusted and respected his commanding officer, he found her actions difficult to rationalize. A sensible captain would've been trying to make contact with base or other US ships, not gallivanting across foreign waters in search of pirates.

"Whatever you're thinking over there, just remember your leg," Miranda cautioned.

"My leg?"

"That infection would've spread. They gave us antibiotics. Not only did you survive, but you kept your leg, and you owe that to them."

"They're slowing," Damon said, peering back into the screen. Miranda followed suit, easing back on the throttle. Through a pair of binoculars she could now make out the speedboats' apparent target––a several-hundred-foot barge cutting through the swells ahead. The wind was pushing twenty-eight knots, a near gale force that was creating choppy, uneven waves.

"That barge isn't stopping. I think they're pushing full throttle trying to keep those pirates from boarding. Looks like it's a Witness ship, too."

"How can you possibly tell?" Damon asked.

"They've got a bunch of guys in life vests and hard hats on deck with water hoses trying to keep the pirates away."

"Water hoses?"

"Yeah. It's a non-violent solution, but effective. It's hard enough to board a ship in high seas, but nearly impossible when you've got a water canon pointed in your face."

"What, the Witnesses don't believe in guns?" Damon asked.

"Nope. That was something they mentioned when we were aboard their rig. I didn't believe them at the time, but not once did I see any armed personnel, or holstered weapons, or mounted guns. Any other organization out here would've spent millions on a private army, but not these people. I'm telling you, Damon, they're something special."

"Special is one way of putting it," the younger man scoffed.

Miranda ignored him and leaned back into the throttle, her expression hard set.

"What are you doing?" Damon asked.

"We're going in."

"But why? You said they were holding their own just fine!" Damon insisted. Miranda just shook her head and ignored him.

***

Alvin struggled with the hose. The muscles in his arms were beginning to tire with the constant strain of trying to control the stream. The thick tubing in his hands was alive, thrashing this way and that as a stream of foamy water rocketed from its nozzle. Alvin wanted to call for someone else to replace him, but there wasn't anyone available. Every hand on deck was busy at some task, each station carefully prepared for just such an incident.

But not everything could be planned for; no one had expected the pirates to be so brazen as to board their ship in daylight, and no one had foreseen just how difficult it would be to maintain control of a hose after nearly fifteen minutes on a deck swaying in high seas, a task made all the more impossible by the slick, wet surface at the men's feet.

But then, all at once, it stopped. Alvin felt the hose go limp in his hands as the gush slowed to a trickle.

"What's happened to the water pressure?!" Alvin shouted, his hands and arms buzzing numbly. He was cold and nearly soaking wet. Behind him, brothers looked dumbfounded at one another until someone emerged from a stairwell.

"Pump is offline!" shouted the man.

"How long to get it fixed?" Alvin asked, but the man made a hopeless gesture before disappearing. Alvin let the dead hose drop to his feet and neared the bulwark of the barge, where a grim sight below awaited him. The two speedboats were now only a dozen meters away, and their occupants were armed.

"Keep away from the edge!" Alvin shouted at the brothers as a barrage of bullets pinged off of the metal bulwark. "Stay down! Stay down!" he ordered. The brothers hit the deck, lying prone on the soggy metal deck to keep from getting nicked by stray bullets.

Carefully, Alvin brought himself to a crouching position and began pushing the men towards the doorways leading below decks. They crawled, scampered, and otherwise made their way to the entrances. There was no sense now in trying to keep the pirates away, Alvin knew. Without the hoses it would only be a matter of time before they boarded, and he was sure they'd be angry and dangerous. It was a risk he couldn't take; there was only one option left.

"Below decks!" Alvin shouted. The throng of soaked brothers complied, huddling close to one another as they squeezed through the doors. Once everyone was down below, the hatches were locked and the disquieting wait began.

***

The USCG cutter sliced a path through the cold, choppy waters. Less than a mile ahead, the pair of pirate ships were inching closer to the barge. Without functioning water canons, it had become an easy target.

"We're running out of time," Miranda said, willing the Coast Guard ship to go faster.

"Surely they've got some defensive measures besides the fire hoses," Damon said.

"I wouldn't count on it," Miranda said. "But maybe we can help to distract them."

"What are you thinking?"

Miranda gave it a moment of contemplation. "Get on the LRAD. Make it unpleasant," Miranda said, tossing Damon the ear protection. He nodded and exited the pilothouse, where he climbed up to the bridge wing and started up the pivoting, disk-shaped device. Designed for crowd control during riots, the long-range acoustic device doubled as a powerful non-lethal weapon and was especially effective against aircraft and sea vessels. At peak performance, the device could disturb the equilibrium in the inner ear, leading to dizziness, headaches, and fainting.

At the LRAD's controls, Damon slipped on the ear protection, selected the frequency, and flipped the switch. He aimed the dish in the direction of the pirates. The effect was nearly immediate. Ahead of them, the speedboats broke from their course beside the Witnesses' barge. They zigzagged haphazardly over the waves like insects doused in pesticides. But then something unexpected happened—they turned and headed directly towards the cutter.

"Incoming!" Damon yelled down at the captain, who could just barely hear him through the opened pilothouse windows. She said nothing in response and maintained course. Damon gripped the LRAD on either side and pointed it like a cannon at the oncoming vessels, hoping he could pull off the trick a second time. Instead, the boats appeared to be speeding up.

***

Rafael was furious. He was drenched, cold, and nowhere closer to boarding the ship and reaping his spoils. And now this! An American Coast Guard ship! And so far outside of its jurisdiction that it was almost laughable! And with some confounding sonar weapon that was sending waves of vibration through his skull and chest. He could hardly walk, let alone think straight.

He struggled his way back into the cockpit of their speedboat, the automatic weapon still slung over his shoulder. He located a latched plastic case under a bench beside his brother in the cockpit and began rifling through its contents.

"We need to disable that thing, whatever it is," Stefan yelled above the deafening thuds of the LRAD. Rafael said nothing. He removed a couple of small black items from the case and stuffed them into his jacket pockets.

"What do you think you're doing?" Stefan objected, glaring at the grenades in his younger brother's hands.

"No more games. I will teach these people a lesson. They will learn not to stand up to Rafael Sosa."

"You have any idea what a grenade does to a ship full of fuel?"

"I know exactly what it does," Rafael said coldly. "It completely destroys it."

"You're willing to wage war on an American military vessel?"

"If the stories we've heard about America are true, there will be no one to retaliate. Besides, that ship is far beyond its boundaries. I say it's fair game."

Stefan thought over his brother's proposition for a long moment, a difficult task with the persistent ringing in his skull. The fillings in his teeth stung.

"Fine. But you'd better not miss."

Rafael said nothing as he stormed back out of the cockpit and prepared himself to face off with the USCG cutter.

***

"Look alive, they're almost on us!" Damon yelled at Miranda as he lunged back into the pilothouse.

"Yes, I see that," Miranda said with unusual calm.

"And? What's your plan?" asked the younger man, frantic.

"Let them come. Better for them to waste their time trying to fight us than going after that barge."

Damon could only shake his head.

"We're much faster, much more maneuverable," Miranda was explaining.

"And out of ammunition, Miranda. If they try to board…"

"I'm well aware, Damon. I say let them try."

Damon grit his teeth together in frustration and left Chief Petty Officer Miranda Sachs at the helm by herself. Maybe she didn't mind dying this way, but he certainly did. He was just twenty-nine years old. Feelings of regret filled him: his decision to join the academy, his decision to enlist with the Coast Guard, and most notably his decision to stick by his commanding officer when he knew full well she was not fit to serve. He'd had a chance and he'd given it up and now he would suffer the consequences.

Still, Damon Valdez was loyal—perhaps to a fault—and mutiny had never been an option. If he had to go down, he'd do it fighting. Back in his quarters, he rifled through his drawers for the last loaded firearm on the ship, holstered it, and returned to the bridge just as the speed boats made their first pass. As they roared past, Damon saw the bright flashes of the pirates' guns. He drew his weapon but thought better of using it now. He was down to his last clip; every shot needed to count.

The speedboats flew past them, the roar of their supercharged engines filling the air. Damon watched as they sliced curves in the seas and looped back for a second pass. It was only a matter of time, Damon knew, before they caused irreparable damage to the cutter or succeeded in boarding. He had to think of something.

CHAPTER 22

"Did you see that?" Rafael yelled at his brother as he leaned into one of the speedboat's cockpit windows. He was standing on the outer deck, the rifle still flung over his shoulder, like a madman in an action film. Stefan couldn't keep from grinning.

"See what?"

"That Coast Guard ship looked empty! I only saw a single officer aboard her deck. I don't even think they fired off a single shot at us!"

"What are you thinking?" Stefan asked.

Rafael pulled out one of the explosives from his vest pocket. His grin was devilish. Stefan said nothing. The plan still worried him. If the grenade missed its mark and bounced back, it would be a big problem. Even a small crack in their boat's fiberglass hull could put them underwater in a matter of hours. If, on the other hand, he succeeded, the Coast Guard ship would be rendered inert. Perhaps they could even board her and salvage whatever supplies she was carrying once they'd dealt with the officers.

"It's the only way," Rafael said as if reading his brother's thoughts. "Just get me near the transom. It'll be an easy toss."

Stefan thought it over for another moment and nodded silently. He radioed the plan to the other pirate speedboat which had fallen into line behind them. Stefan pushed back into the throttle and felt the bow of their speedboat lift into the air with the acceleration.

***

"They're armed, Miranda, and they're returning for a second pass," Damon shouted up from the deck of the cutter. The LRAD had been switched off; it was useless trying to hone in on such a fast moving target at variable distances. Plus, Damon didn't want to be standing upright, fully exposed, when there were pirates with guns trying to shoot at him.

"Let them come," Miranda repeated, eyes glued to the approaching dot on the radar before her.

"I need to know that you have some sort of plan," Damon.

"Trust me," his commanding officer said.

"I do. But this feels like a suicide mission."

"If that's what it takes, then so be it," Miranda said. Damon could hardly believe his ears.

"This isn't what I signed up for, Captain. I want to go home."

"Home?" Miranda asked, scoffing. "There is no 'home' anymore. It's all gone."

"You don't know that."

"Yes, I do," Miranda said softly. She reached into a drawer beside the console and removed a well worn notebook. She handed it to the young man. Damon took the book in his hands and began flipping through the pages. On them, Miranda had scribbled notes and call insignias. The details were disturbing—reports of fires and other disasters from areas ranging from the tip of the Florida Keys to Myrtle Beach and beyond. News became sparser as the locations went inland.

"Radio transmissions?" Damon asked.

Miranda nodded. "Every night I scan the airwaves and try to get the latest news. It was much more frequent at first. But now the broadcasts are few and far between. A lot of the HAM operators that were regularly broadcasting have gone silent. I hardly hear anyone anymore. They're all gone."

"Maybe they've all gone somewhere else—maybe there's some kind of safe house," Damon suggested, trying to convince himself.

"Those radio operators were mostly survivalists—guys who'd been preparing for an end of the world scenario with bunkers under their houses and huge shelters in their backyards. They were the only ones equipped to survive something like this, and there's no way they would've left willingly. So if they're gone…"

"What about other countries? Surely there's got to be someone left?" Damon said, struggling to cling to the last bit of hope he could think of, but Miranda was shaking her head.

"I haven't stumbled on a single non-American independent radio operator for weeks. The only ones using the airwaves are government entities, and it's all the same chatter."

"And what's that?"

"The same mission we were given: to bring the Witnesses back into their territories, presumably so they can be prosecuted and locked up. It's either that or talk of coordinating a big attack."

"An attack?"

Miranda nodded. "Something big in Southern Africa."

"Southern Africa... Isn't that where the Witnesses are headed?" Damon asked.

"It all fits together, doesn't it?" Miranda said quietly. "The governments of the world decided they didn't want religion around anymore, and somehow the Witnesses knew something big, something inexplicable and horrendous was coming. They got out in time, and their governments let them go. Now those same governments have changed their mind, and they're hell-bent on exacting their revenge."

Damon shuddered as he felt a chill go up his spine.

"What is it?" Miranda asked him.

"Just had this crazy flashback to Sunday school," Damon said strangely.

"Oh?"

"Were you a religious kid?" he asked. Miranda shook her head.

"I just recalled this story that the lady that taught our Sunday school class liked to tell us, about Moses leading the Israelites out of Egypt. Pharaoh let them go, but then he changed his mind. He sent the Egyptian army out after them, and it looked like there was no way out until God split the Red Sea. The Israelites crossed, but when the Egyptians went in after them, the sea collapsed back onto them, drowning them all."

The two fell silent. There was only the sound of the sea wind howling over the cutter's deck and in through the pilothouse window and the menacing roar of an approaching speedboat.

***

Rafael spotted no one on the aft deck of the USCG cutter. No officers in wraparound reflective sunglasses shouting commands into a bullhorn, no uniformed men and women pointing automatic weapons in their direction. It was almost too easy.

Stefan nudged the speedboat ever closer to the rear of the large, white and orange vessel. His eyes combed quickly over the surface, looking for a place to toss the grenade so that it wouldn't bounce right back. He found it at the rear of the ship, where a ramp once occupied by a patrol boat led up into a loading area beside a gantry crane. The pipes, walkways, and railings here would surely catch the small explosive, Rafael thought to himself. Turning back to look over his shoulder, he signaled to Stefan to bring them in closer.

***

Gazing out the pilothouse window through a pair of binoculars, Damon Valdez watched as the pirates' speedboat bounced through the waves. And he did not like what he was seeing.

"I think they are going to try to grenade us," Damon said in disbelief. He watched as one the pirates perched himself on the deck of speedboat. He clung to the railing precariously with one hand while holding the small black explosive in the other.

"Come again?"

"They've got grenades, and I think they're planning on using one on our ship."

Miranda reacted instantly, leaning into starboard, rapidly putting distance between themselves and the smaller vessel.

"It's no use," Damon said moments later, watching as the smaller, more agile boat trailed them effortlessly across the water. "We're far too big to evade them."

What few options were at their disposal flashed quickly through Miranda's head. The possibilities were not encouraging. Suddenly, a large blast erupted from the rear of their ship. Miranda knew by the sound that it had not been a direct hit, but it was close. Damon was hyperventilating at the window.

"That was a near miss, Captain. The grenade bounced off a railing and exploded in the water."

"Damon, you might want to hold on to something," Miranda said, her mind made up. Beside her, the younger man took his seat obediently.

Miranda pressed her eyes tightly together, gripped the wheel between her hands, and banked hard in the direction of the speedboat.

***

"I thought you said you could make that throw," Stefan

256

growled out the window of the cockpit, where his brother was still perched outside.

"Not as easy as it looks," Rafael shouted back.

"Well, you'd better get it soon. They will have heard that explosion. And we don't have many grenades to spare."

"I will not miss again," Rafael vowed. He pulled a second grenade from his vest. It was a precarious maneuver, trying this on the bow of a speedboat rocketing through the waves, but he didn't mind it. It made him feel like a movie action hero. He grinned at his little fantasy, pulled the grenade towards his face, and bit down on the metal pin. The Coast Guard ship before him would soon be in flames and tatters, and before long would be sinking to the ocean floor, a thought that brought Rafael much satisfaction.

He pulled the grenade free of the pin and whipped the small explosive into the air. It arced high, and for a brief moment he thought it would again miss its target, but it did not. The grenade bounced directly where he had intended it to, but there was a problem.

The cutter was turning hard to port, quickly closing the distance between the two vessels. Rafael turned to scream some sort of warning to his brother, but it was too late. The steel wall of the cutter's hull closed in on them like a speeding train. Deafening cracks and pops split the air as the fiberglass frame of the Sosas' speedboat cracked and shattered. The side of their boat disintegrated like a plastic toy smashed by a hammer as a slanted wall of steel pushed them down under its wake, where the force of the water did the rest of the work, tearing the small ship apart.

In another split second, a section of aluminum railing came free of its screws, yanking away with part of the speedboat's hull. At its end, a curved bit of metal whipped in the air past Rafael, snagging the strap of the rifle still slung over his neck. Screaming, Rafael was flung with the destroyed section of ship and his gun overboard and into a raging sea.

Stefan did not last much longer. As his beloved speedboat was torn to pieces at his feet, his final sight would be falling through the shattered deck into the cabin below, and witnessing a chaotic scene of flying bits of glass and plastic, and of course, his Louisiana alligator trophy, whose black, dead eyes seemed now to be laughing at him.

The second pirate ship did not stick around. Seeing their boss' boat shredded apart by the cutter's hull, the men turned away and sped off.

***

The sound of rending metal and fiberglass was tremendous, even from their positions within the pilothouse. The Coast Guard cutter rumbled and groaned with the collision, but Miranda was not overly concerned. So long as she managed to avoid any debris getting caught in their propellers, they would live to see another day. She quickly pulled the wheel back to starboard, the horizon before them tilting at an unnatural angle as they sharply changed course.

Chief Petty Officer Miranda Sachs turned to grin victoriously at Damon. "See?" she said confidently. "I told you I had a pl—"

But she was cut off by a new noise, one that put ice in her blood. It was an explosion, and it had come from within their own ship.

"What was that?!" the captain demanded.

"I… I don't know…" Damon said, racing back to his position at the rear pilothouse window, where a black plume of smoke was rising steadily into the air. At the ship's helm, Miranda felt the engines die. She slammed her hands into the console.

"Not good. Not good. Not good," she kept repeating, rising from the console and leaping down the stairwells to check the damage. Within a minute, both she and Damon Valdez found themselves staring in horror at the sight before them: the aft section of their ship was a blackened, mangled mess. The outer deck had been destroyed, and the engines below had taken irreparable damage. But what was much worse was the fire.

It did not take them long to realize that the second grenade had ignited an oil drum kept on deck to service patrol boats. The explosion had destroyed the drum and sent fiery, black oil onto every imaginable surface. Miranda and Damon ran for fire extinguishers and did their best to battle the blaze, but it hardly mattered. For beneath their feet, in unseen compartments far below decks, their collision with the speedboat and subsequent damage from the blast had weakened the steel joints. They were taking on water, and fast.

It took them nearly an hour to extinguish the burning oil, a task that had required every fire extinguisher available. Emptied red tanks were littered about their feet, and before them stood the jagged, smoldering remains of what was once their proud Coast Guard cutter. But Miranda was too exhausted to cry. Whatever happened next, she would accept it. She glanced at her side and realized all at once that the water level had risen drastically.

"We're sinking," she said to Damon, in a voice that sounded more curious than horrified. Damon stood, panicking, and ran below decks. When he returned, he was wet from the waist down. His face was pale and hopeless. He tried to open his mouth to say something, but there were no words. Everything that had piled up on his shoulders over the last few months had come to this. Nothing had mattered, he realized.

"Sit with me," Miranda said quietly. Damon relented numbly, taking a seat beside his captain. The two gazed off into the horizon, where the barge they'd managed to protect was only a faint dot receding into nothingness.

"I keep thinking about that Bible story you mentioned earlier," Miranda said.

"I can't get it out of my head, either," Damon said. "Do you believe in God?" he asked.

"I think I do. And I think he's with His people. And if that's the case, then He saw what we did here today."

Miranda broke her gaze from the horizon and lifted her eyes towards the setting sun.

"Maybe He will remember the good we did and not just the bad," Miranda said, a single tear streaking down her face. Damon nodded slowly.

"Yeah. Maybe."

***

It had been a strange day. The attackers that had arrived so suddenly, nearly sending *The Chariot* into a complete panic, had disappeared just as quickly, never to be seen again. As a precautionary measure, the brothers had kept the hatches sealed until late that night, when they could confirm that no other unknown ships had surrounded them.

"And no one knows what happened to them?" Joyce asked Alvin as the two prepared for bed that night. She slipped into her nightwear as she peeked cautiously out the porthole at a violet colored ocean.

"Only guesses," Alvin said, yawning as he slipped between the sheets into his bunk.

"I heard someone in the infirmary talking about a strange noise. They said it sounded like a low hum."

"Yep. We all heard it. The entire outer hull of the ship was vibrating. It was strange."

"You don't suppose…" Joyce said, trailing off.

"What?"

"Well, you know… Could it have been an angel scaring them off?" Joyce blurted, feeling slightly embarrassed at the suggestion.

"It's possible, I suppose."

"Yeah?"

"Sure. I mean, you're certainly not the first to mention it."

"Oh?"

"A few others suggested it when we first heard the sound. It was eerie, I'll give you that. That, coupled with the fact that after it started, the speedboats simply turned right around and disappeared, is admittedly a bit suspicious. But who knows? And what difference does it make, really? One way or the other, the result is the same."

"But I mean, what are the other possibilities? If it wasn't something supernatural, what option would that leave?"

"Well, there's still that Coast Guard ship somewhere out there."

"Well, that even makes *less* sense to me," Joyce objected. "Why would a military vessel be helping us? Aren't they supposed to be attacking us?"

"Jehovah can use our enemies to destroy one another. Just look at what happened to the Ammonites and the Moabites in Seir."

Joyce shook her head slowly with a blank look.

Alvin shrugged. "Perhaps you have some reading up to do."

Joyce pulled her husband's iPad from its charging station on a bedside table and thumbed through the app to the *Insight* book. She turned to ask her husband how to spell *Seir*, but by then it was too late. He was already fast asleep.

The Chariot trudged on through the dark sea.

PART III.

CHAPTER 23

Chad had never seen anything like it before. Stretched out on the horizon before him as far as the eye could see stood a vast battalion of warships, everything from aircraft carriers to destroyers, battle cruisers to frigates. Above them, fighter jets roared, arcing through the air in tight, precise formations. Military choppers ferried officials from the deck of one vessel to another as plans and alliances were built and solidified. Over the loudspeakers, national anthems blared as soldiers marched and sang. The few families of these forces who'd been brought aboard watched supportively from the sidelines, some caught up in tears as the songs came to their triumphant climaxes. High above the tower of the aircraft carrier, a giant American flag swayed in the wind. Other massive flags just like it streamed atop other ships in the fleet.

Everyone was here: Chad spotted flags from China and Japan, South Korea, Taiwan, Mexico, and Canada. Never before had world governments seemed so unified and determined in a single purpose. It was a new dawn, and Chad was there to welcome it. He slipped on his aviators and red, white, and blue baseball cap and grinned to himself.

He'd never been a patriot; he saw nationalism for what it was––a tool to control the weak-minded masses, just another cog in the propaganda machine. Of course, he suspected that the governments and politicians that ran the world knew this as well. Everyone had an agenda, and if he had to blend into this scene to find his place among this new world order, he would become a chameleon.

Chad Harkett opened his mouth wide, filled his lungs with air, and joined along heartily as the next song blared from the speakers. He placed his hand over his heart and gazed up at the giant, waving flag, wondering to himself just how many of ol' Union Jack's stars would need to removed once the dust settled.

Much of the land would be in ruins, of course, but with so

many millions dead there would be much for the taking. If he played his cards right, he could take his pick of whatever remained. He'd been a king of his industry in the past, and deep down he knew he would be king once again.

King Harkett, Chad thought to himself, singing all the louder as the song swelled to its finale. Beside him, Chad was surprised to find Driscoll standing there. They hadn't talked much since their departure from Hunters Point a month before. Driscoll had been busy, and Chad had spent the weeks familiarizing himself with the carrier, learning the military lingo, and keeping his ear to the ground. He knew they were only a week or so away from making landfall in Africa.

"Harkett," Driscoll said with a nod. There was an eager look in his eye.

"Afternoon, sir," Chad replied. "Any news?"

Driscoll nodded. "Walk with me."

Chad followed the man into the tower of the aircraft carrier, where a personnel elevator took them several stories below deck. From there they walked down a long grey corridor to a dark room. A man in military regalia stood under a single light source as he motioned to a large screen at his side. It showed a black and white satellite image. Before him sat dozens of uniformed men and women.

"As you can see," said the man in a booming voice, "a total of five colonies are up and running, with an estimated eight million residents and counting."

The crowd murmured, shifting uneasily in their seats.

"Due to the geography, we plan on dividing our attack into three separate strike forces. Team Anvil, headed by a joint task force of American and British troops, will be in charge of the attack on the largest colony, which we know to be the capital, a city called Bismarck, as well as the southernmost colony, which they call Grunau. We have high-altitude drones on twenty-four hour surveillance and will be keeping a close eye on the situation as we approach.

"We are not expecting much resistance. Our arrival there is imminent, and they probably know it. Up till now they appear to have been a step ahead of us, but their luck won't last forever.

"The first stage of our mission will be a land deployment of a combined two hundred thousand troops. We will make landfall here," said the man, pointing to a new image. On the screen, an eerie, otherworldly desert cliff dropped suddenly into a dark blue sea covered in a blanket of mist. Unnervingly, several old shipwrecks could be seen littering the sandy shores.

"From here, troops will move inland, following the train tracks left by the Witnesses themselves. If anyone's unlucky enough to be on one of the incoming trains from the cities, they'll be fair game for our soldiers, and you can bet we'll be commandeering that train," the man grinned devilishly with a low chuckle. The audience followed suit.

"The train tracks branch off here in the canyons," said the man, motioning to a new slide. "From this point our forces divide into two teams—one headed to Bismarck and the other to Grunau. Much of the land here is situated in a low-lying basin surrounded by hills and canyon cliffs. We're assuming they did this to put them closer to the riverbed, but strategically it's suicide. They've put themselves in a compromising situation and they'll pay for it. The plan is for our troops to wait just outside the cities. The heavy lifting here will be done by our Navy F-16s. They'll flatten the colonies' key facilities before our troops head in on foot."

"I want to stress here that although the terrain isn't ideal, it's about the only disadvantage we're looking at. This is an easy victory. So get in, get the job done, and get out. You'll be home before you know it, and you can bet you'll get the hero's welcome."

The crowd burst into animated conversation as soon as the debriefing had finished. The air was supercharged with excitement. A new dawn was on the horizon, and these men and women were to be its harbingers.

***

Stacy's eyes stung with the bright, orange light streaming in through the windows. She felt pressure at the back of her head, but there was no pain. More than anything, she felt stiff all over. Stiff and thirsty. Very thirsty. Where was she?

Stacy gazed at the room around her, gathering the details slowly as her mind tried to work it out. She looked down at her hands, two featureless, bandaged stumps. She could feel nothing underneath the cloth, but perhaps that was for the best. She did not at first recognize the woman who appeared at her side. The face was still blurry as her vision adjusted after months of disuse.

"Stacy, is that you?" said the blurry head. Stacy parted her lips to speak, but a stinging pain spread over the corners of her lips. She could feel tiny tears forming in the dry, papery skin.

"No no, don't talk, dear," the woman said, gently placing a hand on her shoulder. She wet a towel and gently dabbed Stacy's face and lips. The moisture was revitalizing. Slowly, her vision began to clear.

"Joyce," she said in a soft, raspy voice, now recognizing the familiar face before her. "Where?" she struggled.

"We're aboard a giant barge called *The Chariot*. It's part of the convoy."

"The convoy?" Stacy asked, frowning.

"Our brothers and sisters. They found us on your sailboat after the accident," Joyce explained, glancing down sadly at Stacy's hands.

"How bad are they?" Stacy asked. Joyce shook her head.

"Second and third degree burns. Serious," Joyce said.

"I see."

"But the good news is that it's almost behind you. You can look forward to new hands on the other side, Stacy."

"How far are we?"

Joyce turned to gaze out the windows at the vast expanse of water beneath them. "The brothers said we'll be arriving in another couple of days."

"Africa."

"That's right. A new beginning awaits."

The two women were quiet as they watched a flock of seagulls outside the window. They had matched the speed of the large vessel and were peeking curiously at the passengers within.

"How long was I out for?" Stacy asked.

"It's been a while. Your system went into shock after the burns. We had to transfer you from one vessel to another. This is the third ship you've been on since the sailboat. We weren't able to save it, by the way. The flames had taken far too much of it. I'm afraid it's floating somewhere off—"

"You stayed with me the whole time?" Stacy asked quietly.

Joyce nodded. "Of course. You think I'd leave you?"

Joyce was surprised to see her friend's eyes redden and fill with tears. "I was so scared when we left Seattle, Joyce. I thought we were dead in those waters. No light, fuel running low, we were nearly out of food. When that fire started, I just knew it was over. I should've never made you leave that harbor with me. It was suicide."

Joyce brought the towel again to Stacy's face to wipe the tears away. "We both did regrettable things, Stacy. We should've never left the camp in the first place."

"You know what went through my mind, when that fire started on the boat?"

Joyce shook her head.

"That video from the convention a few years ago about Lot's wife. That look in the sister's eyes as she looked back and began to turn into a pillar of salt. That was me. I was the one who looked back."

Joyce lowered her head and drew a deep, labored breath. She had had the same recollection, and to this day it sent chills up her spine.

"We both looked back," she said quietly. "But what matters most is what we do going forward. We were given another chance, Stacy, and we can't mess this one up."

"I won't," Stacy said with a hard, determined look.

***

Dietrich gathered his wits as he marched up the winding driveway to the military complex perched atop the canyon walls just outside of Bismarck. A palisade surrounding the barbed wire fence had been constructed sometime since his last visit, and that was not the only recent addition. The complex appeared to be spilling over its own borders; Dietrich could tell from some distance that the initial boundaries had been moved generously outward to accommodate the steady influx of military vehicles and personnel. The brothers and sisters had remained calm so far, but the tension was beginning to take its toll, even for Dietrich Nash himself.

"Identification!" hollered a soldier at the gate, lifting a rifle to his sights as Dietrich rounded the bend in the road and came into view. With one hand still held high above his head, he carefully retrieved the badge he'd been given by Commander Ngoma on his last visit. The guards eyed it over suspiciously, flipping it over multiple times in their hands as if it might be faked. Finally, one soldier performed a pat-down while the other eyed the visitor suspiciously, weapon still held at the ready.

266

Dietrich was pushed through the gate and escorted to the Commander's quarters. It had changed considerably since Dietrich's last visit: what used to be a simple military tent had been replaced by a permanent wooden structure. A giant HD television with a curved screen stood on the far end in a nest of cables and wires. At another wall, an elaborate surround sound system appeared to have been hastily rigged up. Two bulky leather recliners sat in the center of the room facing the TV.

Ngoma entered the room with a jovial look at his guest and motioned around him. He raised his eyebrows, inviting Dietrich's appraisal.

"It's impressive," Dietrich relented. "Where'd it all come from?"

"Here and there, Mr. Nash," Ngoma said with a chuckle. "Whiskey?" he asked, pulling a decanter from a chilled electric cabinet.

"No thanks," said Dietrich. It was eleven o'clock in the morning.

The commander helped himself to a generous serving of alcohol and sat. Dietrich thought it looked more like a throne than a recliner. For a long moment, the only sounds heard in the spacious tent were the clinking of ice in Ngoma's glass and a chopper somewhere in the distance.

"My people have been watching your trains closely," Ngoma said finally. "It seems the traffic has slowed somewhat in the last week. Am I to assume that this means your colonies are nearly filled to capacity?"

Dietrich nodded cautiously. "Most of our brothers and sisters have already arrived."

"But there are more?"

"Some are still crossing the Atlantic, yes."

Ngoma smiled, closing his eyes and tilting back his head as he savored the expensive whiskey. "I have to give you and your people credit, Mr. Nash. I never imagined that such a feat could have been accomplished. When your people first submitted their proposal for using this land, no one believed that it could be done. More than ten million people living in the desert!"

"It wasn't done on our own power," Dietrich said tiredly.

"Meaning what?" Ngoma asked, pouring himself a second glass of whiskey.

267

"You know this land better than I, probably better than most of our own residents. It's been transformed, and not just by the building projects on the surface. Something greater is at work here. Rainfall this year is unprecedented. A healthy river flows where none existed in hundreds of years. The entire region is thriving. Less and less water is required from the towers."

"Your point?" Ngoma growled.

"My point is that our God, Jehovah, has had a hand in this project from the start, and he will continue to bless his people."

The commander scoffed derisively. "God is dead!"

"The false gods are dead. But not the true God. Nothing can kill him."

"I used to say the same! I always hated the churches, you know. Hated the witchdoctors, too. I used to fear the ones in our village when I was just a little boy, but I came to see them for what they were in the end. Charlatans and tricksters, all of them. But gods all the same. Gods that couldn't be killed, just as they couldn't be trusted. But then it all changed! Churches, gone! Witches and shamans, all gone! The first real miracle I've seen!" Ngoma laughed.

"It was foretold—" Dietrich began, but Ngoma held a hand in the air, halting him.

"They are *all* false gods, Mr. Nash. I do not care what color their skin is, what emblem they wear, what rites are used to worship them. They are dead to me, and soon they will be dead to the rest of the world."

Dietrich repressed his urge to say more. He was, after all, here for an entirely different purpose. "I wanted to ask about your drones," he finally said.

"Yes? What about them?"

"They've been… causing disturbances for our friends."

"Disturbances?" Ngoma asked, helping himself to a third glass.

"When you mentioned surveillance, I don't recall you mentioning that it would involve drones spying on our brothers and sisters."

"Is there a problem?" Ngoma asked.

"It is when they are in their private spaces when the drones show up, especially in their own apartments. It's a little unnerving, having a flying robot taking a video of you while you try to sleep, wouldn't you agree?"

"Surveillance is surveillance, Mr. Nash. How effective would

268

it be if it only happened on terms your people were comfortable with?"

"Then may I ask, in all these weeks of surveillance, have your men turned up any details that would incriminate us in what you accused us of?"

"I never accused! The Americans were the ones who accused you! And the British, and the Chinese, and all the rest of them!" Ngoma said, wagging a finger in the air. He was beginning to sway slightly and his eyelids were drooping. "I'm an enforcer and nothing more, Mr. Nash."

"All I'm asking for is a little propriety, sir," Dietrich said, sensing a lost battle. He turned as two armed guards entered. They saluted the commander and stood at attention.

"A call on the station satphone for you, sir," one of them said, glancing distrustfully at Ngoma's guest. The commander struggled to his feet.

"The guards will escort you back to the gate," Ngoma grumbled as he made his way unsteadily to the door. And without another word, he was gone. Dietrich quietly gathered his things and left.

***

It was nearly four AM and Chad found himself aimlessly wandering the endless maze of corridors deep in the bowels of the USS *Ronald Reagan*. He was not alone. It seemed that every other open space he passed was filled with either passengers, crew, or military personnel. Perhaps it was the excitement from the previous few days, the result of constant national rallies, that had everyone so wound up. Or perhaps there was something else.

Chad's mind wandered along with his feet. He grabbed a cup of stale coffee from a cart at one of the ship's sprawling galleys and sat. His thoughts went inexplicably back to California, back to his mansion in the hills of Palo Alto, back to the prestigious name he'd made for himself when names still meant something. There was no sadness for lost things, however. Instead, Chad felt a deep, dark rage roiling from within him. He wanted the old life and its wealth back, yes, but more than that he wanted revenge.

He wanted Thiago. Though it had been months since their last contact, Chad hadn't forgotten. And how could he—he'd sunk a hundred and fifty grand on the so-called professional and had nothing to show for it. The man had vanished without a trace. As Chad had learned so many times before, if you wanted something done, you had to do it yourself. Chad stood, emboldened by his anger, and tossed his half-emptied Styrofoam cup into a trash bin. Cold coffee splashed over its rim and onto the floor. A uniformed janitor yelled something unpleasant but Chad ignored him.

Back in his room, Chad decided to give Thiago's phone one final try. No one had picked up in weeks, but perhaps this time would be different. As unlikely as it seemed, there was always the possibility that Thiago had been forced to lay low for the entirety of his stay on the rigs. Either that or he'd been captured. But even if his captors were the ones to answer the phone, Chad was confident he could extract the information he needed.

Chad pulled the satellite phone from his backpack and sat heavily on his bunk. He dialed the number by memory and waited. It rang twice. Five times. Ten. Chad could feel his frustration reaching a boiling point. If he ever crossed paths with Thiago again, his revenge would start then and there, and it wouldn't be pretty.

On the fifteenth ring, Chad pulled the device from his head, his finger poised to end the call. But the ringing had stopped, and someone answered.

Chad recognized the voice immediately.

***

Overall, Evan Parry had enjoyed his time in Namibia. It wasn't anything like California, obviously, but it wasn't too bad, either. There were plenty of other kids to play with, and they were a whole lot nicer than the ones he used to go to school with. The animals, of course, were his favorite part. He'd been able to tag along with his mom once to help feed the baby baboons, and ever since then he'd been begging to let the overseers assign him a job with animal care. *Sorry, maybe when you're a little older*, she'd said. Mom's *usual* answer.

Evan huffed at the words echoing in his head and kicked off the sheets. It was an early Sunday morning and he was alone. Ever since they'd left America and stepped onto those boats, his mom had been spending more and more time with Ted. That wasn't a bad thing, really. Ted was cool and funny and Evan could tell that he made his mom happy. Like, really happy. Happier than she'd ever been with his dad, even.

Dad. Evan rolled over on his bunk and gazed out at the rising morning sun. He wondered what his dad was up to right now. Evan knew he wasn't a good father, or a good husband, and probably not much of a good man period, but it didn't change the fact that he was *Dad.* And Evan missed him.

The boy strolled into the kitchenette and rummaged through the cabinets, preparing himself a simple bowl of toasted oats. If there was one thing he really missed from home, it was definitely the food. He missed waking up late on Sunday mornings and having a big bowl of Cinnamon Toast Crunch and then sitting down for a morning of *SpongeBob* or *Gumball* before it was time to get ready for the afternoon meeting. As fun as the bonfires and the live music were here, nothing could compare to just curling up on the couch with a bowl of his favorite cereal and flipping on the TV. He missed it.

Evan washed breakfast down with a bottle of orange juice from their tiny refrigerator unit. He puttered around the small apartment aimlessly until he remembered his suitcase. He hadn't sifted much through the contents of his bag since their arrival in Grunau. In the beginning there'd been simply too much going on and they were rarely at home anyway. Evan crouched beside his narrow bed and reached below the bunk, pulling the hard shell suitcase out on its rolling wheels and zipping it open. There were mostly just clothes inside: sweaters and jackets and gloves he'd probably never use again. Evan stuck his hand beneath them and rifled around until he found it—a small, black device that he'd had with him since their time aboard the oil rig.

It was a phone, of course, though it didn't look at all like the slim, shiny rectangles everyone had in their pockets these days. It was made of a thick, heavy plastic, with colorful, rounded buttons and a black plastic antenna that could be extended from its top. Evan wasn't sure where it had come from; he'd only discovered it when he'd been hiding under their bed back on the rig, when that scary man had burst into their cabin and taken his mother away. Evan had run off down one of the corridors, only to come back to the cabin a few minutes later to find it empty. He hid in the crawlspace under the bed, something he'd always done when he felt anxious.

That's when Evan had first noticed the device wedged

between the wall and the bed, as if it had fallen there. Maybe it had belonged to the bad man; Evan wasn't sure. But he'd left it there and went with Peter and Rachel and forgot about it until days later, when his mom was found and he was able to move back into their cabin like normal. That's when he'd remembered the little black device and stuffed it into the bottom of his suitcase. He wasn't sure why; it just seemed like a cool thing to have. It made him feel like a super spy, like he was on some kind of top secret mission.

Evan turned the small phone over in his hands, tugging on the antenna and tapping the buttons playfully. The screen lit up, but it wasn't very colorful or bright. Evan pressed several of the numbered keys and pressed the call button; nothing happened.

He walked to the front door and peeked out the window, making sure his mom was nowhere to be seen. Then, leaning his back into the wall and slinking down into a crouching position, he narrowed his eyes and began glancing surreptitiously over his shoulders.

"Agent *E* here," he whispered into the device. He pressed it up against his ear, hearing an imagined response. "Yeah. I accept the mission. But it's gonna be *super* dangerous," he said, lowering himself onto his elbows and inching across the floor back towards the bed. "Yeah, yeah, copy that. Roger, sir," Evan said into the phone. "Over and out."

Then Evan Parry nearly jumped out of his skin. The phone dropped from his hands and tumbled onto the ground. It was ringing.

CHAPTER 24

"Evan? *Evan*? Is that you?" Chad asked, hardly believing his ears.

"Dad?" came the frail voice on the other end.

"Yeah, it's me. Where are you?"

A long silence.

"I'm… I'm in our apartment."

"Apartment? What, back in California?"

"Um, no. In… In Africa."

"*Where* in Africa?" Chad pressed.

"We're in one of the colonies, I guess," Evan said sheepishly, his voice barely audible.

"Speak up, son. I can't hear you. I asked what *part* of Africa."

"Grunau. The colony is called Grunau. It's in Namibia."

Chad pulled a pen from his pocket and jotted the name down on a napkin. He thought it sounded familiar.

"Angelica with you?" Chad asked.

"You mean mom?"

"You know *another* Angelica?" Chad snapped, feeling his patience wear thin. He never understood how his genes could have produced such a dull child. Perhaps he took more after his mother.

"Um, she's out with Ted, I think," Evan said feebly.

"Ted? Who's *Ted*?" Chad demanded.

"He's an elder. He and mom are friends."

"I'm sure they are," Chad sneered. Then he thought of something. "Wait… Ted? Is his last name Watkins?"

"Um… Yeah," Evan said. Chad's teeth clamped down on his lip, drawing blood. He held back his fury. He could not explode; not yet. There was more he needed.

"I see," Chad said, seething quietly. "So, Evan. Tell me, how's life there? How are you?"

"I'm ok, Dad," Evan said. "I mean it's not like California at all, you know? But it's not too bad once you get used to it. I like the baboons a whole lot."

"Baboons, huh?" Chad asked, wholly uninterested as his son began regaling him with some tale regarding the animal life there.

"Look, Evan," Chad said suddenly, cutting Evan off mid sentence. "I want to make sure you and your mom are safe."

"Ok. Well, we're pretty safe, I think."

"Can you tell me what part of Grunau you're located in? Do you know if it's the north part, or the east part, something like that?"

"I don't really know," Evan said quietly.

Of course you don't, Chad thought. "What about landmarks? Any interesting landmarks you can tell me about nearby?"

"Well, there is this one hill. Sometimes we go up there and have picnics. The hill overlooks the railroad, and sometimes when the trains come in there are baboons on the roof. One time I even saw some of the baboo—"

"That hill have a name?" Chad asked impatiently, his pen hovering over the napkin.

"I don't really know, Dad," Evan said. "I just know it's the only hill by Block D2."

"What's Block D2?" Chad asked.

"Oh, it's our apartment block's number."

Chad pursed his lips in frustration and shook his head. Of course the boy hadn't thought to mention this. "Apartment block number, huh?" he said.

"Yup. Apartment Block D2, room 502. Mom made me memorize it so I'd never get lost. I got a pretty good memory. Did you know that? I already memorized all the books of the Bible, and—
—"

"Yeah, look sport, I gotta go," Chad said, jotting the address down and circling it vigorously.

"Oh. Um, ok. You at work?" Evan asked.

"Um. Yeah, sure. You could say that."

"Hey Dad?" Evan asked.

"What?"

"Am I gonna see you again?"

"See me again? Of course, I'm sure you'll see me sometime. Maybe soon."

"Oh, ok. That's good. Because everyone here is talking about Armageddon, and they think it's coming pretty quick. And you know, if you're not here when Armageddon happens, well. That's it."

"Right, kid."

"So you should get here soon."

"I'll see what I can do," Chad said, and hung up.

***

By the time *The Chariot* arrived with the final evacuees off the shores of the Namib, Elizabeth Bay looked much different than it had when Peter and Rachel has disembarked from their rigs months prior. The tumultuous surf was now circumvented by a series of broad, elevated platforms and walkways that weaved through and around the floating oil platforms. These platforms, in turn, had been put to good use over the months, their cranes lifting various items and supplies from the barges and tankers below.

For two full days, Alvin and the others stayed aboard their barge, ensuring that the passengers and crew were safely moved ashore. It was no small task. *The Chariot's* manifest included many elderly brothers and sisters, dozens of small children, and a handful who were wheelchair bound, including Stacy Owen.

Alvin and Joyce Tucker, along with Claire Aberdeen and Stacy, were among the last to disembark from their ship. They climbed the gangplank and made their way across the platforms towards the shore. Below them churned powerful, thrashing waves, a sight they were keen to leave behind as they put the sea to their backs and headed inland.

The train ride into Grunau was uneventful. All four were exhausted from their months at sea and the last few days of frantic work: Alvin working with the other overseers to coordinate everyone's safe passage; Joyce tending to the last of the patients in the infirmary; Claire at her side, performing various odd jobs and errands; and Stacy, undergoing a gradually intensifying regiment of physical therapy as she prepared to disembark. In the five hours it took their train to chug across the Namib, they were awake for very little of it. They missed the baboons perched atop the canyon walls, staring and hooting curiously at the giant metal snake slithering over its tracks, and they missed the orange sandstone canyon walls, glowing all the more vibrant with the setting sun's crimson rays. But it mattered not. This was home now, and there would be many more

275

opportunities to behold the landscape surrounding them.

Joyce stirred awake as their train's carriage came to a hissing stop. It was dark outside. She glanced at her watch; it was almost eight PM. Alvin's heavy, sweaty head lay still on her shoulder. She patted his leg to rouse him.

"I think we're here, hon," Joyce whispered. Her husband's large, sleepy eyes opened and gathered the scene around him. Witnesses were standing and pulling luggage from overhead racks. Some were gathering sleeping children in their arms. Everyone looked exhausted.

"All right," Alvin said tiredly, standing and stretching the kinks from his back. "Let's get this show on the road."

On the bench across from him, Claire stood obediently and was helping an older couple retrieve their bags from beneath their seats. She held back a yawn as she helped Joyce and Stacy with their bags. Alvin couldn't help but smile.

"Thanks, Claire," Alvin said, grabbing the luggage from the young girl.

"No worries." Claire smiled in spite of the bags under her eyes.

Alvin could feel something welling deep within him, something that brought tears to his eyes. A realization finally surfaced, at this moment, that soon after stepping from this train, Claire would be reunited with her family, and they'd have to part ways.

From the beginning, Alvin had suspected that Joyce's attachment to Claire stemmed in some ways from the loss of their daughter, Jasmin, years ago. But in Alvin's mind, nothing could replace Jas, and he'd been careful not to let Claire get too close. It hadn't worked. Their time together on the barge before Joyce's arrival had shown him how much she was willing to change, grow, and learn. Her honesty about the mistakes in her past had proven that, and her diligence in whatever assignment she was given had only drawn him closer to her. Whether he liked it or not, she'd become like the daughter he'd lost, and he was dreading saying goodbye.

Claire caught the look in his eyes and frowned. Gently, she set her bags down on the bench as the friends around them began filing down the aisles headed for the exits. She took a step towards the large brother and wrapped her arms around his chest. The two of them said nothing for a long moment.

"All right, all right," Alvin said, brushing the wetness from his face. "You're holding up the crowd, Claire" he teased. Claire merely nodded, pulled away, and picked her bags back up to head for the door.

***

Rachel could hardly contain herself. For the past week, ever since they'd had confirmation from the brothers at Elizabeth Bay that Claire's barge would soon be docking with the rigs, reuniting with her little sister was all that she could think of. It had been years since the two had seen each other, and never in a million years could Rachel have pictured the scene before her eyes now: her and her husband, Peter, waiting at a dusty train platform on a cool evening in the middle of Namibia. She shook her head at the very thought of it; it still seemed so surreal.

There was so much she wanted to say, and so much she wanted to hear about. The time Claire had spent away at college were some of the most stressful Rachel had had to endure, but now she was coming home and Rachel could hardly stand the excitement.

"Shouldn't their train be here by now?" Rachel said nervously. She was fidgeting on one of the waiting benches, a large gift box bouncing on her knees as she leaned forward, staring down the quiet stretch of railroad.

"It's a long ride, Rachel," Peter said. "You remember how it was for us."

"Oh, you don't think they got caught in a sandstorm too, do you?" she asked worriedly.

"Possible, but doubtful. If anything happened, the brothers would've announce it to us so we could come back in the morning."

"That would be awful," Rachel groaned. "I don't think I could wait another day." Peter chuckled. "Let's hope for the best, then."

The train pulled up thirty minutes later and Rachel was nearly jumping up and down. Peter would've been embarrassed but for the simple fact that she wasn't alone: the platform and surrounding area had quickly become filled with Witnesses eager to reunite with friends and family. Many waved *Welcome* signs with names written on them, while others held balloons and flowers. It reminded Peter of an international convention he'd once attended, although the energy and love here were even greater.

When the train finally came to a stop and the first of the

277

passengers began to emerge, the tears flowed. Some passengers from the train simply dropped their belongings as they ran into the arms of long-separated loved ones and cried quietly together. Tiny white flashes filled the air as countless photos were snapped. Rachel peeked over the heads of the crowd and scanned every face as it exited the train.

And then she saw her: Claire, her baby sister. Instinctively, Rachel dropped the gift box in her arms and ran. She ran as fast as her legs could carry her, her arms spread wide.

"Claire! Claire! Over here! Over here!" she yelled, hot tears already filling her eyes as her sister looked around, trying to locate the voice.

"Right here!" Rachel said, emerging from the thicket of bodies. Claire dropped her bags and began crying, too. The two sisters embraced tightly. It felt like the happiest moment in their lives.

"I can't believe it's you! It's really you!" Rachel said, stroking Claire's hair and face with her fingers. "I missed you so so so much!"

"Me too, sis," Claire said, nearly sobbing now, her face wet with tears.

"There she is!" Peter said, appearing at the girls' side. He scooped Claire up in his arms in a bear hug and she squealed. When he set her down, Rachel saw the tears in his eyes as well. She would remember this moment for the rest of her life.

"I need to introduce you guys to some close friends of mine," Claire said, wiping her eyes and brushing the hair from her face as she turned back to look at the train. A trio of friendly faces emerged onto the platform, watching quietly with big smiles. A bulky middle-aged brother with an armful of luggage was followed by a woman pushing a wheelchair. Peter and Rachel recognized her instantly from the call months ago. It was Joyce.

They helped her with the wheelchair and began introducing themselves.

"Name's Alvin Tucker. You must be Peter and Rachel," Alvin said with an air of formality.

"Brother Tucker, you don't know how wonderful it is to finally meet you two," Rachel gushed.

"Thank you so much for all you did for Claire," Peter said. "I hope she wasn't too much trouble," he said, winking at his baby sister-in-law.

"No trouble at all," Joyce said, wrapping her arm around Claire's shoulders. "Truth is, we're going to miss having her around," she said, casting a sidelong glance at Alvin, who was silently biting his lip.

"I'm trying not to think about it," Claire said, looking sadly at the couple.

"I don't think we've met your friend here, yet," Rachel said, smiling at the sister in the wheelchair.

"Hi all. Didn't want to interrupt the reunion. I'd offer to shake your hands, but..." the sister paused with a smirk, raising her bandaged arms in the air. Alvin, Joyce and Claire chuckled at the joke, signaling to Peter and Rachel that it was ok. This was just Stacy's sense of humor.

"This is Stacy Owen," Joyce said. "She's from our congregation back in Washington. She's a close friend."

"*Attention, Seattle groups!*" announced a voice suddenly from a loudspeaker. "*The escort to your apartments will be arriving soon. Please be ready at the designated location outside of the station and board the busses marked A14.*"

"Well, that's us," Alvin said, drawing a deep breath.

"Here's our apartment number and line," Peter said, pulling a scrap of paper from his pocket. "Once you get settled there, we'd love to get back in touch."

"Absolutely," Joyce said. The new friends embraced once more and Alvin, Joyce, and Stacy were quickly whisked away by the crowds. Peter, Rachel, and Claire watched them go.

"Hungry, Claire? They've got a late dinner crew working tonight. What would you say to a hot meal?" Peter asked. But Claire's mind was elsewhere. She was still peering into the crowds leaving the platform. Suddenly, she dropped her bags.

"Be right back!" she yelled as she disappeared into the crowds.

***

"You ok, hon?" Joyce asked quietly as she walked beside her husband towards the waiting line of buses.

"Of course. Just tired, is all," Alvin said, grunting as he readjusted the luggage in his arms.

"Uh huh," Joyce said. "Claire is pretty special, huh?"

"Sure," Alvin said. Had it been physically possible, he

would've shrugged.

"Well, we've got their info. We should take them up on their offer and try to get together soon. I want to hear their story. I'm sure they've got plenty to tell."

"If we get time, we can think about it. It's gonna be busy, though. We'll have to focus on other things."

"I'm sure Claire would appreciate it."

"Eh, she'll be fine. She's where she belongs now. With family."   "I saw that look in her eyes, Al. She's really gonna miss you."

"Miss me? Nah. She'll forget all about me. You, maybe. Not me."

"Oh, I wouldn't be so sure."

"Give it a week or two. It'll pass," Alvin said, trying to think of something else when a voice caught his attention. It sounded an awful lot like Claire, and she was yelling his name.

"Alvin! Alvin!" he heard the girl shouting. He set down his bags and turned just in time to see the young girl leaping at him, tears in her eyes. He caught her; she disappeared in his arms.

"Thank you so much, Alvin," she said quietly into his ear. "You have no idea how much I needed you."

Alvin tried to respond, but he couldn't. There was a knot in his neck where his vocal cords used to be. He could only grunt an ambiguous sound. Claire laughed as he set her down. She wiped the tears from her eyes and shook a finger at him with a stern look.

"You have Peter's number, so you'd better keep in touch. I need you guys close by, ok?" she said sternly. Alvin smiled as a single tear trickled down his cheek.

"Ok, kid. You got me. I'll call."

"Good," Claire said. "Now hurry or you'll miss that bus!"

***

"Do you realize what you're asking?" Driscoll asked the man standing before him. Chad might've been dressed in military garb, but he was no soldier.

"Of course I do," Chad said.

"You want to be on the front lines when the attack happens. Why?" Driscoll asked, puzzled.

"I want to be there before the attack. It's personal business."

280

Driscoll said nothing as he studied the man before him. He was an enigma. He'd been useful to them when the USCC was still a functioning entity, but he'd never sensed much patriotism in him until recently. Frankly he didn't trust the man.

"I'm not asking for preferential treatment here. I'll travel with the rest of the ground troops."

"That's a given. I'm just wondering what your angle here is, Harkett."

"No angle. Like I said, it's personal."

"Someone in the colonies?"

"I'd rather not say. But I need to do this, for my own sake. I won't pose any kind of risk to your men. That's a guarantee."

"The troops deploy right after we make landfall."

"I'll be ready."

"Anything else?"

"If you can spare a few firearms, I'll take those as well."

"You're standing on a floating arsenal, Harkett."

"I didn't think it'd be an issue."

"And you understand that if something happens to you out there, there'll be no one to swoop in and save you?"

"Granted."

Driscoll thought for another moment and scratched the side of his head. Chad's early departure would mean one less mouth to feed, one less body using hot water. Besides, he wasn't sure how much use there'd be in the foreseeable future for tech gurus and AI specialists.

"Fine," he said simply. "But you're on your own."

"Understood, sir" Chad said, and with that he disappeared back into the corridors to finalize his plans.

CHAPTER 25

Rachel, Peter, and Claire stayed up late into the night catching up. The topics were endless. They exchanged tales of their evacuations, rescues, and travels across the Atlantic. Claire regaled them with her recent close encounter with pirates at sea, an event that still puzzled most of them, though angelic interference was the popular explanation.

Delicately, Peter navigated the topic to an earlier time, when Claire was still in college. To their surprise, she was frank about her mistakes. There had been a boy and things had gotten physical. She regretted it with all her heart, and had come clean with the full story once she'd become comfortable with Alvin Tucker aboard their barge. The elders had met with her a few times, and over time she'd recovered. It was still a stain that she felt would never leave her past, but she was determined to keep focused on the future. Peter and Rachel couldn't have been more proud. The outcome was better than they could've imagined: it wasn't just their baby sister coming home; it was a changed sister, a more mature Claire.

Peter finally called it quits at three AM in the morning. The three had been talking non-stop for hours over dinner and a bottle of wine, but there was a new day just around the corner and plenty of work waiting.

The next morning, Claire decided to tag along with Rachel on her animal care duties. Despite the previous full day of travel she was full of life and ready to work, an attitude Rachel hadn't seen before.

They met with the animal care crew that morning, as usual, and were briefed by the overseers on the list of tasks that needed to be completed before sundown. A pack of hyenas had been making the rounds to the east of the colony and appeared to be waiting for handouts; another pair of cheetah cubs had shown up out of the blue and needed care to the south, where a sister had taken them in; an aging elephant by the name of Rufus had gotten too close to the river bank and was now stuck in the mud. The volunteers immediately knew it would be a busy day, and they were quickly divided into teams to tackle the tasks simultaneously. To their utter delight, Rachel and Claire were selected to care for the cheetah cubs.

"Cheetahs?" Claire asked. She was clearly unsure.

"They're amazing, you'll see." Rachel said. She was already up from the bench and filling her thermos at the tank.

Within five minutes Rachel was behind the wheel of one of the department's jeeps. Claire laughed at the logo on the side of the jeep's door—someone artistic within the department had cheekily designed an emblem for the fleet of vehicles, a logo highly reminiscent of a certain dinosaur movie franchise. The circular emblem featured the silhouette of an elephant's head, its trunk held proudly in the air before a red and yellow banner.

"Welcome... To Grunau Park!" Rachel joked, hopping in the driver's seat and cranking up the engine.

"We spared no expense!" Claire fired back.

And they were off, their four-wheel-drive bounding over the dunes, tires throwing blankets of sand into the air behind them.

"So. Cheetahs, huh?" Claire asked.

"Yep, and just cubs. My favorite kind."

"And people just take in wild animals here? Isn't that kind of dangerous?"

"In the case of the cubs, either someone takes them in or they die of starvation. They aren't able to survive on their own." Rachel went on to explain the same thing she'd been told by Karen on her first day on animal duty: baby animals were showing up all the time due to accidents or illegal hunting.

"So they're pretty tame then?" Claire asked.

Rachel was nodding. "Sort of like a mix between kittens and puppies. They're constantly chewing on things, testing their coordination, looking for things to play with. They can be very precocious."

"Sounds fun."

"You have no idea!"

But no sooner had Rachel finished talking up the cheetah cubs than the radio at her hip began squawking. She pulled the jeep over and answered the call.

"Rachel here," she said.

283

"Rachel, you anywhere near Kebbel's Canyon?" one of the overseers asked.

"Gimme a sec to check," she said, pulling a laminated map from the console compartment between them. She ran a finger along a jagged brown line in a sea of beige. "Not far. I'd say it's four or five kilometers from here."

"Hate to throw a wrench in your plans, but it's gotta be done."

Rachel winced. She had a feeling she knew what was coming. "Go ahead."

"It's a carcass. It was sighted between the upper ridge of Kebbel's Canyon and the train tracks."

"Got it," Rachel said, glancing at her younger sister, who was frowning. She clipped the radio back onto her hip and started the engine. "Sorry, Claire. The cubs will have to wait a bit longer. Duty calls."

***

Ted's heart was racing. It was silly, to be so nervous about what Evan would say when Ted revealed his plans to him, but there it was. He wasn't sure what he was fretting over; after all, he and Evan were good buddies and had gotten along fine as long as they'd known each other. But the transition of friend to the role of a stepfather was a difficult one, and Ted wasn't sure how the boy would react. Ted knew Angelica was the one for him; he'd known it for ages, and there was little sense delaying the proposal, even if it was a strange time to be getting engaged. But he wanted everything to be as perfect as possible, and that meant getting Evan prepped for the big question.

Evan had been quiet for most of the trek up the hill leading to the west canyon wall. Ted hadn't pressed him, but he was beginning to wonder. Evan was always chipper and willing to talk, but now there seemed to be a dark cloud hanging over him. Then again, perhaps it was just early puberty rearing its head.

"How about we take a breather at the tree up ahead?" Ted asked, catching his breath as he looked back. He was surprised to see that the gap between him and the boy had tripled since he'd last looked. When Evan finally caught up, he seemed miserable.

"Feeling ok?" Ted asked, trying to take Evan's backpack from him to lighten his load, but the boy shook him off.

"I'm fine," he said flatly, eyes at his feet. Ted was confused. He'd never seen the kid like this before.   "We've still got a ways to go. You still up for it? I mean, we can rest whenever you want."

"I said I'm *fine*," Evan snapped. "Let's just get this over with. I can take it."

"Of course, buddy. Whatever you say," Ted said. He was surprised at how much the boy's tone stung. They'd always been on such good terms, even back in California. Why had things suddenly changed? Had he done something wrong? Had he been spending too much time with Angelica lately? Maybe Evan was feeling left out?

"Hey, Evan, why don't we just take five minutes? Grab a little water, open a granola bar, I think we'll feel a lot better after."

"Do I look like a little kid to you?" Evan snapped suddenly. The question caught Ted completely off guard.

"No, buddy. You're not a little kid anymore. I didn't mean it like that. I just don't want us to push it too hard in this heat. Gotta keep hydrated in this sun, you know?"

"You act like my *dad*."

"Your… your *dad*?" Ted asked, bewildered.

"He thinks I'm weak. And you do too. You're both the same."

"Whoa, hold on there," Ted asked, not able to let the snub go. "Like your dad? Really?"

"You act all nice around me all the time, but it's just because you like my mom. I'm not stupid. You're fake. Dad was fake a lot, too. He just acted a certain way to get what he wanted."

Ted's mouth fell open. Never had he imagined to hear these words coming from Evan's mouth, and never could he have imagined how much they'd hurt. He was too shocked to form a response. He shut his mouth and watched in silence as Evan walked past him, leading the way to the top of the canyon ridge.

***

In the months that Rachel Burton had been assigned to the animal care department, she'd come across her fair share of carcasses. Upon arrival at the scene, she knew what to look for to determine the cause of the animal's death, and usually it was clear within moments of examining the carcass. But today was different. What she saw now was both puzzling and disturbing.

At her feet lay a full grown male caracal. The body was intact, ruling out the likelihood of trophy hunting. It was, however, riddled with tiny holes. Whatever had shot after the animal had triggered its instinctive flight response. It had tried to flee for cover but had ultimately failed. Rachel couldn't help feeling sad and angry for the small, helpless cat.

Claire crouched beside the carcass, clearly unfazed by the scene. "You said there are hunters out here?"

"Yeah," Rachel said, frowning. She spun and gazed at the hills around them.

"Just killing for sport?"

"Usually, yeah. But something tells me this is different. And they don't usually go for caracals. These animals are incredibly fast and agile—it would've been running away at full speed. The hunters would've had to chase after it. How is that possible?"

"Maybe they were in a jeep like ours," Claire suggested. The two exchanged a look and began combing the premises looking for signs of another vehicle, but there was nothing; no tracks in the sand, no dark puddles of leaked oil. After ten minutes, they returned to the jeep with the plastic tarp and got to work. Rachel had numbed somewhat to the task but was surprised at how little her sister objected. They were back at the jeep in another half hour sterilizing their gloves and wiping down the equipment.

Rachel got on her radio to report the odd discovery to her overseer before starting the car back up. She was surprised by the response.

"This isn't the first time," the brother said sadly.

"It isn't?"

"No. Third this week, in fact. Everything just as you described—tiny holes that looked like they came from bullets found all over the carcasses."

"Any idea what it could be from?"

"Not too certain, but I think it's best you finish up out there and get back as soon as you can."

"Understood. On our way," Rachel said, frowning at the urgency in the overseer's tone.

Back at the center, the overseer was waiting for them at the entrance of the cafeteria tent with a pair of binoculars. He seemed relieved at their arrival.

"What is it?" Rachel asked. The overseer was quiet for a few tense moments as he scanned the perimeter with the binoculars, then said:

"Let's talk indoors."

He led them inside to a back room attached to the rear of the cafeteria. The place was lined with folding metal chairs; it was clear from a glance that a meeting had been held not long ago. The overseer pulled two of the chairs up to a desk and invited the sisters to sit. From a cardboard box next to the desk, he carefully removed a mangled piece of plastic and wires and set it on the desk before taking a seat himself.

"Either of you recognize this thing?" he asked the two women before him. They exchanged a glance and shrugged.

He lifted another part from the box. It appeared to be a motor of some sort; a propeller was attached to a protruding plastic sprig. "It's a drone. We found it crashed near the tracks north of the compound, not far from where you found the caracal today."

"Is there some kind of connection?" Rachel asked. The brother nodded solemnly and turned the main section of the device over in his hands delicately. A thin, metal barrel protruded from the drone's underbelly.

"We think this is a gun," the overseer said.

"They're flying drones with guns now?" Rachel asked.

"Who is?" Claire added.

"We can't be sure yet, but we believe it's the Namibian military. You've heard of the drones up in Bismarck? The Namibian and South African joint forces have been surveilling the friends with drones that look almost identical to this one. This is just the next step, arming them."

"But why kill animals? What would they gain from it?"

"Not too sure. They could be trying to send a message, showing the kind of power they have. It could be target practice, trying to hone their skills before, you know... They come after us."

"You sounded worried on the radio," Rachel said. "You told us to come straight back. Do you think it's safe for us out there?"

"It wasn't my call, actually. The committee in Bismarck asked us to keep the brothers and sisters away from the outskirts of the camps for the time being."

"What about our assignment?"

"We'll still tend to the animals as needed, but no more going far out into the unpopulated areas. It's just not safe anymore."

Rachel and Claire exchanged a look and nodded.

"He said *what?*" Angelica asked. She was cleaning out a dirty pan from the evening dining crowd. Her brief stint with the animal care department had come to an end when the kitchen crew put out an announcement for helpers. With all the recent expansion, they'd been working around the clock cooking and cleaning and needed extra hands.

"I know. I could hardly believe my ears. He said I'm just like your ex," Ted said.

"Chad? Chad Harkett? Psychotic, selfish, manipulative Chad? It must've been a joke."

"Oh, I don't think so. He was angry, Ange. I'd never seen him like that before."

"Well, I'll just have to talk to him, then."

"I'd give it some time. He wasn't ready to talk this afternoon. He ended up just leaving me behind before we got to the cliff and then heading straight back on his own. Wouldn't even stop for a break."

"Strange. I wonder what it could have been."

"There was one thing he asked that really stood out: he wanted to know if I thought he was a little kid or not."

"He is a little kid," Angelica said.

"I think it was more than that. I think he was asking if I thought he was weak or something. It really upset him when I tried to help him with his pack."

Angelica mulled over this point silently as she stacked the large, clean pan on a stack of others and covered them with a dry cloth.

"Any idea why that would've bothered him about that?" Ted asked.

"Years of emotional abuse from his father, probably," Angelica said quietly.

"How so?"

"Chad was always pushing Evan to do better. Better in school, especially. He wanted to enroll him in a bunch of after school sports, too, try to toughen Evan up. He was constantly belittling our son for being so quiet and mild. Chad had such a predatory nature about him, Ted. It didn't matter if it was at work or within the family. He was quick to jump on others' weaknesses and exploit them. And I think when he saw Evan, he saw nothing but weakness. He had a hard time accepting him as his son."

"Poor kid," Ted said sadly.

"Eventually Evan sort of developed a shell around him to protect himself. I think that's one of the reasons he's so quiet, why he enjoys spending time on his own so much. It's easier when it's just himself. His father ruined his sense of self-respect."

Ted was shaking his head. He helped Angelica carry a second batch of pans from the dining area to the kitchen and donned a pair of rubber gloves to assist with cleaning. Angelica grinned at the sight of the large man before her wearing a pair of pink gloves and a baby blue apron.

"Can I ask you a question, Angelica? It's a little personal, but I'm really curious."

"Shoot," Angelica said, pausing to look up at the large man beside her. She brushed a strand of hair from her eyes with the back of her wrist, revealing the scar she'd sustained at Chad's hands months before. Ted glanced at it, not minding. Oddly, he thought it only made her more beautiful. It reminded him of how tough she was.

"Why did you do it? Why did you marry that monster?"

Angelica's smile faded somewhat as she turned back to the dishes and thought.

"Sorry. You don't have to answer that if you don't want to."

"No, it's fine. I don't mind," Angelica said. She gave the question a bit more thought before formulating an answer. "You have to remember that I was a different person back then. We were still in school at the time. Chad was charming and smart. And he was different back then, too. He didn't come from money and he hadn't started up his company yet. He was a nobody. Sometimes I think it was the success that changed him, made him more ruthless, more cold. And the pressure of all that success drove him to drink more, which made him violent. It was a cycle. He became someone else."

"I'm sorry," Ted said.

"I am too. But when all is said and done, without Chad there'd be no Evan, and I can't imagine life without him."

Ted said nothing as he wrapped an arm around Angelica's shoulder and gave it a squeeze. He gently rested her head against his chest, hearing his powerful heart pumping. She thought it sounded a little fast.

Ted slipped his hand into his pocket where he felt the tiny, velvet box. He'd been waiting for the perfect moment to present it to her and wondered if this was it. But then his thoughts went to Evan and the strange way things had transpired that day. No, Ted decided. The time wasn't right. He wanted to be sure about the boy first. Everything had to be just right.

Ted pulled his hand from his pocket and gave Angelica a quick pat on the shoulder. "Let's get these dishes finished. It's been a long day," Ted said, lifting the final stack of trays from the serving table and heading for the kitchen.

***

Dietrich Nash peered down the dusty road beside the Bismarck office headquarters; a cavalcade of shiny Cadillacs and Land Rovers was approaching in the distance. He could hear the faint, distant hum of boisterous engines. For the dozenth time that morning he said a quick prayer of entreaty. He needed courage, strength, and wisdom.

The shiny government convoy came to a halt just outside the office complexes, a cloud of dust settling around them. Drivers and attendants in dark suits and military uniforms emerged, holding the doors open for their entourage.

Dietrich recognized Adani Ratief, Chief of Namibia's Tax Bureau, but just barely. The man had put on considerable weight in the last few months and had grown his curly hair out. It was slicked back in a sheen of grease. He removed a pair of gold Ray-Bans from his face and nodded. Dietrich thought he looked more like a celebrity than a government official, with the rings on his fingers and his shiny pocket square.

"*Goeie more*, Mr. Ratief," Dietrich said respectfully. Adani eyed him for a long moment.

"We meet again, Mr. Nash," Adani said without offering his hand. He snapped his fingers and one of his attendants raced to fetch him a chilled bottle of sparkling water.

"Shall we get out of the heat?" Dietrich said, motioning to the air-conditioned office complex behind him. The tax official gave it a dismissive glance and shook his head.

"We Africans have no problems with the heat," Adani said,

snapping his fingers again. More attendants appeared, setting up a pair of folding chairs and a large umbrella on the side of the road. Adani motioned to the chairs and Dietrich sat.

"So, how are things in Windhoek?" Dietrich asked. He'd heard that over the last few weeks, the once prospering city had finally begun to feel the effects of what the rest of the world had already been facing for months. With global trade and tourism practically eradicated, everyone was suffering. Everyone, of course, except for the Witnesses.

"We will survive it. I have seen worse," Adani said proudly. "I see your people are doing well."

"We've been blessed."

"I hear that all your people have finally arrived."

"That's correct. Everyone is here."

"And now what happens?"

"We keeping working, and we wait."

"Wait for what?"

"The attack."

Adani shifted uncomfortably in his seat and looked away.

"It's true, isn't it? That there is an attack planned?" pressed Dietrich.

"I have heard nothing," Adani said stubbornly.

"We know it's coming. It's all there in scripture. Just as with the attack on false religion, and the forming of a coalition of nations. We will be protected."

"By what? You have no weapons, no defenses—not even a wall around your perimeter," Adani said with a shake of his head.

"By our God, Adani. Jehovah has blessed and protected us this whole time. Just look around you."

"People can accomplish much when their mind is set on it," Adani said, but Dietrich was shaking his head.

"But they can't change weather patterns, and they can't control the sun and stars."

"Our country was never affected by any of that," Adani said, knowing full well what the brother was referring to, but his voice was quieter now, his resolution weakened.

"I know you heard the reports, Adani. I'll bet you saw footage, too. What happened was supernatural, no other way to explain it. I believe your country was spared because God's people were here."

The two men let this sink in for a quiet moment. Then Adani

said, "It is not good for a government man to be talking of religious things. For years my people struggled with their superstitions and malevolent deities. But we have resolved to put that behind us." Adani sat upright now, straightening his uniform and donning the golden sunglasses once again.

"There's a line being drawn in the sand, Adani. It divides two distinct sides. And when this is all over, only one side will remain. The time left to choose sides is dangerously close."

"I could say the same thing to you," Adani said.

"But you didn't."

"Would it have made a difference?"

Dietrich slowly shook his head.

"The problem, Mr. Nash, is that we are both stubborn men. Two bull elephants, horns locked," Adani Ratief forced a laugh, struggling to lighten the mood.

"I suppose you are right," said Dietrich sadly, reaching for Adani's outstretched hand.

"Of course, it is possible that we are both wrong. I suppose that would be the best outcome of all of this."

Dietrich made a noncommittal grunt and tried to smile. Suddenly, Adani pulled him in close for a hug. As he did, the African man began speaking quiet, quick words into Dietrich's ears.

"You can make this all go away, Dietrich, but you *must stop speaking of God and religion*. Call yourselves a company, a nation, anything but a religion. They are watching. You are in danger."

Adani pulled away just as suddenly as he'd embraced, his expression unchanged, and in another two minutes, he and his entourage had vanished in a cloud of dust.

CHAPTER 26

Dietrich Nash watched the caravan leave before heading back up to his office within the complex. A part of him wanted to mourn over Adani. From the moment he'd arrived to prospect the land for the organization, he and Adani had gotten along well. Adani seemed to appreciate Dietrich's understanding of African culture and thinking, while Adani had proved indispensable in the early days of getting the colonies up and running.

Of course, there'd always been some measure of pride and greed in him, but for years Dietrich had hoped Adani could overcome this and accept the truth. After all, in the near decade since the organization had first purchased the land from the Namibian government, Adani had witnessed so much. In a continent brimming with corruption, civil war, and disease, the Witnesses had remained honest, peaceful, and healthy. Dietrich had always prayed that these experiences would be enough to sway the man's allegiances, but he'd been wrong. In the end, the pull of wealth and power was simply too great.

Dietrich shook his head sadly as he climbed the stairs back to his office just as the whirring propellers of a surveillance drone were heard somewhere overhead. This was yet another reminder of how close their enemies loomed just over the horizon; eyes and ears everywhere, but Dietrich could not focus on this now. His once frequent visits with the Namibian officials, including Commander Ngoma, had brought about nothing. The officials had shown time and time again that they were willing to twist and bend the law to whatever degree they pleased. They'd extorted, harassed, and surveilled the brothers, and there was little left to do now but wait and endure and pray for Jehovah to take swift action. No one knew exactly when things would come to a head, but it wouldn't be long. Things simply could not go on like this much longer. A storm was brewing on the horizon and everyone on both sides knew it.

Brother Nash entered his office on the fifth floor and returned to his laptop, where the blinking cursor of a blank word processing document still waited. It had been this way for weeks; the distractions had been endless. He could simply not get his mind on the interview he'd been asked to give. As greatly as he'd been anticipating this convention, he couldn't help but feel that the time simply wasn't right. There was still so much work to be done: building projects to be completed, paths to be laid, departments that needed restructuring to accommodate new needs and new arrivals. They'd simply grown too fast to give the required attention to each challenge as it presented itself. To Dietrich, it felt like a constant game of catch up, and he was already exhausted.

Dietrich glanced down at a memo pad on his desk where a to do list stared back at him. He sighed. There was so much work left to do. He said another prayer, took a moment to collect his thoughts, and ignored the buzzing drone watching him from just outside the office window. Then he began to type.

***

When the battalion of coalition ships finally arrived off the western coast of Namibia, it was a sight unlike anything seen in the history of the world. In all the wars and battles and conflicts fought throughout man's history, never before had so many troops, ships, and war machines been gathered in a single location. More incredible still was the fact that they were united on a single front and poised to strike at a seemingly defenseless target.

By now, the fleet numbered into the tens of thousands, boasting representation from over one hundred nations. An elaborate ceremony was held aboard the lead ship, a newly commissioned, Nimitz-class aircraft carrier and the only one of its kind in existence. World leaders gathered atop her polished, gleaming deck, delivering carefully written speeches meant to rouse the troops and galvanize their resolve to carry out to completion the task at hand. Yes, difficult actions would need to be taken; yes, many would die, but it was a step that needed to be taken for the good of mankind. The hope of humanity hung in the balance. In the year since the eradication of most religion, the world's nations had finally managed to cooperate, and this was surely a tiding of things to come once the rest of religion was brought to its knees.

The president of the United States—also the chairman for the coalition itself—spoke last. In a strong, booming voice he promised the eradication of the people who'd managed, by trickery and by fraud, to evade legal and military attempts to wipe them out. He reminded the audience of the Witnesses' call to action, their looming predictions of the end of the world, when governments themselves would be overturned. The president paused here, his chest puffing out as he spread his arms outward, gesturing to the flags and banners streaming in the air around him. The crowd cheered and applauded. Surely nothing could break these bonds now, he proclaimed. These were not the signs of a faltering world rulership but rather the precursors of unprecedented unity and cooperation. Their time had finally come to shine as one, united world! And the Witnesses, like a hunted, injured animal who knew its time was near, had fled into an open and exposed area. Now it was time for the hunter to take its trophy.

"Never before have the world's nations been so united and dedicated in our pursuit of a single purpose. Never before have our brave soldiers stood with such solidarity at one another's sides. And never before has success been so assured," the president said. He paused with a purposeful look over his shoulder. The crowd gasped.

Behind him, a giant flag was hoisted into the air by a team of soldiers, their movements perfectly synchronized. Emblazoned on the face of the flag was the seal that had been adopted by the coalition ever since its announcement a year prior. A ring made up of smaller flags belonging to the countries of the world encircled a golden crest of a large eagle beside a bear. The flag was even larger than that of the United States. The crowds erupted into applause; foghorns and air horns shrieked and bellowed in the distance. Bottles of champagne were opened; streamers and confetti littered the skies.

Within ten hours, the first of the land troops were deployed atop a sand bank off of the northernmost section of the skeleton coast. The coalition's militaries had carefully chosen vehicles suitable to this terrain; armored cars with powerful engines and large wheels rumbled by the dozens from transports, braving the shifting sands and surmounting the dunes with ease. One after another, the personnel vehicles were ferried onto the continent, the intrepid ships slicing through the raging surf.

Chad Harkett could not help but smile as his truck slithered up the dunes and over the plateau. He'd made it to the ends of the earth on just his wits and his instinct for survival, and victory for him was just over the horizon. He joked with the soldiers in his company, all of whom wore the same eager expressions. The president was right, of course: this was the dawn of a new era, and despite their difficulties in getting here, they would emerge from the ashes and claim their stake in a new world order.

They sang and played poker and drank as their convoy headed to the southern colony of Grunau.

**

It had long been rumored that a special convention would be held once the colonies had been filled and every evacuee had been accounted for. As encouraged as everyone felt just *being* here, there was much work left to be done and plenty of encouragement needed. Many had sacrificed nearly everything. Even those like Peter and Rachel Burton, who'd evacuated with a sizable load of personal belongings and supplies had, over time, shared many of these items with others or consumed them themselves, so that little was left by the time they arrived in Namibia. But these were the fortunate ones.

In many lands, military checkpoints manned by corrupt officials had confiscated much of what the evacuees had been carrying. Some acted out of malice, others out of their own necessity. In other places, Witnesses had been robbed, or had found themselves bargaining for their lives with treasured family heirlooms, jewelry, and electronics. Witnesses traveling from these lands were especially feeble and exhausted when they stepped off the trains, arriving with little more than the clothes on their backs. But they were glad to be alive.

And so, aside from the normal weekly meetings, more was needed. Something *special*. The convention was announced at meetings; special notices were put up all throughout the colonies. It was to be a one-day program based on the words of Exodus 14:13: *"Stand Firm and See the Salvation of Jehovah"*.

Behind the scenes, brothers worked around the clock to arrange the massive event. Logistically, it was a seemingly insurmountable challenge. While the brothers wished to hold the program simultaneously in every possible language, there was simply no way to accommodate everyone; even with every meeting hall and available arena combined, the number of attendees was simply too large. And so, after much deliberation, it was finally decided that the newest arrivals—those in need of the greatest spiritual assistance—would attend in person at the halls, while the majority of the Witnesses would watch live broadcasts in cafeterias or in courtyards near the domestic units that had gradually come to serve as community centers and town squares for the friends.

For the injured and the infirm, special viewing areas were assembled in the medical wards. And for the few that could not make it even to these areas, portable radios were delivered and tuned in to the appropriate local shortwave frequency. It was the first time such a gathering had ever been possible, and the first time in the history of mankind that so many had been gathered together in the worship of the true God at the same moment. And thus the 'Stand Firm' super assembly was to become a landmark in theocratic history that would never be forgotten.

In Grunau, Peter, Rachel, Claire, and the others in their block gathered in the D2 courtyard. Their clothing was casual but clean and respectable, a dress code many areas had grown accustomed to before and during the great tribulation when their meetings had been pushed underground. For those with parts on the programs, slightly more formal wear was provided to wear. Still, with so many cultures, languages, and peoples assembled in one place and under such unique circumstances, suits and ties had become a rarity.

The program began early in the morning, at 6:30 AM, long before the hot daytime sun had climbed into the desert sky. For many, it was not an especially difficult time, as they had by now adjusted to an earlier morning routine. At 10:30, a four-hour siesta would allow time to return home, eat, rest, and take shelter from the more intense hours of sunlight.

After the opening song and prayer, the program began. In a welcome address, the chairman rattled off a series of statistics: the number of countries represented in the territories, the number of separate viewing locations, how many had arrived in the final month, and so forth. The figures were astronomical and difficult to comprehend, but no one doubted them. It was clear from just a glance around them that history was being made, that Jehovah's spirit was operating upon his people as it never had before.

"But as happy as we all are to be among our brothers and sisters," the speaker said, pausing for the thousands of simultaneous translators to convey the thought, "this is not the time for self-congratulations. The attack of Gog is now imminent."

The brother read a passage from Ezekiel and summarized the events that would soon unfold and, indeed, waited just on the horizon. "As we hold this very convention today, military entities carefully observe our every move. Army bases have even been constructed on our very own property, despite this being a clear violation of our rights to this land. While we have tried, in a spirit of peace, to resolve these issues, we have not been surprised to find our repeated requests denied."

Next, the chairman outlined the program that would ensue. The parts prepared today would help the brothers and sisters strengthen their determination to remain faithful to Jehovah despite whatever trials awaited them. It would seek to further bolster their unity, with an entire two-hour symposium dedicated to promoting unity and forgiveness among differing cultures and languages. Finally, it would build their expectation for the near future, when, after Armageddon, a thrilling new task would await them.

The brother's address was twenty minutes long, but to many held in rapt attention, it felt like much less. When he finished, the arenas, assembly halls, and apartment blocks broke out in thunderous applause that echoed through the valleys and the canyons and could be heard for miles into the desert.

***

Chad Harkett sat upright as the odd noise ricocheted off of the rock walls around him. It was a distant, hissing noise, like an approaching swarm of locusts. He waited and listened and felt an uneasy tension. The sooner he left this desert, the better. As glad as he was to be off of the ocean and away from the cold steel interior of the *Ronald Reagan*, the terrain here was barren and uninviting—an endless stretch of white desert.

Their convoy had stopped to replace a flat tire. Above them, a jagged line of silhouettes danced on the canyon edge: baboons watching on curiously. Annoyed, one of the soldiers shouldered his weapon and fired off a few rounds in the monkeys' direction; they scattered away unharmed as the noise of the bullets echoed off the rock walls.

"Something about this place gives me the creeps," Chad mumbled, wiping a dusty streak of sweat from his forehead.

"This isn't a great position, tactically speaking," replied one of the soldiers. He was leaning against the hood of the truck with a cigarette between his lips.

"Relax," quipped another soldier. "The Witnesses have nothing to attack us with down here. There's nothing to be worried about."

Chad grunted an acknowledgement. No one spoke another word until the convoy was moving again. The canyon walls eventually gave way to sloping rocky formations followed by massive orange dunes of sand. Eventually, the convoy stopped; before them stood an entourage from the local military force. A thin black man decked out in military regalia stood, arms crossed, beside a gleaming black SUV. He introduced himself and shook hands with some of the Americans.

Chad exited his vehicle behind the tight knot of soldiers. They were quickly filled in on the situation.

"You are at the southernmost edge of Grunau," the thin man said, glancing behind him and pointing in the direction of the valley. "We have conducted thorough surveillance on each of the colonies and there is no reason to expect any surprises. All is as planned. They are defenseless. Easy prey."

"We heard some noises when we were stopped in the canyons, sounded like it may have been aircraft overhead, but we didn't spot anything," one of the soldiers asked.

"They are holding a religious assembly. It is being broadcast everywhere," the sergeant scowled.

"Your men are ready?" asked the soldier.

The sergeant nodded proudly, chest stuck out. "Of course. We have collected all of the information as your generals required."

"Fine," the soldier said, glancing at the time on his wrist. "Give us two hours to get into position. We'll have eyes on you from the sky. You can be ready to move then?"

"Absolutely," the man responded.

The soldier nodded, saluted the commander, then ordered his men back into the transports to press on through the shifting dunes.

CHAPTER 27

Dietrich Nash dried his sweating palms against his khakis as he waited offstage for his cue. In spite of years of speaking before various Bethel families and congregations, he'd never quite gotten over his fear of public speaking, and the unease he felt now was unparalleled. This was no typical meeting or assembly; his face and voice would be broadcast to millions, and likely recorded for the future viewing of countless more. This was a historic day that would be meticulously documented, and Dietrich would have preferred to not be included. He'd always seen himself as a behind-the-scenes kind of brother, content with keeping the cogs running in the machine. But the brothers had decided otherwise, and here he was, standing behind a tall, swaying curtain waiting to be interviewed.

"Next," Dietrich heard a voice say, "we'd like to interview a brother who's been a part of the colonies from the beginning, long before most of us even knew they existed. With over forty-five years in special full-time service, many of those years spent here on the African continent, I'd like to introduce…" Dietrich felt the muscles in his gut tense and his feet move him forward. He found himself sitting, moments later, on a sofa across from the interviewer, a brother he'd known for years and a much better orator than himself. His name was John. They shook hands and began.

"So I understand, Dietrich, that the colonies here have quite a few stories behind them. Perhaps you can share a little of how you became involved with the project?"

"I'd be happy to," Dietrich said, struggling to ignore the thousands of faces in the audience around them and the cameras hovering above, allowing millions more to tie in. "I got the first call back in 2015. The branch requested me to try to locate a tract of land here in Namibia. At the time, I had no idea what it was for; I assumed it was for some sort of school or possibly a remote translation office, though the size of land they asked for seemed much larger than anything we'd actually need."

"Do you remember how big it was?"

"Yes. Originally, twenty-thousand square kilometers. But that quickly grew. To be honest, it seemed absurd at the time."

"How did the officials react when you met with them to purchase the land?"

"They were delighted. They had no use for the land—no one did. To them it was like free money, and that was good, because we had our own set of requirements. It was important that Witnesses could enter the country without visas or passports. To their credit, the Namibian government agreed to provide a simple form for our brothers to fill out that made visa-free travel possible."

"What else can you tell us about those early days of the building projects here?" John asked. Dietrich had relaxed somewhat by now; this was beginning to feel more like just a conversation between two friends.

"I think all of us were shocked to hear what plans were in store for this place—it just didn't seem humanly possible to relocate everyone and stick them in one place, and a desert at that! However, it became clear to us that things were falling into place very quickly.

"For example, one of the biggest challenges we faced in the early days was a lack of manpower. There was an incredible amount of work to accomplish and we really didn't think we'd have enough volunteers to get the first phase of the building off to a good start. And with a project as massive as this, that start is a crucial step. But it just so happened that as we were praying for volunteers, civil war broke out in two adjacent countries—Angola and Botswana— sending thousands of refugees out of those territories and looking for a place to settle. Obviously, we welcomed our brothers and sisters with open arms. Of course, it wasn't easy in the beginning and conditions were not ideal, but our dear brothers and sisters from those lands were so thankful to be alive and safe that it didn't matter. They set to work immediately and the next stage of our project got underway right on time."

Next came a video, a short documentary that had been filmed over the course of several years and edited on site. It started with a time lapse showing the laying of the foundations for the main buildings, the cranes being assembled and moving supplies from the train carriages to the construction sites. Several overseers and workers were interviewed briefly on camera, explaining just how they'd seen Jehovah's hand in the work, from the perfectly-timed delivery of building supplies to the effect of the brothers' multinational organization on the native tribes. When the video finished, few eyes were dry, and the applause lasted for nearly a whole minute.

***

It had not been a difficult thing to spot the woman and child among the crowd gathered on the grass staring up at the monitor perched atop an elevated platform. Evan had, after all, been explicit with his description of their address—Block D2, room 502. Fortuitously, the block numbers were painted on the corner of the upper level of apartments. It had taken Chad only fifteen minutes to spot the correct block, at which point he'd slipped into more casual attire and a generic baseball cap and begun making his way down into the colony. Transfixed by whatever was happening on the monitors, no one gave a second thought to the man slipping in among them, making a bee line straight for the spot where Chad had spotted Angelica and the boy.

Chad knew he didn't have much time. The commander had given him only thirty minutes to get in and get out. Beyond that, he wouldn't guarantee anything; as soon as the Namibian and South African joint forces took action in Bismarck, things would move quickly. Chad tried not to think about what would become of him if he got caught in the stampede that was sure to take place just minutes from now.

He slipped around the perimeter of people, their eyes glued to the screens around them, and made his way quietly to his target, half wondering if he'd run into Thiago somewhere out here as well. It was a risk, coming alone like this, but it was the only chance he'd get. Soon, he imagined, this whole area would be leveled, reduced to burning, smoking ruins.

Chad neared his target. It wasn't that he was especially close to Evan, but this wasn't about sentiment, and it wasn't about family. It was about winning. For all his life, Chad had been a winner. Even when the odds had seemed insurmountable, he'd always adapted to his surroundings and remained the hunter. And now here he was, at the farthest reaches of the globe, where his ex had no doubt imagined he'd never find them.

But he had.

***

"I'm sure the friends would love to know, having worked on the projects here for so long, and having witnessed everything you've seen, what lessons do you feel you've come away with?" asked the interviewer.

Dietrich Nash paused for a long moment, his gaze wandering out over the mixed crowd.

"Jehovah has everything under control," Dietrich said simply, his pulse slowing as an unusual calm settled over him. "As imperfect humans, we tend to view things with physical eyes. We see challenges before us and imagine them to be insurmountable, simply because the solutions aren't obvious to us. I'm sure many of our brothers and sisters here today can attest to this—some of you probably had no idea how you would be able to evacuate from your hometowns on the other side of the globe and relocate to some unknown, foreign place. Some of you are disabled, or bedridden, or came from poor villages with no form of public transportation. But in every instance, Jehovah provided a means of escape, and here we all are.

"Whatever challenges come next, it's important to view them with eyes of faith. Just as Jehovah has cared for each of us till now, he will continue to provide a means of escape then. We do not need to fear, but only to stand firm and see the salvation of Jehovah. All is under—"

Brother Nash was cut off as a loud explosion went off somewhere behind him. He and the interviewer turned to look as the audience gasped. Just behind the curtain, a white cloud of gas was rising into the air. In a moment, the mood of the entire arena had changed. Armed soldiers forced their way onto the stage, toppling microphone stands and shoving the speaker's podium from the stage, where it crashed onto the floor and splintered. Shocked, many in the audience stood from their chairs, glancing worriedly at one another, trying to determine what to do. In just moments, the brothers on stage and the attendants rushing to their aid were wrestled to the ground and handcuffed by the soldiers who carried them off to armored vehicles waiting nearby.

Moments later, a large Namibian official wearing a jacket of

303

shining brass badges stood at the center of the stage. He bent down to lift one of the microphones from the stage and spoke in a deep, booming voice: "By order of the Namibian South African Defense Force, this assembly is adjourned. Return to your homes immediately for further instructions. Any who resist will be arrested."

***

Alvin and Joyce Tucker sat staring up at the large screens in the Grunau North assembly hall, shaken and stunned. Joyce felt her husband reach over and squeeze her hand as the two shared a look. Outside of the open air arena, military trucks were skidding to a halt in the dirt. Armed soldiers poured from the vehicles and began barking orders at the brothers and sisters.

"This is an illegal assembly!" one of the soldiers was shouting angrily into a bullhorn. "Disperse immediately or you will be punished!" A line of brothers tried to block his path to the stage but were quickly apprehended by burly soldiers holding riot shields and batons. The crowd shrieked as several of the brothers' faces were sprayed with a red liquid and carried off into the waiting trucks.

"Oh my," Joyce said, looking to Alvin for some kind of action. Her husband merely shook his head.

"Jehovah has everything under control," he reminded her softly as he began gathering their belongings. Obediently, the crowd made its way to the doors. The room was remarkably quiet for what they'd just witnessed.

"I sure can't wait till they get what's coming to them," Stacy muttered under her breath as she hobbled beside the Tuckers towards the doors.

"Easy, Stacy," Alvin cautioned.

"What? I can't look forward to that?" Stacy shot back.

"Just watch what you say," Alvin said as they passed through the doors. A guard stationed there held a camcorder to his face, carefully filming each Witness as they exited.

"You there!" someone shouted as Alvin emerged. He looked up as a pair of officers accosted him, grabbing his arms and pulling him out of the crowd.

"No!" Joyce shrieked. With lightning speed, the guard holding the camera drew the back of his hand across her face. She toppled backwards into Stacy, where the two of them were caught by a small group of Witnesses. Something flared in Alvin's eyes and his mouth opened, but he quickly clenched his teeth together and turned away from the scene. A quick prayer was all that kept him from striking back at the soldier, a man smaller than himself.

"Is this you?" asked one of the soldiers, holding up a blown up image of a face on his tablet. Alvin glanced at the photo and nodded.

"It is."

"You will come with us, then," the soldier said, slapping a pair of metal cuffs onto Alvin's wrists and signaling for a pair of soldiers to haul him off.

Barely able to stand on her own feet and still reeling from the soldier's blow, Joyce squinted at the hazy image of her husband vanishing into the back of the soldiers' car and stretched a hand out to him, but he was already gone.

***

Peter squeezed his way through the crowd of brothers and sisters. Most of them were now standing at full attention as the screens around them broadcast hissing static. A brother in a baseball cap passed by and Peter briefly made eye contact and nodded. The face seemed familiar but he couldn't place it, and no wonder: the last few months he'd met hundreds of new brothers and sisters; it was difficult keeping their names straight, let alone remembering where he'd first met them.

"Ok, back to the apartments," Peter was saying as he approached his group, his eyes roving over the small crowd that had congregated around him. Similar groups had formed around their respective overseers. Tension in the air was unmistakable, but Peter didn't sense fear. They'd been expecting this, after all. Peter took a quick headcount. Rachel and Claire stood at his side expectantly, as did Ted and Angelica. But Angelica did not look well.

"Has anyone seen Evan?" she asked, eyes wide and wild and she shot glances around them.

The group began searching, calling out his name, but it was hopeless. Hundreds of other Witnesses—including many small children—were filing out of the courtyard towards the apartment pods in every imaginable direction.

"When did you see him last?" Rachel asked.

"It couldn't have been five minutes ago—he said he needed to use the bathroom, and I saw him briefly when he returned, but then... He just vanished."

"He could've gotten turned around in the crowd," Peter suggested. "Might be with some other group."

"No," Angelica said adamantly with a shake of her head. "Not Evan."

"Maybe he just went back to your pod," Ted said with a shrug.

Angelica frowned. "I'm going to check. But please keep an eye out for him just in case, would you?" Angelica said to the group. They nodded in return and continued the search while they made their way to the apartment blocks. Overhead, a row of surveillance drones whirred by.

Rachel gave them a quick glance and grimaced. "I sure hope he's ok," she said quietly to her husband. Peter didn't respond. Something at the back of his mind was bugging him but he wasn't sure what.

"He's a smart kid," Ted was saying. "He wouldn't have gone far." Ted stopped briefly to call out Evan's name over the sea of heads flowing around him.

Peter had stopped in his tracks, too, but for an entirely different reason. Something had clicked, a realization that sent an icy chill up his spine.

"Oh no..." he said softly. The rest of the group stopped to turn and look at him.

"What is it?" Rachel asked.

"Chad," Peter said simply, casting a worried look at Ted.

"Chad? Angelica's ex? What about him?" Ted asked.

"I bumped into someone in the crowd just moments ago. A familiar face. He was wearing a baseball cap. I didn't place him at first."

A deep crease formed in Ted's forehead. His shoulders tensed as he leaned forward. "You've got to be kidding me."

"I'm pretty sure it was him."

"If he even lays a hand on either of them—" Ted cut himself off, eyelids pressed closely together as he shook his head. His fists were squeezed into tight clubs at his sides.

"We need to find them," Peter said, his pulse beginning to race. "Rachel, Claire—you two go get Angelica and bring her to our apartment. It's not safe where she is."

"How could he have possibly found us here?!" Ted said, his head reeling.

"That doesn't matter right now, Ted. What matters is getting the boy back safe."

"What should we tell Angelica?" Rachel asked.

"No sense keeping the truth from her. But get to that apartment and lock the door. Go. Now!" Peter ordered as the women ran off to find Angelica.

"How?" Ted asked through gritted teeth once the women were gone. But Peter ignored him.

"I was standing right over there when I saw him," Peter said. "Seems he would've been coming from that direction." Peter pointed towards one of the distant hills.

"There? But there's nothing out there but sand dunes," Ted protested.

"I wouldn't be so sure of it. Come on, we'd better hurry."

And as the words were leaving Peter's mouth, he noted a sudden change in temperature. An odd, southerly wind had picked up. It was cool and damp and felt like nothing he'd experienced in all his time in the Namib. Above them, the color drained from the sky as a dark storm front began its approach.

CHAPTER 28

The dirt walled cell was nearly pitch black, the only source of light a thin sliver that leaked from an uneven seal in the doorway at the top of the stairs. It was dusty and hot, but perhaps not as bad as it could have been had the cell been located above ground, where the incessant Namibian sun could beat down on it for hours. At least they had that.

"Is anyone injured?" asked the muffled voice of Dietrich Nash. None of the thirty other men in the room responded. A good sign. Immediately following their coordinated arrests throughout the colonies, black hoods were slipped over the brothers' heads as they were shoved into vans and escort vehicles and moved to this cell.

"Perhaps we can take turns each saying our names and where we're from," brother Nash suggested, curious about who'd been arrested. He introduced himself briefly, although with his reputation it was hardly necessary. Everyone in the room had seen the broadcast of his interview. One by one, the others followed suit.

The brothers found themselves seated on a semi-circle of rough wooden benches, their wrists handcuffed together and chained to steel pegs driven deep into the ground beneath them, making it impossible to change positions or even to sit up straight. It was uncomfortable, and unpleasant to contemplate how long they might be stuck like this. They'd been told nothing.

There was a loud bang from one side of the cell as the door whipped open and several pairs of boots descended the stairs. The brothers could hear the jingle of keys and the creak of leather. An overhead bulb clicked on, and beads of light appeared within the brothers' hoods, though they could discern nothing from the blurred shapes beyond them.

"You should see yourselves now," said a deep, powerful voice that Dietrich recognized instantly. "So sure of yourselves for so long. So convinced that God was on your side. But just look at you! And would you believe that not one of you put up any resistance? Not so much as a struggle with the military police that brought you here. Isn't it your Bible that says that 'God only helps those who help themselves'?"

Ngoma paused for a response but was met with only silence. Under his hood, Dietrich was shaking his head quietly, but it was enough to catch the commander's attention.

"Speak up, Mr. Nash! Or have you finally come to your senses?" teased the commander.

"We have nothing to say to you, Commander," Dietrich said.

"Oh? Is that so?" Ngoma prodded. "Because my own men were listening quite attentively to your little speech this afternoon, and we did not appreciate your threats to our military and our government."

"They were not threats, sir."

"Shall I bring the recording in for you? Do you need to hear with your own ears the words you spoke less than two hours ago? Or would you deny them even then?"

"He's telling the truth," came another voice from across the room. Dirt and gravel crunched under Ngoma's heels as he turned to face the other brother.

"Who are you?" Ngoma demanded.

"You should know—your men had my name and photo in their database. I'm Alvin Tucker. What Brother Nash is saying is true. He wasn't threatening anyone. He was merely quoting a Bible prophesy."

"Such stubborn people!" Ngoma said, forcing an obnoxious laugh. "After all this—after every church and temple and shrine has been wiped clean from the surface of the Earth, still you stick to your old religion."

"We are not ignorant, Commander," Dietrich said. "We know what lies over that horizon. We know about the ships and the planes waiting to attack."

"And yet you've done nothing," Ngoma said scornfully.

"To the contrary. We've done everything we could to keep our people safe."

"Keep them safe! And how do you expect to do such a thing when you've failed to keep even yourselves safe?"

"We protected them until the end. Our God Jehovah knows it, and he will take care of the rest."

"Some God!" boomed Ngoma. "Unwilling even to protect you all! I would not bet on him doing much for the rest."

The brothers were silent. There was nothing left to say.

"Commander," came a distant voice from the corner of the room, where the stairs led up to the ground level.

"Yes?"

"The Americans are on the line. They say it is time."

"Fine," said Ngoma in a low, solemn voice. He took in the room of hooded men once more before chuckling to himself and climbing up the stairs and out of the dirt cell. When the light had been turned back off and the cell door had shut, Dietrich spoke to the group.

"Perhaps," he said quietly. "one of you brothers would be willing to represent us in prayer."

***

Evan could not remember ever having felt as conflicted as he did now. On the one hand, he was thrilled to see his Dad again. It had been months since they'd last seen each other, and longer still since the two had shared any kind of meaningful time together. Now it seemed that he was getting all the Dad time he'd ever hoped for.

"So you mean that you were in another one of the colonies this whole time?" Evan asked, trying to keep pace with his father's long strides up the sandy hill.

"Yeah, that's right," Chad said. "Another colony."

"Whoa. So, you're studying, then?" Evan asked.

"Studying. Yeah, sure. Whatever," Chad said distractedly with a glance at his watch.

"Man, mom must be pretty happy about that!" Evan said, delighted. "I never thought both my Mom and Dad would become Witnesses!"

"Look, Evan, can we have this conversation a little later? We need to pick up the pace if we're going to make it back to base in time."

"Oh. Yeah, sure. Ok," Evan said, happy to comply. But then he frowned. "What base?" A handful of jets holding in a tight V formation soared overhead and the two paused to squint up at them.

"See those planes?" Chad asked.

"Uh uh."

"They're from the base. Same place we're headed to."

Evan's pace slowed as he watched the planes vanish behind a thick wall of clouds.

"Those planes? But aren't those from the military?" Evan asked his father.

"Well yeah, sure. But it's part of *our* military. The Witnesses' jets, you know?"

"Our military? But we don't have a military, Dad," Evan said softly.

"Son, can we have this conversation another time? We're really running out of time here."

"But I don't get it, Dad," Evan said, stopping in his tracks. "The Witnesses don't have jet fighters. We don't need them. Jehovah is going to fight for us during Armageddon. We just had a talk about it. Didn't you see it?"

"Evan! Please, not now! Just keep moving!" Chad snapped. Evan recoiled, a look of doubt and fear beginning to well in the small boy's eyes.

"Actually, I don't think I want to go that way, Dad," he said softly.

"What did you say?" Chad snarled, glaring at his son. He took two steps toward him, his hands balled into fists.

Evan felt a knot forming in his throat, as a cold sheen of sweat formed on his face and arms. His tongue was swollen; words were impossible. He could only shake his head slowly.

"You're telling me that I came all this way for nothing? Is that it?!" Chad demanded, yelling down at the child. But Evan wouldn't budge. His eyelids were pressed tightly together as he prayed fervently to Jehovah.

"Answer me!" Chad screamed, drawing back the palm of his hand to strike the boy. But then, gazing up, he stopped. Two figures had appeared in the distance. Chad squinted. Were they soldiers?

He waited a few moments as the distance between them shrank.

***

Peter and Ted and followed their instincts, which led them out of the south end of the valley and up the hills to the desert plateau. The land turned barren here, the fertile, sloping valley walls giving

311

way to a parched white landscape where skeletal trees rattled in the breeze, branches chattering like teeth.

It was mercifully cool; the desert sun had vanished behind a swirling curtain of grey blue clouds, the color of a stormy sea. In the distance, they spotted them: two figures, a man and a child, walking side by side.

"That's them," Ted said with certainty. The two picked up their pace, though neither had a plan.

At fifty meters from Evan and his father, the pair of brothers stopped. Chad had turned and spotted them. His dark eyes scowled beneath his baseball cap.

"Not a step further!" Chad Harkett shouted over a gusting desert wind. In the distance they heard the rumble of thunder.

Peter and Ted came to a stop, palms held above their heads. "We're not here for a fight," Peter called out. "We just want the boy."

"He's my son. He stays with me," Chad said, pulling Evan by the sleeve of his shirt and pushing him to one side. The boy nearly tripped over his own feet.

"How did you even get here?" Ted Watkins asked.

Chad grinned. "By aircraft carrier," he said, letting the words sink in. But the men didn't react. "Sailed all the way from California. There's an international fleet of ships out there, all waiting to attack."

Evan looked up at his father and frowned. The boy said something that neither of the brothers could make out. "Just shut up and stay with me," his father hissed in response.

"Let the boy go, Chad," Peter shouted.

Chad responded with a laugh. "You think I'm forcing him? You see any chains? He wanted to come; he hates it here. This was a rescue mission."

"Is that true, Evan?" Ted asked. The small boy's wide blue eyes blinked a few times as he looked up at his father, then at Ted and Peter, and then over his shoulder. He frowned and slowly shook his head.

"I want to go back," Evan said finally.

"Congratulations, you successfully brainwashed my kid," Chad said, shrugging it off with a sneer.

"The end is close, Chad. Let him go and be with his mother where it's safe," Peter said.

"Safe!" Chad said, throwing his head back for a laugh. "You people have no idea what's coming, do you? None of you are safe! This whole area is about to become a giant smoking crater in the middle of the desert. It's over, guys, and so is this conversation." With that, Chad reached behind his back and removed a small black gun. He aimed it directly at the brothers and pulled the trigger.

***

Peter and Ted dived for the sand as the bullet whizzed past them. Evan was screaming, the wind was howling. Covered in dust and sand, the brothers raised their heads to see Chad approaching slowly, the barrel of his gun pointed at them as he chambered another round. There was nowhere to go, no cover in sight. A sharp crack rang through the air as the second bullet was fired. It landed with a thud in a puff of sand just inches from Ted's head. They heard the metallic click as Chad prepared his third shot. His feet crunched along the gravelly sand.

"NO! Dad, stop!" Evan was yelling, pulling at Chad's shirttails, trying to dig his heels into the sand. Chad turned and threw the boy off of him. His face was cold and expressionless.

"Should we make a run for it?" Peter asked Ted.

"I'm not leaving without Evan," Ted said. Peter nodded. Wind blew stinging sand into their faces, into the creases of their clothing and down the necks of their shirts. It was warm and gritty.

Overhead, the clouds were parting just enough for the sun to be visible once again. An odd, ethereal greenish haze hung in the sky around it. Clouds of dust now raced across the plateau, making it difficult to see. The figure of Chad's body moving slowly towards them wavered intermittently through the dust. Ted and Peter laid their heads back down in the sand, ears pressed into the earth, eyes shut tightly. An odd sound rose up from the ground to meet them, a rhythmic thudding noise not unlike the hooves of galloping horses.

"You hear that?" Ted asked.

"Yeah," Peter replied, opening an eye to stare up at the sky, hoping to see an angelic horseman coming to their aid. But the sickly, swirling skies were empty.

"It's getting louder!" Ted said excitedly. He raised his head from the sand to gaze out into the dunes. In the distance, lithe grey shapes were racing towards them. Ted shook Peter's shoulder.

"Look!" Ted said. Peter looked.

Chad was now just a few meters from them, an elbow arced over his face to shield it from the thrashing sands and dust. His eyes smiled as he came into range, lifted the gun one final time, and prepared to fire at the men lying in the sand.

But the cheetahs were too fast. The large male cat was merely a blur as it leapt high into the air, snatching at its prey with sharp claws and teeth. Chad's final shot went wild as his body flew to the side with the sudden impact of the predator crashing into him. He screamed once—a terrified, unbelieving yelp as his fingers clawed the sand—before the cat's long fangs clamped down.

Peter and Ted were too stunned to move. They laid in the sand gazing up into the creature's large, yellow eyes just a few feet from their faces. Its black nostrils flared, chest swelling, spotted coat rippling in the wind as it caught its breath. Slowly, it lay down in the sand beside the fallen body to rest. The other cheetahs gathered around the body quietly and sat.

Ted rose slowly from the ground, eyes locked on the cheetah as he stood and backed away. The creatures looked up at him curiously but made no effort to move.

"I guess that's that," Ted whispered to Peter. Carefully, he and Peter left the scene, found Evan, and returned to camp.

***

"Chad? You there?" Driscoll barked into his transmitter. His forward base had just set up camp in the eastern plains of the Namib, not far from the canyons leading into Bismarck. He knew Chad was somewhere far to the south, at another one of the Witnesses' colonies in Grunau, though his exact location was unclear. He waited a few moments, but nothing came through. He'd been trying to contact the man for the last five minutes, but so far the radio had been silent.

"Fool," Driscoll said under his breath with a shake of his head. After all, he'd told the man not to trek out there. Not to ground zero, and not so close to the strike time. It was suicide, and now he was gone. Beside him, a scrawny technician wearing fatigues two sizes too large gave Driscoll a look. He was waiting for an answer. Driscoll glanced at his wrist.

"Forget it. This'll be on his head," he muttered, nodding to the tech. The tech nodded back and typed something into a laptop computer balanced on his lap.

The strike zone was clear.

Hundreds of miles away aboard the USS *Ronald Reagan*, two F-16s were scrambled and flung via aircraft catapults from the deck. Their noses pointed up into the sky, jet engines flaring blue as they climbed to meet the holding squadron above. Strapped beneath their wings and fuselage were their fully loaded payloads. The squadrons formed up high in the air, circled once, and oriented themselves towards the dunes and the colonies beyond.

***

Within the situation room of the aircraft carrier, a refrigerator fully stocked with expensive champagne had been wheeled in from the galley and stuck in a corner. Banners and flags hung from the doorways and the ceilings. Not long now, Driscoll thought, and the celebration could begin. At a large table in the center of the room, uniformed men and women from various countries—admirals, generals, and a handful of politicians—sat around with laptops and satellite phones. Cigar smoke drifted lazily in the air as they joked quietly amongst themselves, casting occasional glances at the large high-definition screens bolted to the walls behind them: live feeds from the SANDF drones, a high-altitude feed from the Americans' UAVs, and live images from the fighter pilots now making their way over the desert plains towards Bismarck, the Witnesses' capital city.

"Not long now, gentlemen," the president said with a grin, helping himself to a bottle from the fridge. Chilled waves of condensation wafted from the champagne as he set the bottle on the table and prepared to open it. At the top of the screens, an ETA read out the digits *1419*. Fourteen minutes nineteen seconds.

"I won't bore you all with another speech," said the president, eliciting mild chuckles around the table. "So consider this a kind of pre-toast." The president reached beneath the table, where a mahogany cabinet held tall, crystal champagne glasses. A secretary stationed at the corner of the room scurried over to help but the president shooed him away.

Behind him, the screen read *1344*.

"It's been a long ride for all of us, and the road ahead will no doubt be tedious and riddled with its own problems. But seeing how

315

we've all managed to come together gives me faith that this truly is the start of a new era—a new world order, if you will."

1310.

The president peeled away the foil from the top of the bottle and freed the cork with a thumb. It released with a pop into the air and the seated men and women gushed and applauded. The president took it upon himself to pour each of his guests a glass and passed the drinks around the room.

1203.

"I have faith that without religious interference, without this plague that has dominated our species for so long—" the president pointed to the screens over his shoulder, "our cooperative efforts will continue. We will rebuild, and we will thrive! To the future of the world!" said the president, lifting the glass of golden champagne over his head, and the others did the same.

***

"What happened? Where did you find him?" Angelica asked as Peter and Ted entered the apartment with Evan in tow. Rachel and Claire stood in the kitchen looking over Evan for bruises and cuts. He was dirty and dusty but unharmed.

"We'll tell you later," Ted said with a sidelong glance at Peter. "The important thing is that we found him."

"And that we're all together," Peter added, looking around the room at each of the faces. "Any announcements?" he asked.

"Nothing," Rachel said. "It's been eerily quiet out there. Everyone just fled to their apartments and have kept out of sight since."

The group fell silent as thunder rumbled ominously in the distance.

"What do you think will happen to the brothers who were arrested?" Claire asked.

Peter shook his head. "Jehovah will take care of them one way or the other. We don't need to fear for them."

"What if they take you two?" Angelica asked.

Ted and Peter exchanged a look. "We're prepared for that," Ted said.

"You don't think Jehovah will actually let it go that far, do you?" Angelica asked.

316

"I don't know. But I'm convinced he'll act exactly at the right time."

Rachel crossed the room to her husband, wrapping her arms tightly around him and pressing her head against his chest. She could hear the thud of Peter's heartbeat against her ear; it was surprisingly slow and steady.

In the apartment below them, a sound was vibrating up through the floor. The sound of singing. The group exchanged looks and began nodding.

"I think they've got the right idea," Peter said. "Let's get our devices out."

CHAPTER 29

The group of hooded brothers sitting in the dark were halfway through their fourth song when their cell door creaked open once again. They immediately fell silent and waited. A pair of shoes shuffled down the landing and paused in the middle of the room.

"Dietrich?" asked a mild voice. "Dietrich Nash?"

"Over here," Dietrich responded. The feet shuffled over and he felt a rush of cool air against his face as the canvas hood was pulled away. He found himself staring into the eyes of Adani Ratief. Sweat dripped from the man's brow and he was clearly out of breath.

"I came as soon as I heard about the arrests," Adani said, wiping his face. "Did they hurt you? Are any of you hurt?"

Dietrich shook his head.

"I told you this was coming. I wish you'd listened," Adani scolded, shaking his head as he looked around the room at the others.

"We made the right choice, Adani," Dietrich said simply.

"How can you say that? Just look at you! Look at your friends!" Adani said with a dismal look. "And this is only the beginning! You did nothing to protect yourselves and now these men will come in and take it all from you. Everything—everything you worked so hard for, Dietrich."

"It isn't over just yet, Adani."

"Oh I'm afraid you're quite right about that, Mr. Nash. It is going to get much worse before it is over."

"And is that what you came to tell me?"

Adani's eyes narrowed as he took in the sight of the helpless man chained to the bench before him. He raised his eyebrows and sighed.   "No. There is something more. A bit of good news for you and your friends." Adani paused here to open a briefcase he'd carried down the stairs with him. He set it on a folding metal chair and began rifling through papers inside. "As you know," he explained, "I have many connections within the Namibian government, and I have been fostering relations with the NSADF. They are difficult men to deal with, but you will be pleased to know that we have reached an agreement."

"What agreement?"

"Terms for your immediate release."

"And what are the terms?" Dietrich asked. In response, Adani set a document on a chair before him. Dietrich began reading but didn't get far.

"I'm sorry to disappoint you, Adani, but I'm not signing that form."

Adani Ratief stared at the man blankly, wide white eyes blinking in the dimness of the room. "You cannot be serious."

"I'm afraid so. And I won't change my mind."

"I don't understand, Dietrich. Do you have any idea what it took on my part to prepare these documents? If Commander Ngoma and the others had it their way, you would've all been *hung*—likely on the very stage on which you held your assemblies! Would you have preferred that? Your execution broadcast live to all of your followers?"

"I would take death over signing my name on that paper, yes," Dietrich replied. "And they aren't my followers. My death will have little consequence on how things play out here."

"You stubborn, stubborn man. Fools! All of you!" Adani said, whipping his head around to chastise the men, all still seated quietly on their benches.

"We've been over this many times before," Dietrich said. "Nothing means more to us than our loyalty to our God, Jehovah. Not our belongings, nor our land, nor even our very lives. Jehovah can give that all back to us, but he cannot restore our integrity once we have forfeited it."

"You thankless man!" Adani screamed, drawing back his hand and striking the defenseless brother on the cheek. Dietrich reeled from the impact and its surprising force. Only the metal cuffs locked around his wrists kept him in place; he felt the sharp metal bite into the skin as his body lurched to the side.

"Fine. I give up. I give up on all of you," Adani said, stuffing the documents back into his briefcase and charging up the staircase. The lights shut off, plunging the room back into darkness. The men heard the door creak, but before it shut completely Adani turned back to them and spoke. "What happens next... It is on your heads!"

319

The room was silent for a long moment until quiet sobs could be heard in the darkness. It was Dietrich.

"Are you ok?" someone asked.

"Yes. Yes, of course," Brother Nash managed.

"Not hurt?" someone else inquired.

"No. I am fine," Dietrich replied, struggling to catch his breath. "Just... disappointed. I've known that man for years. I'd always hoped he'd come around. I was wrong."

***

Strike Force Delta reached its target precisely on time. As the Time-On-Target clock in the situation room of the USS *Reagan* struck 0000, the squadron was circling at 8,000 feet with visuals on its target below. This particular team of Navy pilots had been specially selected for their nearly immaculate flying record. In their nearly twenty-thousand combined hours of Navy flight time, they'd downed over fifty combatant fighters, neutralized thousands of ground targets, and had never once lost an aircraft. They were national heroes, thoroughly decorated, and about to score another notch in their belts. None of them expected resistance. This would be easier than shooting fish in a barrel; this was more like lighting a stick of dynamite in a fish tank.

The lead pilot, who flew by the handle ZAG86, took a quick inventory of the planes in his squadron—a visual once-over at first, glancing over at the jets he could see out the window of his cockpit on either side of him—and then a radio call-in, confirming that nothing was amiss with his pilots. Everything checked out, there were no surprises. It was time to check in with the Mission Intelligence Coordinator back on the *Reagan* for final confirmation to strike.

"ZAG86 to MIC."

"MIC copies," replied the tower.

"Delta team in position and holding at eight thousand feet. All systems go."

"MIC copies. Do you have visual on the compound?"

"On screen, roger."

"Copy that, ZAG86. Lower to strike altitude and await further instructions."

"Roger that, MIC, Delta Team copies."

ZAG86 eased the tip of the F-16 downwards, and that was all it took. It had plummeted to five thousand feet in minutes. The pilot relayed their position back to the base and waited. No one expected to hear the next voice that was piped through their headsets.

"Hi guys, this is your president speaking," came the familiar voice. "Just wanted you all to know that everyone down here is rooting for you and can't wait to welcome you home. You're heroes already, but after this mission, you'll be legends. This isn't an opportunity that just comes along every day. You're making history today. This is bigger than D-Day, bigger than the A-bomb. This is the day we saved the world."

"Thank you, Mr. President," ZAG86 said. "We'll do our best."

***

The first bottle of champagne had not lasted long; neither had the second. The men and women gathered in the situation room had by all counts already begun celebrating their assured victory. After all, this was essentially a one-sided battle. They talked idly among themselves as the jets lowered altitude and began their final approach.

"Ladies and gentlemen, this is where the fireworks begin," the president announced smugly as he held a refilled glass of sparkling liquid to the crowd seated around the table and smirked. It was to be a historic day, not just for his country and its military, but for himself. He would forever go down in the books as the man who put the final nail in the coffin of religion. An unthinkable title only a decade ago, he realized, but how much had changed in the last few years. It hadn't been pretty, but as they said, all's well that ends well, and if the end of this whole fiasco meant his likeness immortalized in a bronze statue on the courtyard of some future university, then all was certainly well. He took a seat in his chair at the head of the table, spun around to face the monitors, and smiled giddily.

On one of the screens, live drone footage revealed the strike target—the Witnesses' main office compound and effective headquarters at the center of their capital city, Bismarck. This first strike would be what the Navy and Air Force liked to call a *hammer*, a powerful, decisive blow used to demoralize their enemies. Their capital fortress in ruins, the Witnesses would flee in horror and confusion, where strategically placed platoons and outposts would either pick them off or take them into custody, depending on the disposition and instructions given by that particular nation's military. With so many countries tied up in their coalition, it was hopeless reaching any sort of consensus on what to do. In the end, of course, it mattered not. The end result would be the same: the Witnesses would be gone forever.

"ZAG86 to MIC. We are in position," came the tinny voice over the speakers.

"MIC copies. You are go for strike," the tower responded.

For the following moments, the room fell silent. There were no clinking of champagne bottles, no muffled grunts and chuckles between the commanders, generals, and dignitaries, no sounds of preemptive congratulatory remarks. There was only anticipation. On the screens before them, the men and women in the dark room watched eagerly as the bombs were released from the bellies of the jet fighters and plummeted towards the ground.

***

"Bombs away. Repeat, the payload has been delivered," ZAG86 barked proudly into his microphone. He glanced quickly back and forth from his controls to the downward aerial cam feed, where a black-and-white screen showed the dark device shrinking to nothingness below. ZAG86 counted down in his head. 3. 2. 1.

BAM.

The pilot glanced back to the screen but there was nothing to be seen, the strike zone was out of frame. He would need to rely on confirmation from the UAVs' feeds.

"MIC, how we looking?" ZAG86 asked the control tower. Their response was not immediate.

"Stand by, Delta Team. We've got other comms coming in."

ZAG86 frowned. He looked over each shoulder at his fellow pilots flanking him and saw them return the expression with a shrug. Perhaps the bomb had failed. Even with all the cash Washington threw at their military tech, duds weren't unheard of, which was one of the reasons they had come prepared with backups.

"MIC to ZAG86, please confirm your coords," the tower finally said. The pilot's frowned deepened. What did the tower want with his coordinates? Had they attacked the wrong building? He checked and double-checked the numbers and called it in.

"Copy that, ZAG. Command is recommending you return to twenty thousand feet and hold. Please standby,"

What was going on? thought ZAG86.

***

Back in the situation room aboard the USS *Ronald Reagan*, the air was filled with the ringing and buzzing of phones. The champagne glasses had returned to the table. Something had gone terribly wrong. A young female Navy tech flew into the room and nearly crashed into the table. She signaled to the admiral and general. She had news, and it didn't look good. The president joined the trio in the corridor just outside the doors.

"What is going on out there?" the general demanded.

"The fleet is under attack," said the young woman, her face pale and covered in sweat.

"An attack? By whom?"

"Not sure yet. The Russians are saying one of their destroyers was hit from above. She's covered in flames. She's taking on water fast."

"You're telling me someone conducted an airstrike over this fleet and no one has any idea who it was? How is that possible!" hissed the admiral. The woman's entire body was shaking.

"Gentlemen, if I may," the president said, drawing irksome stares from the military brass. "I think we ought to consider the possibility that the attack was launched by some other party to this fleet."

"A coalition military attacking another member? And the point of that would be?" the admiral snapped.

"An old grudge, perhaps, or maybe some political play. Crazier things have been attempted."

"You're talking about an act of war—that would be suicide in these waters," said the general.

"I'm just saying we need to consider the possibility. We may have a coalition at the moment, but things can change in an instant. Once this threat is dealt with, we need to consider the possibility of a power struggle. There's a bigger picture here we can't ig—"

The president was cut off as the young tech from the situation room burst into the hallway, looking even paler than before. The men braced for the worst.

"We have a situation," he said simply, eyes locked to the floor. "You need to see it for yourselves." The men followed him back into the room and stared up at the large monitors in shock.

Another warship was in flames. This one belonged to the Chinese Navy. The president glanced at the representatives from the Chinese and Russian governments who'd previously been smiling expectantly at the screens, champagne in hand. Now they stood in opposite corners of the room, their backs turned to the others as they spoke on secure private lines.

"Tell me exactly what just happened," the admiral simmered. The tech was expressionless.

"It was a plane," replied one of the Chinese delegates from behind the table. "We all saw it. One of your American jets crashed into our ship."

"Impossible," the admiral said, but the Chinese were already gathering their things and heading for the doors.

***

ZAG86 couldn't explain it. One moment he'd been soaring high over the desert city of Bismarck, and the next he'd found himself back over the Skeleton Coast. He glanced over his shoulders through the cockpit windows only to discover that he was alone, the rest of his squadron nowhere to be seen.

"ZAG86 to base, something's going on here," he said uneasily into his mic. There was no response. He continued anyway: "Not sure if I blacked out... or... something. My location is way off here. I'm back at the coast. And I'm alone."

"MIC to ZAG86, we have a situation. Return to base ASAP, mission has been scrapped," came the curt reply.

Nothing made sense. The pilot checked his watch, double-checked his position, and proceeded back to the carrier. Suddenly, a pair of red lights began flashing on his control panel. He was nearly out of fuel. This didn't make sense either—they'd topped up their tanks before takeoff; checking that he had a full tank of fuel had been part of the checklist required for launch. It had been more than enough to take him inland and back, so how was he running low? Was there a leak? Was it instrument error? The pilot didn't know, but he struggled to push the questions from his head and focus on the task at hand—landing his plane back on the deck of the USS *Ronald*

324

Reagan.

Then something else caught his eye. Below him, two yellow and orange pillars of fire were erupting from the sea. Ships were on fire. The fleet was under attack.

"ZAG86 to MIC, I have eyes on a couple of ships that appear to be on fire. Please confirm clear for carrier landing, over," the pilot requested. He felt the sweat begin to cover his skin beneath his flight suit in spite of the cockpit's air conditioning. He waited ten seconds, then twenty. There was no word from the tower.

He dipped the nose of the plane down towards the horizon and felt the sea drift up to meet him. At five hundred feet, he leveled out. His carrier was right below him, and things didn't seem right there either. There was far too much activity on deck; no one seemed prepared for his landing. From the looks of it, the foreign representatives were trying to board their escort helicopters, ostensibly to head back to their countries' ships. It didn't look good. Something was definitely wrong.

ZAG86 tried his best to ignore the creeping sense coiled in the pit of his stomach. He wouldn't be able to land until the deck was clear and he had clearance from the tower, but he wouldn't last long circling in the air without fuel. It was beginning to look like he'd need to eject, but he'd need a safe spot to point the ditched aircraft in to avoid a collision with one of the fleet's ships. Time was running out and his options were few. He tried the radio again but there was no response from the tower.

Frustrated, the pilot decided to head once again to the dunes, where he could ditch the jet and somehow find his way back to the carrier. He leaned into the controls to steer the ship towards his new destination and realized that there was another problem. The stick wouldn't budge. He tried the pedals next, almost by instinct, but discovered a similar problem. They were stuck. He was unable to steer the plane. Stranger still, he could feel himself speeding up. With a glance at his air speed indicator, his fears were confirmed. It was as if the plane had been taken over by a third entity. The pilot knew all the rigors the Navy went through to keep their planes safe from these kinds of attacks, but everything was connected these days and nothing was failsafe. Now the nose of the plane dipped even further past the horizon, and ZAG86 finally had clarity. Dead center in his HUD was the command tower of the *Suzhou*, China's largest aircraft carrier and the crown jewel of her Navy force.

Desperate, ZAG86 conveyed the situation to base on his radio and tried everything he could think of to pull his jet off course, but all of it was fruitless. He jettisoned the canopy and ejected.

CHAPTER 30

The scene aboard the deck of the USS *Ronald Reagan* was total chaos. It was as if every good intention and proud proclamation had come back to bite them, and indeed, it had. The coalition was dissolving as quickly as it had been formed just months before. Red-faced dignitaries and military officials fled back to their ships by the droves, under strict instructions to have no further contact with the treacherous Americans. It had clearly all been a ruse, a trick to usher in an unprecedented era of world domination. Within five minutes of the *Suzhou* disaster, China had placed a secure call to the Russians pleading for a military pact against the Americans and British, but Russia refused. It no longer trusted anyone but itself.
Representatives aboard various ships were being herded in by the dozens. The sky was awash with buzzing helicopters.

They would fall from the sky next.

No one knew who shot first, only that once it started, it triggered an unprecedented naval battle. High caliber bullets and explosives were arcing and whistling through the air, shredding the airborne craft to pieces. Heaps of fiery metal fell lifelessly from the sky into the waiting waves below, but this was only the beginning. For those with aircraft carriers, more jets were scrambled with orders to bomb whatever they could. But most would never leave the runway, as the expansive tarmac made for easy targets by the enemies' turrets and mortars.

The sky filled with choking, black smoke as the ships began to burn. Oil leaked from burning wreckage, sluicing out over the surface of the water and eventually igniting. Some of the smaller ships managed to separate from the fray and flee, but they would meet their own fate soon enough.

***

The radio tech stared wide-eyed at the notes he'd been jotting down on the pad before him. Surely there had to have been a mistake. Surely this could not be happening. His fingers trembled as he finished transcribing the message. He yanked the headset away, stood from his desk, and ran down the bunker's dimly-lit corridor. They were thirty meters below the surface of the Tatischevo Airbase, a Russian military facility five hundred miles Southeast of Moscow. The men had been stationed here for this exact scenario, though they'd never once dreamed that the day would finally arrive.

At a junction in the corridor, the tech came face to face with his superior officer, a man not much older than himself who wore the exact same expression—one of abject horror and disbelief. But orders were orders. Together they ran farther underground until they reached the officer's quarters just outside of the launch site.

They carefully relayed the instructions. The codes they provided were accurate.

Within fifteen minutes, four nuclear warheads had been launched from submarines off the coast of the North American continent.

Of course, at the very same moment, similar things were happening around the world. No one wanted to be the first to push the button that would launch a global nuclear war. But it would be much, much worse to be the last.

***

In their apartment pod, Peter Burton crouched down to get a clear line of sight up at the sky around them. The storm had arrived; it was spitting droplets of rain against the glass. The greenish, purple sky bulged and blistered with tempestuous clouds ignited by intermittent bursts of lightning. The ground shook with every bout of thunder.

"The fighter jets still out there?" Ted asked, joining Peter at the window as the two stared up at the bruised clouds.

"Not too sure. Haven't seen or heard anything. It's like they just disappeared."

"Maybe the storm scared 'em off," Ted shrugged. Angelica walked over to join them at the window; Ted placed one of his large arms around her shoulders.

"You don't think that was it, do you?" Ted asked.

"Armageddon? I was expecting more."

"Me too, but who knows?" Peter said. He walked to the phone on the wall of the kitchenette. "Lines are down," he reported.

"I guess we just sit and wait this thing out, then," Ted said.

"Maybe we can do some reading together. An account actually just came to mind."

"Which one?" Rachel asked, joining the other three. Claire and Evan had fallen asleep together on the sofa. It had been a long day for everyone.

"One of the Gideon accounts, when he was up against the Midianites."

"Gideon and his 300 men," Angelica said. "Must've read that story to Evan a million times. It's one of his favorites."

"Remember how it ended?" Peter asked.

"They broke water jugs and make a lot of noise to confuse the enemy camp."

"And it worked. They began killing each other and fleeing."

"Whoa. You think that's what's happening out there?" Ted asked.

"It's possible. But I guess anything is," Peter said. The four made their way to the small kitchen table and began reading *Judges* chapter seven.

***

Driscoll and the other commanders and officers had grown increasingly impatient. Little was certain but for the fact that clearly the airstrike had run into trouble. Their air cover had since vanished, possibly due to the storm. But what made things worse was the complete lack of communication from their base. It was as if the lines had been completely severed, as if the satellites had fallen out of the sky somehow. There was no one out there but the other ground troops' and bases' chatter. Strong winds were beginning to blow sheets of sand over their men and the vehicles; for the past hour they'd resorted to moving the vehicles every few minutes or so to keep them from being buried in the sand.

Driscoll shook the warm desert grit from the folds of his jacket and walked to the other end of the tent, where an army sergeant sat hunched over the radio waiting for instructions. The thick green canvas making up the walls of their command center billowed and flapped around them with the fierce outside winds; Driscoll half expected that at any moment the whole thing would blow away.

"Still nothing?" he asked. The officer shook his head.

"We have our orders, regardless," Driscoll said.

"I'd prefer knowing what happened with the birds," the officer said, grimacing.

"Can't fly in this weather. Even F-16s have a limit. No surprises there."

"Doesn't explain the radio silence."

"Technical glitch," Driscoll said with a casual shrug.

"Maybe. I don't want to send the troops in blind," the officer said with a stony look at Driscoll, but the man was unfazed.

"This is hardly a battlefield. You saw the intel: no resistance expected. These nuts haven't even bothered putting up a perimeter fence and guard patrols."

"I've been trained to trust my gut. And something isn't sitting well with me on this one. Too many things are off."

"You're superstitious," Driscoll said.

"It's not that. This is quantifiable. My concerns are justified."

"It's *exactly* that. I know you were tuned into their religious meetings—an offense that could get you discharged, I might add."

"It was surveillance," the officer argued.

"It was *beyond* surveillance. So what were you before all this? Catholic? Protestant? Baptist, maybe?"

"I'm non-religious. Never have been."

"But curious all the same. I've seen that look. You start having doubts about the mission, maybe your conscience begins to prick you. You start listening in. Surveillance is your job, after all. But then those words start getting in your head. *Maybe God is on their side*, you start to think. Then the weather changes, our air cover retreats—"

"That wasn't a retreat, sir, and you know it. We have recorded drone footage. The jets… they simply… *vanished*. How do you explain that? And then this radio silence? Who knows what's happening back at base."

"Like I said, superstition."

"I saw them disappear with my own eyes!"

"You *think* that's what you saw. What you *really* saw was a glitch—a hiccup in the live feed, a few dropped frames from the live images that made the jets seem to disappear."

"Then how do you explain the bombs? We saw them drop. Where were the explosions?" the officer asked.

"Weapons malfunctions! Listen to yourself! Do you really think that *God* is fighting for these people?! Is that what you're telling me? Because if it is I'm prepared to slap a pair of cuffs on you and throw you in the back of one of the transports and we can wait for a military tribunal to decide your fate while I take your post—is that what you're asking for?"

The sergeant blinked his eyes rapidly, his shock at Driscoll's outburst momentarily overshadowing his misgivings.

"No... No, of course not," the man said, his attention returning to the equipment before him.

"Then let's finish this."

***

It had been decided prior to the deployment of ground troops that the enemy would be engaged primarily at close range. As much as possible, they were not to damage the structures making up the five Witness cities. After all, their compact, efficient design was clever and economical, and many of the nations suspected they would be able to find some use for them once rebuilding began in their home countries.

And so, in spite of the howling wind in their faces and the ominous, swirling clouds above, the troops were roused and ordered into position at the top of the canyon walls and dune plateaus. For many, it was the moment of combat they'd been waiting months for. They'd left everything behind to participate in this historic attack. Glancing up at the skies, some were now questioning whether it had been worth it. Still, the only way home now was forward, down the rock and sand embankments into the valleys below. They'd been told how heroic their actions would be. Some believed this, some did not, but on this particular day no one would question orders, no one would stay behind. When their commanders and captains gave the order to advance, they would unreservedly charge down into the apartment blocks and begin firing their weapons.

Of course, they did not know that it was already too late. Most of the homes and people they'd left behind had already been incinerated in nuclear blasts, entire cities and neighborhoods swept away like a fine layer of dust by a strong wind. In remoter areas, raining fire and sulphur, earthquakes, lightning storms, and tsunamis would wipe away what the atomic destruction missed. By the time the ground troops were finally given their orders, the coalition's military forces were all that were left of their old system, and they would not last long.

***

Peter Burton and Ted Watkins found themselves in one of the courtyards when the wall of soldiers appeared. The two elders had been conferring with overseers from nearby blocks to see if anyone had news regarding the Witnesses in Bismarck or the disappearing jets. As usual, theories flourished while little concrete information was known.

Suddenly, one of the brothers pointed and shouted. All at once, the conversations halted as the throng of brothers stared out at the distant hills. In every direction, swarms of soldiers were descending the slopes, rifles in hand. The sky above rumbled.

Peter took in the sight. He was awestruck—not for the fact that the armies were impressive, but for the fact that scenes just like this had been pictured before in the publications he'd read. His mind flashed back to years before, where he found himself sitting in a Kingdom Hall during a Watchtower study, distracted for a moment as his gaze lingered on an illustration of the attacking armies of the Gog of Magog. And here he was, he *himself*, witnessing the very event that would be the sure climax of Jehovah's war against Satan's system. Bible prophecy was coming to life before his very eyes, and he could not contain the thrill he felt to have made it to the end. He turned to the brothers, wondering if similar thoughts were racing through their minds.

"This is it!" he said, feeling his pulse race. There was no fear, no terror, only anticipation.

"Armageddon is upon us!" shouted another overseer. Thunder rumbled again, this time even closer, as if in response.

"Brothers, it has been an honor and a pleasure serving by your sides, and I will never forget this moment for as long as I live. These are the final moments of this old system. All we have left is to stand our ground and wait on Jehovah's armies."

Peter could not contain his emotions any longer. Hot tears

bulged in his eyes, and similar expressions could be found on each of the faces before him. Brothers' lips trembled, smiles widening as the realization sunk in that this truly was the end. In the distance, the battle cries and screams of the soldiers began to echo into the valley. They were strong and powerful, but a glance up at the roiling clouds reminded each of the brothers that they were nothing compared to the dynamic force that was on their side.

"We have nothing to fear!" Peter said, turning back to face the incoming wave of soldiers. And then he began to walk. *No weapon formed against you will have success*, he thought. *There are more with us than there are with them.* His feet continued leading him forward, all the way to the perimeter of the apartment block, where the faces of brothers, sisters, and children were pressed against the windows. Some were frightened, he realized.

And so the brothers sang. They sang as they never had before, their praise and entreaty lifting up to Jehovah above the sand and the dunes and drowning out the battle cries of the incoming soldiers. They sang for courage, for strength, and for endurance, the lyrics readily coming to their minds. Soon the sound of their singing had spread to the entire block of apartments, so that even within the pods the friends joined in the song, eyes watering, lips trembling as they waited on Jehovah.

And Jehovah did not disappoint them.

CHAPTER 31

When the soldiers finally found themselves within range, they fell to the ground, muzzles pointed at the brothers. Whatever reservations some may have had about shooting on unarmed civilians vanished in these crucial initial moments of combat. Their stance had been taken, and with it their fates were sealed. High in the skies above them, figures began appearing, men on horses, men armed with swords and bows and arrows, shining weapons held high in the air as if poised to strike. But the ground troops did not hesitate.

All at once, thousands of automatic weapons began firing, their tips exploding in furious white and yellow flashes. Emptied brass bullet casings spun and flung in the air as the crowd was sprayed with automatic weapons fire. Many of the bullets missed their marks entirely, burrowing into the earth in a puff of sand. But many shots were true and on target.

Still, they seemed to be having no effect. The soldiers scanned the lines of men standing below them; not one had fallen.

Confusion began to set in. Had the ammo been switched out somehow for blanks? Were the guns faulty? Soldiers and their captains began shouting at each other. Nothing like this had happened before. The command was given to advance and try again. Dutifully the men crawled forward a few meters, their hearts now racing, as they reloaded and launched a second assault.

***

The president and the few surviving members of his cabinet ducked for cover behind an overturned steel table. Along with all the rest of the mayhem of that day, the electricity had gone out, and now they were being fired at on their own ship. He covered his ringing ears as bullets pinged and sparked around him. He hadn't seen or heard anyone enter the room, but it felt like they were being assaulted by an entire army.

"What is going on here?! How are there so many of them?!" the president screamed over the barrage of bullets. But there was no answer. He shimmied along the floor on his belly to the general, but the general was still and unresponsive. The man's uniform was wet to the touch. The president recoiled in horror. He screamed again, but his only answer was the roar of more bullets.

***

"They can't hurt us," Peter heard Ted say over his shoulder. "It's like there's a protective wall or something between us!" he said, mesmerized. Testing the theory, Peter reached out his hands in front of him but could feel nothing. On the hills before them, the soldiers appeared to be arguing. After their second attack they had stopped firing and were apparently considering a new tactic. The brothers watched curiously while the men conferred angrily.

***

"We're doing this the old fashioned way," Driscoll shouted with a scowl, staring down at the confused troops on the hill below him. "Get out your blades, boys." Obediently, the soldiers shouldered their guns and began unsheathing their knives.

"Let's see them stop this," Driscoll grunted smugly to himself as the soldiers continued their advance, albeit much more slowly and cautiously than at first. The surrounding troops took notice and followed suit, abandoning their firearms for deadly, serrated blades. Step by step, they moved closer to the wall of stalwart brothers.

***

In spite of everything, Peter felt his pulse quicken as the mass of soldiers slowly descended the valley walls, knives glinting in their hands. Some were shouting taunts and howling. Many wore grins on their faces, clearly enjoying the prospect of what was about to occur. It was unnerving and disturbing, a sight that took all of Peter's resolve not to back away from. At that very moment, he felt an arm slipping into his own. He turned to find himself looking into the

335

determined face of Rachel, his wife. The two of them said nothing as they gazed into each other's eyes before returning their focus to the approaching enemy.

At less than twenty feet, one of the male soldiers pulled a short, jagged knife from a pocket on his thigh. He pinched the blade between a pair of fingers, flipping it in the air and catching it in his other hand. He wound his arm back, as if pitching a fastball, and threw the knife directly at Peter's chest.

Peter felt his heart skip a beat as the knife spun dizzyingly straight at him. But before it could make contact, it vanished. Just as the bullets had. Just as the jets and the bombs had.

Still, it seemed to make no difference to the soldiers. Now they charged again, faces red, eyes wide and wild as they ran, screaming, knives flashing in their hands.

Peter winced as the soldier who'd thrown the blade ran straight for him, knife clenched tightly at his side. Teeth bared, nostrils flaring, he was more wild animal now than man. But as he thrust forward, blade in hand, a look of confusion filled his eyes. He stood, frozen, for a moment, arm stuck out like a statue stuck in time.

And then, slowly, a form emerged as if stepping from an enshrouding mist. It bore the resemblance of a man, but its body shimmered like the surface of water in the sunlight. What looked like golden condensation fell from its shoulders in waves. It towered above the soldier, its hand outstretched, holding the man in place.

The soldier's eyes widened for a brief moment, his mind struggling to process what was happening, before the angel began glowing even more brilliantly than before.

Before their eyes, the soldier disintegrated.

The glowing figures in the skies descended all at once, falling upon their enemies in a curtain of glimmering light. The soldier's weapons were raised above their heads, muzzle tips igniting with pinpricks of light as they attempted to ward off the attack, but it was hopeless. The bullets passed harmlessly through the figures, the clothing of their garments rippling like wisps of smoke. The skies shook with thunder, their supercharged clouds whirling with otherworldly colors as tendrils of lightning scattered through the hills.

But it was no ordinary lightning. It bounded over the ground, spreading and expanding like an electrified net, seizing the soldiers caught within. They glowed brilliantly for a split second before falling, lifeless, to the ground. Panic seized the soldiers who remained. Many dropped their weapons and helmets, struggling to remove an excess weight as they turned to flee back up the embankment. But they would not make it very far before their eyes caught sight of what awaited them on the canyon walls and the crests of the sand dunes.

All around them, in radiant, glowing clothing, angelic horsemen stood poised to charge. The air filled with the bellow of unearthly battle cries, a sound that shook the ground and brought many of the remaining soldiers to their knees. The thudding of the war steeds' hooves against the rock and dirt were nearly deafening as they charged towards the uniformed men, raised their weapons, and attacked.

That the true God was protecting His people was an inescapable fact.

Commander Daniel Ngoma could hardly think straight. After he had witnessed the drone footage of the coalition's warships firing on each other, he had come straight back to his quarters—the opulently outfitted barracks he had set up for himself in the compound just outside of Bismarck. His men were scattered somewhere among the canyon walls preparing their ground attack with the Americans and the Russians, but as soon as they heard of what was happening at sea, Ngoma knew, anything was possible. He raced to the small command center at the edge of the room—a long table stacked high with expensive computers, surveillance equipment, and radios.

"Show me our soldiers," Ngoma demanded of the young technician sitting in one of the chairs. The man cast an uneasy glance over his shoulder before complying. His fingers danced over the keys as the image on one of the monitors came to life. But Commander Ngoma could hardly make out what he was seeing. The image was staticky and shaky.

"Why can't I see anything?" the commander grumbled.

"I... I don't know... Technical difficulties, I think, sir," stammered the tech.

"Get closer, then, and get me a clear image!" Ngoma said.

"Yes, sir!" shouted the tech, switching stations to manually pilot the drone. He banked left and then right, testing the controls. He could see the image panning this way and that. Clearly the image was still a live feed. Perhaps, he thought, there was some sort of interference. He brought the drone lower to the ground, and as a layer of low lying clouds lifted away from view, the two men gasped.

The hills were filled with the bodies of dead soldiers.

"No… It cannot be," Ngoma said, eyes wide as he stared at the monitors. "They can't all be dead! Show me more!" he screamed.

The tech obeyed silently, nudging the controls forward as the drone panned over the dunes. But it was all the same. As far as the eye could see, piles of lifeless uniformed men littered the hills.

"How? How is it possible?" Ngoma shrieked, fingers gripping the hair at the sides of his head.

Suddenly, the drone's live feed began to shake violently.

"What now?" Ngoma said.

"I don't know, sir! I don't know!" the tech said hopelessly as they watched the image slowly come to rest. Before the lens of the drone's camera sat a stretch of sand leaning at an odd angle. They could still see the outlines of fallen soldiers in the distance. And then, something entered the frame, the foot of a creature. It lowered its head, gazing straight into the lens with its large, yellow eyes. Ngoma felt a shiver race up his spine; it was as if the caracal was looking straight at them. It bared its fangs and pounced, and the live feed went dead, the monitor showing only blackness.

With that, the tech ripped the headphones from his head, stood, and raced for the door.

"Where are you going?" hissed the commander, but it was already too late. The man was gone.

What a mess! the commander thought furiously to himself, wiping a sheen of sweat from his face as he crouched behind the leather sofa in his quarters and accessed the safe. He had no plan in place yet, nowhere to go and hide to wait out the chaos, but that could wait. All that mattered now was *getting out*. He reached his arm into the safe and swiped its contents into a black garbage bag. There were diamonds and Rolexes and several other precious items here—mostly bribes he'd acquired in the previous two years. He reassured himself that they would be worth something in the days to come before tying a knot in the mouth of the bag.

A noise caught his attention—a muffled cough from the doorway—and he remembered the prisoners beneath his feet. For a moment he contemplated the thought of setting them free, but decided against it. There was nothing to be gained from their

338

survival.

Ngoma paused to glance wistfully at the expensive surround sound system, the 8K television, the mahogany wet bar—items too big to take with him—before stuffing the plastic bag of valuables into his pocket and exiting his quarters.

Outside, Ngoma stared up at the swirling mass of clouds. He ran as fast as his thick legs could carry him to his expensive Land Rover. But before he could reach it, his vehicle was destroyed. He stared in shock as the expensive SUV disintegrated before his eyes, the metal eroding away, exposing the interior. Layer by layer the car was turned to dust, a chaff instantly carried off by the winds.

Lifting his head to the skies, the commander screamed and cursed. He spat and snapped his teeth at the looming clouds and turned to run down the hill. There was no plan in his mind now; all that was left was a desperate attempt to save his own life. But at the bottom of the hill he came to a stop.

Just ahead of him, a glowing figure had appeared to block his path. It held a long, fiery sword in its hands. Ngoma fumbled in his pockets for the plastic bag, dumping the contents onto the road and falling to his knees.

"Please, sir. Take whatever it is that you want. I beg you. I have more of it hidden away in the city. I can take you there! Just—"

But the angel said nothing. His mighty blade swooped once, and it was over.

***

An eerie, green haze settled over the waters off of Namibia's desert coast. The sea blazed with fire, thick black smoke billowing into the sky, flecks of ash and ember drifting endlessly. Most of the vessels—the destroyers, gunships, tankers, frigates, and a handful of remaining aircraft carriers—had already been crippled far beyond repair. Their thick, steel hulls buckled and bowed in the heat of the fires.

Of the soldiers who remained, most had resigned to their fates. It was clear to all now that their war—a seemingly efficacious attack—was already over. When the angels appeared to finish Jehovah's day of vengeance, few had any fight left in them. Any attempts to flee were pointless. Giant, glowing angels towered over them in the water, firing flaming arrows at the ships that remained, rending them into pieces that quickly sank in the oily waves.

In the few remaining governmental facilities around the world, the final vestiges of Satan's system were trampled by flaming steeds that stood as high as skyscrapers, their muscles bulging like the waves of tumultuous seas. Mighty angelic soldiers armed with bows and swords marched through cities in mere moments, their feet as large as houses. With each step, their sandals left behind an imprint of crumbling molten rock and fire. In a single swoop of their broadswords, city blocks crumbled to ash.

Windhoek, the capital city of Namibia, was no different. The officials and politicians who'd so carefully orchestrated the attack on the Witnesses now huddled together in a small room. Screens and bulletin boards on the walls around them served as evidence for all they'd planned: the remaining diamond deposits within the Witnesses' territories carefully marked and parceled among the men, red Xs on the parts of the maps where the airstrikes were to have occurred. The ambush had been their ticket to unimaginable wealth and prestige, but now it would never be realized.

Adani Ratief stared numbly out of the windows as the others in the room argued and blamed one another for their failures. To Adani, though, they were all to blame. They'd had years to see the signs that the Witnesses were unlike any other group of people on Earth. There had been no shortage of evidence to support their claims of Divine blessings. Still, they'd let their greed and ambitions blind them to the truth, and now they would pay.

Adani Ratief took one last breath before closing his eyes tearfully and resting his forehead against the warm glass window separating him and the advancing heavenly armies.

And then it was over.

CHAPTER 32

The brothers had passed the time in the dark, sweaty cellar sharing experiences and singing songs. It was impossible to doze off, chained as they were to their backless benches. The muscles in their necks and backs ached, but there was little point in complaining about their discomfort. They were thirsty and tired and hungry, but they could only sit and wait and listen to the puzzling noises above them—soaring planes, marching troops, scampering boots, tires spinning in the dirt. Of course, there were also the noises of the storm, powerful gale force winds that rattled the walls of the structure above them, thunder that tumbled through the valley.

And then, suddenly, it was all over, and there was only silence.

The chains fell off all at once, the metal pins and screws holding the cuffs together coming loose and falling softly into the dirt. The brothers said nothing as they quietly nursed their chafed wrists and ankles, removed their black hoods, and blinked their eyes in the dusty darkness. A bluish sliver of light squeezed past the door at the top of the steps, a light of a different quality from the one they'd seen when they'd been thrown in the cell hours before.

Dietrich stood, somewhat unsteadily, half expecting the chains at his feet to yank him back into place, but he found he was completely free. Iron chain links lay burst open in a pile between his feet. Cautiously, he made his way up the creaking staircase and pushed against the door. It swung open freely, letting in a cool, refreshing evening breeze.

The air was awash with the sound of crickets and the distant cawing of hawks.

Dietrich scanned the horizon. Piles of unrecognizable, charred metal were all that remained of the munitions stocks and war vehicles that had once stood in their place. Overhead, he spotted the familiar shapes of circling vultures and knew instantly what their presence meant. Farther in the distance, thin trails of black smoke climbed into the night sky.

"What do you see?" someone asked from within the pit. Dietrich closed his eyes and took a deep breath.

"A new world," he said.

One by one the brothers climbed from their underground prison, taking in their surroundings and breathing in the cool desert night.

"There they are!" shouted a voice from downhill. "I see them!"

Dietrich and the others walked down to meet their brothers, arms over each others' shoulders, emotions too deep and complex to put into words. They passed an odd pile of expensive gold watches and precious stones and ignored it. Further on, they met the team of brothers and sisters who'd been dispatched to find them. The two groups exchanged tearful hugs, but few words were spoken. The weight of all that had transpired was too great for conversation. Questions could wait.

***

Ted and Angelica Watkins were married on a cool, August evening. Evan, of course, had been the one to present the wedding rings, and Peter delivered the talk. Their attire was casual, with Ted wearing a white open-collared shirt tucked into a pair of ironed khakis. On her head, Angelica wore a wreath of flowers grown by a sister in a nearby nursery.

They enjoyed a generous spread of locally grown foods under a clear, starry night. A small band of brothers and sisters played music on a wooden stage—jazzy tunes spruced up with local African percussion instruments with plenty of original songs and Kingdom classics thrown into the mix. The wedding party danced on into the night.

"I don't think I've ever attended such a beautiful wedding before," Joyce said, complimenting the newlyweds across the table from her. Angelica squeezed herself into Ted's chest as he kissed her on the forehead.

"Thank you. And would you believe, we didn't even have to take out a loan for it!" Ted joked. The table laughed.

"Oh, the things I won't miss about the old world," Rachel said serenely, her shoulders swaying to the music lolling in the background.

"Taxes, mortgages, health insurance, car insurance," Peter said, counting off items on his fingers with a grin.

"College debt," Claire chimed in. The others just smiled and shook their heads with distant looks in their eyes.

"You know," Alvin Tucker said. "You two might be the first couple to be married in the new world. Had you considered that?"

Ted and Angelica shared a look. "I guess not," Angelica said.

"I had," Peter said. "That's why I had to edit the talk's outline a bit. No more "for long as we both shall live" in the vows. For better or for worse, you two are stuck together!" Peter said. Everyone laughed again.

"So, any big plans for you two?" Rachel asked.

"Actually, yeah. We were thinking of heading out with the salvaging crew to Windhoek. We heard there's quite a bit of work to be done out there."

"Windhoek? That's far," Joyce said.

"They're setting up a small camp on the outskirts of the city, so we'd be living there for a while, wouldn't need to commute back and forth."

"That's a big change. How does Evan feel about it?" Rachel asked.

"I think he'll be fine," Angelica said, glancing at her son, who played with a baboon in the grass with another small group of children.

"And we aren't moving right away," Ted added. "The railroads are still damaged in some places, so the transportation department needs to get them completely repaired before any work can be done in the city."

"It's a big job, going into the city like that. Every building will need to be inspected for safety before the volunteers can go in and start salvaging. Sites deemed unsuitable for entry will have to be torn down," Alvin explained.

"What's the timeline on something like that?" Peter asked.

"Couple of years at least, maybe more."

"And after that? What's the plan?" Rachel asked.

"I guess we'll move on to the next city, then the next one after that, spreading out until we've covered the globe."

"Sounds like a huge task," Peter said, whistling, but excited about the prospects of the work that awaited them.

"It's ok, we've got time," Alvin said with a wide, toothy grin, an expression that made Claire giggle.

"I've been hearing rumors that during Armageddon, several of the nations launched nuclear attacks on one another. Did you hear anything about that, Alvin?" Ted asked. Alvin nodded.

"I can confirm that. We were sitting in an underground cell when one of the soldier's radios went off. They were in total panic when it happened."

"So what happens to those cities that were hit? Aren't they going to be radioactive for hundreds of years or something? And come to think of it, what about nuclear power plants and places like that? Doesn't something go terribly wrong if they aren't constantly being run by scientists or something?" Claire asked.

"I wouldn't worry about it," Alvin said, taking a sip from a glass of wine and wiping his mouth.

"We saw what those angels were capable of," Peter said. "I'm sure they can handle containment of a little radiation."

"It'll get taken care of," Ted agreed with a determined look.

"Wise words," Alvin said. "It's amazing to think how things unfolded, isn't it? How we all ended up here together and how Jehovah took care of us every step of the way."

"Still doesn't feel quite real," Peter said. They paused for a moment to gaze over at the crackling bonfire. Tiny embers swam into the night sky and vanished, and for a long moment they relived the breathtaking moments of Armageddon.

"This spot taken?" asked a voice over their shoulders. It was Stacy Owen. They welcomed her and she sat. The bandages were off of her hands now, the flesh fully restored. Joyce poured her a glass of wine as she congratulated the newlyweds. Across the table she handed them a pair of envelopes.

"What're these?" Angelica asked.

"Tickets. Not sure if you've got the honeymoon planned or not, but if not, maybe you'll consider me as an option," Stacy said, grinning.

"What do you mean?" Ted asked, peeking into one of the envelopes.

"I'm with the coastal care department now. We're doing cleanup on the Namibian shores: disposing of wreckage from the military ships and planes, dismantling rusty old shipwrecks on the coast, that kind of thing."

"Must be a big job," Angelica said, raising her eyebrows.

"It is, but to be honest, we're having a blast. Guess what I get to pilot?" Stacy asked, eyes roving around the table waiting for guesses. But none were offered. Stacy pulled her phone from her pocket and pulled up an image. The group peered at the screen, not comprehending it at first.

"It's a submarine," she said excitedly. "The brothers salvaged them from a military installation farther up the coast and repurposed them for the cleanup of underwater wrecks. Cool, right?"

"So what are the tickets for?"

"If you're looking for a getaway, there's nothing cooler than taking a sub ride to check out the wrecks. It's already teeming with wildlife. Absolutely stunning!"

Ted and Angelica shared a look and shrugged. "We'll keep it in mind," Angelica finally said, and the friends laughed again.

***

Hand in hand, Peter and Rachel Burton meandered through the quiet apartment blocks back to their home in the valley. The night was cool and breezy and the Milky Way spread across the sky in a hazy purple band above them.

"Mind if we take a detour?" Peter asked his wife.

"Sure," she said.

Peter led his wife onto the small trail behind their apartment, up into the hills. They found the bench atop the rocky outcropping and sat. Before them lay the yellow lights of apartment windows below.

"I've never been up here before. It's beautiful." Rachel said.

Peter nodded. "Marcus brought me here the last time we talked."

Rachel gazed over at her husband and silently laid a hand on his arm. He looked at his wife and smiled. "Don't worry. I'm ok."

"I miss him too," Rachel said.

"You want to hear something crazy?" Peter suddenly asked, smirking at his wife.

"What?"

"You remember that soldier who attacked us with the knife?"

"Of course."

"And you remember that angel that came to our defense and stopped him?"

"How could I forget?"

"Before the angel materialized in front of us, I saw him somewhere else. Just for a moment. You know where he was?"

"Where?"

"Up on this hill, behind the line of soldiers. He was sitting right on this bench."

Rachel drew a sharp breath. "You think…?"

Peter could only shrug. "I like to think it was him."

"That's incredible, Peter," Rachel said.

"I know. I can't get that image out of my head. The angel with the glowing robes sitting here, and then, an instant later, appearing in front of us like a wall. And then I just keep thinking about how amazing Marcus's new life must be. Can you imagine? Working side by side with Jesus and Jehovah? Inhabiting a spirit form, seeing Earth and humans and the universe the way the angels do? It must be… indescribable."

Rachel smiled as she laid a head on her husband's shoulder.

"I'm so happy for him, Rachel. He was faithful to the end."

"And so were we."

"I keep thinking back to our old life in California—years of working the same territory over and over. Going to the Kingdom Hall week after week, even when we were tired or not feeling well. Of everything that happened once the evacuation orders were given, of all that we had to leave behind and everything we went through to get here."

"It feels like another lifetime, doesn't it?"

"Yeah. It really does. But all of it was worth it. I lay awake at night staring up at this sky through our window and just keep thinking how grateful I am for it all. Every sacrifice, every act of obedience, every time we trusted in Jehovah at some expense to ourselves. Everything was worth it."

Peter felt his wife's warm hands in his own and gave them a squeeze. They gazed up once more at the endless expanse of stars before them, and Peter offered a prayer.

AFTERWORD

What a ride this has been! For the last three years, Peter and Rachel Burton, Joyce and Alvin Tucker, Claire Aberdeen, Ted Watkins, Angelica Parry, and all the rest of the *FLEE* ensemble have been such a big part of my life, and ending their stories means saying goodbye, something which is always hard to do. Witnessing their growth through the novels was a special experience, and one that mirrored my own.

The past few years have not been easy. The persecution of our brothers in Russia has reached a fever pitch, a wave of Satanic resistance that seems to be spreading to nearby territories. In the past two years, friends of mine serving in certain territories were captured by police, interrogated, and expelled from the countries they were serving in, in some cases not even given the opportunity to return home to collect their belongings or say goodbye to friends and Bible students.

It's been bad, but of course it is only the beginning. As we near the tribulation, we can only expect conditions to spread and worsen. Perhaps that is what most motivated me most to press on with this series. While it is a work of fiction, I've always maintained that if anything can be taken away from the stories, it's the way the characters react and grow. The situations they face force us as the readers to imagine how we might react given the same scenarios.

Of course, as readers we have the luxury of being able to skim through the pages to the last chapters of the stories to reassure ourselves that all ends well, but real life is different. Lacking foreknowledge, we plunge into each day like a blindfolded diver, not knowing what lurks beneath the surface of the water. It is this uncertain future that most necessitates faith.

And perhaps that is the central theme here: faith. Faith that things will turn out well so long as we obey and persevere. Faith that the direction from Jehovah's organization is always right, even if it feels very wrong. Faith that nothing lost now is lost forever.

Part of the challenge of writing this trilogy was in trying to figure out how all the pieces involving the great tribulation and Armageddon fit together. This was not done in an effort to push a certain agenda or make predictions, but to bolster the integrity of the story and make it believable. It was also an opportunity to brush up on my own knowledge of our most current publications and their depiction of the events just ahead.

That said, I expect that some readers will come away with questions or concerns regarding certain scenarios presented in this series.

In the past, some readers have commented on the violence portrayed in this series. I feel that a certain degree of violence is required to evoke the horrors of the coming tribulation and the execution of Jehovah's enemies during Armageddon. Still, I have done my best to refrain from gratuitous violence, such as graphic descriptions of gore and death. Of course, I completely understand that every reader must use his own conscience to determine what is acceptable entertainment, and as always, I urge readers to use discernment in recommending these novels to others, especially those sensitive in this regard.

I have made a conscious effort in this series to depict a range of attitudes towards the Witnesses among unbelievers, including those who eventually attack true religion. Some, like the characters Chad Harkett and Driscoll, truly hate the Witnesses and yearn to see them completely destroyed. Others, like Commander Daniel Ngoma, become complicit primarily due to their lust for power and riches. Still others, like Adani Ratief, act out of cowardice. In spite of seeing the signs, they make unwise choices that ultimately cost them their lives. While we do not know if such ones will exist during the final moments of this system, (perhaps all will resemble the former type of enemy) I have included them based on the existence of similar characters in the Bible record.

I anticipate that some readers will take issue with the character of Luis Escobar, the Venezuelan smuggler who joins Alvin and Joyce on *The Chariot* and abandons his old life to join the Witnesses. Perhaps some will find it unfair that an unbeliever would be given such an opportunity to change at the last moment. Others may feel that once the great tribulation starts, there is no longer an opportunity for honest-hearted ones to join true worshippers.

However, in researching our recent publications, I was unable to find such a claim. (Especially helpful information on this topic was found in the *Kingdom Rules* (*kr*, 2014) book, chapter 21, and the *Pure Worship* (2018) book, chapters 17 and 18, and *The Watchtower* (2013, July 15, pages 3-8).

As always, I urge readers to view these books for what they are: not dogmatic predictions, but rather entertaining diversions that keep our minds fixed on the things ahead while we eagerly await the real thing.

Finally, I'd like to thank my tireless editors, who offered countless valuable input to help bring to fruition the story you hold in your hands now. It would not be what it is without them. So thank you, Ruth, Veronica, and Lisa.

-EK Jonathan

46884792R00207

Printed in Poland
by Amazon Fulfillment
Poland Sp. z o.o., Wrocław